MW01127156

DORMANT

龍 Curse

BY

John Ellis

neodigm
press

Published by Neodigm Press
Austin, Texas
www.neodigmpress.com

This book is a work of fiction. Names, characters, companies, and incidents are the products of the author's imagination, or are used fictitiously.

Use of company or product names is not an endorsement.

Cover Design by Blue Mustang, LLC

Publisher's Cataloging-in-Publication Data

Ellis, John.
Dormant curse / John Ellis.
p. cm.
ISBN: 978-0-9836360-0-7 (hardcover)
ISBN: 978-0-9836360-1-4 (pbk.)
ISBN: 978-0-9836360-2-1 (e-book)
1. Cyberterrorism—Fiction. 2. Terrorism—United States—Prevention—Fiction.
3. Cults—China—Fiction.   I. Title.
PS3605.L466 .D67 2011
813—dc22   2011911368

Printed in the United States of America
10 9 8 7 6 5 4 3 2 1 0

Acknowledgements

Jennifer, my greatest fan, thank you. Without your love, trust, and honest feedback, I couldn't have gotten through this. I love you.

Robbie Dale Carl Joseph Kesselring, you know this book wouldn't have happened without your prompting and constant encouragement. I don't know what this world would be like without your friendship.

To my reviewers and critics: Kat, Wyatt, Dad, Mark, Scott, Martha, and Rich. There's no way to repay you.

Joe and Matt: You're always in my heart.

To Rebecca, my editor: I made the right choice with you.

Chapter

(Zero)

*"**H**urry…hurry…hurry now!* They're coming!"

The small boy studied his mother's face with interest and confusion. Her eyes were wide, screaming at him, while her voice barely made a sound. It was almost like watching a silent movie. But the tension in her tone still came through, making her panic palpable. This was unlike anything he had seen from her before and he was struggling to make sense of what was happening.

"Qiang…now! With Lien-Hua!" her mouth whispered and face yelled at him, as she frantically pointed to the small cubbyhole in the kitchen. Qiang's mother wanted him to take his little sister and hide. Pain, fear and anger wrenched his mother's beautiful face.

Running to the kitchen, dragging the baby girl by the hand, the four-year-old pushed his little sister into hiding. With her safely in the crawl-space, he stood looking back at his parents and older sister, Bao-Yu. They were scurrying to roll Bao-Yu under their canopy bed, flipping the sheets back down to touch the floor and then smoothing over the wrinkles in the fabric on top of the covers. Nothing must look out of place.

The dark cubbyhole was once used to store extra bags of rice, now long depleted during the siege of their city. Their side had surrendered. The enemy was coming. The Japanese were going door-to-door to find Chinese soldiers attempting to escape by blending back into the community.

As the boy backed his rear onto Lien-Hua's face and into the storage space, she asked, "Are we playing a game?"

"Shhh!" Qiang sharply whispered back. "This isn't a game. Be quiet or you'll get a bad spanking!"

Reaching to pull the door shut, he could hear Bao-Yu say from under the bed, "But they won't hurt us, Father, will they? They want the soldiers."

Qiang stopped moving. He wanted to hear the answer. He studied his father's face as best he could from two rooms away, looking for any hint in his reaction.

His father pursed his lips and looked at his wife. She shook her head as if to say, "don't tell her." He nodded.

"Bao, they want to find any soldiers hiding out," said Father, feigning confidence. "But I don't want them to see such a beautiful girl as you and think they can take and marry her. They would be fighting each other for your hand in our own house."

"Oh, Father," Bao-Yu said in a hushed tone, "I'm not that beautiful! But I'll stay here and be quiet until they leave."

The boy could see the tears in his mother's eyes as his parents looked at each other in fear and hopelessness. He now knew what Bao-Yu could not see from her hiding place: his father had lied.

His mother looked past her husband, into the kitchen. When she saw that Qiang had not yet closed the cubbyhole door, she realized that he had seen and heard their conversation. She pointed at him wordlessly, which caused Qiang's father to turn and face his young son. His look of disappointment was quite easy for Qiang to discern.

Qiang saw what was coming and backed hurriedly into the cubbyhole, pulling on the door as his father, now almost sprinting from the bedroom, made his way through the foyer and into the kitchen. When their eyes met, his father's look was one of sadness, not anger.

Why such sadness? thought Qiang.

Father reached Qiang just as the boy caught the door's edge with his hand and was starting to pull it closed.

His father grabbed Qiang's arm before he could draw the door shut.

Qiang cringed and ducked his head down, expecting a slap from his father's hand as a reaction to his disobedience. Instead, when he looked up, he saw the calmness that had come over his father. Father leaned into the hole, gently pulled little Lien-Hua close enough to kiss the top of her hair, and drew his head back out.

Now with his hand gently on Qiang, he looked his son squarely in the face and said, "Keep yourself and your sister quiet, no matter what you see or hear. Promise me this."

"Promise me" was clearly not a question. It was both a plea and an order. Qiang nodded in response.

"I love you," he said, as he kissed Qiang on the forehead and swiftly shut the door.

All went immediately dark for the children. His sister couldn't help but whimper.

"You heard Father. Quiet or I'll make you be quiet," Qiang whispered his harsh reminder.

After a few moments, Qiang's eyes adjusted to the darkness. Through a thin gap between the door and the cabinet edge, he could see just a little slice of the entry room.

With the cubbyhole door shut, sounds were now muffled, but even so, he thought he could hear screams and gunshots drawing closer.

Were these the Chinese soldiers the Japanese were looking for? Why did they scream so?

He saw his father's figure go past with a cup of tea in hand, trying to appear as if nothing was amiss. Surely this wasn't a game after all, was it?

Bang-bang-bang-bang on the door followed by a shout. "Open the door or we'll break it down!"

The voice came in broken Chinese. It was the Japanese soldiers.

"I'm coming!" his father responded.

Qiang strained to see anything through his private viewing hole. Nothing.

"Brother, who is it?" came the hushed query from behind.

"Quiet. No noise."

"Where are they?!" demanded the soldier.

"Who? We are the only ones home."

"You lie!" said the soldier. The thud of the butt end of a rifle could be heard as it struck against Qiang's father's back.

"No, no...I'm not lying!" he said pleadingly.

"Look for the knapsack marks," commanded the soldier in charge. Heavy knapsacks used by the Chinese soldiers would dig deep marks into their shoulder that would be visible for hours. These soldiers were looking for evidence.

Qiang heard the tear of ripping cloth.

"Humpf. No marks. So, you won't die...yet."

There was silence for a few moments; Qiang held his breath, hoping the next sound he would hear would be the door closing and his parents coming to pull him and Lien-Hua from their hiding place.

"So, I see your wife is quite lovely. What will you pay me to keep her? I will not ask again."

The soldier's broken Chinese made it hard to understand what the soldier was asking, so his father was hesitant in his response.

Pay him? thought Qiang. Mother didn't belong to the soldier. Why such a strange question?

"I have food…"

There was a long pause.

"No! Don't take her, I have silver! Let me get it!"

"Well, that's more like it. Get it now or we leave with her!"

Qiang glimpsed his father dashing into his bedroom to retrieve the silver he had stored in the ceiling. Moments later, he saw his father dart back into the entry room.

"Very well. You can keep her, but both of you will come with us! You carry the silver, and while you are at it, carry that chair over there. I want it, too," the soldier commanded.

"But you said—" his father protested.

Another thud made it clear that no arguing would be tolerated.

"I said you could keep her. I didn't say that either of you would stay. Now, let's go!"

Next to him, Qiang heard the sound of his sister building up a sob. He realized from her breathing that she had been crying, though he could not see her tears.

"No sound!" he fumed. Rationalizing that his parents might return after they carried the stolen goods for the soldiers, he continued, "They will be back soon." He hoped this would quell his sister's panic. He almost believed it himself.

Qiang's father walked past the viewport, carrying the chair on his back and the silver in a knapsack on his shoulder.

The door slammed shut.

The sound of the soldiers' yelling and commotion moved down the street.

Qiang decided he would wait for his big sister to come and get them out of their cubbyhole. He was much too afraid to move right now.

His little sister had a different idea.

"Let me out! Bao-Yu! Help!" she yelled.

Immediately, the door to their small house slammed open and the sound of a soldier's voice was heard. "Stupid Chinese! I knew you were in here! Come out now! I heard you!"

Qiang was quick to cover his little sister's mouth before she could make another noise.

"There you are!" came the next voice.

Oh no, they've seen us! thought Qiang.

"You look much older than your voice sounds…"

"What do you want?" came the reply. The voice was Bao-Yu's. She must have come out from under the bed when she heard Lien-Hua's cry.

"See what you did!" Qiang seethed to his little sister, tightening his grip on her mouth to silence her.

The soldier didn't reply, but instead laughingly called out the door to his other compatriots in Japanese. Qiang couldn't understand what was being said, but the call quickly drew three or four more soldiers' voices. He saw their shadows pass by his viewport on their way toward his parents' bedroom.

"No, don't! Please don't!" Bao-Yu cried.

A slap, a scream, and more soldiers' voices in Japanese. Laughter, threats, and his sister's screams intermingled together.

"NO!! Please, NO!!" she yelled again and again.

Qiang wanted to cover his ears, but he was afraid his little sister would make a noise when he uncovered her mouth. The tension and fear caused the pressure on his grip to grow, which, in turn only increased the fight she put up against his hand and arm.

This went on for what seemed like an eternity, with pauses in screams and cries every few minutes, followed by more laughter and taunting and slaps.

What are they doing to her!?

The shadow of a soldier crossed in front of Qiang's view again, but this one was different. It had a knife drawn by his side, in a fighting stance.

Is someone finally going to rescue my sister? Qiang thought hopefully.

After the next pause in screams, it all continued again. The shadow moved into the room. Rather than the screams stopping, they increased in intensity and pitch. Yelping, hollering and taunting increased as Bao-Yu's scream became one long death-cry of agony.

Only then did Qiang realize that his little sister had stopped fighting him completely.

The sound of Bao-Yu's screams blended with and eventually became a voice from the Hua Dan, a Chinese opera whose shrill tone had triggered memories of the childhood atrocity.

"Sir, Leader, we are here…sir? Leader?"

The Leader was in a trance. His bodyguard never knew what would set off these spells—it might be a sight, a smell, or a sound.

The bodyguard would have to wait until it passed. Realizing that might take a few moments, he motioned for the limousine to pull into the waiting area next to the hotel entrance and for the music to be silenced. They were arriving at the Shanghai Grand Hyatt for important meetings. Now was not the time for any difficulties.

The Leader, who had been staring blankly forward, expressionless and barely breathing, now called out, "Bao!" before snapping into the present. He blinked, took deep breaths and looked around frantically. The bodyguard knew the Leader's exit from whatever trance he was in was usually marked by some reactionary response, however transient.

Chapter
(One)

Michelle pressed her lips hard against Greg's. Kissing, licking, then biting his lower lip.

"Greg, I want you now…" she whispered.

Michelle's figure was silhouetted in the moonlight as they stood on the beach, just beyond the reach of the lights from the bar. Her bright yellow bikini took on a muted tone as her sheer, white shawl flowed gently over her tan skin in the ocean breeze. Greg's tall, muscular frame stood in complimentary contrast next to Michelle's diminutive build. She fit him perfectly.

Caught up in the moment, and feeling Michelle's ample chest now pressed against him, Greg almost forgot where he was.

"We can't, not here on the beach in front of everyone," he whispered back hoarsely.

"They can't see us, Honey. Not out here in the dark. Besides, don't you want me? Don't you want me now? Your body says you do," Michelle said with a playful smirk. "At least, it's giving me that impression."

Greg felt tingles all over. Of course his body was responding. How couldn't it? Michelle had him wrapped around her finger. All of five-foot-two and one hundred five pounds, with curves in all the right places—she had him mesmerized since his freshman year.

Michelle had her own buzz going. After a couple of Mai Tais, she would start to lose control. The meds pretty much controlled her impulses, but with some alcohol, her manic side would start to kick in. She was going to have her way, even if it got them arrested.

"Well, *part* of your body is extending an invitation," she whispered as she licked and tugged at his earlobe, "and here's my RSVP."

She started to slowly kiss his neck, his collarbone, and then work her way down his chest. The fear of being caught and the excitement he felt made Greg think he was going to explode.

Buzz… Buzz… Buzz… Buzz…

What? Where was that sound coming from?

Buzz… Buzz… Buzz… Buzz…

Greg wasn't on the beach. He wasn't even near the ocean. He was laying flat on his back in bed.

Greg slapped the snooze on the clock and tried jump back into the dream. It was no use; he was much too worked up to sleep now. Making sure the alarm was shut off, he rolled over to Michelle, who lay in a deep sleep next to him.

Michelle could sleep through anything. Ambien had that effect on her. But it was five in the morning, when most normal people were sleeping. Still, it was worth a try.

Greg brushed his fingers over the nape of Michelle's neck, down to the arch of her back and then back up again, seeing if she might stir without much effort.

"Mmmmm…" came the response. "That feels nice."

Greg was hopeful as he continued to kiss the back of her neck and gently rub his hand down the curve of her side.

"Oh, Honey," Michelle cooed. "When does your plane leave?"

"I have some time," responded Greg, trying not to let the anticipation show in his voice. It was going to be a quick, two-day review with their regional office in Dallas, but it had been days since they had last made love and he needed relief now, especially after that wild dream had left him aroused and unsatisfied.

Still lying on her side, spooning, Michelle took Greg's hand and moved it up to her breast as she pressed her ass into his thigh. Greg's body responded eagerly.

"Mmmm…OK, Honey, I'm still groggy…so…mmmm…you're gonna have to do all of the work," Michelle whispered softly.

Pulling her close, Greg sighed heavily and sensuously as he pulled Michelle's body firmly onto his.

Chapter

(Two)

Security was tight for anyone entering or leaving the assembly and packaging plant in Shenzhen. The facility, owned by Hon Yao Industry Group, was responsible for the manufacturing of high-tech gadgets, devices, phones and computers, and serviced many customers. The parts list used in specific products was classified. Secure work sections were implemented to ensure no individual worker had access to the complete assembly information for any one product.

One section of the facility literally had processed silicon wafers going in and plastic integrated circuit packages coming out. The workers familiar with this section called it "No-Man's Land," for only a few personnel were required to run the fully-automated area. When a piece of equipment needed repair or service, the area around the equipment was curtained and cordoned off, allowing the technician to see and work only on what was necessary to get the job done.

Each day at the Hon Yao factory, a nondescript worker arrived at precisely 7:15 a.m. Where most workers would merely use their key cards to enter the plant, this privileged individual was met by security and allowed to enter anonymously. He carried a locked aluminum briefcase, and was allowed to bypass the typical inspection process forced on every other employee and visitor arriving at the gate. Unless someone was looking specifically for the deliveryman and his guard escort, he blended seamlessly into the surrounding busyness of the factory, undetected.

Once inside, the worker was escorted directly to the inner sanctum. No-Man's Land. Once there, he delivered his unique package to the material stocker holding the days' supply of silicon wafers.

Most other wafers were products from the US, Korea or Taiwan. These wafers contained leading-edge microprocessors, GPS receivers, Wi-Fi and Bluetooth circuits, DRAM and Flash memory. These were made everywhere but

China, on large 300mm silicon disks the size of a 12-inch vinyl record. The wafers were ground down as thinly as possible, sometimes as thin as a sheet of paper. After grinding, the wafers were diced into individual chips, which were then stacked and combined into one package. This was a relatively new technology called 3D integrated circuits, or "3D ICs." It made for incredibly small devices, and reduced cost and power usage. Any company not using this technology was left behind in performance and cost competitiveness.

The downside to 3D ICs was that one couldn't inspect between the individual chips—called dies—very well. It was difficult to examine when things were stacked perfectly and all of the individual connections between the thin silicon chips were lined up and fused together.

No one in No-Man's Land knew what was on the special set of wafers that were delivered, nor did they have any identifying marks. All they knew was that the dies appeared to be made in China, and from the looks of them, had a somewhat simple design. For those who caught a glimpse of a special wafer, it looked as if nothing was on it but the connections. Perhaps it was just a simple die that routed circuit traces between other chips? No one really knew or cared. After thinning the wafer and cutting and assembling the die into the stack, it was hard to discern it was even part of the stacked assembly. However, this seemed the intent.

In No-Man's Land, anyone who asked questions beyond how to do their immediate job was at once removed from the section and made to work on rather mundane activities. They knew better than to question. Getting selected for a job in this section was an enviable honor. Only loyal employees with substantial service with Hon Yao would even be considered, and significant raises and bonuses were sufficient incentive for volunteering. Sometimes the pressure of working in the inner sanctum and keeping the secrets of No-Man's Land took a toll. Some staff ended up committing suicide—or so the factory rumors said. Young workers jumping to their deaths became a fairly common occurrence, though the behavior was blamed on high stress. Workers in the factory doubted this cover story, but they knew better than to question their authorities.

Amidst all of the commotion of the factory, the mirrored windows of the management office overlooked the overall operations. Even the factory manager didn't know exactly what was on the unique wafers that were brought in each day. He only knew that the special die went into the stacks with GPS, and that its presence didn't seem to have any impact on system performance. Beyond that, there was nothing else to know or question. The managers knew that their livelihoods depended on obeying government orders. If one had forgotten for a moment that this was ultimately a communist, state-controlled system, it took only a terse meeting with the local party officials to remind them of the benefit they received from being allowed to run the factory. They needed to work with the officials to ensure it ran smoothly, lest it not run at all.

Most finished products from Hon Yao were complete end systems: smartphones, tablets and netbooks bound for the United States or Europe. Hon Yao also shipped assembled chips to final integrators that would use the circuits on in-flight and in-car navigation systems. With the cost efficiency of 3D IC technology, it was difficult for other assembly and packaging companies to compete. Financial incentives given by the Chinese government, in return for Hon Yao's cooperation, ensured that no one else ever would.

Chapter
(Three)

***P*hones off already?** Why do airlines still have this stupid rule?

Michael James was on his way from Atlanta to Salt Lake City to visit his grandparents. It was much too early in the day for him, so he was already in a foul mood. He wasn't too thrilled with the announcement to shut off all electronics.

Everyone knows the phones don't interfere with anything, he thought. Control freaks.

Sitting in the aisle seat of row 34, it would be easy enough for Michael to just stand up and slip his phone, still on, into the side pocket of his carry-on.

It's irritating enough that I'm sitting in the last row on the plane, with seats that don't recline and that for some reason that damn oxygen bottle is taking up my overhead space. Don't they have some special compartment for that? I've had enough impositions. I'm not gonna shut off my phone, he rationalized.

Michael was dressed in sloppy, low-hanging pants, the kind his mother hated, with an Ozzy Ozborne t-shirt, Converse All Stars tennis shoes and a buzz cut. His large, strong frame betrayed the fact that he regularly exercised. He didn't really fit any stereotype—punk, rocker, emo or preppie. But that was Michael. He defied categorization, except "rebellious;" his look vastly different from the one he sported in his days as a Boy Scout. His parents hoped he would grow out of it, but at 18 years old, it didn't look very promising.

Having said his goodbyes to Mom and Dad before boarding the plane, Michael was looking forward to getting out of Georgia and spending time with Pops and Grams before starting a job in California. His grandparents always accepted him for what he was—whatever that was. He usually left their place feeling pretty good about himself. It was going to be an excellent trip.

As he stood up to slip his phone into his bag, he made sure his Blather account was up and going. He didn't want to miss any good updates from Lady Gaga while they were taking off, before he could get on the on-board Wi-Fi.

Sitting back down and trying to get comfortable, Michael looked around the plane at who else was traveling on this early flight. It was mainly businessmen, but a few families were on-board. He spied a tattoo on the arm of a jet-black haired beauty about four rows in front of him.

That's what I'm talking about, thought Michael.

Quickly that thought came into check as Michael remembered his girlfriend, Jill, and how she would have disapproved of his glance.

He was taking the job in California so he could move in with Jill. She had graduated a year earlier from Milton High and was the love of his life. When he was a Junior, she had her sights set on him, won him and bagged him. She was his first, though she had been around the block a few times. She had his head spinning with the way she made him feel. The spinning didn't stop for a whole year, during which his grades, social life and relationship with his family tanked.

After graduation, Jill was done with Michael and ready to move out of the state and onto bigger things. Having no real interest in academics, Jill started full-time work in a Pleasanton tanning salon. However, that hadn't worked out so well. Within a few months, and disillusioned with her low-paying job, she started calling Michael again, forging a long-distance relationship, much to Michael's parents' dismay. They had hoped the destruction Jill had wreaked over the past year was done and that their son was back on the right track. The phone calls and text messages from Jill had been in secret, but his parents knew something was up as Michael's grades began to slide again and his mood became more irritable.

Mid-way through a miserable school year, Michael announced that college was not in his plans and he was moving to California after high school. No amount of encouragement, cajoling, or threats by his father to cut off financial support could change his mind. At least Michael graduated. Still, his performance was a far cry from the promise he showed as a young teenager, when he was learning science theory and building advanced computer projects in his school's gifted program.

Jill had selfishly taken much more than Michael's heart and virginity. It appeared that she had also taken his future. The job at the local Safeway in Pleasanton he'd secured wasn't the future he or his parents had envisioned a few years ago, but with his income and Jill's combined, they'd have an okay life. His vision of the future now included only the next few weeks and dreams about being back with Jill. He thought about how good he would feel again, being completely intimate with her in every way like he had always wanted, but never could under his parents' thumbs.

Michael settled into his seat, closed his eyes and let his mind go.

Chapter
(Four)

Greg arrived at National in a sweat. Making love with Michelle was so distracting and all-encompassing that he'd almost lost track of time.

That would be just great, Greg thought to himself. My first chance to show my skills and I miss my flight, and my only excuse is that my wife sidetracked me.

He wasn't that late, but with the number of passengers trying to get a flight out, security was worse than he'd expected.

Greg Cannon was a bright, young electrical engineer working for the National Transportation Safety Board. The NTSB headquarters were in Washington, but he was on his way to a regional meeting at their Texas office near DFW.

Greg was usually pretty quiet, but he was always ready with a warm smile or "hello" for anyone willing to acknowledge him. To those who took the time to get to know him, Greg was quite a character. He had a dry sense of humor and was good at making people feel comfortable. His biggest flaw, though, was his tendency to worry. If he dwelled on a problem long enough, his mind could blow things out of proportion.

Greg had just graduated with his Master's degree from the University of Illinois in December and felt lucky to have a job, considering the shape of the present economy—unless he wanted to work near Des Moines, back on the family farm. This was his first trip with NTSB, and his supervisor, Dennis, was travelling with him. He was to report on some commonalities he had been researching regarding Cessna 207A's electrical systems failures. It was not all that interesting to Greg, but it was a way to get started with the agency.

Dennis Wright was a middle-aged man, though the lines on his weathered face made him look older. His life had been hard. The deep scar above his right eye that separated the eyebrow into two distinct pieces, confirmed the blows he'd been dealt.

From the little that Greg knew about Dennis, it seemed that Dennis just made things tough on himself. In some ways, Dennis was kind of an old crust. Not that he was difficult to work for—he could hold very interesting conversations and wasn't nearly as unpolished as most engineers. But you had to get used to his straightforward, blunt style. Dennis had never been married, at least according to the office grapevine; no one could put up with such a curmudgeon. One thing everyone knew was that one didn't ask Dennis about his personal life.

The line through security was long, and Greg was getting more concerned about missing his flight. The 80-year-old grandmother in the wheelchair six passengers in front of him had been randomly selected for screening by TSA.

Isn't there a way to un-profile a case like this? She looks really dangerous to me, thought Greg sarcastically.

The poor woman had a very difficult time and looked a little lost throughout the process.

Once on the other side of security, Greg checked the departures schedule. He still had 45 minutes before takeoff—not nearly as bad as he'd thought.

As he walked toward Gate A-14, Greg thought he saw a familiar face. There was Dennis, already camped out in his seat. He looked like he had been there a while.

"Boy, you sure like to cut it close," quipped Dennis in his gravelly voice.

"Well…never mind, it's a long story, and I need to run to the restroom before we get boarding. Can you watch my stuff?" said Greg.

"Sure, Greg. Just don't get lost, and get me a Coke while you're up and about—here's a five," came the gruff reply.

Great, something else to slow me down, thought Greg.

Dennis saw a little anxiety on Greg's face as he left.

He thought to himself: This new kid sure is uptight about the trip. I hate breaking these new guys in, but that's life in lower management.

Dennis kicked his feet up on the chair across from him and tried to get back into the book he was reading. He had learned long ago that he couldn't worry about things that were out of his hands, especially a late employee. He wasn't about to start worrying now.

All his life, Dennis had known he wanted to leave a mark on society. He wasn't doing a good job of it so far. The goal of most engineers was to work themselves out of engineering and low-level management by the time they were fifty. At his current pace, Dennis would be lucky to make it by sixty. Half of his friends had left NTSB to start their own businesses. Dennis had been promoted to supervisor two years ago. He decided to give it a shot, even though he figured he was offered the position more out of his seniority than the management's desire to see him move up.

Waiting in line at McDonald's for Dennis' Coke, Greg wondered who would drink a Coke so early in the morning? He started to run his fingers through his short, blond hair as he grew impatient. He had developed this nervous habit as a kid and had never grown out of it. His mom used to tell him that he would lose his hair prematurely if he kept it up.

From the airport TV, Greg overheard a CNT world report.

"…coming up next, China's saber rattling in Asia. Is an invasion of Taiwan imminent? What is the US's responsibility in negotiating a settlement to ongoing disputes? And we'll cover the latest developments with Iran: do they really have multiple nuclear weapons ready for deployment? What are the implications for the US and Israel if reports are accurate?"

Can't anyone just get along? Greg thought. I'm so tired of the national and religious conflicts in the world.

"What'll you have this fine morning?" asked the attendant.

"I'll have a large Coke. It's not for me; it's for my boss. He's addicted to the stuff," replied Greg.

The girl looked at Greg carefully. "And you're his buyer for this addiction—I see how it is," she said with a bright smile. "Too much information," she smirked as she turned to get his order.

Ugh, that did sound strange, thought Greg. I need to settle down.

Part of Greg's nervousness was because he felt he just didn't know enough about his job. Most staff in his department were experts and aficionados in aviation, aerospace engineering, meteorology, and, well, all things related to flight. His specialization was in semiconductors. He had taken this job because most jobs related to his field required moving to Singapore, China, India, Taiwan, the United Arab Emirates or Korea. In fact, the position at the NTSB had been the only reasonable job offered to him in the States.

It was obvious from his few months at HQ that Greg had a lot to learn. Half of his on-the-job training was learning to deal with contrary personalities. No course in college prepared him for office politics.

Rumor was that Dennis would be close to Director by now if he would play the political games like everyone else. From Greg's experience with Dennis, he could see that. Dennis was extremely intelligent, but he spoke his mind. From the subordinate's perspective, that made a great supervisor. You knew exactly what he expected, and he didn't make any promises he didn't intend to fulfill.

Dennis was asleep and snoring when Greg got back. How could someone sleep in an airport?

All around, people were trying to find one of the few seats left in the gate area. Well-dressed businessmen in Priority Class were beginning to line up at the gangway entrance. A young mother sitting with a child on her lap across from Dennis was obviously miffed that he had the gall to take up three seats: one for himself, one for his feet and one for his luggage.

It's obvious Dennis wasn't looking after my luggage very well, Greg thought. Looks like it's all here, though.

Greg tried to step over Dennis' sprawled out legs and take his seat without disturbing him. Dennis woke with a start.

Dennis felt the hot glare of the woman sitting across from him.

"What's with her?" Dennis mumbled to Greg as he sat up, moving his feet.

"Don't know, maybe she's had a rough morning," Greg said under his breath. The woman quickly moved her luggage to the vacated seat before it was snatched up.

"You get my Coke?" asked Dennis.

"Sure. Here you go. Hey, you seemed pretty relaxed there," Greg said with a grin. "When did you get here anyway?"

"I spent the night, couldn't you tell?" replied Dennis.

It was pretty tough for Greg to judge Dennis sometimes. Obviously, he hadn't been there all night, but it looked like he had certainly been there for quite a while. Greg noticed a few empty Coke cups and junk food wrappers under and around Dennis' seat.

Boy, this guy needs some help in his personal life, thought Greg.

"Dennis Wright, please report to the check-in counter," came a call over the intercom.

"Got my upgrade," said Dennis as he hopped up.

Lucky, thought Greg.

Over the course of Dennis' long career, he had saved a few hundred thousand miles. Government employees weren't supposed to use their miles for flights, so Dennis used them for upgrades whenever he had a chance. Nothing like investigating airline accidents to keep you accumulating lots of miles.

"American Airlines Flight 367 to Dallas Fort Worth is now ready for pre-boarding…"

Greg hadn't planned to tackle any work or reading on the flight, but he wasn't necessarily prepared for a nap, either. Thoughts were competing for priority in his mind—those of his stimulating dream and real climax of passion this morning with Michelle, and those of his presentation and how it would be received by the regional office. Once comfortably in his seat, Greg would be able to relax. Even without an upgrade, he still managed to get a reclining exit row, which gave him more leg room.

Once in row sixteen, the stately gentleman seated next to him smiled politely and offered Greg part of his paper.

"Thanks very much, sir," Greg said as he took the front section.

Once again, he was reminded of the ongoing tensions in the Middle East and Asia.

China invading Taiwan? he thought. Not a chance. We'd never stand for that.

From his semiconductor training, Greg knew that the leading-edge foundries in Taiwan made a ton of high-tech integrated circuits that were used in all electronic products. China had been trying to get their own leading-edge chip manufacturing capabilities, but so far they had only been successful in luring Intel there to build processors using legacy technology. They had also secured low-cost assembly and packaging facilities. In contrast, foundries in Taiwan controlled over fifty percent of the global market for specialized chips, including many used in US defense systems. The US would protect that supply from China's control at all costs.

Issues like these were way above his pay grade and what's more, they were way outside of his control. He went back to thinking about Michelle. Once the plane climbed to altitude, the steady hum of the engines lulled Greg to sleep.

Chapter
(Five)

The room was hushed and the lights dimmed in the Polaris executive meeting room on the 53rd floor of the Grand Hyatt in Shanghai. There were sixteen designer, leather chairs stationed around the high-gloss, walnut conference table—eight of which would soon be occupied by sharply-dressed Chinese businessmen in dark suits and ties. Upon arrival, each guest presented his engraved invitation to the guard at the door, who shone a handheld UV light on it to ensure the appropriate symbol of the secret clan was stamped on the card at the intended location. The guard requested and received cell phones and all other potential transmitting or recording devices from each guest and placed them in a partitioned cabinet labeled with corresponding seat numbers. Passing through a metal detector in the short hall between the inner and outer doors, the attendees entered and promptly took the pre-assigned seats indicated on their invitations. Though there was a door at the far end of the meeting room, it was locked and guarded. There was only one way in and one way out.

No one really looked at each other, and they certainly did not speak. They just stared at the front chair, waiting purposefully. Soft music played in the background to mask any conversations that might have been taking place between the organizers as final details were being prepared.

The symbol on the invitation—the symbol of the "Zhonghua Nine"—had deep meaning and a long history. Behind the Chinese characters for Zhonghua and Nine on the group's symbol was the image of a dragon. For the men in the room, Zhonghua had two connotations. *Zhonghua Minzu* meant the "One China" they had always believed in, a notion of a unified country that included and assimilated all ethnic communities and lands that were Chinese in name and history. Zhonghua was also the name of the most famous gate in the city wall of Nanjing, known as the China Gate. It was built during the Ming Dynasty and for these men, the gate not only symbolized the strength of China and its history, but also held their attention for the massacre that had occurred in that city at the hands of the Japanese in 1937. Though the Japanese would have expunged the violence of those days from the record of the world's collective mind, the Zhonghua Nine's mission was to ensure that no one forgot.

The number nine, the last and greatest single-digit number, was historically associated with the Emperor of China. The Emperor's robes often had nine dragons, and Chinese mythology held that the dragon had nine children. When pronounced, the number nine sounds like the Chinese word meaning "long-lasting." Nanjing was one of the earliest established cities in Southern China; it had been the capital city of various dynasties over the millennia. It had been destroyed and rebuilt many times, and it was now one of China's largest commercial centers. "Long-lasting" was an appropriate term for Nanjing.

Finishing off the symbol design, the five-clawed dragon used in the background represented power, strength and good luck. These were all characteristics desired for the group. Together, the combined symbols represented the beliefs and desires of the collective group of nine.

One had to be chosen to join the high-ranking sect. None of the members knew of its existence before being approached, if "approached" is really the right word for it.

Once the Zhonghua Leader had selected a loyal, influential and powerful man to join the secret group, a message went out to the cult members to establish contact and begin compulsion. The man selected couldn't be just anyone; he had to already hold a unique position or possess certain potential to be promoted to a position in the military, government or university that would afford the Leader the skills, political savvy, and power needed to fulfill the cult's mission. The selection of the Nine was a well thought-out and essential process—the Leader's team was his arms and legs to do his work. He considered himself the soul and intelligence behind the movement, but each member of the team had his own superior intellect to support the operations.

As the selected one could not be allowed to expose the group, he was typically kidnapped, gagged and brought to a secret location where the discussion would begin. After a full history of the sect's formation, purpose and structure, and his proposed role in the organization, the conscript's choice was simple: either join the sect with full loyalty to the Zhonghua Nine, its Leader, and its goals, or face immediate execution. Fortunately, the prospect had already been fully investigated for his sympathy to the Nine's premises, principles and loyalties.

In the twenty years since its formation, only three men had chosen execution. Two of the sentences were carried out immediately, the bodies dumped discretely in the Huangpu River. However, the other's execution was the day after his indoctrination. It was clear he planned to alert the authorities and expose the Nine. Collisions between pedestrians and buses are, unfortunately, common occurrences in Shanghai, and the pedestrians almost always lose. If the potential conscript had been able to testify, he would have said that he was tripped and pushed at the same time; but with thirty other hurried, pushy pedestrians on the same crowded street corner in the Pu Dong district, it would have been difficult to prove his story, even if the man had lived.

Moments after the last attendee took his seat, the curtains to the expansive windows were automatically lowered, as if on cue, cutting from view the evening lights of the shimmering city and magnificent Pearl Tower.

Now securely out of sight of any potential witness beyond the group, the Leader walked in, slowly and deliberately. An old, crippled man, the Leader was escorted to his place at the head of the massive table, at which time the eight followers rose to attention and bowed to him in unison. At the same time, the guards exited the room and stood in the short hallway between the room and the outer door.

Though the Leader had founded their movement and society twenty years ago, his life, history and memory were much older. In fact, at 81 years old, the Leader even remembered the Rape of Nanking, as the massacre was then called. As a four-year-old during the invasion, he was lucky to escape with his life. If it were not for the Safety Zone set up by western missionaries and businessmen, the Leader would not have survived.

Experience with the government that abandoned the city during the Japanese invasion, as well as the ensuing insanity meted out by Mao's government during the Chinese Revolution, showed him that government could not be relied upon.

The current openness in the government—and its willingness to do business with the very nations that had tried to destroy their culture, history, and people—left the Leader with no choice but to recruit trusted allies with similar views and similar power with the aim of taking matters into their own hands.

When the Zhonghua Nine was formed, they didn't know how or when they would be able to seek their vengeance for past atrocities, and establish the rightful Zhonghua Minzu and its dominance in the world. They assumed that their destiny was assured, as they were guided by the good of the nation, its people and the principle of justice. They thought that greed, power and exploitation, which were once the foundation of domination they had experienced, would eventually be the seeds of destruction for these same adversaries. In their minds, they were in the right, and as their July target date was approaching, things were lining up on all fronts.

The Leader outstretched his gnarled hands and motioned downward as he said, "Please sit."

After the eight were seated, the Leader stayed standing and continued, "The time has come."

After a lengthy pause, he breathed deeply and deliberately, raised his fist, and stated: "Dormant Curse preparation is now complete and ready to be released."

Everyone in the room knew what project Dormant Curse was. It was the ultimate weapon. The Nine were instrumental in its development, design and deployment. Four years in the making, the ability to design such a pervasive and secret weapon only came to fruition with the latest development in high-technology, not developed in China, but assembled there for other purposes.

"The testing at our target city in the Midwest United States was completely successful. The test city allowed us to assess the impact on aircraft, homes, hospitals and vehicles, including ones just passing by town on the interstate highway. Seward, Nebraska is a town of only six thousand, barely the population of a city block here in Shanghai."

The Leader smiled broadly, obviously very pleased.

"The death count of ten was small enough that it did not catch the attention of the Federal Government. However, one plane, fifty homes and over one hundred vehicles were either disabled, damaged or destroyed. As a rural town, the Dormant Curse weapon was not as pervasive as it will be in higher-value target areas where people use advanced, leading-edge technology."

The Leader's smile turned into a small chuckle as he continued. "The Americans think that a freak magnetic pulse destroyed the processing and communication capabilities for the city. The article in the news said that a solar flare, sunspot or magnetic field anomaly was responsible. No additional investigation has been done, so they won't be any further along in figuring this out when the real attack happens…"

He paused for full effect.

"…which will be in precisely 15 minutes, at 7:30 a.m. on the East Coast of the United States."

This unanticipated announcement caused the energy in the room to suddenly rise as the cult members took it all in. Each of the eight wanted to talk, but decorum and respect demanded their silence.

The Leader could sense their tension, and expected it. He motioned for them to stand.

"Zhonghua Nine, my faithful and loyal sons, you have all known the parts you have had to play and have not questioned the overall plan. Have continued faith that this is the destined path toward glory, strength, power and vengeance. But please, ask questions if you must."

There was anxious silence in the room. No one wanted to be first to speak.

"Zhonghua Two?" asked the Leader as he extended his crippled hand toward the follower on his right. Names were not used among the sect, so as to not absentmindedly slip and expose an identity. "Do you have a question?"

Zhonghua Two quickly bowed toward the Leader and graciously asked, "Leader, may we know where is this next target?"

The Leader replied slowly. "We had considered attacking multiple targets at once, but then decided on a large section of a major US City…a city that would receive both public and Federal attention. I cannot tell you the city, but you will know shortly. Three…any questions?"

Zhonghua Three likewise bowed, and with a more nervous voice, asked "Leader, has the order already been given?"

"Yes, it has. Dormant Curse is now in motion and cannot be stopped, even by me. In fact, we will all sit in the room and watch the American news channel to see the results." The Leader's reply was serious, but he wore an underlying grin. "Zhonghua Four—any questions?"

Zhonghua Four detested his number. In Chinese the number four sounded much like the word used for "death." Most Chinese tried to avoid this number if at all possible. The Leader, astute man that he was, reserved this position for the most ruthless of the group, ensuring that the number assigned most closely matched the personality of its recipient. Zhonghua Four secretly suspected this, and likewise resented it.

With a crisp bow to the Leader, Four asked, "Will this demonstration be sufficient? Will we be allowed…I mean, will we *possibly* be required to perform another demonstration?" his own words revealing his sadistic tendencies.

"Zhonghua Four, remember that we are only using the weapon as a means to gain our ultimate goals. Our goal is not to destroy or permanently injure the United States. However, if the attack is insufficient to meet our needs, yes, we will be required to attack again. Once the initial attack occurs, it will be a race between the Americans discovering the source of Dormant Curse and our ability to attack again. We must act quickly on all other plans in order for our destiny to be fulfilled. However, we will only inflict injury to the extent required.

"The time for discussion is done; we have five minutes. Let us sit and face the display."

At the Leader's command, they turned their chairs to face the display at the other end of the room, which had been tuned to CNT.

"Now we wait," the Leader said with a sigh.

Thousands of miles away in a nondescript apartment in San Francisco, a rogue programmer was preparing unique messages to be sent through the top one hundred most-followed Blather accounts. Joe had been jilted in the initial public offering of Blather, and grew angry when he thought that not only should he be retired right now, but he should have been given credit for creating the core code Blather was based upon.

However, a friend he'd made last year who intended to start his own social networking company had asked Joe to help send out hacked Blather updates. It was supposedly a means to send hidden messages to his staff in the field who needed a way to get fast, secure information over otherwise public communication forums. Joe didn't feel too badly about making some money off the backdoor openings he had put into the system. The hacks were originally for testing, but he had never had a chance to seal them up before being forced out of the company. The money was good, a few hundred thousand a year for a few messages a month. Whoever was behind the operation had deep pockets and didn't want to be found out. The messages were so few and far between, Joe would never get caught, so he didn't really care who was paying him.

Today was unusual, though. Instead of a random message on a specific account, two messages were going out on many. The first message was clearly bogus and confusing, plausibly from someone playing a prank. The second, to come precisely two hours later, was either more gibberish from a celebrity or an apology from a politician recognizing the miss-sent message. The first was intended to go out early in the morning, when most followers wouldn't even read it. However, almost everyone in the Internet-connected age left computers, phones and iPads on all night to catch emails, texts and messages. All of these systems would still receive the coded message even if the owner was asleep.

Joe had already sent the first message and set his alarm to wake up ten minutes before the next one was due. He waited impatiently until precisely 4:30 a.m. to finish the job. He wasn't used to getting up this early and was looking forward to hitting Send and lying back in bed.

"55, 56, 57, 58, 59, Send!"

Joe hit Enter and waited for the messages to come full-circle, back to the accounts he was following. There they were, just as he had sent them.

All done, he thought as he quickly closed his lid, flopped back in bed and pulled his pillow over his head in one swift motion.

Little did Joe or anyone else but a few members of Zhonghua Nine know that a whole team of disconnected, disgruntled, independent programmers and hacks in the San Francisco Bay area had sent similar messages on Facebook, Twitter, Blather and other social networking sites, all simultaneously.

Dormant Curse had been released.

Chapter

(Six)

"Pop... pop, pop... pop..." Smartphones and tablet computers popping and smoking sounded like microwave popcorn. But the smell developing on the plane was anything but appetizing—the space suddenly reeked of burning, melting plastic. Yelps and cries for help came from across the plane. Within seconds, the cabin was being engulfed in smoke.

Michael had been dreaming about Jill and how good he felt when he was with her. He woke with a start. It took him a few seconds to realize where he was and what he was seeing.

"Mayday, mayday, mayday, this is American 1225, requesting emergency landing. We have a fire on board, I repeat, we have a fire on board," came the frantic call from the pilot.

The emergency request was met only with static on the receiver.

Again, the pilot tried to reach air traffic control: "Mayday, mayday, mayday, this is American 1225 requesting emergency landing. We have a fire on board!"

Suddenly, the radio sprung to life. "Mayday, mayday, mayday, this is Delta 289, we have a fire in the cockpit, I repeat, we have a fire in the—"

The transmission suddenly stopped.

"For God's sake, what's going on?" exclaimed the pilot.

"Jack, look at that!" Shouted the co-pilot as he pointed to a bright flame in the distance.

"Fred, we're going to land NOW. It's clear no one is listening on the other end and we're not going to try to make it to a runway." Jack accessed the PA system. "This is the Captain speaking. Prepare for emergency landing. Put on your seatbelts and oxygen masks. Hang on tightly."

Oxygen masks dropped from the ceiling and passengers frantically pulled them toward their faces to escape the toxic smoke.

In the cabin, though, smoke was already filling the space and burning lungs and eyes. Michael jumped out of his seat to help the flight attendants extinguish many of the fires. Blankets, drinks, and pitchers of water were all used to combat the smoke and flames.

Passengers whose seats were quickly becoming uninhabitable unbuckled their seatbelts to scramble for safer parts of the plane, clogging aisles and abandoning the safety of their oxygen masks in the process.

The captain, a skilled ex-military pilot, was acting quickly and decisively to push the descending plane to its limit. So far, the smoke and fire in the cabin had not made it into the cockpit. The trouble was determining where to land. Without contact with air traffic control, Jack was on his own. He aimed for the closest ribbon of highway he could see. The navigation system's last reading placed them over Northern Alabama, so the city off in the distance was likely Huntsville. Ominous smoke-trails on the horizon let him know that other planes were going down. There was no time to waste in coordinating a landing; he just needed to get on the ground.

Though it could hardly be noticed with all of the other commotion going on, there was a thin trail of smoke coming from the overhead bin in row 34. Michael's smartphone, left on in his bag, had also fried. The smoldering side-pocket had burst into flames.

In the meantime, the flight attendants, assisted by Michael and a few other courageous passengers, were succeeding in smothering the many fires. They were soon getting thrown around the plane, with their ears and sinuses screaming, while the pilot was making extreme descent maneuvers. But in the adrenaline rush of the moment, none of that was registering in their minds.

We may make it, thought the co-pilot as the highway came closer into view. The sun was up, but Jack hoped that his landing lights would be visible to the few cars on the road below.

"Passengers, prepare for landing!"

In the intensity of the moment, he had almost forgotten to warn them.

"Place your head between your knees if you can, with your hands clasped on top of your head, or brace your forehead against the seat in front of you. Now!"

Michael quickly ran for his seat. The tattooed beauty who had previously run to the back of the plane in a panic was now sitting in his place. Fortunately, her seat was still empty. He made eye contact with her and saw tremendous fear. Michael tried to smile reassuringly and mouthed, "It will be OK." It seemed to make an impact as the fear disappeared from her face, even if only for a moment.

Quickly jumping into the seat and buckling the seatbelt, Michael curled up into a ball as best he could. He knew that protecting his head and brain were key.

In the cockpit, there was no more time to talk or give further instructions to the crew or passengers. The highway was right below them and there was a curve in the road a little over a mile away. Jack knew he either had to land now, or try to line up for the next straight portion of road. Under normal circumstances, they needed nearly five thousand feet of runway to stop the heavy aircraft. The image of the other planes Jack had seen plummeting to the ground flashed through his mind. He backed off the engines and brought the nose up.

"This is it!" Jack exclaimed.

Cars on the highway that were behind the plane had quickly clued into the fact that something was up when they saw the body of the MD-80 rapidly descending over them. Some slowed and some hit their brakes or pulled onto the shoulder. In front of the plane, it was a different story. The few drivers that had seen the plane in their rear-view mirrors either grabbed the exit or ran off the road into the grassy median. However, one new Mustang GT decided his best chances were to accelerate. Going from 70mph to 180mph in about five seconds, he was quickly pulling ahead of the danger. The few cars that didn't see the plane at least saw the other cars' erratic driving, awoke to the danger and followed the others' paths—some with only seconds to spare.

The landing was hard, but the wheels stuck to the ground and gave Jack ample ability to hit the brakes and reverse thrust as hard as he ever had. The plane shuddered and groaned under the stress. It was only the plane's design that held the engines to the wings and kept the landing gear from collapsing.

As quickly as the plane skidded to a halt, the passengers in the emergency exit rows were pulling the doors out and leading others off the plane.

As he jumped up, Michael looked back toward the girl who had taken his seat. She looked almost petrified and wasn't moving very quickly. It was just then that Michael saw the smoke billowing out of the bin above her head—as the plane was now depressurized and the oxygen levels normal, the fire inside the overhead had more fuel.

Shit, that oxygen bottle! thought Michael.

The aisle was full of frantic passengers, so Michael jumped over the few empty seats between he and the girl. Her surprised look made it plain that she had no idea what in the world he was up to.

There was no time to explain. With her seatbelt already undone, Michael grabbed her by her tattooed arm and yanked her up out of her seat. She was a tall, thin girl, and with the momentum gained from Michael's strong pull, the girl flew by him in the space he created by shifting to the right, in a move almost as graceful as something he'd seen in "Dancing with the Stars." Pushing her in front of him and pulling her close to protect her with his own body, he tried hustling her toward the emergency exit.

In any other situation, the girl would have thought she was being assaulted. But Michael's heroic efforts in fighting the fires as well as the calming, winsome smile he had given her somehow left her trusting whatever he was doing.

There weren't many thoughts going through Michael's mind. He was acting on instincts that came from somewhere he couldn't have predicted. It was almost as if a force outside himself were using his body, leading his mind—providing him with speed, energy and strength.

All this time, the fire in the overhead in row 34 had been steadily growing behind the closed compartment door. The oxygen bottle had heated to its combustion point. A small micro-crack in the canister, caused by a stamped date code embossed into the side, provided the added stress that allowed a fracture to rapidly grow, releasing the pure, flammable oxygen. The explosion from the oxygen bottle was deafening, but Michael didn't hear it. All he saw was a flash and stars.

Then darkness.

Chapter

(Seven)

Greg had slept for a while by the time the coffee cart reached his row.

"Would you like something to drink?" the flight attendant asked with a bright smile.

"I could use some coffee, with cream and sweetener," Greg replied, weakly returning the smile as best he could.

While the attendant prepared the coffee, Greg pulled out the dinner tray from the arm of the seat and unfolded it in front of him.

"Here you go, with two creams and two sweeteners. I'll let you prepare it how you like it, hon."

"Thanks much," Greg responded.

As the passenger next to him was fast asleep, the attendant moved on to the next row. Greg causally sipped his coffee while looking through the in-flight magazine. There it was, right on the inside cover: The new Honda Galaxy. Though it sounded a little too much like the old Ford Galaxy, this car was anything but. The new Galaxy was a hybrid with 60 miles per gallon, leather seating, a long warranty and a full entertainment system with built-in 4G capability; passengers could browse the web, watch YouTube, keep up on Facebook, and get updates from Blather while traveling. Of course, other cars already had a lot of this capability, but 4G was the big plus. The network served as a gateway to the Internet through built-in Bluetooth for all other devices a driver carried. Being the gadget freak he was, this car was like a dream for Greg.

Greg suddenly heard the engines change pitch as the nose of the aircraft tipped ever so slightly downward.

Whoa, descending already? thought Greg.

Greg looked at his watch. It had only been an hour. We've got two more to go, he reasoned. At the same time, he noticed a flight attendant speaking with a big man who got up to take a position outside the cockpit door.

Is that an Air Marshal? he thought. Something was up.

"This is the pilot speaking," came the overhead announcement. "There's no need to be alarmed, but we have been requested…well, ordered to make a landing in Huntsville. I know this is an inconvenience, and I don't have the details, but we know there is a good explanation. This order is in effect for all planes, that is, all planes must land at the nearest accessible airport. We are a little different in that we have a couple passengers onboard from the National Transportation Safety Board who are needed in Huntsville; otherwise, we'd be landing in Omaha.

"The good news is that Huntsville will be a decent airport for us to get out of once we know what's going on and we are allowed to take off again. We appreciate your patience.

"In the meantime, would Greg Cannon please press the call button above your seat?"

It took Greg a couple of seconds to realize that his name had just been called. The flight had started to feel somewhat like a dream. They were descending early with no real explanation. There was an Air Marshal guarding the cockpit, and now Greg's name was being called. As he pressed his call button, he noticed Dennis stand up from his seat in first class. Since the attendants had his name and seat recorded for meals, he had already been identified. Dennis looked back and made eye contact with Greg. He looked at the marshal, pointed to Greg and motioned for him to come to the front of the plane. Some relief came over Greg as he realized he wasn't being singled out for any crime, but instead this request was likely related to his job. Something serious had to be going down for NTSB to find them on this plane and redirect their flight.

Greg chugged the remaining portion of his coffee, snapped his tray table back into place and slowly made his way toward the front. At the same time, an attendant, apologizing profusely, directed a passenger in first class back to Greg's seat, where the call light was still displayed. The passenger, a short, slightly balding, middle-aged businessman wore a mix of confusion, embarrassment and fear. He smiled awkwardly at Greg when they met at about the sixth row, near the bulkhead.

Dennis slid over to the window seat to give Greg the aisle in the first row. With his laptop open, Dennis was using Skype to have an online conversation with headquarters.

"Greg, this is serious. You know me well enough now to know I don't shit around," Dennis said in a hushed tone without even looking up from his Skype conversation.

Dennis never talked in a hushed tone, that wasn't his style, which made Greg pay attention even more, if that were at all possible.

"We've had some type of disruption or attack. We don't know what happened exactly. We have about a five-mile radius around the Hartsfield Airport in Atlanta that's been impacted. There're cars, trucks, houses, commercial buildings and schools that have been hit. And we've got planes down, as in crashed, with no likely survivors. What's strange is that some planes that took off from Atlanta were in completely different locations when they got hit, which makes an EMP highly unlikely. Something may have happened to them while in Atlanta."

Dennis finally looked at Greg straight on before continuing.

"So we're off to Huntsville. We have a plane from Atlanta that managed to survive the attack and land there. Oh, it got hit, and they almost lost it. But HQ says they landed on a highway east of town. Good thing it was before rush hour and on the slow side of the city, or we'd have an even bigger mess to look at.

"Where's your laptop?" Dennis asked.

In the heat of the moment, Greg had left his bags in the overhead above row 16. It hadn't dawned on him that he was coming up here to work.

"I'll go back and get it," explained Greg as he took off his seatbelt.

"Well, hurry, we have a lot of prep work to do before we land. The highway is closed off and I don't want anyone touching that plane. It's a crime scene, and anything they mess with could jeopardize the investigation."

Greg stood up and made his way back to his original seat. With this new information, his head was spinning even more. Cars had been hit? What did that mean? Dennis had pretty much already ruled out an electro-magnetic pulse, and

Greg would have to agree. This seemed like something that affected everything in a specified area. Did it happen all at once, or had it spread from some central source? If so, how? The number of possibilities seemed endless.

Greg realized that a number of passengers were watching him very closely. Perhaps they were trying to pick up from this obviously important individual whether they had cause for concern. Others were clearly irritated at the prospect of the detour, which would surely disrupt plans for the day, and were partially blaming Greg. After all, wasn't it Greg who was called to the front immediately after the pilot's announcement? Wasn't it Greg who was responsible for the first class passenger having to give up his seat?

Greg quickly gathered his computer bag and returned to first class. He thought it best not to bother with his carry-on, given that he didn't know if there was room in first class for it, nor did he want to draw any more attention to himself.

Safely in his new seat, Greg opened his computer, waited for it to come out of sleep mode, and logged in.

Dennis updated Greg on the rapidly developing situation.

"We've got a number of casualties, Greg," Dennis whispered. "With the severity of this incident and our need to keep this in confidence, I'd like to use only Skype to communicate between us as well, though I know how strange that sounds right now with you sitting next to me. Just trust me on this."

Greg's computer was up and running now and he'd signed onto the onboard Wi-Fi access point. He dutifully opened Skype and waited for Dennis' instant message. This did seem a little strange, Skyping the person sitting right next to you, but within a few lines, he began to understand the seriousness of the situation and why it was important not to alert nor alarm the passengers.

"little info from ATL," Dennis wrote.

"lots of planes down, car wrecks. fatalities. communication knocked out."

"at 7:30. 10 planes hit. 9 crashed. likely no survivors."

"current ATL cond unknwn. ATL office handling."

"U and I dissect huntsville plane. it's locked down. this was an attack."

Dennis looked up from his keyboard to look Greg full in the eyes. Dennis usually looked pretty serious to begin with, but the look Greg saw now was severe and determined. The reality was that Dennis was prepared for an incident like this. It was about time that a national security crisis occurred. He had somewhat expected it, though the expectation was more like dread. As such, Dennis was already down the path toward eliminating possibilities and solving the mystery behind the attack.

"We're gonna solve this, Greg," Dennis said. "We can't let this happen again, whatever the cause."

"Passengers, prepare for landing," came the call over the speaker. Both Greg and Dennis begrudgingly put away their computers, sat their seat backs upright, and willed the plane to land.

Chapter

(Eight)

Numerous calls into **911** from frantic motorists alerted the Emergency Services Unit at the Huntsville Hospital of the emergency landing; operators dispatched MedFlight and ambulances to the scene. Huntsville Hospital, the area's only Level One Trauma Center, was hardly prepared to handle the size of the emergency they were now facing.

What the emergency crews found when they arrived was surreal. It took them a moment to understand what had happened and assess what steps to take next. The MD-80 had skidded to a halt in the middle of the highway, just past the Madison County High School. Most passengers were on the ground outside the plane, with some screaming that others were still trapped inside. Quickly onboard with their equipment and self-contained breathing apparatus, the emergency crew extinguished a fire at the back of the plane and saved a few of the passengers who were on the floor of the aircraft. But for seven passengers at the rear, it was much too late. An explosion onboard had knocked many unconscious and smoke inhalation had finished them off.

Michael was one of those knocked to the ground in the oxygen tank explosion. So was the girl he'd rescued from his previous seat in row 34. While the girl had merely been stunned by the blast, Michael had been knocked unconscious. Along with the explosion came shrapnel and a shockwave induced concussion. Those stuck behind row 32 didn't survive the immediate injury and ensuing fire and smoke. Shards of the blown-apart oxygen bottle ripped through the overhead bin and sliced through fragile flesh while the extreme heat sealed the fate of those nearby.

Since Michael had made it a few rows further up the aisle, he didn't suffer the full impact and heat from the explosion. Having been knocked to the ground, his unconscious body was below the initial flames and resultant ceiling of smoke. His fall likely kept him alive and saved the girl's life.

Michael didn't remember the firefighters who made it onto the plane and carried him out to the waiting ambulance. He wasn't aware when the IV was placed in his arm or the breathing tube shoved down his trachea. He wasn't even conscious when they wheeled him into the ER. As is the case in most bombings, the full extent of some patients' injuries only became apparent after the fact. Michael was badly injured.

The Alabama State Patrol had been first on the scene. They made certain everyone's identification was obtained before anyone left, whether they left on their own power or were carried off. They even got Michael's driver's license information and recorded which hospital he was being taken to before the ambulance headed out.

Sergeant Cooper always hated making these calls, but he knew if his son were in trouble, he'd want to know right away.

"Mrs. James? Are you the mother of Michael James, from Milton, Georgia? Mrs. James, I'm Sergeant Larry Cooper with the Alabama State Patrol. I'm so sorry to be calling you with bad news, but there's been an accident..."

Chapter
(Nine)

*T*he **breaking news** of the Atlanta incident was starting to hit news channels, and the Zhonghua Nine were watching CNT intently to see the extent of the damage.

It wasn't a coincidence that Atlanta was hit with the first real attack. And it wasn't luck that limited the strike radius to just five miles around the airport. The Leader had thought through every detail. Atlanta was the global headquarters for CNT, and the radius of the attack brought the damage to within a mile of the network news station's door. If they wanted to observe the damage, all they had to do was drive a mile or two to see it firsthand. And for the past decade or more, Hartsfield-Jackson Atlanta International had been ranked as the busiest airport in the world. More than two thousand planes took off each day from its runways to destinations all across the United States.

So it was with glee that the Leader broke into a broad smile as the morning stock market forecast on the channel was interrupted by the breaking story from Atlanta, accompanied by live images of fires erupting and downed planes.

"Zhonghua Four, I hope this answers your concerns about whether the attack was sufficient to get the public's and government's attention," said the Leader. "The US public loves a good crisis movie. They love to be scared and worried about disasters. They will be glued to their televisions today. Now is the time to give the order to begin troop movement. The US will think we are going after Taiwan. They are sorely mistaken. We effectively already own Taiwan. When they figure out our real destinations, it will be too late to act, and if they even think about intervening, we will hit them again. And again."

When a few of the Zhonghua Nine heard the word "destinations," they wanted to ask the Leader what was meant. That word seemed confusing for them. As far as they knew, there was only one destination: some small, nondescript islands in dispute between China and Japan. Did he mean the multiple islands? Or did he mean something broader? As much as they wanted to ask, they kept silent in respect and obedience.

The islands, if one were to call them that, were called *Diaoyutai* in Chinese and *Senkaku* in Japanese. These rocks were yet another symbol of the history of strife between the two countries. A series of eight tiny lumps of land, with a total area of barely eight square kilometers. Except for a small lighthouse some zealous Japanese citizens had erected in the early seventies, there was little to suggest any type of habitation. The history of the islands traced back hundreds of years, with China having significant claim to them until they were, in the Leader's view, taken by force by Japan with the Treaty of Shimonoseki in 1885. China was coerced into ceding many islands, including Formosa, which was thereafter known as Taiwan. That treaty was rendered null and void after Japan's loss in World War II and their co-signing of the Treaty of Peace in 1952.

It wasn't until oil was discovered in the area in 1968 that anyone really seemed to care about the subminiature islands and how all of these treaties affected ownership. The discovery started a three-way battle over the mineral rights to the find, with Taiwan, China and Japan all laying claim. To make matters more confusing, the US, which had been in control of the islands following Japan's loss in World War II, yielded control back to Japan in the early seventies. Given that the original Treaty of Peace was between China and Japan—the US decided to let them sort it out.

Since the matter had not been resolved in courts, ongoing conflict remained. If China won the argument of ownership, it would strengthen their claim that the continental shelf off China extended far out into the East China Sea giving them ownership. If Japan won, their Exclusive Economic Zone would extend to the disputed reserves.

The problem was that the conflict appeared to be escalating. Where Japan and China had seemingly ironed out some of their differences, even going so far as to sign joint exploration agreements, the constant changeover in Japanese Premiers caused frequent shifts in the political landscape. With the latest hostilities, along with additional, significant natural gas reserves discovered, and China's ongoing, increasing demand for energy, China was running out of patience. To make matters worse, the 2011 earthquake and resulting tsunami damaged Japan's nuclear power plants, causing some to be permanently shut down. This further drove Japan's need to find new sources of energy. They weren't going to let the islands and reserves go without a fight.

China developed many new markets and trading partners in India, Vietnam, Singapore, Malaysia, Africa, South America, North America and, in particular, certain states in the Mid-East, including Iran and Syria. Japan's influence had steadily dropped in China, partly due to China's new dominance in the renewable energy, electronics and automotive industries. Their steady, decades-long strategy of forcing hopeful foreign businesses to set up joint ventures with local Chinese companies had paid off. More and more businesses were becoming not just mindless manufacturing extensions of the goods they produced, but bona fide developers and creators of unique goods and services sold all over the world. With this landscape, China was growing ever more powerful as Japan's influence waned.

In the Leader's mind, this was the perfect time to retake what had been stolen and begin the first steps in what would be long-term dominance over Japan as punishment for Nanjing. Very few in the United States, Europe or the United Nations understood or cared about the issues surrounding the Diaoyutai islands. Amid the chaos unleashed on the US today, taking possession of a few small rocks in the sea would seem of little consequence to anyone.

Unknown to the rest of the Nine, yet another scenario was starting to play out in the Middle East and in the US stock markets. The Leader was involved in many plans, all hinging on this one day. He saw no reason not to have some personal gain from the crisis he knew was to unfold. Any benefit he received was, in his mind, a just reward for his loyalty to the Spirit of Zhonghua.

The Chinese President, Li Zhuàng, was completely aware of the plans for Dormant Curse, and had waited for the command to be issued to the Central Military Commission (CMC) to begin the assault. The Leader had the President's ear and was partially responsible for his rapid rise in responsibility and authority. The President felt honored to be China's leader while positioning the country for future growth and security. He didn't feel as strongly as the Leader about past atrocities, but knew the Leader's passion for revenge could be used for China's gain.

President Li was also the Chairmen of the CMC and had the authority to issue an attack order. His CMC Vice Chairman was also the Commanding General in China's People's Liberation Army, whom he looked to for direction. The General was none other than Zhonghua Three. Three didn't know that the President was aware of their cult and of his role in it, which was misinformation the leader intended. There were many layers of secrecy to the Leader's plan and its execution, allowing various participants to focus on their specific roles while allowing plausible deniability.

The President placed orders for a portion of the strategic missiles along the coast, once solely aimed at Taiwan, to be redirected toward the US military base on the Japanese island of Okinawa. Okinawa was only two hundred miles from Diaoyutai and was a wild card in the mission, which is why Dormant Curse was so important. Dormant Curse was the secret weapon that would force the US to stand down. The missiles were merely a backup plan.

Japan and Korea had been putting up with China's military exercises in the East China Sea for some time. China used these exercises as a display of might as well as an illustration of what lengths they would go to in order to protect the oil and gas reserves. So it wasn't a surprise when China's flotilla of ships began making their way into the East China Sea. This movement was only a diversion from the real target. This launch was no exercise.

The Chinese military leaders in charge of the flotilla recognized something different in the orders this time. There was an unusual sense of urgency from the ranking officer's command to launch, along with an atmosphere of excitement, fear and importance among the ranks. The ensuing order to turn in all communication devices, cell phones, smartphones and the like was also highly unusual. Very few in the ranks could afford such devices, but in case a real assault occurred, the military was taking no chances that anyone would be tipped off.

The Leader now had a peaceful, anticipatory look on his face. It was time.

"Zhonghua Three, give the order."

Zhonghua Three placed his call from the Shanghai Hyatt to his subordinate in the CMC.

"Begin Dormant Curse immediately," he commanded.

The key words triggered a series of calls, transmissions and orders that filtered through the Chinese military system. While it wasn't a surprise that the attack order had been given, it was still extraordinary since no one currently in command had seen real combat in their lifetimes. This was a real order. This was not a drill. Initial movement toward Taiwan was to commence immediately. Ships participating in war games about two hundred miles southeast of Shanghai in the East China Sea were to set sail toward Taipei, on the north end of Taiwan, then pull short and aim for the Diaoyutai islands at full speed.

When Zhonghua Three dialed his call, a guard in the Polaris room quietly slipped out to make his own preset call at the Leader's request. The guard's call went to the Iranian Embassy in Beijing. The message to the Ambassador was short: "Dormant Curse has begun." That call, in turn, began a whole series of calls and responses thousands of miles away in Iran.

The Leader, taking advantage of his knowledge of the date and time of the attacks, had done some of his own behind-the-scenes preparation by shorting US telecommunications companies' stocks and prearranging the immediate payment of five hundred million US dollars from the Iranian government into a Swiss bank account. Neither the Chinese President nor Zhonghua knew of this addendum to the Leader's plans.

Chapter
(Ten)

*A*s soon as **Dennis** and Greg landed, they quickly got their rental car and headed from Carl T. Jones Airport in Huntsville toward the landing site. It took Dennis about fifteen minutes to get through to the local FBI office to see about getting an escort to the plane. Fortunately, when Dennis finally got through, the local office was more than accommodating. They were already onsite, and would send a special agent to escort them through the mess developing on the highway. They would meet at the intersection of Wall Road and Highway 72 before the roadblock at Moontown Road, a mile or so away from the plane.

The FBI's hazardous devices school was located at Redstone Arsenal, right outside Huntsville. Instructors from the school scoured the wreckage and had given the "all-clear" that there were no remaining bombs, improvised or otherwise, onboard the plane. While this knowledge gave Dennis some sense of calm, it also left him concerned that the site had been disturbed, potentially mucking up evidence that might have helped him determine what had happened during flight.

The highway had been shutdown and traffic was pretty well backed up. News about the incident travelled fast and frantic parents, receiving calls from teenagers at the nearby high school, tried to make their way over to pick up their kids. Of course, there was some sense of voyeurism that went along with this; parents wanted to see the action for themselves. Radio and TV stations picked up the news, but also heard the appeal from State Patrol and FBI telling listeners to stay away from the area—that there was no danger to the community, nor to the students, and that coming out for a look would just cause more problems.

Agent Tony Donovan parked by the side of the road, waiting patiently for Dennis and Greg to show up in their rental. It was a new Cadillac DTS, a little glitzy for Dennis' taste, but one of the only cars they could get quickly, making it easy for Donovan to pick them out in the crowd of cars lined up. Once he spotted them, Donavan quickly got out of his SUV and motioned for them to drive on the shoulder up to where he was parked.

"That looks like our guy, over there on the shoulder," Greg said, seeing Donovan waving them over.

"He didn't say he was black, I'm not so sure..." Dennis said.

"Like that matters. There's not a whole lot of other officers looking straight at us and waving us forward."

"Good point, but where's his FBI jacket?" Dennis countered, observing Donovan's dark, unmarked jacket.

"That's only on raids, Dennis," Greg said, shaking his head.

"I'm just messing with ya. I told him what car we were driving, so that's got to be him," Dennis said, giving a raspy laugh.

Donovan's salt and pepper hair indicated an age somewhat in conflict with his well-built physique. His stern gaze signified that he was all business today, if not always.

Dennis rolled down his window.

"Agent Donovan?"

"Yes, that's me. Cannon and Wright?"

"That's us."

Dennis looked over at Greg with a smirk.

Donovan wasted no time in getting down to it.

"Look, we've got a mess of traffic building up, kids locked down in school and a national crisis in the making. I'll explain more when we get to the site. Right now, I need you to follow me. Across the intersection we have a Trooper who's gonna give us a fast escort through this initial backup, past the roadblock, then down to the plane. OK?"

Dennis had questions, but he'd save them for later. "Sure, we appreciate the help."

"No problem. Frankly, I think you got your work cut out for you. There's no evidence of a bomb, though it appears we had an oxygen bottle explosion. It looks to me like the plane just self-destructed. This is the only plane that survived what we presume to be an attack. So you have some fast work you've gotta do to figure this out. OK, let's go," said Donovan before jogging back to his black Suburban.

Once they were escorted by State Patrol, they reached the site rather quickly. Besides the police cruisers, ambulances and fire trucks still stationed around the wreckage, the first thing Greg noticed about the plane was the large hole in the starboard side. It looked like the plane had been hit by a small missile, but the metal was twisted open from the inside. Clearly this was the explosion Donovan had referred to. But with a hole that size, the plane would have totally decompressed and passengers would have been sucked out. That certainly didn't fit the description they had been given before landing.

Donovan wasted no time in relaying the current plan. "OK, guys, we've gotten all passengers and crew off the plane and the injured are either already at one of the local hospitals or en route. We've cleared the plane for explosives—there weren't any—and secured the perimeter. What we'd like you to do, unless you discover something that conflicts with this plan, is gather any and all evidence and photos that you need that would be disturbed by us moving the plane.

Dennis nodded.

"The plane looks intact to us, except for that gaping hole in the side, and I'll explain our theory on that in a moment. If you concur, we have permission to move the plane over to the Baptist church parking lot over there," he said, motioning to the facility with the white roof and steeple just up the road, "which we'd like to do as soon as possible to get traffic flowing again and get the kids from the high school back to their parents."

Dennis took a slow look around, taking in the surroundings.

"Couldn't have picked a much better place to land this bird," Dennis said. "You've got utility poles on the other side of the road that would have snapped off a wing, somersaulted the plane, spewed fuel and created a nice fireball had he landed there. This here is a nice straight stretch of road, and it looks like nothin' worth mentioning happened on the ground as far as damage or injuries. Having a parking lot to move this beast so close by doesn't hurt either.

"Let me and Greg get onboard and get anything documented that might be disturbed during a move, like you said. I'm particularly interested in the cockpit. But I don't see why we can't get that done quickly and get things set up over at the church so we can begin investigation in earnest," Dennis concluded. "The sooner we can get that going, the better.

"By the way, it's really important that we interview as many of the passengers and crew as possible while everything is still fresh in their minds. Are there still some here to talk with while the plane's being moved?"

Donovan had looked pretty upbeat until Dennis posed that question.

"Yeah, well, that's kind of a problem, actually," he said with a frown. "None of the passengers intended on landing in Huntsville, so most are trying to find another way outta here. The crew has been given orders by the airline not to talk with anyone until their lawyers get here, which is completely ridiculous. American clearly doesn't want to open themselves up to liability, so they're getting all their ducks in a row."

Dennis cussed under his breath. When there are survivors in a crash, he knew the best way to discover the timing of events was to immediately interview eye witnesses. This was going to make things tough, or at least slow. In his mind, they had absolutely no time to waste.

A news helicopter nearby caught Dennis' attention and distracted him from his train of thought.

"Donovan, try to clear this airspace, OK? We don't need that going on while we're trying to get an investigation done," he said, pointing toward the copter.

Regaining his thought process, Dennis continued, "What about the injured? Do we have anyone in good enough shape to be interviewed?"

"Let me check on that and get back to you. We certainly have passengers in local hospitals right now. If we have to, we'll get some agents over there right away to take down statements."

"Thanks for your help, but I'd like to interview some myself, if possible. One last thing—I'm assuming all luggage is still onboard?"

"Yeah, well, mostly," Donovan replied. "There were a few passengers that had left purses or billfolds onboard, and of course they needed these for getting to cash and credit cards. Once we draped off the area past row 32, for obvious reasons that you'll see, we escorted passengers one at a time to retrieve critical items. Everything else is still intact. We went through some items during the bomb search, but it's all there."

"My gut tells me maybe there *was* an *onboard* electromagnetic impulse device—just local to the plane—so I'm assuming the EMP generator will still be there, if that was the cause," replied Dennis.

Greg had been listening intently but also thinking logically through things at the same time.

"Agent Donovan, before you leave and we start our work, I'd like to know more about that explosion," interjected Greg.

"Oh, right. Well, word from the passengers is that the explosion took place after the plane landed. Go figure. They've landed, they're getting safely off the plane with no serious injuries so far, and then *kaboom*, the oxygen bottle blows up. We noticed a lot of fried smartphones and iPads onboard, too. I'm not talking just heated and melted, either; these devices were *on fire* and *started fires*."

"That's consistent with an EMP, but that oxygen bottle is not...and neither is the fact that the plane's electronics were intact enough to land," Greg said, thinking out loud. "An EMP would have taken them out as well."

"Like I said, you've got your work cut out for you," came Donovan's reply. He wasn't sure he really liked Greg too much so far.

"We've got enough tools to get started. Let's collect the data we need before the plane can be moved and let local law enforcement do what they need to do. I've got confirmation our full set of gear will be out here within the hour. We'll do what we can for now."

Chapter
(Eleven)

*T*he **President of the** United States called an emergency meeting of his National Security Council as soon as word reached him regarding the attack on Atlanta. Many things were happening at once, and it was not only unclear what was going on, but who was behind it. The President had utterly mishandled the last big disaster, and being mid-way through his second term, he didn't want to be remembered for his failures.

The Secretary of Homeland Security, Carl Johnson, had just arrived in the Situation Room and was prepared to brief him on what they knew so far.

"Mr. President, what we know is sketchy at this point, but we have all our agencies on the ground investigating each and every aspect of this incident. If you'd please turn your attention to the screen."

The projected image displayed was one that looked like it had come out of a war zone.

"This is an image of I-85 about three miles due west of the Atlanta airport. What you're looking at is the burned-out fuselage of a Boeing 757 with maybe twenty cars completely obliterated nearby. At approximately 7:32 a.m. today, cars, buses and planes were all hit with some type of impulse that caused most of them within about a five-mile radius of the airport to self-destruct. This was devastating for both inbound and outbound flights. Most planes that were in the air when they got hit were not able to land safely. Full fuel tanks made crash sites instant infernos. We're talking almost two thousand passenger and crew fatalities and possibly more than that on the ground. The commuter traffic was possibly the worst it could have been. Only one plane was able to safely land and with very few casualties."

The President and Security Council members squirmed anxiously and murmured as they talked among themselves. They all wanted to ask questions at the same time. The President, sensing this, raised his own hand and motioned to the staff to keep quiet, for now.

"We're looking into every possible cause. As the geometric center of the attack is the airport, we have local police, FBI, ATF and NTSB all onsite, scouring the area for anything that might look like an electromagnetic impulse weapon. As the area is under great duress, you can imagine the difficulty in getting things organized. To that end, we've asked the Governor to call up the National Guard and State Patrol to bring some order to the developing chaos."

The President had too many questions running through his head to keep quiet any longer. Always one to worry about control, he interjected, "Carl, are you in total charge of the operation?"

"Mr. President, we anticipated such an attack and already had a plan of action. Each agency involved has a counter-terrorism plan in place, coordinated by the Department of Homeland Security. Though no plan fits perfectly with every incident, we do have a plan of action, chain-of-command, and roles and responsibilities defined for our response—"

"So this was a terrorist attack? Do we know that for certain?"

"Mr. President, while we don't have a group claiming responsibility, it has all the marks of an attack. Our investigation might uncover some natural phenomenon that would explain the incident or a fundamental flaw in some electronics, but I would say that's highly unlikely."

"So we have to assume this could happen again."

Carl nodded.

"Any motive that we know of?" the President asked, looking around the room.

The Director of National Intelligence, Henry Cline, spoke up. "Mr. President, if I may?"

"Sure, Hank."

"Well, we have a few things going on globally that we've picked up on our overheads. At about 8:30 a.m. Eastern this morning, we detected significant movement of the Chinese Navy toward Taiwan. Along with this, we detected a lot of chatter on the airwaves in the East China Sea. Unfortunately, most of it was encrypted and it will take time to translate."

"What makes you think it's not a typical war game?"

"Mr. President, three indictors. First, the chatter I just mentioned. In addition, where they typically have one 'team' pitted against the other in their exercises, this is the whole fleet moving in concert. Finally, the speed and trajectory of the fleet are all lined up...directly at Taiwan."

"What do your operatives report?"

"We have a few agents in the Chinese Navy, but the ones deployed on this latest set of war games have indicated that all electronics were being confiscated before this latest mission. We have no contact with them now. However, our agents in Shanghai indicated that they have no reason to suspect a strike on Taiwan. This doesn't quite add up for us."

"Are they anywhere near Okinawa?"

"Yes, Sir."

"General, what are we doing in response?"

"We've scrambled P-3s stationed in South Korea for reconnaissance. We'll be receiving details within the next thirty minutes. We put Okinawa on alert as well. They're standing by for further orders."

"Excellent work, everyone," said the President. "Anything else?"

The Director raised his hand.

"Yes, Hank?"

"Actually, there's more."

"My apologies. Go on."

"Our overheads have also detected movement of troops in Iran. They're taking up positions along the border with Iraq, specifically near the border crossings at Shalamche, Mehran, and Khosravi. The movement is slow but deliberate. In this case, our overheads and listening posts in Iraq have detected and decrypted some of the transmissions. We clearly have a build-up of some sort. The exact nature of it is still undetermined."

This update further heightened the President's concern. The withdrawal of troops from the Middle East had been a tenuous affair. The stability of the region wasn't quite where he had wanted it to be before pulling out, and having Iran enter Iraq, filling the void, was something they tried to monitor closely. Iranian troops in Iraq would give them control of tremendous oil reserves and place them one nation closer to Israel. Shia sympathizers in Iraq weren't likely to put up much of a fight, either.

The President looked hard at Henry; this was a lot to absorb at once. After some contemplation, he finally spoke.

"OK, let's see if we have this straight. We have a terrorist attack on Atlanta of unknown cause, origin, or party of responsibility. We have movement of the Chinese Navy toward Taiwan, which doesn't take a rocket scientist to figure out—no offense Carl. And we have Iranian troops gathering on the border with Iraq. Connect the dots, gentlemen—all indications are that we have some type of coordinated effort taking place, unless you believe in extraordinary coincidences on a global level."

There was silence in the room as everyone took it all in.

"We'll reconvene in one hour. I'll be making calls to our allies, to the Iranian president—if he will speak to me—and to China's President Li. As always, Hank, I want voice analysis on each call to detect stress and truthfulness. I expect we'll know much more on every front when we reconvene. Compartmentalize whatever you can. If there aren't any other questions? Okay, let's get to it."

The Council members dispersed purposefully.

"Ned," the president called to his Chief of Staff, "I need this room set up within the hour. I don't expect we'll be leaving here for the rest of the day. You know the drill."

Ned gave one last statement. "By the way, Mr. President, the attack was basically on CNT's doorstep…news is flowing out faster then we can manage it."

"Yeah, but there's no news out there on Iran or China. We need to keep it that way for now. And if you think it was a coincidence that CNT had a front-porch view to this scene, think again. There's more going on than we know. A terrorist would have claimed responsibility by now. Let's get to the Oval Office and set up some calls…."

Chapter
(Twelve)

Dennis and Greg had been photographing every inch inside and outside of the plane as quickly as possible, making voice memos as they went along to try to document each aspect of the scene in case something went wrong when the plane was moved. Of all of the locations on the plane, the cockpit was relatively unscathed, which was some sort of evidence in itself; they just weren't sure what it meant quite yet.

In Dennis' experience, one didn't jump to conclusions too fast, even if he had done a little of that already. He had to gather all of the evidence, interview whomever he could, and then let his mind synthesize all the pieces together. Sometimes, he would wake up in the middle of the night with an "ah-ha" moment after his brain worked out a solution. He always slept with a pad of paper next to his bed.

Greg was trying to synthesize as he went. Some evidence he saw would point him in one direction, then another piece would rule out his latest mental theory and put him on a different track.

When Greg pulled back the curtain set up to cordon off row 32 and beyond, he was taken aback by what he saw. While mindlessly browsing websites at home, he had occasionally seen gruesome pictures of accidents, but this scene was the real thing, and it was nauseating. He quickly took pictures, and fought the urge to vomit during the course of the work. He tried to suppress his feelings and follow through with what he had been trained to do. If any areas were to degrade in the course of the investigation, this death zone would be the most impacted as the residual flesh, blood and bone deteriorated. This was a key location to document.

As they were wrapping up, Greg had an epiphany.

"Dennis, I need to take a few things off the plane."

"You know that's not part of our normal process, Greg."

"Yeah, but does this all seem normal to you? And I see something that I can start investigating right away while they're moving the plane and you're interviewing survivors."

"OK, what is it?"

"Well, as I was taking pictures of the overhead bin around the front bulkhead, I noticed an undamaged Dazzle phone lying out—it must have been pulled out as FBI was doing their sweep for bombs. Funny thing is, I saw an identical phone in the row in front of the exit row."

"That would be row 11. So?"

"OK, row 11. The phone in row 11 obviously blew out. It was scorched, but looked like it got put out rather quickly. It wasn't totally destroyed like the other phones we saw in the burned-out rows. Whether it didn't get the full impact of the pulse, didn't have as full a battery or whatever, it was only partially damaged. Point is we have two identical phones. One impacted, one not at all, from its appearance. If I can find out the difference between these supposedly identical phones, I think it will point us in the right direction."

"Well, what if the difference is that one was on and one was off?"

"I guess I would find that out when I turn it on."

"Whoa, then we have destroyed evidence," said Dennis.

"OK, what if I pull the battery and take them both apart to look for physical evidence only?"

"This is why we need to be working together. You really can't be doing this stuff without other advisors. If you turned the phone on and it toasted, that error in judgment could cost you your job on a highly visible case like this. I know you're new to this, but everything—and I mean *everything*—you might do from this moment on is in the public eye. Expect that once you walk out the door, there's a camera somewhere, filming you. Whether you're picking your nose or turning on a phone that explodes in your hands, it's all public. I've been through this before. If a scapegoat is needed in the future, you don't want to give the press or management a reason to make you one.

"So, yes, take the phones. But get an evidence bag to do it. We'll bring them with us and figure out how to start processing them as soon as we can. If I didn't suspect this could happen again, and happen very soon, I wouldn't be bending the rules like this. We have to get to a solution quickly—and not just a conjecture or a made-up solution to appease the press."

Greg quickly ran to collect the two phones, placing them in an opaque evidence bag, to keep anyone from seeing what was being taken from the plane. As Greg and Dennis exited the craft, they saw Agent Donovan standing by a plane dolly absconded from the airport. They were ready to move the plane once Greg and Dennis were done.

"Having a party in there?" Donovan said as Greg and Dennis stepped down the ladder.

Greg gave him a confused look.

"Well, you took long enough. See all the local police lined up over there? Traffic has become a nightmare and we have parents up in arms…"

"Donovan, don't get me wrong," Dennis started, "I like you and all, and your help here has been instrumental in getting us in quickly to document…but you have no idea what the fuck we're dealing with here! I know parents want their kids back home safe, and they'll get that, but we have a likely terrori—"

Dennis noticed the camera crew on the side of the road, about a hundred yards away from the plane. He quickly turned his back to the camera and swung Donovan around to face the same direction.

"What are *they* doing here?" Dennis said under his breath.

"We could only hold them off so long. They're looking for some type of statement, but we're not giving them anything."

"Hell, you get someone over there right now and take whatever tape they just made. We don't need what I just said to you broadcasted," he said in a deliberate, hushed tone.

"Hey, this is the modern age—this is all transmitted back to their station. It's not live, but likely the 'tape' is a hard drive back at their office."

"Greg, let's get going. Walk with your back to the camera. Get in the car," Dennis said. "Donovan, come with us and we'll discuss our next steps there. In the meantime, have one of your agents shut down those assholes filming us. No more recording. As far as I'm concerned, this is security breach."

Greg hadn't ever seen Dennis act this way. Sure he was gruff sometimes, but this was over-the-top.

As Greg and Dennis loaded their vehicle, a hulking agent walked over to the camera crew on Donovan's orders. They continued to film the agent's approach; this was good material, and they weren't going to pass up the opportunity to film until the agent took the camera out of their hands, if necessary.

Donovan quickly joined them in the DTS.

When he closed the door, Dennis quickly flipped on the radio and manually adjusted to an AM channel with only static on the line. He turned up the volume to mask whatever conversation they were about to have.

"Look, Donovan, when that crew showed up, you should have let us know they were around immediately. I'm praying this doesn't get picked up by the main networks anytime soon. You know as well as I do that anyone who's had a hand in this—if it was actually a terrorist attack—is watching the news channels closely. We don't want to tip them off to our investigation. I would have just as well have had no one know that a plane even survived, let alone that we were recovering evidence from it. I want you to call the station and see about getting any video retrieved. I imagine it's live by now, but you never know. It could be that the chaos in Atlanta is taking all the eyeballs.

"I also need you to call the hospital while we're en route and locate any and every passenger we can interview. Keep them from being released. We're heading over there now. Time is of the essence, so we could use an escort, if possible."

Greg could see Donovan's jaw clench, and sensed him swallowing the retort he wanted to give Dennis. Instead, he cleared his throat, looked down at his fidgeting hands, and said, "Yeah, let's, uh…let's get you two to the hospital. I'll see what I can do about the press."

Greg got a last word in: "Donovan, is there a university here? One with an Engineering department?"

The lack of any accent in Greg's voice reminded Donovan that he wasn't from the South. "Yeah, there's a pretty good one—The University of Alabama, Huntsville."

"Great, I'll need to get access to some of their labs right away."

"Sorry, guys—not in my jurisdiction. I'm sure you'll figure it out," he said sarcastically. "Now, let me get you that escort...."

Bahram was in a foul mood today. Since it was summer break, he let his wife and two grade-school-age girls sleep in. As always, he got up very early to prepare his breakfast and pack food for the day—or so he planned. Now, in the middle of a hot and late afternoon, he found he had forgotten to pack dinner. With his income driving a taxi, buying dinner wasn't a luxury he could readily afford.

His mind had been preoccupied that morning, and he found himself still distracted during the course of the day. Something was up, and something big. His suspicions were raised a few nights ago with a late night pickup.

Bahram had been on his typical search that night, scouring the streets for rides in his 20-year-old Peykan, the taxi of choice in Tehran. Though many Tehrani had cars, most chose to keep them at home, leaving the combat-like driving and ensuing collateral damage to the experts, like him. Later that evening, over near the Azadi tower, Bahram picked up a group of three men who flagged him down. The Shahrak-e Gharb district was upscale, nothing like his family's small quarters downtown—the air was clean.

I would so love to live here, he thought.

"Where to, men?"

"Daneshkaden Afsari," came the cheerful reply.

Bahram raised his eyebrows.

The military academy, he thought. But it looked like these men had been drinking. That wasn't allowed, certainly not by military men. Besides, it was just the beginning of the week—partying was for the weekends. Moonshine, he surmised. Vodka was the drink of choice for men in Iran. The religious police generally turned a blind eye.

He was uncertain whether to start his typical chat with his passengers, or just let them be. They started the banter on their own.

"Amir, lighten up. We won't be gone long. After this, you'll be famous," came a remark from one of the more jovial men.

Looking into his mirror, Bahram guessed that Amir must be the soldier with the scowl on his face.

"Shut up!" said Amir, making a motion for the man to zip his lips.

The other soldier jumped in, "Oh stop it, by next week, you'll want everyone to talk. Your wife will be proud."

"She'll be angry! This week was to be the beginning of our vacation; there will be no understanding on this."

"You signed up for action, and now we have it. Parsa and I are excited, right Parsa?" he said to his fellow, amicable soldier.

Action? thought Bahram. Oh no, not again. Bahram had lived long enough to remember many wars; the Iranian people were tired of war.

"I said to stop talking," Amir seethed under his breath. "Besides, you both are young and single. I have a pregnant wife."

"Which is why you are the commander of our team—experience!"

"Which is why, if any of you say another word I will cut your tongue out. As your commander, I gave an order. I *knew* going out tonight was a mistake. Tomorrow comes early."

Parsa winked at Amir and said, "But it may be our last outing together, so thank you…" Sensing continued irritation from Amir, he finished, "…and I'll shut up now."

No one had ventured to speak the rest of the ride.

Bahram had been hoping for days that this was a fluke…the puffed up talk of inebriated military men. But his heightened sense of foreboding was either playing tricks on his mind, or had helped him pick up on something in the works. Everyone seemed to be acting strange today.

Chapter
(Thir-teen)

Michael couldn't open his eyes. In fact, he couldn't even move. He felt as if he were waking up from a long dream, but the pain he was feeling in his body assured him this was real. It seemed that there was some type of goo on his eyes, but when he tried to move his arm to lift his hand to his face and wipe the substance away, it wouldn't respond.

Where am I? he thought.

The last thing he remembered was getting on a plane to visit his grandparents in Utah.

He groaned audibly, but was unable to speak.

"Michael? Michael, can you hear me?" came a voice.

The voice seemed distorted and distant. He tried to mouth a "Yes" in response, but could only groan again.

"Nurse, please give him something for the pain"

Michael recognized his Mom's voice. He tried to speak, but again, could only manage a groan. Something was blocking his throat.

Another voice said, "Mrs. James, I'll give him another dose by pushing this button here. At some point, Michael will be alert enough to do this on his own. I know it looks pretty rough right now, but he's going to make fast progress. He's young and strong. We'll know more within a few days on the damage to his lungs, spine and his overall prognosis."

Michael could barely make out what the voice was saying over the din in his head. He thought he heard "spine" and "damage." Was he in a hospital? What had happened?

As he was trying hard to comprehend what was going on, Michael felt a warm peace sweep over his body from his shoulders, down his arms to his fingers. The world settled back into blackness.

Chapter
(Four-teen)

As Greg followed the escort on the relatively short drive over to Huntsville, the mood in the car was pensive. Greg was already trying to piece together the images and data he had so far. It was too much to process with not enough information and not enough time.

He was pulled out of his intensity by Dennis' call to Headquarters.

"Darcy, yeah, this is Dennis. Hey, sorry I have to dispense with the pleasantries and all, but I need some numbers ASAP. I need to get a list of the flights in and out of Atlanta from five to nine this morning. The whole list…yeah, that's right, even private and commuter. Poll our favorite contacts over at FAA. No, I don't have anything concrete yet, I just feel we're gonna need all that.

"And as best you can, try to itemize the damage for each plane. Just send the data as you get it and copy Greg, OK? You're a gem.

"Wait, wait—one last thing. Send me that info as quick as you can, and afterwards, please look up each type and model of plane, OK? Thanks, Darcy."

Dennis turned to Greg.

"Greg, look…I know you think I probably overreacted back there with Donovan and the news crew and all…"

Greg nodded once, slowly.

"…I worked TWA Flight 800. The flight that conspiracy theorists claimed was taken down by a missile. That was a fucking mess of an investigation. It all unfolded fast, but by the time we got on deck, FBI, Navy, CIA and FAA had buried everything. All we had were bits and pieces to work with—frankly, there were a lot of things that looked suspicious. Our formal conclusion was that there *was* no conclusion.

"I've never told anyone this, but that formal statement was bogus. It wasn't internal NTSB's conclusion at all. Things were covered up and distorted so much that I had no idea what data was real, what was doctored and what data we just didn't have. A good friend and colleague suspected it was an errant Navy missile and asked for ship whereabouts. His request was leaked to the press...."

Dennis' voice drifted off for a second as he recalled the intensity of the situation.

"Let's just say that was the end of his career, and the end of us getting anything further on that facet of the investigation.

"Greg, I'm telling you, this investigation's gonna get crazy. It's gonna get political—and if my instincts are right, we have limited time to collect all the data before the FBI starts hiding things.

"FBI usually does interviews on this, but they're understaffed here, and most agents likely got directed to Atlanta, which is a bigger mess."

The patrol officer they were following pulled into the emergency room entrance of the hospital.

"OK, Greg, get your recorder going. We can't afford to miss anything. And I want you to back everything up to your laptop just in case...well, in case of anything. We may only get one shot."

"Dennis," Greg finally interjected, "dissecting the phones we pulled off the plane is just as important as these interviews. Before we get started inside, I just need to make a few calls. I have some contacts in Austin that are used to tearing apart phones to see how they work and what chips are inside. I need to talk with them about this Dazzle and see if they've taken one apart already. And I need them to buy one off the shelf and rip it apart as well. We need to see if there are any physical differences. What type of budget do we have, Dennis?"

Dennis looked at him incredulously.

"Greg. Buddy. For this investigation, frickin' spend now and ask questions later. If your people in Austin can shed any light on this, and I mean any at all, get them on it right away. Tell them to drop everything else. Man, we may have only hours."

Dennis paused, remembering Greg's lack of real-world investigation experience.

"While we're at it, I need you to shift gears. This isn't a term paper or report. If you've got a hunch and someone can help, consider HQ at your disposal. Consider any company you can pay to help at your disposal. Your hunch doesn't have to be right, just act on it.

"Tell you what, let's take a couple of minutes right now and walk through our 'hunches' so far, then make our calls. I'll start. I have a feeling that only the flights in or out of Atlanta, one or two hours before 7:30, got hit. I don't know how or why, but that's why I called Darcy to get the list. Now, what's your first gut feeling?"

"Well, I have a feeling there's something in one of the phones that wasn't in the others—that something was added, likely hardware. I want to see inside, even inside the chip packages. I'd like to compare these two phones because I want to see where the short was and where the fire started, but I don't have the time or resources."

"OK, so that's why you're going to call Austin and talk with these folks…?"

"Teardown dot-com."

"Sounds appropriate, I guess," Dennis said. "And you're gonna do it right away. Now about the phones you have with you, what about the Engineering department at the university, can they help?"

"Well, I don't think they'd know how to take them apart."

"Can you walk them through it?"

"Not really, I'd need help as well…"

"OK…can Teardown talk them through it?"

"Great idea, I'll get them on that. They may have to sign a Non-Disclosure Agreeme—"

Dennis interrupted, "There's no time for that—seriously. Stress to them—no, actually, demand, in your nicest voice—that they help out. Tell them this is a national security issue, and highlight the fact they can't talk with their buddies or the press, whether they find something or not. If you have trouble, call me and we'll escalate this."

Greg was feeling a little more control over things now. He had felt like his brain was going to explode before walking through these next steps.

"OK, you make some calls," Dennis said, gathering his things. "I'll go inside and find out where the patients are and which ones we could possibly get the most out of. I'll call you when we're ready. See if you can get one of the professors to get his butt down here and pick up these phones. You have a blank check and no time. So…*buy* us some time."

Chapter

(Fif-teen)

*T*he atmosphere in the Situation Room was somber. In the past hour, much had transpired.

The President was late entering the room. Apparently he had been stymied in his attempts to get through to other dignitaries, but orders were that his staff would continue to try to reach the Iranian and Chinese presidents. If and when they got through, the President would be pulled out of the meeting to have a discussion and try to determine the intentions driving their latest movements.

Things had gone from bad to worse in Atlanta. In addition to the damage from the attack, the developing aftermath was far from stable. From the Council's perspective, this was a well-planned incident. In one fell swoop, the attackers disabled one of the largest airports in the nation and at the same time ignited a powder keg of chaos in the city, within miles of—but without damage to—the broadcasting ability of a huge global news network.

To make matters worse, the area around the airport, particularly just north, had one of the highest crime rates in the nation. The 30310 zipcode had ten times the crime level of the national average, and almost three times the violent crime rate for Atlanta, which was already several times the national average. Reports of arson, looting and random violence, began to spread across the city as residents learned that their neighborhood had been singled out for attack.

"Let's start with Homeland Security. Bring us up to speed, Carl."

"Well, Mr. President, we have five main thrusts going on right now. First, we have the NTSB investigating the downed planes to determine actual cause of failure. The word I've received in the past few minutes is that we have a team in Alabama that's with the plane that survived the incident. This is going to be an important piece of the puzz—"

"Excuse me, Carl, did you say Alabama? What's it doing there?"

"It seems that planes that left Atlanta quite a bit prior to the 7:30 incident were still hit at 7:30. None but this one plane survived, however."

"So we're looking at a non-local weapon," the President reasoned.

"That's why we have our expert investigators on it, Sir," replied Carl. "Second, we're about done scouring the airport, which was at the epicenter, for any type of weapon. We've found nothing. Except for the critical staff at the airport, it is fundamentally empty at this point. We took names, numbers, initial reports and sent people home."

"Are we calling this an 'incident,' Carl? Don't we pretty much know this was an attack of some sort?"

"We are still being cautious about stating that as fact."

"I understand," said the President, nodding.

"Well, third, we have…"

Just then the door to the Situation Room opened and Ned barged in.

"Mr. President, we really need to watch what's developing on CNT right now. If I could just interrupt—"

The Chief of Staff approached the console without waiting for the President's approval. The large flat screen on the side of the room lit up and immediately, a live feed to CNT was displayed.

"…and this breaking news from our affiliate station WAYA TV in Huntsville, Alabama. In the continued confusion emanating from the attack on Atlanta this morning…"

"Damn. 'Attack'—is what the news is saying," noted the President, under his breath.

"…there appears to be yet another twist. In Huntsville, nearly an hour after it had taken off, an American Airlines flight had to make an emergency landing on a busy highway just east of town. The plane appears to have caught fire while in flight, and the pilot had no choice but to set down as quickly as he could. This is the only known flight to have survived the attack, which is why local FBI, police, and State Patrol officers have been investigating the scene. We have WAYA reporter Gerald Manning on the feed with some revealing footage. Gerald?"

The scene quickly shifted to a rural field with a highway and what looked like a plane far off in the background. The highway had been cordoned off and traffic was obviously backed up extensively.

"Cynthia, the scene here is one of confusion. FBI agents had originally allowed us to get close to the scene, but suddenly asked us to leave, and firmly but politely asked for the video we were shooting at the time. Fortunately, the video was fed back to our station, and the request was just that, a request—not a demand.

"From the information we've been able to gather, American Airlines Flight 1225, was DFW-bound from Atlanta. We haven't been able to talk with any passengers or crew at this point, as all have been either taken to the hospital for their injuries or to Huntsville Airport to make travel arrangements. Our calls to American Airlines for a statement have gone unreturned.

"While authorities have been tight-lipped, examination of our feed revealed what could be critical details about what happened here today…"

"Carl," the President hissed, "who the hell gave permission for a news crew to get that close to a crime scene? What about the protocol?"

The Secretary of Homeland Security hadn't heard anything about a potential information leak, and indicated as much with a shrug and a head shake.

"Let me describe what we're seeing," Gerald continued. "Here you see the side of the plane. It's clear that an emergency landing has taken place. We have the emergency doors removed and the slide deployed. As we move our way from the front of the plane to the rear, you can see a huge hole in the side of the plane. It looks like a missile likely hit at this point. I'd say the plane was lucky to stay airborne."

"Gerald, sorry to interrupt. Did you say authorities suspect a missile?"

The President turned to glare at Carl. "A missile?" he repeated. "You never said anything about a potential missile. Why am I just hearing about this from CNT?"

"Mr. President, that is clearly not a missile strike. The explosion came from onboard. If you look at the hole, the skin of the plane is ruptured from the inside out. A missile would have taken the plane down."

The President rubbed his hands over his face, a signal to those close to him that he was feeling the stresses of the day. He turned to Ned, "Get a hold of John and get a briefing set up for this afternoon. Two o'clock. Maybe that will quell things for now if CNT knows we'll be talking soon."

"…and if you listen very carefully to the plainclothes agent speaking to the local FBI agent, you can hear him make a shocking statement. Be aware, some colorful language is used, so if you have children watching, please use discretion."

The President snapped his head again to look at the Secretary. "And I want to know who the hell that plainclothes agent is. He's not wearing FBI garb, NTSB, or any identifying gear like he should be. What the hell kind of operation is Huntsville running?"

The volume on the news crew's video had been amplified substantially, so that even the shifting of the cameraman's feet on the gravel beneath him was being picked up, aggravatingly so.

Though muffled somewhat, the dialogue was clear: "Donovan, don't get me wrong, I like you and all, and your help here has been instrumental in getting us in quickly to document…but you have no idea what the fuck we're dealing with here! I know parents want their kids back home safe, and they'll get that, but we have a likely terrori—"

Gerald's voice resumed its narration: "Cynthia, the plainclothes agent now notices our crew, as you can see, and turns his back and pulls the man we've identified as Agent Donovan, to face away from the camera."

The camera had zoomed in closely on Donovan and Dennis's faces, to the point where it was easy to discern the scar that split Dennis' right eyebrow into two parts.

"Cynthia, Donovan is with the local FBI office in Huntsville. My colleagues tell me that we've had a cordial relationship with Donovan in the past, which likely explains why we were allowed so close to the plane."

The video now showed a rather large agent on his way over to the news crew to shut them down.

"As we see Donovan's colleague coming over and the look in his face—you can tell he's not happy—I went ahead and stopped the video. We pause this last scene to point out a few things to you in the studio and to our at-home viewers. Notice the plainclothes agent and his partner walking over to an unmarked vehicle—the Cadillac DTS. We didn't have a good angle to get the license plate, so we aren't sure if it's government issued, or if these are more deeply buried agents…"

"Deeply buried agents?" exclaimed the President. "Carl, do you even know who that is? And what the hell is he doing stating this is a terrorist attack? On national—no, let me correct myself—on *global* television?"

Carl was silent.

"Get that man identified. Get his name, notes, computer, whatever else. He's not the only guy working on this case, so unless he's the equivalent to Einstein on this, pull him. And if he is Einstein, lock him up and feed him the information without letting him get anywhere near a camera crew. He has no business being out on the street."

The President was silent for a moment. He knew that time was still ticking away, and decided it was best to try to return to the original agenda. He signaled for Ned to turn off the TV, thanked him and dismissed him with a nod.

"Carl, as pissed off as I am at your agencies right now, we need to hear the rest of your report.…"

Chapter
(Six-teen)

The first call Greg made was to Michelle. He was used to talking with her every day, and texting and calling her all the time while traveling. With the unlimited calling and texting from his government-issued cell phone, it was easy to stay in touch. His original flight was supposed to land a couple of hours later, so he was hoping to hedge some of his own anxiety more than hers.

"Hi, Honey, I'm so glad I was able to reach you."

Michelle was a substitute teacher. She didn't get calls to work at the school district all that often and was a little ambivalent when she did. Sure, they could use the money—they were saving towards getting a place of their own—but substituting always meant dealing with a bunch of unruly kids. It was better for her when the high school called, since it meant there was a good chance she'd be called into a science or math class, subjects in which she had some background, and the kids were usually more serious about their work. However, that was not the case today. Michelle had gotten up around eight and although moving pretty slowly she was already caught up with the latest news when her phone rang.

"Hi, Sweetheart. I didn't expect to hear from you so soon. I thought you'd call tonight after you checked in."

"I know…we had had some change in plans."

"Really? Are you coming home? Please say your meetings got cancelled and you're going to be back home tonight. I really enjoyed this morning, you know. You were so strong and forceful with me, you know I like that. And I love it when you—"

As much as Greg hated to, he had to cut her off: "Michelle, actually, it's a little more complicated than that. Believe it or not, I'm in Huntsville, Alabama."

Greg remembered the paranoia that Dennis had about anyone knowing what they were working on and quickly backed off on what he was about to share.

"Huntsville? Are you serious? How did you end up there?"

"Well, I don't know if you've seen it on the news, but there have been some planes with engine trouble…"

"Yeah, I saw that! There's crazy stuff going on, Greg, especially in Atlanta. Is your plane OK? Are you OK?"

"Honey," Greg said, aware of the rising panic in Michelle's voice, "yes, I'm OK. But we did have some trouble," Greg said, stretching the truth. "We had an emergency landing here in Huntsville and I'm not sure how long it will be until we get another flight out."

"Greg, I'm so sorry. It won't be long though, right? Will you be coming home or going to your meetings?"

"Well, that's just it, I'm not sure. In fact, I need to go find Dennis to try to figure out what our plan is, but I wanted to call you and let you know what was up so you wouldn't be worried."

"Oh, Greg, I wish I had gone with you like we planned…"

"I promise I'll call you right when I know what's up, OK?

"OK, stud-muffin." Michelle always laid her compliments on thick when on the phone.

"Well, Gorgeous, I'm so glad you miss me already."

"How could I not with the wake-up call you gave me this morning?"

"I hate that I have to do this, but I have to go. Really. I miss you."

"I miss you, too. Call when you can."

When Greg hung up, he was hurting inside. He missed Michelle so much all of a sudden. Maybe it was the urgency of the current situation, or the potential danger to all of them that had him feeling especially emotional. He knew he needed to put that aside, however, and get moving on calls to the various experts that could help him buy time on the investigation.

Greg got on his T30 smartphone to "Google" Teardown.com's contact information. Just as he opened his browser, a pop-up showed that there was new mail from Darcy, Dennis' admin. The message read: "Dennis, had to jump through hoops, threaten a few people, even open a can of whoop-ass to get this done. You owe me. And this time, you will actually remember to pay. Enjoy. Darcy."

Greg quickly glanced over the data in her spreadsheet. Any flights that left after 5:30 a.m. had been hit, even if they were in-flight. It was almost as if some virus or Trojan had been planted at 5:30 and then triggered at 7:30, and any plane that was at the airport during those two hours caught the bug. This was good information. Darcy had done well. But now, Greg conjectured, it was time to figure out the bigger plan and how it was pulled off. First, he had to rule out anything with hardware, which was why he needed to call Teardown and the university as soon as possible. The next angle was a virus, or maybe a Trojan Horse. Could someone inject something over Wi-Fi or a 3G network in such a localized manner? Who could he call to find out? First things first, Greg told himself. It's time to call Teardown, and fast. As Dennis had said, he planned to "use money to buy time." Greg was going to make Teardown an offer they couldn't refuse.

After dinner, fares had ramped up nicely for Bahram. He was well into the early evening rush where his keen driving skills could be put to the test. For passengers, the traffic delays made this a most frustrating time of day. For Bahram, it was his chance to shine; he knew the backstreets like the back of his hand. His astute skills would often earn him some handsome tips, especially from the government types wanting to get somewhere in a hurry. Besides, the adrenaline rush helped make up for the dullness during the slow part of the afternoon.

The banter Bahram had with his passengers was a welcome respite from the time spent alone in his cab. He would claim that he could drive the city blindfolded, and could get around any obstacle in his path. Bahram had heard in America, taxi drivers sat silent while driving their fares. What a way to make a tough job a miserable job. In his opinion, the taxis were the lube that greased the workings of the city. It gave him a mission. It also gave him a finger on its pulse.

Today, the pulse was high. Either the city's body was sick, or it was very nervous. Typically, passengers headed for the government offices were cordial and relaxed, even if in a hurry. After all, a posh job in the government meant you were well taken care of, and likely some of your relatives might stand to benefit from some contracts coming their way. There was no relaxation today.

Picking up a somber, older gentleman from the Tehran Bazaar area, he expected to be giving him a ride home, to a relative's house, or to a hotel.

"The Ministry of Defense," stated the man.

Bahram thought he should maybe bite his tongue, but decided to make a statement anyway.

"It's time to go home. Isn't that the wrong direction?" he said, offering the biggest smile he could muster.

No response was offered.

Suddenly, after looking at his phone at presumably a text message that had come through, the man spoke.

"I'll triple the fare if you get me there fast."

"No problem, sir."

A likely government-type giving him permission to break the law? This was going to be fun.

Bahram was entirely focused on getting his ride to the Ministry as fast as possible. Only a few times was he able to look back at the gentleman, who was holding on while still being glued to his phone. It took only a glance to recognize the man's smart phone as the new Taha, the tPhone-Five.

Humpf, he thought.

All the government-types had tPhones. The Republican Guard, the protector of their countries' Spiritual Leader, was trying to make sure everyone in Iran used one. The tPhone had internet, GPS, and the Holy Quran—it could even tell you when to pray each day and which direction to face toward Mecca, no matter where you were in the country. Rumor had it the phone could also tell whether you stopped to say your prayers and report if you didn't. Despite the spying aspect, everyone wanted one, and eventually, if Bahram saved and the price dropped, he might be able to get a tPhone, too. Besides, it was less expensive than a black-market iPhone.

Arriving at their destination, Bahram felt proud of his skillful driving. Even by his own estimate, he made it in half the time. It was only then, when he saw the campus entirely lit up and the parking lot full, that his stomach sank.

Oh no, something is not right…please no war, Bahram thought.

The man paid him triple for his efforts. Between the pay and his now-developed premonition of danger, he just wanted to go home. The city would survive without his taxi the rest of the evening.

Chapter
(Seven-teen)

*T*he **President's National Security** Council was not the only executive team
that had observed the report on CNT. Still holed up in the Polaris room,
Zhonghua Nine was carefully observing every update. They had received word
that the Chinese Navy was well on its way—they would be on target within three
to four hours.

After hearing about the events in Huntsville, the Leader was getting
somewhat concerned. Obviously the government had brought in a specialist, and
had an intact plane to investigate. It would only be a matter of time before they
determined any discrepancies in smartphone hardware, which would likely lead
to the source of the attack signal. Things would need to be both accelerated and
delayed to accommodate this unexpected turn.

On the one hand, the timetable for additional attacks would need to be
advanced. If the source of the attacks were uncovered before the Chinese Navy
was in control of the Diaoyutai Islands, all would be lost. If the US military was
not forced to stand down, China would have to confront the US forces supporting
Japan.

On the other hand, "delay" meant activating a local sleeper agent. The agent
was to disrupt the investigation.

"Zhonghua Two, send out the notice to your social networking agents that it
is time to move into the next phase of Dormant Curse. Rather than staying with
the original schedule, the next attack will need to take place by 4:00 p.m. Eastern
Standard Time. Tell them they must gather the networking drones immediately to
prepare for the next phase.

"Zhonghua Five, determine what operatives we have available in Alabama.
We need disruptions and delays throughout the investigation in Huntsville.

"In the packet provided to you at the door, you will find your room key. If you haven't guessed by now, you won't be leaving the hotel tonight," the Leader said with his characteristic smirk. "Fortunately, you don't have to sleep here in this room all together," he added with a chuckle. "The guards will lead you to your rooms. Zhonghua Two and Five, you'll stay for a bit. I want you to make your calls from here.

"The rest of you are free to go to your rooms. You'll find you have every amenity to which you have grown accustomed," the Leader stated with a wink. Some of the Zhonghua Nine had developed questionable habits with their increase in influence, as often happens to the rich and powerful. The Leader made it a point to know each of the men's weaknesses and strengths—using it all to his advantage.

Since the Polaris room was one floor below the lobby, where the main hotel elevators were located, they rode an escalator up one floor before boarding one of the six high-speed elevators in the lobby. They arrived on the 58th floor, where escort-guards ensured each man was led to his room in an orderly fashion. The hallway on each floor at the Grand Hyatt followed a large circular path, which made it difficult to see very far ahead. As the group passed each potential exit, a loyal Zhonghua guard was stationed there, doing his job in keeping the floor secure. Each of these guards would nod to the escort guards as they passed. At this stage in the game, the Leader didn't want any of the sect members getting cold feet. He expected that with the escort detail, guards clearly stationed at the elevators and stairs, and the enticements awaiting each member in his room, he would not have much trouble.

As Zhonghua One arrived at his room, he was greeted by one of the most amazing looking women he had recalled ever seeing. His first thought was that she must be from Suzhou, where women are renowned across all of China for their beauty. As she smiled and bowed before taking his hand, One could only look back at the guard and smile politely, and somewhat sheepishly, as the door slowly shut behind him.

And so it was with each member who was led to his room, to look forward to whatever gift the Leader had provided.

Back in the Polaris room, Zhonghua Two and Five were making calls on opposite ends of the meeting room.

Two's phone call was short and to the point. He detected no inability to deliver on the new timetable. After his call was complete, he updated the Leader on the status and made his way to the door, where an escort was ready to lead him to his own unique lair, prepared specifically for him.

Zhonghua Five's job was tougher. He first had to make calls to determine what sleeper agents were available anywhere close to Huntsville. He wanted an agent with training and access to serious weapons—someone who could literally take out the target seen on CNT, but, from a safe distance. What he got wasn't anything close. Instead, this sleeper was well trained in the art of seduction, drugging and poisoning, but possessed limited firearms skills beyond a pistol. She would likely have to get close to get the job done.

It was going to be difficult to identify the hotel where the target was staying, and equally challenging to track the man down. Nevertheless, Five gave the deployment order, knowing that she might be the only chance they had to cripple the investigation. Once deployed, however, he might not be able to use her again, if things went badly.

Five called the agent's handler in the United States. The call was short, direct, and to the point.

Shelly's cell phone rang at work. It was a special number that only her lover knew. She grew a little excited.

"Hi…" Shelly said, with anticipation.

"Shelly, it's me," came the deep, sultry voice in response.

"It's so good to hear your voice. I've been thinking about you."

"Aw that's nice, Babe. Hey, I've got something special for you. Can you come home for lunch?"

"Of course. When's lunch?"

"Well, I kind of have plans for us—how about you take off the rest of the day?"

"Hmmmm…that sounds nice. How about I come home right now?"

"That's what I was thinking, too."

"Be right there."

Shelly was a tall, gorgeous, light-skinned African American. A model employee, it was unusual for her to request the rest of the day off, but her boss understood. A sister in the hospital was something he'd want to be there for, too.

When Shelly got home, he was already at the door, waiting expectantly. Steve, an Asian man twenty years older, with a little gray around the temples, was nothing remarkable compared to this twenty-five-year-old exquisite beauty. It was clear from her broad smile that she was totally in love with him.

"Babe, hey, it's not quite time for lunch, let's go have some fun, I'll show you how much I love you."

An imperceptible twitch flashed across Shelly's face.

"Sure, anything you want is what I want...I want you now," she said seductively.

A smile came across the man's face, looking forward to what was coming next.

Thirty minutes later, Shelly and her man made their way from the back bedroom to the dining area. The delicious smell of pot roast and potatoes captivated their senses. In the center of the table was a white vase and a single red rose.

"Oh, for me, Honey? Thank you!" Shelly said, hugging her lover.

"Is Celine joining us?" Shelly inquired of the setting for three.

"Yes, she's made lunch for us. It should be ready soon. Let's sit down."

An older Asian woman with a stern look soon came out from the kitchen with a ceramic pot, steaming from the heat.

"Shelly, I'm so glad you could come home for lunch. Did you and Steven have a good pre-lunch meeting?" she asked, setting down the pot.

"Oh, Mommy, Daddy's always so wonderful. I'm so glad you all love me so much."

Celine smiled at her daughter and came over behind her, gently massaging her neck as she came close.

"Oh, still sweating I see. You need to dry off better after your next session."

Now out of Shelly's direct view, Celine gave her husband a firm nod.

Slowly and deliberately, her father stated, "Shelly, Baby. There's something I need you to do."

From the look on Shelly's face, it was like a switch went on. The smile fell and she stared blankly at her father.

"Yes, Dad?" she replied.

Inside Shelly's head, she was trying to fight the memories that particular phrase conjured up. She felt like she was floating, as she had in the dark, suspension tank as a child.

"I need you to listen carefully. And I need Mary inside there to listen as well. There is a job I need you both to do. I think you are going to really like this one...."

Shelly's mother now broke into a broad smile. It wasn't a happy smile. It was pure evil.

Shelly had been kidnapped as an infant, selected for her good genes and likelihood of blending into southern US society. Her "adoptive" parents were paid well by Zhonghua Nine to create a cold-blooded, yet seductive, killing machine. Well-documented techniques used by the CIA in Top Secret "Project MKULTRA" were used by Shelly's parents to create an alter personality. Sensory deprivation with LSD was the fastest way to a guaranteed split, which was forced into existence by age six. Her alter personality was given the name "Mary."

While Mary was trained to be a world-class assassin, Shelly was regularly abused by her father, perverting the normal parent-child relationship which helped her parents to mold her into a seductive and deceptive, yet obedient agent.

Mary's training started at age seven. She learned quickly, and with her intense, angry personality showing glee when inflicting pain, her trainers called her Mary Death, though not directly to her face. The training involved as much development of mental acuity as it did physical training. Martial arts enhanced with moves designed not only to protect, but to go on the offensive, gave her the ability to disable and kill within the first few seconds of contact. Lessons in anatomy and physiology went along with the practical aspects of killing, and soon Mary learned not only the key nerves and arteries but what drugs would work best to have the desired impact and how to protect herself while administering them.

No training could be complete without ongoing, real-world testing to prove her new knowledge and ability. Mary kept Shelly's memory from the guilt and occasional grisliness of the test killings. Starting with random, walk-by assaults outside the Western Hills Mall in Fairfield, Mary progressed to well-orchestrated drive-by shootings, then poisoning. The poisoning started with hookers she and her parents would find on Highway 78, but progressed to unsuspecting, random citizens they would target in swanky restaurants in downtown Birmingham. By the time Mary's training was finished, she was fully capable of planning and executing almost any type of hit.

The generous funding from the Zhonghua Nine ensured that Shelly's family was always available to fulfill the roles they needed to play.

Living in Birmingham and working at the McWane Science Center, Shelly became a normal part of the community and her neighborhood, though she was far from normal.

After finishing their meal, Shelly's father gave her only sketchy details about her target, for now. She would make the short drive to Huntsville in her own car and await further instruction.

It was now 1:00 p.m. Shelly's goal was to identify her target and make initial contact by six that evening. She quickly collected her gear and tools, including her prized Glock 26, a 9mm pistol that was compact and reliable. The attachment would likely come in handy as well—a Gemtech Trinity silencer that made a kill virtually undetectable. Subsonic ammunition and a laser sight made it a perfect package. Of course, she packed her three favorite poisons: cyanide, anthrax and ricin—though she considered that ricin and anthrax might act too slowly for her purposes tonight. Scoline, a fast-acting muscle relaxant, could take someone out in seconds with a good overdose, but since she had to inject that chemical, it could be difficult to use unless she could get very close. Shelly thought about that for a moment, but added a vial of it to her collection anyway, just in case.

After packing some clothes and putting things in the car, Shelly set her sights on getting to Huntsville quickly. It was a straight shot up I-65 and over Highway

72 to downtown. In fact, unbeknownst to Shelly, her father's Google Maps directions would take her to within a mile of Greg and Dennis.

Back in the Polaris Room, Zhonghua Five finished his discussion on the phone. He was exhausted. The Leader was still in the room, waiting patiently for the conclusion to the conversation.

"It appears we now have someone en route to disrupt the investigation," he stated.

"Yes, my Leader. However, I am concerned about any possibility of success. We don't yet know the identity of the plainclothes agent, nor where he is staying. Our only hope is that somehow he will be identified by the American press during the course of the day."

"Zhonghua Five, have faith. Their press rarely lets us down. They smell a headline story, and will not let it rest until they have uncovered the agent's identity. Rarely do they care about their story's impact on their country.

"Someday, their government may understand that when the masses learn the truth, you lose control and they can turn on you. We know this all too well in China. Our control of the press and the Internet is for our people's own good, to ensure they aren't exposed to misleading truths. Sadly, the Americans are exposed to so much misinformation that I doubt anyone there really knows the truth about anything."

With a sigh and a dismissive gesture with his hand, the Leader continued: "Zhonghua Five, you've done well. Please rest; it is very, very late and you'll have to be up again in a few hours. We have staff viewing the news channels continuously and will inform you when the plainclothes agent's name is revealed. Until then, get some sleep. We are entering an intense phase of Dormant Curse, and we all need to be clear-headed."

The Leader made his way to the entrance of the Polaris room, where the guard allowed him to walk by unescorted.

Chapter

(Eight-teen)

Once the order went out to gather the drones, a half-dozen agents in the San Francisco Bay area began contacting their hackers with major social networking accounts. Once located via cell phone, the agents ensured that each drone was picked up—sometimes forcefully, if required. From now on, each drone was going to need tighter control—and perhaps additional pressure to comply with requests—for the remainder of the day. The agents had been prepared in advance and made necessary arrangements. While the agents might not have known the ultimate reason for the messages, they knew there was a million dollars for each of them at the end of the mission, which was now so close they could taste it.

The aggregation point for the drones was in a distribution warehouse in Hayward, across the Bay from San Francisco. The Peppertree Industrial Park Building was nothing special, just a quiet industrial park set up with light manufacturing and distribution. But within that complex was a secure set of rooms that had been built out over the past two years—since the development of the social networking facet of Dormant Curse.

The office space reserved for this final phase was made up of an outside reception area, a bathroom, sleeping chamber and storage closet, all connected to the only workroom. If one were to use the space on a daily basis, its setup would seem quite strange. But for the ultimate purpose of the arrangement, it made perfect sense.

The whole facility inside the warehouse was built with metal shielding, rendering it a large Faraday Cage that blocked external radio signals, including both cellular and Wi-Fi. The only signals that could get into and out of the room were through the DSL line distributed via Ethernet on each workstation. The only voice communication allowed was through four phones located on a central table.

Though it was indiscernible from the outside, once one made it through the workroom entrance it was clear that there was only one way in and one way out. The workroom itself was locked with a keypad that required codes for entry and exit. The large, steel door, ensured the integrity of the shielding, as well as provided a means of keeping everyone inside. The door and walls were also well insulated for sound. Since it was anticipated that the coercion of the drones might require extreme measures, the agents were instructed to use physical pain as a means of inspiring compliance, if necessary. These tactics had the potential to get loud.

The main workroom consisted of twelve workstations. Unlike most office spaces, these were not arranged in cubes, rather, they were set up on the perimeter. Each was monitored by agents at a table in the center of the room where they could immediately lock out keystrokes on any drone workstation if they detected something suspicious.

On the near wall of the workroom was a kitchen area, with a fully-stocked refrigerator, a microwave, oven, sink and storage.

In the corner opposite the drone workstations was a door to the bathroom. The bathroom was complete with a shower, two sinks and a toilet. The storage closet had little obvious purpose. Finally, the sleeping chamber consisted of six twin-sized bunk-beds, all stacked three high. Facilities arranged for multi-night lodging for as many as eighteen.

The time from the initial order to collect the drones until the first social network message to go out was about two hours. The accelerated schedule made it very difficult to pull off, even with the detailed advance planning. The order was to send a message at three o'clock EST to prepare for a four o'clock secondary message. It was about ten in the morning on the West Coast, which made it easier to find the drones at their homes or workplace. Fortunately, all were highly motivated by money, and the lure of a hundred-thousand-dollar, one-day payoff, was enough to ensure that the drones, by whatever means necessary, would get to the warehouse within the hour. For a few, however, the flag raised by the central location didn't align well with prior commitments for the day.

In one case, the agent was incredulous that his key social networking hacker couldn't be enticed by the generous offer. As a ploy, he arranged to drop off the information for the drone at his condo on King Street near AT&T Park. The information was too important to send over email or via a text message, so the agent decided to utilize the parking garage next door to the condo complex for their in-person meeting. The difficult drone, Joe, was the same disgruntled Blather founding partner who had previously hacked into the site's backdoor account. Joe's suspicions about a second request, so soon after the first, set off alarm bells in his brain and should have led him to reject the request outright. The easy cash, however, was too much of an enticement.

When the agent met Joe in his garage, he had an envelope full of cash and instructions prepared. He also had a partner. With the amount of money they were dealing with, the extra protection seemed reasonable to Joe. He quickly exchanged pleasantries with his agent and was reaching to take the package when he felt a tremendous pain in his side; his body stiffened uncontrollably. He let out a muffled scream and collapsed onto the garage floor. He had been hit with a Taser.

The agents were taking no chances. Joe was their number one hacker, having access to social networking accounts with the largest reach in America. Accounts included those belonging to the hottest celebrities, musicians and politicians— boasting over sixty million followers between them.

The car's trunk was already unlatched, so it was rather easy to tape Joe's mouth and toss him in without drawing attention. The agents placed their pickup point strategically out of sight of the security cameras. No one had seen Joe disappear.

The remaining drones were relatively easy to gather. In fact, to make things uncomplicated, each was given instructions and an envelope of cash right as they passed the reception desk. A small fraction of the money could be used to make it up to those significant others, co-workers, or bosses they had blown off to get over there without delay.

After collecting money and instructions, and giving up their phones, they were led through the secure door. It became obvious that this job would be anything but normal. Other workers were all seated at one of many workstations lined up against the wall. The workstations were not yet enabled, so each drone was waiting patiently for further instructions while enjoying a soft drink or snack.

Once all the drones had arrived, the lead agent entered the room. It was clear he was the lead by the respect the other agents gave him and his apparent command of the situation.

"OK, everyone, sit down. Time is short and our instructions are simple.

"For all intents and purposes, my name's Ron. And I'll be your 'cruise director' in charge of our activities. I don't imagine any of you thought you would be doing this today, and frankly, neither did I. So it sucks for all of us…let's try to make the best of it.

"This room and the adjacent rooms are completely shielded. Engineers like to call it a ferret-day cage, or somethin' like that. I'm no engineer, so I just like to call it 'The Box of Electromagnetic Silence.' So if you have any other device you haven't given up, well, it's not gonna work in here anyway, just so you know. If you think that's extreme…we're just getting warmed up.

"Each of you has access to a workstation. There are only two programs installed on each of them. One is Notepad. There are four text files on your desktop, named Phase One through Phase Four, with encoded messages you will send to your social network accounts. You will find only one or two messages inside the file. The first one goes first, and if there's a second one in the file, it goes next. Pretty simple. Don't mix them up—you know the drill from your previous work with us.

"The other program is Internet Explorer. You will cut and paste the message into your social networking site as if the message is from your client. Do NOT retype it. I don't want to see any typing going on at all for that matter once you're logged in—it should only be cut and paste from then on.

"By the way, before you all came here, you were given instructions to bring any and all usernames and passwords for your accounts. If you managed to forget to bring those, you royally screwed up. You won't have the time or access to retrieve them. We're on in less than an hour. If you forgot your secure data, you're just gonna have to stay here with us for the duration. Our clients are generous, so you'll keep the money we handed you at the door, but don't expect a callback. We'll find a more reliable body in the future.

"So, as you may have guessed, the stakes are really high. I would advise you not to even bother asking about the intent of the messages. You don't want to know, and I can't tell you. It would just complicate things for us all. And I know some of you are legitimate ghostwriters for your social networking clients—hopefully the messages aren't so strange that you'll get fired over it when you get back, because we'll still need you. By now you've probably figured out that we're not just doing this for fun and games, and today is an important payout day.

"Finally, in case I didn't make it clear before, there will be NO communication with anyone on the outside while you're in here. Calls, emails, messages through your social networking sites—you're to access none of that. And I'm very serious about this. If we observe any attempt to communicate—which we can from our monitoring workstations here on the center table—not only will you lose your stipend, but there will likely be some punishment. And you'll still be required to get your hacked message through. I really hope you save us all any trouble and just do the job we've asked you to do—nothing more and nothing less. Any questions?"

Just then the door to the workroom opened and a somewhat disheveled young man appeared in the entrance escorted by two agents. In fact, it looked like he was being shoved through the door rather than walking in on his own volition. Once inside, he was practically dragged to his seat. Something was clearly different about this guy. It was obvious to everyone that not everything here was really as it seemed, especially with this sudden and spectacular arrival.

"Everyone, meet Joe. I'll expect you will fill Joe in on the details. By the way," Ron stated, looking directly at Joe, "with the insolent behavior I heard about, you'll have close supervision. Ask permission to do anything, including using the restroom. Sorry."

One drone had been biding her time, not necessarily patiently. When Pamela showed up to the warehouse, she thought this was going to be a quick venture. She hadn't planned on staying for more than a few hours. She had left her Xanax back at the office and it would be wearing off long before they were done here. Heavily addicted to the prescription drug, there was no way she thought she could survive without it. After seeing Joe's treatment, she was very polite in her inquiry: "Sir, I have some prescriptions I didn't bring them with me. I don't know that I can be here for very long without taking them."

"Ah, Pamela. You know, we pretty much thought of everything for this mission. You need to know how valuable you all are and how much we respect you and need your help. We've determined each of your needs, and have accommodated appropriately. Over in the cabinet next to the microwave, you'll each find a full prescription of the meds you might need during your stay. In fact, to the best of our ability, we've tracked your personal preferences and made sure we have your favorite drinks on hand. We need you to stay attentive, so there's no alcohol or beer on-site, but we have just about everything else. I know, Rick, in your case with your problem with alcohol, that may become an issue," said Ron as he looked to the drone on the far right. "Rest assured, we have a stash of your brand of bourbon just in case things get too stressful for you.

"We have everything set up to make this mission as comfortable as possible. However, as I stressed before, don't try to contact anyone, or the consequences will be severe. Just get this done over the next few hours, and we'll all get out of here a lot richer and in good shape.…"

The phone on the central table began to ring just then. With there being a single room, everyone could hear any conversation that transpired.

"Yes," came the simple answer from Ron. It was clear from then on that the agent was only listening. He was quiet for about thirty seconds before responding.

"Affirmative," he said, then hung up.

Ron looked around the room to ensure he had everyone's attention.

"We now have the 'go-ahead' for our mission. I want you all to open your Phase One file and log into your social networking accounts. Get the first message ready to go, but wait until I've given the order before sending. We're monitoring each of your screens. The message will go out at precisely noon, so get everything set and then back away from your keyboard for us to observe. If you need to, ask permission to get some food or use the restroom, but just relax and be patient until I say 'go.'"

Chapter

(Nine-teen)

*T*he **White House Press** Secretary kicked things off for the two o'clock press conference.

"Ladies and Gentlemen of the press, there has been quite a bit of speculation and consternation over the tragic events of today. The President has called this press conference to try to set the record straight. With no further delay, here to bring you up-to-date is the President of the United States."

The President made his entrance from the rear "stage" of the briefing room. He looked tired, which was clearly a clue to those in the Press Corps that this was a very serious matter, and it was getting most, if not all, of the President's attention.

"Today, at approximately 7:30 Eastern, there was an incident in Atlanta. The calamity that struck is unprecedented. While we don't fully understand the cause, as you have likely observed on the news channels, the aftermath has been incredibly destructive."

The President paused. Not really for effect, as he might have done on one of his previous speeches where he was trying to be dramatic, or even political. No, this pause was to gain his composure. There was nothing to compare with trying to tell the American public about a crisis that you didn't fully understand and at the same time, hiding the additional crises brewing, such as the escalation in Iran and movement in the East China Sea.

"While we don't understand the mechanism by which the incident transpired, our Department of Homeland Security is leading the effort with the FBI, National Transportation Safety Board, state officers, Georgia National Guard, and the intelligence community. All are working fervently to determine the cause of the incident.

"After observing the conjecture on the news channels, as well as the possible irresponsible speculation by one of our federal employees, I want to bring you up to speed on our official conclusions so far.

"Let me be clear and to the point: We have no evidence that this was an act of terrorism, nor has any terrorist group claimed responsibility for what happened this morning. This incident is tragic, and we all mourn the loss of lives. However, we must get to a thoroughly investigated conclusion. If we find that this was an act of terrorism, rest assured, we will act swiftly and decisively in protecting our homeland.

"I will provide an update, either personally or through the Press Secretary, if we have any additional information or conclusions to share.

"At this point, I'm concluding our press conference. I do not have time for questions. My sincere apologies."

From the look on the President's face, most reporters knew that trying to get a question in edge-wise would be a waste of time, and might even cause some ill-will during future press conferences. However, one reporter from SPOX news just had to get one in.

"President Brunson, what about the plane that landed in Huntsville? There's evidence of a missile attack. What can you tell us about the missile? Was it an attempt to down the plane before it hit a target?"

The President's back was already turned to the reporters by now, but this particular question got the best of him. Turning back towards the room, the President laid eyes on the reporter and stated, "Tim Harvey, from SPOX News, correct?"

Tim answered in the affirmative somewhat sheepishly, surprised that the President knew his name.

"Well, Mr. Harvey, it's interesting that your brilliant reporting has uncovered evidence and conclusions that not even the FBI, NTSB or Department of Homeland Security has information on.

"In your astute observation, did you notice that the metal was perforated from the inside out?" He paused for effect. "I'm not a trained engineer, scientist or weapons analyst, but that's one of the first things I noticed.

"Unless your supposed missile was somehow already onboard and was launched from the inside, there's kind of a problem with your claim, wouldn't you say?"

Tim Harvey was silent.

"I suggest you start reporting the news and what you know to be true rather than trying to make judgment on matters you obviously don't understand. I would have expected you to come better prepared."

With that, the President turned again to leave. There were no further questions.

Chapter

(Twen-tee)

Greg finished talking with Teardown and easily convinced them to take apart another Dazzle phone. They had already done a review on it when it first came out, so it wasn't going to be too hard to identify any differences. In the meantime, their lead engineer, Trey, gave Greg clear instructions on how to take apart the damaged phone he bagged from the plane. Greg looked at the phone's motherboard and saw there was a completely obliterated chip right in the middle. Beyond being charred, the middle of the package was blown through with a large hole. Even the power traces leading to the chip were melted; it seemed like the board was bubbled from the inside out.

The analyst at Teardown quickly surmised that something had shorted the chip, which turned out to be the main processor stack. He explained this was more than a simple processor. This was actually a processor, memory, GPS and a few specialty chips all stacked together in one package to save on space and cost. It was as leading-edge as phone technology could get. The ruined motherboard was probably damaged by the power and ground planes overheating, which shouldn't ever have occurred with all the built-in safeguards. Something must have gone seriously wrong.

The analyst recommended that Greg have someone at the university take apart the chip in his phone to observe what layer might have shorted, but that was a difficult job for someone untrained to do so. Trey volunteered to talk with the university directly to lead them through it, provided Greg could hook them up.

Greg had a better idea—have Teardown locate a professor at the Huntsville campus—use an administrative assistant to find one. Stressing the urgency of the situation, Greg said he would double their fee.

Fortunately, they agreed. Engineers are always spurred on by challenges, and this one was of national importance. The analyst promised to call Greg as soon as they located a professor. In the meantime, Teardown would begin working on a new Dazzle. While they were at it, Trey said they would pull apart another smartphone known to have a similar chip stack.

These guys are good, thought Greg.

Trey warned him that if this was purely software, they couldn't help him out; in fact, it would take a team of experts weeks to solve that challenge. However, if it had any basis in hardware, they had a chance to uncover the culprit quickly.

"Samantha? Samantha Grey?"

Greg spoke softly to the seemingly frail girl resting quietly in her hospital bed. As Greg was much less abrasive and certainly more pleasing to look at than Dennis, the senior man figured he'd let Greg do the initial introductions before jumping in.

Samantha, barely seventeen but mature beyond her years, was the black-haired girl whom Michael had protected from the oxygen bottle blast. Though Greg and Dennis didn't know the details, they had heard that there was some incident after landing that involved Samantha and Michael. Though Dennis hated to bother passengers who were hospitalized, these were the only eye-witnesses they could interview. Everyone else had either disappeared to local hotels or just flat-out left town.

Samantha, fortunately, had escaped major injury. Still, the ER staff wanted to observe her to ensure there was no danger of internal injuries. Greg's soft voice in her slumber reminded Samantha so much of her father's tone, she knew that he would be right there with her when she opened her eyes.

As the room came into focus, Sam realized this wasn't her father, and she wasn't in his house in LA. No, her plane had crashed on the way, and…the landing. *That landing.* Where was that guy who had saved her? What happened to him? And how in the world could she ever thank him for what he did?

"Samantha?"

"Yes? Who are you? What do you want?" she asked somewhat timidly.

"Samantha, my name's Greg Cannon. I'm with the National Transportation Safety Board. I'm here with my partner, Dennis Wright, to ask some questions about your flight from Atlanta. I'm so sorry about what happened on the plane.

It's really important that we gather as much information from you as while it is still somewhat fresh in your mind. Samantha, do you understand what I'm asking you?"

Samantha was fully lucid by now, and understood what Greg had said to her.

"Sure. I mean, yeah. I remember what happened. I think. Can you tell me who it was who saved me? I want to thank him. He protected me. The explosion, it was so loud—my ears still hurt. They're…ringing or whatever. But this guy totally saved me. Is he OK? Is he hurt?"

"Samantha—"

"Hey, just Sam, okay? No one calls me Samantha."

"OK, Sam. We'll check on your friend that—"

"No, he wasn't my friend. I don't even know who he is."

"OK. Well, whoever this man is, we'll identify him and make sure you can thank him. OK? There's a very good chance that he's here in this hospital or one nearby. But for now, try to answer a few questions, if you can. Whatever you can remember will allow us to prevent this from happening ever again."

"Yeah, OK."

"Sam, have you flown much before today? What do you remember being the first strange or unusual thing that happened on the flight?

"Umm, what's your name again?"

"Greg."

"Greg, the flight seemed totally normal. I go to visit my dad whenever I can. I really miss Dad…"

Sam's voice trailed off as she remembered how much she wanted to spend time with him and now how she was stuck in some place she didn't expect to be…she started to tear up.

"I'm sorry. I really am…" Greg said, trying to console the young stranger.

"I'm sorry for crying. I really wish he were here. He always knows what to do. So, the flight…the flight was normal. It was early, at least early for me, and I was going to sleep like I always do. And then all of the sudden, I smelled smoke. Like burning plastic…like when something melts in the dishwasher, you know? That's the smell that woke me up. There was smoke in the cabin and people jumping out of their seats because all their phones and iPads and stuff were getting hot, smoking, and catching on fire. In the row next to me, a guy's iPhone was totally in flames, and…he threw it, right at my feet. I just remembered that. But I freaked out and screamed and stomped on it to put it out, you know. It worked, too."

"That sounds really crazy," Greg commented, trying to visualize the surroundings Sam had experienced.

"It *was* crazy. I was panicking. It was, like, right out of a movie. But I was in it. It wasn't making sense, but I knew I had to do something. After I stomped out the flames, I got out of my seat and ran to wherever it seemed safe, which was at the back of the plane."

Samantha was fully lucid by now and found her mind suddenly flooded with details.

"Go on, please. Sam, what happened next?" Greg asked.

Sam's voice grew steadier as she spoke: "I ran to the back near the restrooms, and looking toward the front of the plane, it seemed like chaos. Well, organized chaos. People were being smart and not panicking too much—using blankets, water and whatever they could to put out the fires."

"So, it was just the devices—iPhones, iPads—that were catching on fire? Anything else?"

"I think that was pretty much it. But maybe it was only phones that were on? Because when I got here I realized that my phone was totally fine, and it was off during the flight. I mean, it's just a phone—it doesn't have internet or whatever—but still, it's totally fine.

"And then the pilot came on the speakers and said we had an emergency and to get on oxygen. That's when the plane started to dive. I was so, so scared. I could only crawl to the nearest seat, which was the last row on the plane."

"Do you remember anything else?" Greg inquired.

"I remember people screaming, my ears popping as we came down so fast. I remember seeing that guy…the guy who saved me. I could read his lips. He looked back at me and said it would be OK. I think I even took his seat. Yeah, it was his seat that I grabbed before we landed. And then I remember the pilot saying to put my head down or something, and feeling the descent, the plane pull up, then hearing the brakes screeching…. We stopped so fast…I've never felt anything like that except on a rollercoaster. I thought I would throw up. And I remember praying. I don't ever pray. But I prayed to God. I prayed that He would let me live, that He would send an angel to protect me."

Sam paused as she thought about what happened and how she had been rescued. As the full implication of what she had just said dawned on her, she slowly and deliberately stated, "That guy was totally my angel." She paused when tears began to well up in her eyes as she took it in. "Please find out who he was. I really hope he's OK. I really want to thank him."

"Sam, this all sounds so intense. So traumatic. I'll help you find out what happened to this guy, OK? Sounds like God might need some thanks, too," Greg said.

He paused for a few seconds to let Sam gain her composure.

"So, Sam, let's keep going. After the landing…what do you remember about that?"

"I remember…well, I remember looking to the front of the plane. People were taking off the emergency doors and starting to get out. And then I remember seeing that guy. He had a really fearful look in his eyes, which didn't make sense. We were on the ground and safe, but he was freaked out! He jumped up, ran back and grabbed me. Lucky for me I was already out of my seatbelt, or he would have ripped me in two, he was so strong. He pulled me up and I just flew through the air. Then he somehow spun me around, held me, and then I felt and heard a huge 'boom' and then…well, then I woke up in an ambulance. And then I came here. That's what I remember."

Sam sighed and was silent.

"Well, Sam, that is all very detailed. More detailed than I could have hoped for, actually, considering all you've been through."

Dennis interjected as gently as he was able. "Sam, again, I'm Dennis. I want to make sure we don't miss anything."

"OK."

"Do you remember anyone out of the ordinary being on the flight? Anyone that looked strange, nervous or suspicious?"

"Uhhh…no. I can't think of anyone strange. Even now. Honestly, no one stood out except the guy who rescued me."

"Well, Sam, thinking back to this guy. Do you imagine that somehow he knew that there was going to be an explosion and he had second thoughts since maybe he was attracted to you? That he tried to protect you from a bomb he set himself?"

Sam looked puzzled for a bit as she considered what Dennis had asked. The meds she had taken made her thinking a little slow, but she understood what he was getting at. Fortunately, Sam had a good sense of humor, and the meds, amplified that.

"Well, I know I'm pretty hot and all and I have guys just falling all over themselves to win me over..."

Greg's face suddenly mirrored Sam's puzzled expression.

Even in her pain, Sam winked at them both and said, "That's a joke, Greg."

For the first time in what seemed like forever, Greg felt himself break into a smile.

"But in spite of that," she continued, "I don't think attraction was any part of it. The bomb or whatever it was had to be right over my head. And that's where he was seated to begin with, you know? He would have blown himself up with that one, and I'm telling you, he didn't look like the type of guy that was depressed. He had a great smile. Yeah, maybe there was a connection there when we made eye contact. But he didn't fit what I expect a terrorist to look like. He was white. He was kind of nerdy. And he didn't cry 'Ali-Akbar' or whatever before the explosion."

Dennis decided that now wasn't the time to explain profiling and the proper Muslim phrase for "God is Great," considering what Sam had gone through. And she did have some good points.

"Sam, thanks for giving us that additional information. You've really helped us a lot. We have some other patients to visit. In fact, the next one is an 18-year-old guy...could even be your angel. If it looks like he is, we'll let you know, OK?"

"Sure. Well, glad I could help. I'm gonna go back to sleep now, I think. I need to turn the TV back on to try to cover up this ringing in my head. The doctor said it should go away soon, but it's driving me nuts."

Sam turned on the TV and closed her eyes as Greg finished his notes. He had his recorder on, of course, but there were a few things he wanted to jot down as well.

Dennis' eyes were fixed on the TV.

"There are FBI reports that the event in Atlanta was not only not isolated, but was a terrorist attack. This breaking news from our affiliate station WAYA TV in Huntsville, Alabama earlier today…"

As he saw the story unfold, he realized they were filming him and Greg.

"…and if you listen very carefully to the plainclothes agent speaking to the local officer, you can hear him make a shocking statement…"

Dennis tapped Greg on the arm. "Greg, look at the TV. Now," he whispered.

Greg looked up from his notebook in time to see himself and Dennis walking over to agent Donovan.

"I can't believe this. This is worse than I'd thought," Dennis said under his breath.

Dennis felt the blood drain from his face as he heard his voice—and his particularly indelicate comments—emanating from the national news network. He looked over at Greg.

As the segment ended, Dennis motioned for Greg to come out into the hall. Greg quickly stuffed his notebook and recorder into his computer bag and followed.

"Greg, this is really bad. This means I'm going to be called back in and probably pulled off this case and maybe you will be, too. The good thing is they'll have to track down Donovan to find out who we are, and Donovan will have to figure out *where* we are. No way am I answering his call since I know his number now. We have to get as much information as we can in the next few hours before we're locked out. Make backups, and make backups of those backups, OK?"

Dennis tried to think through priorities as quickly as possible. He couldn't keep his hands from shaking slightly.

"Greg, we need to talk with this next kid. He's likely Sam's angel, which means he probably knows more than she does—at least he knows why he ran back and grabbed her. And we've got to get the information from Teardown. You make a call to them and I'll see about talking with the boy. Fifteen minutes. Make it quick, OK?"

Greg had little choice but to follow Dennis' lead. They were off any playbook they had previously developed, as Dennis' participation in the investigation likely had a short life. He would make the call to Teardown, he reasoned, but then he would sit down and try to think. Ten minutes of concentrated thinking might be just what he needed to get some insight.

When Greg opened his phone, he saw that he'd missed two calls. One was from Teardown and the other from a local number in Huntsville.

Sure enough, Teardown had located a Professor who could get right on things and was calling to let Greg know. The second call was from a Professor Jones, who worked in the Materials Science department at the University of Alabama. He volunteered to come to Greg and pick up the Dazzle phones, given the gravity of the situation, and let Greg continue his work; he just needed to know where.

Whether it was the money that had motivated Teardown or just the opportunity to serve the national interest, those guys had really come through. He now had top experts helping and that's precisely what he needed. Greg would call Professor Jones first.

Chapter
(Twenty-1)

Shelly made it up to Huntsville and was waiting for further information from her father. She was getting frustrated with how slow things were moving. Mary was waiting anxiously behind the scenes, inside Shelly's head, ready to take control when needed. Shelly set up at Starbucks on Grosvenor and Whitesburg, near downtown. What she had seen on secure email were the images and video of Greg and Dennis gleaned from the report on CNT. Of course, the pictures were to familiarize her with how Greg and Dennis looked, but the video was also valuable for studying any and every mannerism she could pick up. Inspecting her surroundings, Shelly noticed an unusual profusion of white coats and blue scrubs in the coffee shop. Little did she know, this particular coffee shop was merely a thousand feet or so from where Greg and Dennis were preparing to interview Michael James.

After the Zhonghua Nine had seen the special report with Dennis and Greg, they quickly dispatched their own experts to analyze the video. CNT was busy trying to track down other news sources—since they hadn't been able to discern license plates, they moved onto events focused in Atlanta. However, Zhonghua was looking for any other discernable information from the broadcast. After enhancing the video from their high definition feed, they identified a barcode on the rear window of the driver's side, used for inventory control at rental car facilities. A quick check online showed that only two car companies in Huntsville rented Cadillacs, and they both shared the same reservation system since they had merged operations.

Shelly received the call she had been waiting for. Well, not the call to give her the target's name and location, but more information, nonetheless. She quickly gathered her computer and made her way to the Huntsville Airport.

Since she had her luggage with her, she fit right into the landscape of travelers. However, what she was currently wearing wouldn't work for what she needed to accomplish next. Darting into the nearest restroom, Shelly changed into a tight, bright red, low-cut business suit. She was going to turn heads with this one. With the addition of some subdued red lipstick and light purple eye shadow, she looked every part of the network news reporter she was going to impersonate.

Shelly attracted attention at the rental car counter. In fact, with just a few people in line in front of her, both guys at the counter hoped to time things right in order to get to talk with her. Lisa, a young and perky rep also waiting on customers, noticed her colleagues now acting much brighter and more pleasant.

"Next," came the call from Jerry, the smiling agent at the counter, a college student, who had won the race.

Smiling with the nicest, biggest smile she hoped could melt anyone within ten-feet, Shelly sauntered up to the counter. She had been trained for moments just like this. No one who knew Shelly from the science center would have recognized her.

"Hi, Jerry," Shelly said, pointedly noting the rep's nametag. "I'm hoping you can help me out here, can you?"

"Well, that's my job. What can I do for you?"

"Has anyone told you that you have a gorgeous smile? That's got to be a great asset in a customer-oriented business like this. I bet you'll go far with that charisma. Wow."

Jerry wasn't quite sure what to say in response, so he just smiled—somewhat embarrassed, actually—and stared at Shelly.

"Well, honey, I'm not actually here to get a car. I'm here for some information. And if you give me what I need, I'm gonna make it totally worth your while, OK?"

Shelly leaned over with her elbows on the counter and her chin on her hand, looking straight into Jerry's eyes. It was all the agent could do not to steal glances down her blouse—it was such an easy view. The other agents further down the counter couldn't tell what was being said, but they could tell that Jerry was getting somewhat excited.

"S-s-so, you're not here to rent a car?" he stammered.

"Jerry, I'm from WAYA News and I need to get a bit of information that will really help me out. Don't worry, honey. I won't reference you or this company at all in my story, OK?"

Jerry looked a little perplexed. He was a really bright guy, but this was all becoming confusing for him.

Shelly looked at Jerry like she wanted to jump over the counter and start pulling his clothes off right then—a regular cat-girl in heat.

"OK, well, I…I'll try to help. What information do you need?" Jerry responded.

"By the way, Jerry, I was just wondering, a young hunky guy like you—well, do you have a girlfriend?"

"What? Well, um, no."

"We gotta do something about that," Shelly purred. After a pause for effect, and to ensure she had him off-balance, she continued, "Well, honey, what I need from you right now is just a few names. I need to find out who might have rented one of your Cadillac DTS's today."

"Well, we normally don't give out information…"

"Honey, this is not a normal situation. This is a big story and I need to get this information before any other news channel. This will make my career, and it will make your month, at least. So let's make this easy—I'm gonna get those names, and I'm gonna make it worth your while. I've got an envelope here. On the outside is my phone number—you give me those names and they're good, and you and I can get together soon—and inside is something else to try to convince you. But this is my only offer. I can tell out of the corner of my eye that your colleague down the counter might be interested in this offer as well, and since I'm not gonna take 'no' for an answer, you get one chance to look in the envelope and make a decision, OK, honey?"

Jerry nodded. He understood. He quietly took the envelope from Shelly. Looking inside he saw hundred dollar bills—it looked like there must be at least twenty of them—two thousand dollars or more. His face grew hot. He was behind on his rent and his car payment. With that much cash, he could get out from under his debt and have plenty to spare.

"So what did you say your name was again?"

"I didn't," came the answer from Shelly. "I guess that's a 'no.' Please give me the envelope back and I'll move on…"

"No, no. I mean yes. Yes, I'll do it, OK?" Jerry answered quickly, adjusting his tone so as not to draw attention.

"Now that's what I was expecting out of a smart guy like you. I'm glad you were the good-looking guy that got to help me out, honey."

Pretending to be looking for a reservation, Jerry quickly did a search on cars rented that day. Only two Cadillacs had gone out that morning, one as an upgrade.

"Well, we have two that were rented today. One was black and the other white—same DTS model," Jerry stated.

"I'll need the name on the black one."

"There are two names on the booking. Must be government types since no one ever lists their second driver unless they do things by the book. Plus, one driver's license is from Maryland and the other from Virginia…DC area."

Shelly smiled even more broadly, if that were possible.

"Jerry, you're good. Really good. Hot and smart…You make me all tingly inside. So…their names?" she coaxed.

"OK…well…the one's name is Greg Cannon. He's the primary driver from Maryland. Second is Dennis Wright, from Virginia. Look, I'm gonna write down their driver's license information on this sheet of paper. Just casually put them in your bag and I'll loudly say that we don't have anymore Cadillacs in stock to rent, which is true," Jerry stated, getting more nervous all of the time.

Jerry wrote the information down neatly but quickly and tried to discreetly hand the note to Shelly.

Taking the paper from Jerry, Shelly smiled yet again at the young, overheated, perspiring college student. "Jerry, you've done well. Now how hard was it to make some quick cash and a new friend with some benefits? What time do you get off work, anyway?"

"Oh, well, um, ten tonight. Long shift." He felt his face getting red thinking about the prospect of hanging out with this gorgeous woman.

"By the way, my name is Veronica," Shelly said to him quietly. "If this all pans out, you and I'll get together soon and party. I'll buy. If it's not later tonight, then call me."

Of course the phone number on the envelope was bogus. But with the amount of cash she had just given Jerry, Shelly knew it was highly unlikely that he would tell anyone what had transpired. Shelly wondered if Jerry would hold out if pressed by the authorities…her thoughts were cut off just then by Jerry's booming voice.

"Ma'am, I'm sorry but we are just out of Cadillacs. Is there something else you might be interested in?"

Good job, Shelly thought.

She took her cue and responded a little louder herself, so the other rental car agents could hear. "Honey, I had my heart set on a Caddie…you are such a gem to look so hard. But since you're out, I'm gonna try elsewhere for now," she said, turning to go.

Shelly slowly swayed her hips as she sauntered away from the counter, back down the hall towards the ladies' room. She was going to need to change again to ensure no one would recognize her from this latest scene.

When she had handed Jerry the cash, she had a choice of two envelopes she could have given him—one with Anthrax, one without. Shelly thought Jerry was cute and even toyed with the idea of hooking up with him later on. But Mary Death wanted no part of that—she knew he could identify her later if grilled. Plus, Mary was always on the lookout for someone to justifiably kill. Mary won the argument. The cash would keep Jerry quiet for now, but the white powder at the bottom of the envelope would ensure Jerry, and anyone else he came in contact with, would be quiet for a long time.

Chapter
(Twenty-2)

*T*he **President had** no sooner finished his press conference than he was intercepted by Ned.

"Mr. President, I need you in the Oval Office right away. It's Purple."

Purple was their private code for highest priority and highest security.

The President wondered what could be even higher priority than what had already transpired.

It took only a few seconds to make the walk from the Press Briefing Room to the Oval Office. Along the way, various staffers tried to catch the President's eye to either nod their heads in agreement with his job at the press conference or catch him for a second. The look on his face made it clear that now was not the time.

Once in the Oval Office, with the door shut behind them, the President shot Ned a look. A look that said, "OK, give it to me straight."

"Mr. President, we've finally heard back from the Iranian President, through their Washington office. It's not good."

The President was silent, waiting for him to get to the point.

"They didn't really address the issue of the troops gathering on the front with Iraq. Rather, the message was, exactly…" Ned opened an envelope and began reading. "Mr. President, we insist that you resist from interfering with our Middle East activities. Iranian citizens and Islamic people have been persecuted in Iraq and have been pleading for relief from the oppressive government. We must do our duty to ensure Islamic interests are protected, as our Supreme Leader has ordered. Likely you have surmised from your spies and satellites that an incursion of protective forces into Iraq is imminent. We insist you do not interfere in our religious or political affairs. Likewise, we insist that you do not interfere in China's current activities in the East China Sea. Failure to stand down your troops in either location will result in another attack, similar to the one you experienced in Atlanta this very morning, but in multiple cities in the US with an increased radius of impact. The attack on Atlanta was not an accident, and we are prepared to increase the devastation if you do not comply. To ensure you know we have the power to act on our promise, the next cities to suffer will be Dallas-Fort Worth. We await your positive response by 4:00 p.m. Eastern Time."

The President was again silent, taking it all in.

"Mr. President, this memo was officially delivered, in person, by the Chief of the Interests Section of Iran, here in Washington. He also provided exact coordinates for the next strike—DFW Airport."

The President responded immediately: "Call a meeting with the National Security Council. Call it now. We need a plan of action. Immediately."

Chapter
(Twenty-3)

Dennis quickly found Michael James' room. Unfortunately, he had gotten out of surgery only an hour before and wasn't going to be in the best condition to talk with Dennis or Greg just yet. Michael's surgery was to relieve the pressure on his lower spine and protect his spinal cord. Apparently, it was successful and Dr. Fisher, the primary doctor attending, was hopeful. The scope of his lungs looked good as well, leaving Dr. Fisher in an upbeat mood after informing the James' of Michael's progress.

Michael's parents were waiting patiently for any sign that he was either conscious enough to talk, or to see if there were any complications. Though they had little idea what the various tubes and sensors attached to Michael were for, they were quick to notice any change in breathing, heartbeat or alarms.

Dennis and Greg quietly entered the room. Mrs. James was somewhat surprised to see two men at the door she didn't recognize.

"Mr. and Mrs. James?" Greg asked.

They both nodded their heads as Mr. James stood up to greet them, looking concerned. Michael just moaned and drooled.

"I'm so sorry about what happened to Michael—"

"And you are?" Mr. James said.

"Mr. James, my name is Greg Cannon," Greg said quietly. "I'm with the National Transportation Safety Board—this is my partner, Dennis Wright—and we're here to investigate the incident this morning on your son's flight."

Dennis pulled out his government identification while Greg was talking and showed it to Mr. James.

At this point, Mr. James felt all of the emotion of the day start to pour out of him and onto Dennis. He kept his composure well enough on the frantic drive from Atlanta. He had remained calm as Dr. Fisher told him his son might be permanently injured and wheeled him off to surgery. He had even remained strong for his wife, who was scared, upset and angry at the circumstances. But somehow the presence of two investigators who were trying to discern what happened—when they hadn't prevented these tragic events in the first place—just made him lose it.

"So, you're from some government agency and you're gonna try to solve this mystery? Where the hell were you guys before my son was almost killed in this fucking nightmare of a landing?" Mr. James felt his voice getting louder and his emotions growing stronger. "This shouldn't happen in America, and it should never happen to my son. Do you even have kids? Do you know what my wife and I have been through today?"

Mrs. James appeared at her husband's side and rested a gentle hand on his shoulder. She'd seen him lose control before, and it wasn't a pretty sight. She was worried about disturbing Michael, and about her husband's emotions generating even more stress during an already tense and enormously stressful day.

"Honey, shhh, you're going to—"

"Shirley, don't shush me! These guys are probably suspecting Michael did something since he's a survivor. I know how these assholes think."

Greg hadn't anticipated such an antagonistic meeting and was ill prepared for it. Fortunately, Dennis' experience kicked in.

"Mr. James, you're wrong. Michael is a goddamn hero," he said loudly. He was using the same language and tone as Mr. James in an attempt to appeal to the man on some level.

"Excuse me?"

"Yeah, you heard me right. A hero. We're here because your son not only saved a young woman's life on that plane, but because the only way he could have known to save her was to have an incredible presence of mind in extraordinary circumstances."

"Oh…Dr. Fisher mentioned something about a gir—well I—" Dennis had clearly taken some of the wind out of Mr. James' sails, and Michael's father found himself at a loss for words.

"Mr. James," Dennis continued, "the girl he saved is in this very hospital. She would love to meet Michael and thank him when he's able to have visitors. She considers him her guardian angel."

"You'll have to excuse my outburst, I—the day and…we're under a lot of stress today."

Dennis looked at Mr. James with as much understanding as he could muster. "Mr. James, I can't imagine what you have been through today. You don't need to apologize."

"So how can we help?" Mrs. James interjected, raising a finger to her lips to signal for quiet.

"There are just a few key pieces of information that would really help us, when Michael is able to answer a few questions. First of all, let me write down the name of the girl that Michael was able to save. And I'm not at all stretching the truth to say that if he had not pulled her to safety in literally the nick of time, Samantha would be dead right now. Everyone else in that very row, unfortunately, was killed in an explosion that occurred after the plane landed. In fact, Samantha—who goes by Sam—said she had taken Michael's seat in the chaos, it is also Sam who saved Michael's life. If he had been in his originally assigned seat at the time of the explosion, he would not have survived."

"Oh, my word," Mrs. James muttered.

Dennis took a few seconds and wrote down Sam's name and room number on a sheet of notebook paper. He then wrote out three simple questions he wanted the Mr. and Mrs. James to ask their son at the first opportunity.

"There are only three questions, and all are important. When and how did he know there was going to be an explosion on the plane after they landed? Why did he save the girl, Samantha? And what did he do with his phone during the flight? If you can get Michael to give some thoughtful answers to those three, it will really help us."

Mr. James took the paper from Dennis and looked at it for a bit. "So what about what they're saying on the news, that this is a terrorist attack? What do you think?"

Dennis could feel his heart sink. Mr. James had probably seen the very report that had the video of him and Greg and his careless statement, but just hadn't recognized them yet.

"Mr. James, I can't comment on that. I wish I could, but it's just too early in the investigation," he replied. "I'm sure you understand how these things go."

"Yeah, that's what I thought you'd probably say," he countered. "I still had to try."

Just then, Mrs. James moved to Michael's side. She had been watching him through the entire conversation, multi-tasking the way only a mother can. Her husband's voice had caused Michael to stir, and it looked as though the continued conversation woke him up.

"Mom?" Michael moaned.

"Honey, Michael, it's OK," his mom said quietly as she gently touched his hand. "Honey, just go back to sleep…"

"Shirley, if he's kind of awake, let's see if he can answer the questions so these guys can keep going on their investigation."

Mrs. James flashed her husband an angry look. If looks could kill, he would have been dead and sliced into a hundred pieces.

"I know, Hon, believe me—I get it. But if Michael can help these guys, now is the time to try. If he can't, we'll try again later. How about you talk to him, Shirley? You can be as gentle as you want, only…I think we have to try."

"Fine," Mrs. James huffed. "Michael…Michael, Darlin'…"

"Mmmm…Mom…"

"Michael, do you think you can answer a question for me, Honey?"

"Huh?"

He opened his eyes slightly. He had a far-off look as he tried to focus on his mom, and then on everything else in the room. The effort seemed to great, and he let his lids close.

Dennis quietly interjected, "Can you please ask him his age?"

Mrs. James looked at Dennis like he was a Martian.

"Well, of course he's—"

"No, I know his age, Mrs. James. This is to see if he's lucid enough to even try to answer. We need to know his answers are valid."

"Oh..." she said, nodding. She turned back to Michael. "Michael, Honey, how old are you?"

"Mom, you know..." he slurred very slowly and softly, "I'm eighteen."

Mrs. James looked back at Mr. James and smiled. At least something was working right.

"That's good, Sweetie. Thank you. Now there's some fine men here who need just a few questions answered," she said clearly and deliberately. "Michael, do you remember that you were on a plane this morning?"

"Ummm...yeah. It was on fire..."

"That's right. It had some bad problems. But you were a hero on the plane. Do you remember saving a girl after you landed?"

Michael just slightly nodded, "Mmhmm..."

Mrs. James paused a moment to let her son remember. "Why did you save the girl?"

Mrs. James thought she saw a slight upturn in the corners of Michael's mouth—a slight smile. Her heart leaped.

"Beautiful..." came the one-word response.

Mrs. James smiled.

"...scared...she was," he continued.

Mrs. James stayed quiet and just let Michael think. It was clear that words were coming very slowly.

"...explosion coming..."

Dennis was instantly at complete attention. Without interrupting, he motioned to Mrs. James to keep that dialogue going.

"Honey, how did you know an explosion was coming?"

Please remember, thought Greg.

"Smoke above...my seat...oxygen bottle...inside." He was quiet for a moment, and his face contorted as he remembered the scene. "My phone...still on...in overhead...on fire...I saw...saw the glow. Knew bottle was there. Felt it was going to burst," he said haltingly.

It was all starting to make sense to Greg, and it was all he could do not to interrupt and break that flow of conversation, if you could call it a flow. He literally bit his tongue, waiting for Michael's molasses-slow responses.

"Felt…heard…voice telling me to…look back…to the girl…saw the smoke…and glow."

Mrs. James could see that there was emotion building in Michael now and she was getting concerned. Her son didn't need to be getting anxious or worked up. His heartbeat was steadily increasing as he recalled the events. Previously beating at a steady sixty beats per minute, the rate was already up to eighty and rising.

"Felt…heard…'save her'…I…I don't remember…"

Dennis jumped in, "Mrs. James, that's good. Thank you. It is likely that the explosion will make it tough to remember everything. We have enough to go on…"

But Michael continued, "My phone…my fault…"

Tears began to well up in Michael's eyes as he realized what had happened…that it was his phone he had left on that caused the explosion. His heartbeat was racing now, up to one hundred beats per minute.

Mrs. James had had enough; she hit the nurse call button to get something to calm him down.

"The girl…is she?" Michael said, clearly choking up inside.

"Michael, you are a hero. The girl is fine. You saved her. You can meet her soon." Mrs. James said, swift but soothing.

The nurse responded to the call, "Yes, can I help you?"

"Michael is awake and very agitated. Can you please bring something to help settle him?"

At this point, Dennis and Greg had what they'd come for.

Dennis leaned over to Mr. James, "Mr. James, thank you. You've helped us get closer to solving this. This was an oxygen bottle explosion, not a missile and not a bomb. We needed this information."

Mr. James just nodded as Dennis and Greg made their exit.

"Dennis, that was incredible," Greg said, practically bursting with admiration. "You handled that so well…and now we know Michael's cell phone started a fire in the overhead that eventually caused the oxygen bottle to explode. It was probably the one phone on the plane that was still on fire, but hidden so no one knew. It all fits!"

Dennis just nodded in agreement, happy to have another piece put together before he was inevitably pulled off the case.

"But how in the world did Michael know to look back?" Dennis wondered.

"That still bothering you?" asked Greg.

Dennis nodded again, thinking hard.

"Dennis, look, I believe in a higher power. I personally don't doubt that there are angels watching out for us. It fits my world view, so I guess that's why I'm not having a problem with that."

Just then Dennis' cell phone rang. He quickly looked at the number, and his countenance quickly fell.

"Damn, that's Donovan. I knew it would be a matter of time. I'm not answering. I'll just say I didn't hear it. The problem is, he knows we're at the hospital. We parked right out front with that ostentatious Cadillac.

"The only question is whether just I'm being pulled back to Washington, or both of us are. I'll let him leave a message."

Across town, a beautiful woman, dressed in all black, waited patiently at the entrance to the Embassy Suites downtown on Monroe Street. Shelly always dressed in black before a kill. Yes, she was dressed to kill, figuratively and literally. Her tight-fitting knit dress looked like it had been sewn on her, hugging every curve of her body. It was sleeveless, showing off her toned arms, covering her torso in a swathe of fabric that ended in a turtleneck. What was covered up by the high collar was made up for with a peek-a-boo cutout showing her ample cleavage. Shelly had everyone entering the hotel doing a double-take. But one look into her steel-like eyes let them know she was off limits, unless you really enjoyed pain.

Shelly had taken the time to call every major chain hotel, starting from the city center and working her way out, asking for Dennis Wright. It only took her five hotels to hit the right one. She booked a room online, drove to the hotel and found a comfortable chair in the lobby. She knew what Dennis and Greg looked like, and knew very clearly what car they drove. Now all she had to do was patiently watch and wait.

Chapter

(Twenty-4)

"The important thing to determine immediately is whether this threat from Iran is credible. If it is, we have to take definitive action to protect ourselves. First, we must decide if we'll stand-down in response to the threat and inform our allies of why we're not supporting them...."

The President had the National Security Council assembled in the Situation Room. In a way, this was akin to the escalation with the Russians during the Cuban Missile Crisis, where Defense Readiness Condition (DEFCON) Level Two was reached. But in that case, no attack had actually occurred. DEFCON-1 had never been reached in US history, and the President hoped to avoid it now.

"The threat is to attack DFW by four o'clock Eastern if we don't state that we'll stand down. Of course, we know that there are Iranian troops poised to enter Iraq. I want Hank to give us an update, but first, Carl, I need your input on the situation—both in Atlanta and the potential attack on DFW."

Carl gave the President a grim look. "Mr. President, we've had Homeland Security focused on Atlanta since this morning, and we've made good progress. The damage is contained and riots are under control. However, we still don't know the cause or the source of the attack that created this crisis. I do know that Iran has cyber-warfare groups located in Isfahan and Zanjan, but there's nothing in the cyber world we know of that could account for the physical devastation we've witnessed today. This has all the marks of an EMP. But it was a real attack, and right now, Iran is the only country willing to take credit."

The Secretary paused briefly before rendering his opinion.

"Based on this, I think we have to take the Iranian threat at face value, at least for the homeland. We have some time to search for any type of impulse weapon at the coordinates provided in the message, as well as prepare the public for the impact in case the threat is viable."

"Prepare the public?" asked the President.

"Ground flights, shut off computers, phones, cars, any other electronic devices within five miles of the target. The coordinates in Dallas are similar to Atlanta—the epicenter is directly at DFW Airport."

"How could this weapon be so accurate? Could it be satellite based?"

"Mr. President, that is highly unlikely. We know the trajectory of each and every satellite up there, as well as its likely purpose. From a satellite, a pulse would require a tremendous power source as well as an enormous antenna for such precision. With that said, we have to treat this as a credible threat. I'd like to call up our offices in Dallas and start searching and preparing in parallel."

"By offices, you mean…"

"Every agency we have available. FBI, State Patrol, local police…there isn't enough time to bring in the National Guard. We'll have the Governor and each Mayor briefed before cutting into broadcasts with the Emergency Alert System. If we have agreement, I'd like to leave the meeting now, actually, and get started. It will take some time to get the message out and we only have an hour."

The room fell silent. This day—and the decisions they made in this room— would have long-term implications for the country and history. There was no time for frivolous discussion.

"Unless there is strong opposition to this plan, I am going to authorize Carl to move forward."

Henry spoke up. "Mr. President, I am in agreement with Carl. We have to view this as a credible threat and act accordingly. There's no time to waste."

Others around the table nodded in agreement.

Henry continued: "Regarding action in the East China Sea and Iraq—to stem the movement we see from China and Iran—well that's another matter."

"OK, Hank…that can wait until later. For now, Carl, get moving on the plan for DFW."

"Yes, Mr. President," Carl responded as he rose to leave the room.

"Now, to shift gears. What do we do about our troops? We have Okinawa on alert and have ships near Korea as well. My understanding is that we can have fighters scrambled out of Okinawa and on target within a half hour, is that right, Robert?"

Robert Goodwin, Secretary of Defense, nodded in agreement. "We have Okinawa on high alert, which means they're standing by right now. Likewise, the *Washington* is en route from South Korea. The Taiwanese government is well aware of the threat. Logistically, we can do whatever you'd like us to do. The key issues are political. If we stand down, I don't know what message that sends, unless we disclose the entire predicament, which is fraught with problems. Likewise, in Iraq it'll be tough getting troops lined up to intercept within an hour, but we can have Tomahawks and Hornets on target right away. The *Truman* is stationed in the gulf in support of Afghanistan. We also have cruisers, destroyers and frigates in support of each of the carriers."

There was no doubt that the US could respond militarily to whatever presented itself. In fact, what was unspoken in the room was also the possibility for use of tactical nukes. While never used in combat, the volatile situation in the Gulf coupled with potential possession of nuclear weapons by Iran might necessitate this option, particularly if the US was attacked again.

The President spoke. "Certainly I understand the need to be highly conservative with our approach in the US. Carl's taking care of that aspect. However, with regard to our allies, namely Israel and Taiwan, plus the movements of troops and ships, I'm not so sure we shouldn't show some action."

Henry interjected, "But what if that causes Iran to deliver the blow to DFW?"

"Well, Hank, how long should we be held hostage? Homeland Security hasn't found the cause of the initial attack—do we just *wonder* how this is happening at the same time as we concede to *every request* from Iran? What if they really aren't capable of pulling this off? After all, it appears that the technology is beyond what even we have available. I don't think Klingons pulled this off, but I really don't think Iran did, either."

Henry had to agree. There was no way Iran could have been the sole aggressor in this instance. Either they had a carefully constructed web of technology operatives in the US, which was possible but unlikely, or they were working with Russia, China or another high-tech, capable country. Whatever the case, their support was sophisticated. It was also entirely possible that this was all a bluff, and both China and Iran were taking advantage of the opportunity.

Unfortunately, President Brunson had not heard back from the Chinese President, so they could only guess at motivation and cooperation between Iran and China.

Henry continued his assessment. "Mr. President, in any case, we are going to have to inform our allies of our next steps. If Iran crosses into Iraq, we know the Israeli Air Force is ready to strike. And they likely won't limit themselves to the forces crossing the border. They've been itching to take out other Iranian facilities, including those nuclear plants, for some time. This might be just the excuse Israel needs. And you know they can go nuclear if it escalates. But, frankly, I don't understand this potential Chinese strike against Taiwan."

The President nodded in agreement. This was certainly a difficult predicament, to which there was no right answer—only shades of gray and levels of uncertainty.

"If we stand down, we'd better have our explanations in order," Henry finished.

"I know," said the President. "We can't show weakness. At some point, and it better be soon, we'll know the cause of the Atlanta incident. And I'm sure it won't have anything to do with Iran's capabilities. They have none."

After a pause, the President continued: "What I want to do is prepare for a show of force, to both the Chinese Navy and Iran. I want to show that we're not going to back down. We're going to call their bluff. I don't believe they can really hit us, and on the slim chance they do, we'll already have DFW locked down and secure. Get ready to make an assault on both fronts. Is everyone in agreement?"

Ned interrupted, "But shouldn't we try for more diplomatic means with China? We haven't been able to get in touch with them yet. Clearly the message from Iran was unambiguous, but we really are flying blind with China."

"Good point. Continue to try to contact President Li. In the meantime, get ready to strike, monitoring movements as we go. We won't take action unless there's continued threatening movement, and until we know the supposed four o'clock deadline has passed. Send a message to the Iran office in Washington, stating that we're standing down pending further review of their actions in the Gulf."

"But that's not exactly what they asked for," Ned replied.

"I know, but that's the best we can give them. If they move toward Israel, we have to act, even if there's an attack in the US. For all we know, the supposed attack is a spoof, or was already planned. Iran might not have control here," the President surmised. "Are there any other serious objections?"

Various Council members and staffers shook their heads.

"OK. Good luck, everyone."

Chapter
(Twenty-5)

*"O*K, drones, it's party** time. Get ready to send out your first message."

It was 12:15, and they were already behind schedule. The first message was supposed to go out at three o'clock Eastern.

"Go ahead and send it." Ron commanded.

The messages were to be sent an hour apart allowing time to ripple through all the various systems out there—including smartphones and tablets.

Forty-five minutes should still be sufficient, Ron thought.

As the agents carefully monitored each of the screens it all appeared to be going just fine…messages were going out across all applicable social networks. They were innocuous messages that ranged from "I'm having a party" to "I love chocolate so much" to "He's at it again" for some business-oriented sites. All of the messages were pretty much meaningless. However, it was the few scrambled characters spread throughout the messages that had significance. They were being used to set a trigger for the intelligent devices. If the social sites hadn't supported Unicode characters, this wouldn't have worked. As such, binary commands were embedded in each message string with the regular text.

It appeared that each drone had successfully sent their message or messages, on multiple accounts.

"OK, break time. Feel free to get up and stretch or get some snacks…or your meds, Pamela. And Joe, you're allowed to get up now and do what you need to do, but we're watching you closely."

Joe, looking irritated and still disheveled, just had to ask, "So what time is this all supposed to be over? I have a poker game tonight."

"Joe, if you keep up that attitude, we may keep you around all night just to piss you off. I can't tell you when we'll be done; it might be that this extends into a whole 'nother mission. You all now have a ten minute break—then return to your workstations. You can thank your buddy Joe for the shortened intermission."

The drones casually got up and began making sandwiches, getting drinks and using the restroom. In the commotion, one of the drones tried to get a message to the outside. Hitting Ctrl + N on his keyboard to rapidly open a new window, he figured that a quick message from anyone's account would be better than not communicating at all. Maybe he could...

"Hey, Rick," Ron yelled, spying three windows open on his monitor.

As quickly as he heard his name, Rick hit Ctrl + W to instantly close the window. If he had been typing in his main window, the characters would have still been there to give him away.

"What the hell were you doing?" the agent yelled again.

"Uh, nothing."

"Don't tell me nothing, there were multiple windows up. What were you doing?"

The tone in his voice made everyone stop and pay attention. There was anger that no one had guessed could come out of him. This was serious.

"Uh, just checking scores..." Rick lied.

"Really? Well, we have all sites blocked out except for your social networking sites. I think you had another page open, probably to your own account or your client's account."

Rick had been caught. He hadn't realized all other sites had been blocked.

"OK, I was on Blather, but I didn't type anything."

The agent was done talking. He pulled out his list of accounts to see what Rick had been assigned. He had two accounts—one was a "gangsta" rapper and the other was a burned-out Hollywood socialite. Neither was as high in popularity as they once were, though each had a few million followers. He decided to act quickly to send a message to the other drones. If Rick had been assigned Ashton Kutcher or Britney Spears, he might have gotten off with just a punch in the face. For all he knew, though, Rick's accounts were now exposed or suspicious. He wouldn't be using them again anyway.

"OK, Rick, I need to talk with you privately—right now."

"What? I didn't do anything..."

"I don't know that. I gave explicit orders only to copy the messages I provided. No typing once you were on your social site, and no screwing around. I guess you didn't think I was serious. You'd think for the money we've paid you over the past few years and the money we gave you today, you'd just obey your orders. Now, please go over to the utility room—it's the door in the corner over there—and wait for me."

"I'm sorry…really…" stammered Rick as he got up and walked to the door.

The agent's tone and demeanor had changed. He seemed more settled. Rick didn't know if this was a good or bad thing.

The utility room was just that. Actually, it was more like a janitor's closet. There were a couple of chairs inside, some replacement bulbs, a broom and a mop. Not much else. Rick sat down in the closet and waited nervously for the agent to come and reprimand him.

Ron quietly discussed the situation with his subordinates. When done issuing commands, all nodded in agreement and took positions around the room. Four agents fanned out behind the workstations, two behind each table. A fifth continued to monitor the screens from the central hub. Ron made his way over to the utility closet.

Once he opened the door, everyone could hear Rick: "Dude, I'm sorry. Really, I didn't send anything or type anything…"

Ron closed the door.

The drones and agents still in the main room could hear the muffled voices, though they were too faint to really make out what was being said.

Suddenly, Rick's voice got loud—loud enough to hear exactly what he was saying, or rather. screaming.

"No, really, I'm sorry! PLEASE, NO! DON'T!!"

A gunshot rang out. Then silence.

Pamela's voice came first. She let out a blood-curling scream once she realized what had happened.

"WHY!? Why did you shoot him?! You killed him?!" Pamela cried as she fell to the floor as if she had been stabbed, writhing in pain.

Some of the other drones still looked like they were in shock, some were crying, and most were deathly scared.

One of the agents said coldly, "Stay seated and away from your workstations."

As Ron exited the utility room, he turned the light off prior to opening the door so no one could view the scene.

"You're just going to let him lay there?" Joe asked incredulously.

"Yes, Joe," the lead agent said. "Where would you like me to put him? He's dead. I checked. One shot to the temple and it was over. He didn't feel a thing."

"Why did you have to kill him? This is crazy…" said another drone. "I want out, here's your money back. Just take it and let us go!"

"Now you suddenly feel remorse?" Ron scoffed. "How come it was so easy for you to take this money over the past couple of years? Didn't you think for a moment that this much money meant you were up to something illegal or risky? Do you think we'd be dumb enough to collectively fund you all millions of dollars just to send out a few lame, meaningless messages a few times a year?

"You made a deal with the devil and you all knew it. Don't pretend you didn't. Now's when you actually work for all the money we've provided, and the dollar per hour sum is still ungodly. After tonight, we're done. We all walk away from here and never see each other again. If you talk about this on the outside, yeah, we'll get to meet in person, and it won't be a pleasant meeting.

"So, just sit down, don't screw around with your workstations, ask permission to eat, drink or piss, and we'll all get through this just fine.

"And, Joe, I don't care if you have Lady Gaga as your client, if you mess up, I'll take you out just like I did Rick. It made it easier that Rick had some low-scoring has-beens on his client list, but the stakes just got higher. None of you are indispensible."

Ron took his seat at the main table. He motioned for the other agents to take their regular positions. Though he wanted to show strength and composure, the lead had to close his eyes and take a deep breath before collecting his thoughts and getting back on track. He hadn't planned on what had just transpired. If he failed this mission, the quick end he just provided Rick would be a blessing. If he was successful, he too could get out of this mess he'd gotten himself into and retire quietly with his family. Gathering his strength, he opened his eyes and looked at his team and the drones.

"Get your second message ready. Do not send it yet. You'll do it on my command. Get it ready and back away from your mouse and keyboard. One o'clock is the witching hour and it's coming soon. No one test me again."

Chapter
(Twenty-6)

After he and Greg left the hospital, Dennis decided he'd better check the message on his cell phone from Donovan. It was as he suspected; Donovan had been contacted by Homeland Security and was asked to identify and find Dennis. Dennis was off the case and ordered back to Washington immediately for debriefing. Donovan had taken the liberty to check for any evening flights—there weren't any, so Dennis would be leaving first thing in the morning.

"That was the call I expected," Dennis told Greg. "Donovan says I'm off the case and to return to Washington tomorrow morning. The good thing is, he didn't mention your name at all. You can stay here and keep the investigation going. And there was no mention of us not talking to each other, either. Looks like I can sit back and let you feed me information from the field," Dennis said with a grin. "I planned this perfectly," he added sarcastically.

Greg looked pissed. This was going to make things really difficult, even if Dennis was trying to make light of it.

"Fricking news crew," Greg muttered.

"Look, I think I've got all of the information I was gonna get here anyway. We've got a good idea of what happened on the plane. There was no bomb onboard, and the fires were caused by something that blew up a bunch of smart devices all at once. Whatever that something was didn't hit any devices that weren't in Atlanta before around 5:30 this morning. The next, key conclusions depend on what you find out about that phone. I can help interpret those results just as easily from DC as from here."

Dennis paused and gave Greg a supportive pat on the shoulder. "So it's all up to you now, Kid. No pressure," he said with a wink.

Dennis, in spite of his crustiness, had a way of putting people at ease, which is just what he was able to do for Greg.

Greg wasn't so confident.

"I've not handled anything like this before. I really don't know what I'm supposed to be doing next," he said.

Dennis smiled and continued his supportive tone.

"Sure you do. You are already on the right track, just continue on that path. Let's pick up where we last left off."

Greg summarized his calls.

"The professor's only had the phone for about an hour. I don't imagine he's etched away all of the packaging material yet, but he may be getting close. Teardown has their new phone, and is likely well on their way toward tearing it apart. Hopefully, I'll hear something back from both of them within the hour. In the meantime, I sure could use some coffee."

"Great idea. Let's get some and make sure our notes are in order. We gotta make copies of everything. Then I'll give Donovan a call, assuming the FBI isn't waiting outside at our low-profile Caddie. By the way, do you remember where Darcy put us tonight?"

"Umm, I don't think she said. I'll give her a buzz—or actually, why don't you so she can make your flight reservation too?"

"Yeah, thanks for the reminder." Dennis looked a little grim as he dialed. "Hey, Darcy, it's Dennis…. Yeah…we're OK. Things are pretty strange down here, but we've made really good progress…. What's that?… Yes, I've seen the news…. No, I didn't always want to be famous, certainly not this way. Because of that screw-up, I've been told by Homeland Security, through the FBI, to get home on the first flight tomorrow morning…. Yes…really…. I'm kind of not surprised you didn't hear—this came directly from Homeland Security. The problem is that the answers to the Atlanta incident are all right here. Fortunately, Greg's staying…. Yeah, that's the main reason I called, can you book a flight for me?… By the way, where are we staying tonight?… OK, Embassy Suites—downtown?… Good.

"Please do me a favor and call me if you hear anything else. I know it's getting late in the day and you'll be heading out, but I have a feeling this day's not going to be over for us for a while. Thanks, Darcy…. Yeah, I'm sorry too—damn press…well, talk to you later…bye."

"All right," said Greg, "now that that's done, maybe call Donovan to get him off your back? Then we can find a Starbucks and collect our thoughts."

"You know, I've been thinking about things after I heard the message from Donovan. If someone high up in Homeland Security took the time to track Donovan down, and he's got to report back, he's the one that can get our message back to them about there not being a bomb, but rather something that impacted the intelligent electronic devices onboard. If it had been a pulse, it would have taken out the plane's electronics as well. If these guys are looking for an EMP generator of some sort, they're not going to find it.

"In fact, I'll bet that if your professor and Teardown find something new in those phones, either software that takes advantage of a flaw in the hardware, or hardware that went undetected—a timer or something, I don't know. If it *is* software, course, that's gonna be impossible to find."

Greg looked at Dennis in amazement. This guy was smarter than he was letting on. He seemed one step ahead of Greg on theorizing, that was for sure.

"But I just don't know how it got triggered," Dennis continued. "A local signal to the devices just in Atlanta? Injected into the cell phones' signal? But iPads and some other tablets got hit as well...I just don't know..."

Dennis suddenly snapped to attention. "But I do know it would take days to get through red tape in our system and get this information where it needs to go. We have a conduit through Donovan. Tell you what, Greg, you call your sweetheart so she knows you're all right and I'll give your buddy a call. Let's meet back in the waiting room lobby in fifteen minutes.

"And then," Dennis added with a smile, "we'll get that cup of coffee."

Chapter
(Twenty-7)

Government agents from federal and state authorities swarmed DFW looking for an EMP device anywhere near the target coordinates. Others were sent to shut down each and every electronic system they could within five miles of the strike zone. This was proving to be a difficult task, especially since there was little more than half an hour get it done. Local authorities decided the best way to shut down the city was to ensure no one got in or out. Around DFW, that wasn't so easy. There were effectively six highways and interstates that all formed a loop around the airport, including Interstate Highways 635 and 30—some of the busiest roads around Dallas. The police determined that shutting down all ramps and feeder roads would work best. For vehicles within earshot, the police used their vehicular Public Address systems to announce the need to shut off all electrical systems, including cars, cell phones, and any other electronics. It was quickly turning to chaos.

Perhaps most important was the airspace above the strike zone and the potential for planes to be hit. The FAA shut down DFW airport and Dallas Love Field, grounding all planes and redirecting air traffic to Oklahoma City, Houston and Austin.

Fortunately, the Emergency Alert System that the FCC ran was a primary conduit for getting the message to the public. It allowed the President to broadcast on all electronic messaging systems available over both radio and television. However, there was a choice to be made—go on nationally, which the President had the authority to do, or just use the state's local systems. Because the President didn't want to cause panic on a national level, it was decided that a local EAS message would go out to the Dallas-Fort Worth area rather than alerting the entire country. Time was short, and it was important to get the message out quickly.

In the Press Briefing Room, a camera was set up, ready to send out the President's message.

"Ned, I've made a decision," the President said as they were preparing to enter the Press Room.

"Yes, Mr. President?"

The President's tone was ominous, so Ned was certain that this was something very serious, as if the message he was about to deliver wasn't serious enough.

"What time are we on?"

"In three minutes. It will be 3:45."

"OK, we have aircraft standing by on both Okinawa and in the Gulf. We've told the Iranians that we'll stand down, but I don't trust them. I think if they're capable, they'll attack us anyway. I personally believe they don't have the capability. They're nearly a third-world nation, with very little homegrown technology or capabilities. Once we have DFW locked down, I want to launch strikes against both the Chinese Navy fleet and the Iranian troops building up on the Iraqi border. We can't let this threat shut down our ability to defend our interests and support our allies. We have two minutes to go now…call Robert and get the order out. We launch at 4:10."

"Mr. President, are you certain? Is this really the right move? What if it escalates things? What if they go ahead and launch an attack based on our aggressive response?"

"Ned, I'm going to have to take that risk. If we stand down now, I don't think there's any turning back. We have to stand strong and ensure we're protected from further attack…so if we get hit and have to shut down the entire nation's electronics to prevent further damage while we defend ourselves, that's what we'll do. But you know as well as I that Iran doesn't have that type of capability."

As the President walked into the Press Room, he was keenly aware this was no ordinary address. Other times the President spoke to the nation, everything was well set up and staged in the Oval Office. In this case, there was little notice and his speech had been prepared in a hurry. On top of this, there were nagging thoughts on what the repercussions would be if nothing at all happened after the speech. Would it undermine the government's credibility, like they had cried wolf? What if something actually *did* happen and there was another incident similar to the one in Atlanta? It was a no-win situation, but the President would much rather have no incident to later explain to the public than deal with the alternative.

The time for contemplation was over. The President's message, followed by a directive to "Turn off your television immediately," was intended to be repeated continuously every three minutes over the next hour. Radio stations were to repeat a similar message. But the White House reserved the right to commandeer local stations if conditions changed or persisted.

As the President approached the podium, he gathered his printed notes. No teleprompter this time.

This is as real as it gets, he thought.

"OK, Mr. President, we're connected to the local stations now…we have a preamble being delivered…"

"We interrupt your regular programming for an emergency message from the President of the United States. This is not a test. We repeat, this is not a test."

"…and we're live in five, four, three, two…"

The President took a big breath and looked intently into the camera.

"My fellow Americans in the Dallas and Fort Worth areas, as the prior message stated, this is an emergency—it is not a test. The safety and security of you and your family depends on the actions you take in the next few minutes. Stop whatever you are doing this instant and listen to the instructions I am about to give…"

The President's tone was serious and direct. There was a stern look on his face that gave every indication that this was truly a grave matter. In fact, listeners across the region did indeed stop what they were doing to listen. Most had never experienced anything quite like this. The Emergency Broadcast Service had only been activated one other time, in the 1970s, and that was very far removed from the nation's collective memory.

"We have a credible threat that has been made to the communities of Dallas-Fort Worth. Specifically, in the vicinity of the DFW Airport. The attack that we have been warned about is similar in nature to the attack on Atlanta this morning.

Based on this, there are specific actions that you must all take immediately to limit the impact and potential damage."

The President now referred to his notes to ensure that he was reading the instructions carefully and accurately.

"First, you may have noticed that federal, state and local authorities have descended on your communities to both ensure you are prepared for the possible attack as well as search for a potential weapon or weapons. Do not panic, but rather, try to help them in any request they have.

"Second, after you have heard this message in its entirety, you must shut down any and all electrical and electronic devices by three o'clock Central time, and leave these systems off for at least an hour—until at least four p.m. This includes all computers, phones, cell phones, televisions, radios, cars, cameras, stereos and microwave ovens. In fact, if at all possible, please cut the circuit breaker to your house or office immediately. The weapon is likely an electromagnetic pulse device that will impact any and all electrical systems, at least damaging the systems and at worst causing fires and casualties. All flights have been grounded, and all vehicle traffic in the area will be stopped. If you are driving and hearing this message on your radio, find the next safe location to pull over, even if it's on the side of the road, and shut off your car, cell phone, and any other electronic device you have with you.

"I repeat, you must shut down any and all electrical and electronic devices now, and keep them off until at least four p.m. in the Dallas-Fort Worth area.

"Finally, we will provide an all clear air-raid siren when things are safe. As I just stated, shut down any and all electrical and electronic devices now until after four in the afternoon in Texas.

"This message will be repeated numerous times over the next hour. All other programming has been suspended. Resist the urge to turn on any device to check the status of the situation. Wait for the all-clear siren.

"This is a crisis situation, please listen to this message once more if you need to, then take immediate action. This is a credible and immediate threat and time is of the essence in protecting yourself and your family. Please walk to your neighbors to tell them the situation. Do not drive and do not use your computer or phone to make contact. You are all in our prayers. God bless us all."

Chapter
(Twenty-8)

In their fifteen-minute break before meeting in the lobby, Greg got to talk with his bride at length. Dennis, on the other hand, had given up trying to get through to Donovan, and frustratingly made his way to the lobby to meet Greg.

The talk with Michelle was a good break for Greg. She was doing alright. It was a slow day for her. She had been watching her favorite soap operas and keeping up with her college friends through Facebook and Blather.

The conversation was fun, as almost all conversations with Michelle were. He almost felt guilty for walking back to meet Dennis with something of a grin on his face.

When he looked out from the lobby of Huntsville Hospital, Dennis had expected to see Donovan and a host of FBI agents waiting for them at their car. After all, Donovan knew they were at the hospital. It was both a surprise, and maybe even a disappointment that there was absolutely no one waiting when they both walked out of the hospital doors.

"Greg, this is strange. The message from Donovan was so direct and urgent, and supposedly came down from the highest authorities. There has to be something much more important going on for us to get the cold shoulder like this," Dennis said with a scowl. "You know, I even tried to reach him a few times. No luck. That's pretty strange. He's looking for me, leaves me a message, and now doesn't answer his phone, nor return a call…"

Greg breathed a sigh of relief. He wasn't ready to deal with the politics and authority of Homeland Security or the FBI. Getting out of the parking lot without a scene was a welcome relief. Walking to their car, Dennis noticed a Starbucks directly across the street—a perfect spot for their coffee break. Of course, he couldn't have known that just a few hours before, visiting that coffee shop might have cost him his life. But now Shelly was sitting where she was sure to intercept them…expectant and patient, waiting for Dennis and Greg to show up in the hotel.

For those in Dallas-Fort Worth watching his broadcast, the President finished his message and the screen turned to the official Emergency Alert System notice to turn off the TV.

TV and radio stations in the DFW area did what they could to maintain composure. For one thing, it was a really confusing message for them. Were they supposed to shut down their own electronics as well? Well, clearly they couldn't and continue to broadcast the President's message. So, obviously the message couldn't apply to them. At the same time, they all needed to make contact with their families and loved ones to pass along the message as well, in case they didn't have their radios or television on at home.

Not only did the thought of contacting family run through the station employee's minds, but it must have occurred to everyone else who heard the message and had a cell phone with them. Between the calls placed and text messages transmitted in the following few minutes, all cell phone carriers were suddenly and completely deluged with traffic, enough to bring down the entire communication system. The sudden appearance of police, firemen and state patrol announcing the message to shut off all electronics over their public address systems, combined with FBI and other unmarked cars with agents frantically searching the DFW airport, all added to the surge on the system. This, in turn, caused further panic among the general public. If the President's intent was to shut down the city, the real impact was to electronically light up the whole region.

Back at the White House, the President headed to the Situation Room, where his staff was anxiously awaiting him. There was loud discussion going on when he entered the room, with Council members talking over each other in heated voices.

"Damn it, I said we should have shut down the power grid, which was the fastest and most efficient way to deal with this—"

"But Henry, we didn't know what impact that would have on hospitals, nursing homes, and other critical facilities th—"

"Bullshit! You know they all have generators…"

"Just look at the communications grid across the whole US now, let alone the target regions. You can't expect people to do the right thing with this, they're sheep—"

Just then they noticed the President's arrival. The room fell silent.

"Go on, don't stop just because I'm here," the President said. "No, I'm serious," he continued. "I don't have all the answers. I can look at the communications grid projected right there and see what you see. It's not working and we've got ten minutes until time is up—so if you were me, what would you do right now?"

After a few seconds, Carl spoke. "Mr. President, I would demand that public utilities cut power to each target region immediately. It's the only way to ensure that systems are shut down and not impacted by an electromagnetic pulse. But I don't know if we can really pull that off in time."

"What if it's not a pulse?"

"Sir, there's no other source that could cause such widespread yet targeted damage."

"Well, I think you're neglecting to account for the planes that were out of the Atlanta airspace when they got hit, in particular a plane that somehow crash-landed in Huntsville," the President said, with a stern look at Carl.

There was silence in the room again as the Security Council realized they really didn't know what they were up against.

The President broke the silence, "That's what I pay you for, Carl, to have a team understand the threat and mitigate or eliminate it. We'll start shutting down power. Is there anyone else here in disagreement? You've got one minute to voice your objections and then we move forward with Carl's plan."

"We have no other choice right now…" came one response.

"…I agree, let's get the requests out, it may take time…"

"But we don't *have* time…"

The President interjected, "OK, Carl, make it happen, grids off. You've told me that a pulse can't go more than a five mile or so radius with flat terrain unless it's nuclear, so start at the epicenter and work out from there for at least five miles. If this is a real threat, you may not get far before it hits. There's only six minutes to go now. Get on it. And when you're done, call up the National Guard. If this goes down, we're going to need them."

With that, Carl literally ran off to make the calls.

The President let the room soak for about 30 seconds before continuing.

"Before I gave my address, I told Ned to send out notice to be ready for strikes against the Iranian forces building up on the Iraqi border and to send fighters from Okinawa on a low-pass sortie as a message to the Chinese Navy. We see what they're doing and are ready to actively engage."

"Mr. President..."

"Yes, Robert?"

"We've acted on your orders; however, our latest intelligence shows that the Chinese Navy has taken a turn towards the Senkaku Islands. That's likely their destination."

This new information caused the President to pause. He closed his eyes and put his hands to his face in thought. The President knew the Senkaku Islands were highly contested because of their oil and gas reserves, and he also knew that those reserves had become particularly important to Japan, whose dependence on Iranian oil made it difficult for them to impose UN sanctions.

Everyone was anticipating the President's next words.

"If Iran and China are in this together, then China is offering Iran something much greater than their loss of business with Japan. If Iran is leading this, however, they must feel aligning with China is preferred to losing favor with Japan. Perhaps Iran wins alliance with China *and* further dependency by Japan on Iranian oil in one fell swoop; though I'd think Japan would look for a different, more trusted partner. Whatever the motivation behind their apparent partnership, we still need to respond.

"OK, everyone, there's not much time to act. Here's what I'd like to do. We have to stop Iran from crossing their border and send a message to China. Japan is our ally, and we've pretty much cut off their ability to adequately defend themselves, so we have to protect their interests while not provoking China to war. Send a message to China and attack Iran."

"But we said we'd stand down, Mr. President," Henry said.

"Well, we didn't say for how long. At 4:10, we launch."

"Are we declaring war?" asked Robert.

"No, we're defending ourselves."

"That's not really true, is it?"

"Robert, we've been attacked on our homeland. If Iran truly attacked Atlanta, and China was involved, that was an act of war. Iran claimed responsibility and has implicated China. I don't think we need to have concrete and definitive proof—we have a confession and an immediate threat."

"I see your point," Robert said.

Giving orders, the President declared, "Team, it is now 3:58. We have two minutes to go. Robert, get things in order for a 4:10 launch. We'll all remain here to monitor progress. Get on it. Ned, patch us in live to the war room at the Pentagon."

CNT had picked up the local broadcasts to Dallas and replayed them to national and global newsrooms. Commentators were already online, discussing the implications. The Zhonghua Nine closely watched.

Zhonghua One hadn't slept at all. It wasn't that he was nervous or anxious. In fact, when the door closed to his room earlier in the evening, he tried to forget all about Dormant Curse. So when the guard knocked at his door at 3:30, he answered wide-awake, in his bathrobe. The lovely escort, also in a bathrobe, peeked out from behind the wall, looking quite disheveled. Zhonghua One wasn't the most attractive man, so it wasn't often that he was able to find a willing partner to meet his needs. His liaison that evening hadn't known what she was in for. The inner circle of the Zhonghua Nine didn't get to their leadership positions by being passive and weak; they were all competitive and strong, with an intense craving for their particular habits. She felt the full brunt of not only his pent-up desire, but the added intensity of the excitement he felt surrounding Dormant Curse. Needless to say, she was thankful when the guard knocked and effectively rescued her. She was looking forward to showering and scrubbing any trace of Zhonghua One off of her body, getting dressed, and getting out of there.

At 3:50 a.m. in Shanghai, the Zhonghua Nine reassembled in the Polaris Room, earlier than some had anticipated.

"Zhonghua, we are ready to begin the next attack phase on the US. However, we have just seen the President of the United States provide warning to the cities in advance. It is my feeling that we should delay the attack by fifteen minutes. It is likely that many will indeed shut off their phones and smart devices as requested. However, in their 'free' society, they do not respect nor submit to authority. They will grow impatient. Within fifteen minutes they will call or text friends, or try to check the Internet for status. Our signal keeps the attack active for ten minutes, so anyone who turns on their system during that period will receive the trigger message and get hit."

The Leader looked at Zhonghua One. "Zhonghua One, I trust that you have saved enough of your personal energy to place an immediate call to our agents administrating the drones and delay the attack until 4:15 Eastern time," he said with all seriousness. He quickly delivered an easy wink, however, to show that he knew what One had been up to the past few hours.

Zhonghua One promptly and crisply bowed. "Yes, Leader, I will make the call immediately." And with that, he quickly retreated to a telephone at a side desk near the window.

Though no one expressed it, the sect did not understand how the President of the United States could have possibly been informed of the threat. The Leader seemed unconcerned, so they took his direction and quickly put the thought to rest. Only the Leader knew about the message to the United States from the Iranian government. This was Iran's end of the deal, to distract the US from the real source of the attack and cause confusion among the leadership in the US government. He knew that the Iranians were planning on a move into Iraq, then Israel, during this period of attack on the US, but the Leader also counted on the US not believing Iran technologically capable of such an assault. He knew the US had to be readying their forces against Iran. Even if they promised to stand down, the US would have been getting ready for a counter-attack to protect Iraq and Israel, and therefore, would still be culpable of misleading and disobeying Iran's request, even if they hadn't yet launched an overt attack. The strike on Dallas-Fort Worth would ensure that the US would keep out of China and Iran's way until it was too late. Well, at least too late to do anything in the Eastern China Sea.

The Leader had hidden the information about Iranian participation from the rest of Zhonghua Nine; only his closest guard knew anything, and this was only to make a call to the Embassy to tell them a short message about the beginning of Dormant Curse. The Iranian contribution was a detail Zhonghua Nine didn't need to know about. When Dormant Curse was complete, Iran's involvement wouldn't be important to the Zhonghua Nine anyway. Of this the Leader was sure.

Chapter (Twenty-9)

Darcy heard about the message from the President that was going out to the regions. She figured the new development was worth a call to Dennis. After all, news of a possible additional strike on multiple cities had to be significant.

By the time she reached Dennis, he and Greg had settled in at Starbucks.

"Dennis, there's another strike about to happen, just like on Atlanta," she said.

"How did you find this out?"

"It's all over the news. The President used the emergency news system to talk directly to Dallas-Fort Worth communities just a few minutes ago. Those are the targets. CNT picked it up and is replaying it already. Of course, they're also picking it apart with armchair analysts…"

"Did the President indicate how he knew these cities would be attacked? How did he know the time?"

"He didn't mention it, just that there was a credible threat and to turn off all electrical systems, including phones and computers. People here are talking about an electro pulse or something…it was a pretty quick message."

"Darcy, I don't know if you can get in touch with Ben, but you've got to get a message through to Homeland Security. There's no time to explain, but they've got to shut down the Internet in those locations—wired, wireless and cell phone. The President can do it. He has the authority."

"But Dennis, there's no *time*. He said the attack is coming at four o'clock. I don't even know where Ben is."

Ben was Dennis' boss. He had been glad that Ben hadn't contacted him yet, as any news from him would likely have been bad from the slip-up that morning. But now he needed Ben…or Donovan. Dennis was convinced that this wasn't an EMP—the clues just didn't add up. This was something that came from a signal going to phones and computers alike. The only commonality was the Internet. He didn't know how, but that had to be it. Darcy was right, though—there was no time. Ben didn't have the authority to pass a message through the ranks in a little over five minutes, even if Dennis could prove his hunch somehow. A hopeless feeling settled over Dennis, one of inevitability and powerlessness.

"Darcy, please try to get Ben, even if it ends up being too late. I have to talk with him and we have to get our current findings into the hands of someone who can do something with the information. Thanks, Dar."

"There's been an attack again?" Greg asked.

"No, not yet. But the President announced one is coming to Dallas, at DFW and the surrounding area. Now, less than five minutes to go." Dennis looked despondent. "I hope this is a false alarm.

"This probably explains why Donovan is unavailable; FBI has probably called all agents in to get ready for the attack, at least to brief everyone on what's going on. There's no way he's going to return my call anytime soon."

In the disguised warehouse in Hayward, California, the drones were ready and waiting to hit the Enter key for the second message for Phase One. All watched closely for Ron's command. After the cold-blooded murder of a fellow drone, no one dared touch the keyboards without direct orders. At 12:53, the phone rang. Ron jumped to answer it. He seemed a little surprised to be getting a call, with only seven minutes to go. But the call was short and he didn't seem at all perplexed when he came back to the main monitoring table.

"There will be a short delay," he stated matter-of-factly. "1:15 is the new target time, but on my command. Relax until then, or at least try to."

The Secretary of Homeland Security had been making calls to his staff to try shutting down electricity in the DFW area, sector by sector. This was proving to be a more difficult task than anyone had envisioned. The DFW area grid was controlled by one main central distributor, TXU Electric Delivery, and though they generally had a good relationship with the Federal Government, they were a bureaucracy. A call to the President of TXU by Carl found him temporarily out, but his administrative assistant would continue to try to reach him and have him call back immediately. Carl stressed the urgency of the situation, and asked if there were anyone else with operations authority. She wanted to help, but it turned out that the TXU President and his staff were at an offsite meeting at Los Colinas Golf Course. The last she had heard from them was just before the air-raid sirens started their warnings. Her attempts to reach him were met with busy signals as the cell phone system was overloaded with everyone trying to get in touch with friends and loved ones before the 4:00 deadline.

Crap, Carl thought to himself as he got off the phone, what a mess we've created.

In Carl's mind, if nothing happened, they had just created a huge crisis unnecessarily. However, if an attack occurred now, some things were going to be in worse shape. At least the airports and interstates were shut down, so there weren't going to be any incidents happening at high speed.

Chapter
(Thir-tee)

Shannon was anxiously waiting for the traffic to clear. I-635 was the quickest way home for she and her son after daycare let out at 2:30. Unfortunately, she had been caught up in the police blockade. The State Patrol set up a block at mile marker 30, directing traffic off at both exits 29 and 30 on westbound I-635. This forced traffic onto the frontage road leading to the George Bush turnpike. The turnpike fed cars northeast, directly away from the epicenter of the coming attack. However, the frontage road wasn't designed to handle the amount of traffic coming off the interstate. Many cars were stuck as the deadline advanced. The original plan was to shut down I-635 at the I-35 interchange just outside the anticipated strike zone, then redirect the stragglers off I-635 before shutting everything down completely. At 2:50, the police figured time was up, and they closed down all exits. The cars still jammed on I-635 had to sit and wait. Authorities reasoned that it would be better for a sitting car to get nailed by an EMP than one travelling 70mph. This left approximately five hundred cars still sitting on the freeway.

The air raid sirens had started blaring around 2:45 and hadn't let up, causing many commuters to turn on their radios to hear the President's announcement. Shannon was one of those that heard the order to shut off electronics by 3:00. For those that might have not had the sense to turn on their radios, police immediately dispatched a few of their cruisers to make their way down shoulders and relay the command.

This all turned out to be a big problem for Shannon.

Shannon's two year-old, Theodore, hadn't had a very good day at day care. "Shawwee hit me on the head," was his explanation. Sure enough, there did appear to be a red mark on the top of Theodore's forehead. As such, he wasn't in the mood to hang out on the interstate and wait for the cars to clear. The police cruiser coming down the shoulder with his lights flashing was certainly distracting and interesting, for a bit.

Stepping out of the car, as many of the stranded motorists were doing, Shannon wondered what was truly happening. This was like something out of a movie, but it was real.

Shannon's natural instinct was to call her mom in Plano to see if she knew anything more. In her old age, Shannon's mom had found connection and stimulation online. She was likely plugged into what was up. In fact, Shannon was somewhat surprised that her mom had not already called her. Giving into her own impulses, Shannon tried to quickly dial her mom to ask if she knew anything. After three tries with no connection, she gave up.

Perhaps a text message would go through, she thought.

"Stk on 635. sht dwn. do u no whts up?" she wrote. Her mother hated interpreting Shannon's text-message English, particularly since her primary language was Spanish. But she had no problem with this message—she never saw it. The cellular system was so overloaded that the message couldn't go through.

For Shannon, it was surprising not to receive a response after a few minutes. That wasn't like her mom. A lot of things seemed to be out of place.

The sound of Theodore screaming in the background didn't help.

There was that announcement again to shut off cars, radios and phones. Shannon grudgingly complied, hopped back in the car, rolled down the windows, and let Ted out of his car seat. Her Honda Civic had been a gift from her grandpa, and though she was grateful for it, there wasn't much room for Ted to jump around and stretch while waiting for whatever it was that was supposed to happen.

"Ted, it's OK, we just have to wait here for a little while."

Like he really cared. In the mind of a two-year-old, the world revolved around him. He hadn't had a good day and he wanted to go play with his toys at Nana's house.

"I wanna go now!!!" he cried.

"Theodore, screaming is not going to help. Just stop it!" Shannon said, raising her voice.

Just then, Shannon and Ted heard the rumble of a helicopter overhead. It was making a final, low pass over the area using its public address system. That stopped Ted's crying in an instant.

"See, they heard you screaming…if you don't stop it they'll take you to jail for bothering everyone…they told us to turn off our phones and radios and be quiet."

Shannon didn't think her lie to her son would cause long-term damage to his psyche, and if it calmed him down…

With less than a minute to go, the helicopter found an open spot on the median not too far from Shannon's car. She had never seen a helicopter set down so quickly. The pilots cut the engines and stepped out, looking at watches and then up the interstate, as if something was bound to happen.

Greg and Dennis just stared at the home page of CNT and waited, hitting Refresh on the browser to make sure they didn't miss anything new. As much as they hated the news network, somehow CNT was plugged into everything that was going on.

The information was there, but Dennis' issue with it was that their analysts' conclusions always seemed skewed to create the greatest drama and stress and, somehow, increased viewership. Decades ago, news was filtered. Granted, a few important items didn't make it through, but a lot of the filtered information was bad stuff that the public had no control over anyway. And when bad news did come through, the "dyed in the wool" patriotic newscasters tried to put a positive spin on things. Propaganda? Possibly. But Dennis considered what passed for news these days was not only unpatriotic, but just plain bad investigative reporting.

Anxiously awaiting 4:00 to come, Greg and Dennis said little to each other. Greg bounced his legs anxiously while Dennis just sipped on his coffee. His wouldn't have seemed like a nervous gesture if you didn't notice he was taking a sip every ten seconds, like a nervous smoker repeatedly pulling a drag off his cigarette for comfort.

In the Situation Room at the White House, the President and his staff were watching CNT, as well as the various internet, department of transportation, and utility usage maps. While internet and cell phone traffic had escalated in the few minutes following the President's speech, shortly before 4:00 p.m. usage began to plummet. Word had gotten out and people were responding. Cell phones were still being used, but much less frequently than just a few minutes earlier.

"Thank God. People are taking this seriously," said the President as he let go a big sigh.

Carl was back in the room. He wasn't so excited about the usage levels on the map, though he had to admit people were responding. It was only a minute or so until 4:00, so the time of reckoning was imminent. There had to be a way of detecting the weapon, if that's what this was, and disabling it. So far, none of his agencies sweeping DFW had found anything. However, sensors and monitoring equipment had been set up all over the area to pinpoint the source of any electromagnetic fields that burst on the scene—just in case a post-mortem was necessary. Fortunately, some astute scientists on the team realized their own equipment would be blown out by the EMP, and quickly used aluminum foil to create a grounded shield around the equipment. Only the monitoring antenna was sticking out from each hastily made aluminum shell.

All eyes were glued on the monitors as the seconds ticked closer to 4:00.

Even on CNT, the announcer was quiet. Waiting. The channel had set up remote cameras throughout the city as quickly as possible and was getting feeds from affiliates. They chose to keep everything running, figuring the footage gained before things possibly blew out would more than make up for the cost of replacing the equipment they were using. Besides, one of the things they learned from the Middle East conflicts was to turn each of their own remote broadcast trucks into its own Faraday Cage. If it had a fiberglass shell, they lined it with metal. They might lose a few cameras and some auxiliary equipment, but all the feeds were linked into a satellite, so the loss of local stations wouldn't impact their ability to give coverage.

"Please note that we will maintain silence for the next five minutes," the announcer finally stated, if nothing more than to break the incredibly ominous silence that had developed.

Across the US, Americans outside the DFW area were rapt to news outlets on every possible medium. Twitter, Blather and Facebook were going nuts with messages sent from anyone and everyone that had an opinion on the subject.

It was just the kind of reaction the Leader of Zhonghua Nine had in mind.

Chapter
(Thirty-1)

*T*he smile on the Leader's face grew as each minute passed. His gut decision to delay things had been right.

Zhonghua Nine watched the same broadcast as the rest of the world, including the US President, his staff, and even Greg and Dennis via their laptops. They, too, grew more anxious with each passing moment.

The Leader sensed the tension in the room and laughed…and laughed. All those in the room wondered if he had suddenly lost his mind. Those with less sleep and a little less self-control started laughing along with him. It was contagious.

Still laughing, the Leader smiled at Zhonghua One. "Zhonghua One, why are you laughing?" he said through his smile.

Zhonghua One, still smiling, stopped for a second and looked confused.

"Because we are about to win this battle?"

"Is that a statement or a question, One?"

"I don't know!" he exclaimed, as he realized he had no idea what he was really doing.

"So, I will tell you what is so funny, OK?" said the Leader, still smiling. "You felt the tension in the room just a few minutes ago…in fact, I could sense that the tension was almost unbearable for all of you. We are only five minutes past the deadline that was given to the US, and look how much tension you felt!"

As of yet, the Zhonghua had no idea how the President had gotten the message on the timing of the attack; they naturally assumed one of the other Eight had made the call. Overlooking that underlying issue, the Leader had a point, and the Eight almost unanimously nodded their heads in agreement—the laughter had broken the tension, but now their laughter had stopped.

"You welcomed the break in tension that my laughter brought. You may not
have known that this is what was happening to you, but it is precisely the reaction
I had hoped for. The exact same thing is happening right now in the United
States. The lull between the time they expected something to happen and now is
building more and more tension. However, they will not break the tension
through laughter, but rather through communication. They have to have noise
and busyness; they must always be doing something with their minds, talking to
someone, going somewhere. Patience in the US is something the public is not
used to. They have to know what is going on and when to expect it—now, now,
NOW!" the Leader said, doing his best impression of an American accent at the
end.

The rest of the sect understood what the Leader was up to, and were
impressed with the man's genius. Some had thought their mission would lose
credibility for not delivering on time as promised. But this plan might be much
better. They had all felt the anxiety caused by the silence in the room and on the
television. CNT's decision to have airwave silence while waiting only
exacerbated the tension.

As if on cue, at 4:05 p.m., CNT broke the silence, if possibly for nothing
more than to ensure their sponsor, commercials and revenue stream continued.
Recent Gallup poll results showed that less than 25% of Americans trusted the
news stations, but that didn't mean they weren't all watching. CNT knew these
statistics, but also knew that people tuned in to their channel as much out of
boredom as for bona fide news. The more *Jerry Springer*-like they became, the
higher the ratings and revenue, regardless of the drop in trust.

"We are now five minutes past the President's deadline, and it appears that
there has been no type of incident thus far, though it is clearly too early to tell.
We'll keep our remote news crews on live, but we have also assembled two
experts on homeland security and cyber terrorism, prepared to give their opinions
on the current crisis at DFW…"

"See?!" the Leader exclaimed, holding his gnarled hands up to the screen. He
didn't need to say anything else.

In the White House Situation Room, the fact that CNT was already breaking silence and broadcasting opinions was disconcerting to the Security Council. The fact that it was five minutes past the deadline might only have meant the Iranians didn't have their act together and that the attack was delayed, but that didn't slow down people's opinions and restlessness. Americans were used to instantaneous news, and this delay didn't fit well with the instant-gratification society they had become.

"Mr. President, look at the cell phone transmissions," Ned said.

Sure enough, little by little, the area around Dallas-Fort Worth was starting to light up, signifying increased cell phone and internet traffic.

"Why didn't we get power shut down?!" exclaimed the President, turning to Carl.

"Mr. President, we just didn't have enough time. I'll explain later, but we…we hit obstacles," Carl said, shaking his head. "But the fact is that most of those devices you see lighting up the map are battery powered—cell phones, laptops, tablets. Shutting down the grid wouldn't have prevented their use. Most cell systems—their switching systems and towers—are on battery backup as well. You're just not going to be able to shut off communication."

"As frustrating as that is, I understand. It's out of our hands now," the President said.

In the background, the banter of the CNT analysts buzzed, while everyone else in the room was relatively quiet.

"…we don't know where the threat came from, who rendered it, nor if there were conditions placed on it. The President needs to be more forthcoming with his information if he wants it to be credible…"

The President had enough. His determination to stop the insanity made him want to nip this in the bud at the border with Iraq and the Senkaku Islands.

"Robert, it's time to give the order for our strikes. To be explicit, strike the Iranian forces aligned on the border of Iraq—strike them deep and hard to ensure that they are under no impression they can cross the border without consequence. And do a low-pass fly-by of the Chinese Navy headed toward those islands near Japan. If their Navy engages, sink the ship that locks on. These are my orders. This is not a declaration of war—yet. This is in defense of a substantiated threat and bona fide attack on US soil this morning, claimed by the Iranian government as being their own action in support of China."

"Are you sure we can't wait a bit more?" Ned asked.

"Absolutely not. Each minute we wait means that more systems will come back online in Dallas. Let's say there's a half hour or forty-five minute delay? Every system will be live. We'll be in as bad or worse shape than before, especially with rush hour and all the Internet chatter as a result of this. Attack Iran now, hard. Then we'll negotiate."

There was no time to doubt and not enough information with which to argue. This threat had come from Iran. If the country's claims were true, their attack on Atlanta was an act of war and their current intentions were indisputable.

Robert immediately called his staff. Though the President wasn't an expert on war strategy, his directives had been made clear. The Secretary already had plans in place and forces ready for strike. He gave the order for attack.

It was 4:10 p.m. on the East Coast of the USA.

Chapter
(Thirty-2)

Shannon couldn't take the suspense anymore. Ten minutes had passed since the 3:00 deadline, and the silence, heat and tension on the interstate were palpable.

I can sneak a peek on my phone, she thought. No one will see and it will be for just a minute.

Shannon crouched down in her seat and nonchalantly pushed the power button on her iPhone.

It took almost thirty seconds for the phone to boot up, but sure enough, once it was up, she had three bars of signal. 3G locked in and her phone buzzed multiple times, showing she had five text messages and two voicemails. Plus, PUSH notifications let her know there were ten new notices on Facebook and another fifty from the accounts she was following on Blather.

If they wanted us to shut down power, why did they leave the cell phone system on? she thought.

Even before checking any messages, Shannon felt guilty about turning on her phone. Still, she wanted to put in a call to her mom, even if it had to be brief.

It was 3:13 p.m. in Dallas.

F/A-18 Super Hornets jets had been scrambled off the USS *Truman* from the Gulf of Oman and were soaring at their maximum limit of Mach 2 toward the Iranian border with Iraq. They had been expecting the orders, and quite frankly, many of the servicemen had been looking forward to an attack on Iran for a long time. Most knew that Iran had been the source for a significant portion of the radicalism in the Middle East, and they viewed the country as one of the primary reasons why they couldn't return home.

Almost simultaneously, F-22 Raptors stationed at Okinawa, had launched and were quickly en route to intercept the Chinese Navy fleet slowly converging on the Senkaku Islands.

The President and his staff were trying to monitor not only the conditions in Dallas-Fort Worth, but progress of the attack in the Gulf and the fly-by in the East China Sea.

The F-22s were given orders to fire if locked-on. Everyone was hoping the Chinese would back down on their advance and not be foolish enough to act aggressively toward the fighters.

Intercept time at 1300mph: 12 minutes.

Dennis and Greg could take only so much. At 4:10, they found themselves wondering exactly what to do next. Greg could be pressing Teardown for answers to the analysis of the main system package, but he figured they were working furiously since hearing of the potential attack on DFW.

"Dennis, I...I really don't know what to do next. Maybe we can type up our notes from the flight or...or *some*thing...I feel like I need to be doing something. Anything. This suspense is killing me. CNT obviously doesn't know what's going on any more than we do. I think we're likely the most knowledgeable about what's happening, as far as the possible mechanism behind an attack. But it's too early to make a clear conclusion. In fact, who would even listen if we said 'the way to prevent a future attack is to shut down all cell phone systems completely—towers and everything,' even if we knew for certain that it would? It's become our primary form of communication."

Dennis just shook his head. "Greg, it's right under our noses, we just don't see it yet. A unique signal gets into the phone to set something off. Some software...hmmm...but what software can explode a phone? That seems pretty impossible. The only signals to these phones are cell, Wi-Fi and Bluetooth, right? Bluetooth works phone-to-phone or device-to-device...that path would have to be viral with a connection made between the devices. No way. Cell phone coverage doesn't work for planes in mid-air, generally. But Wi-Fi, that's ubiquitous, even on the planes now. But how can being hooked to Wi-Fi blow up a phone or iPad? It just doesn't make sense."

In the drone's warehouse, the tension had grown high. The room was silent, except for the sporadic buzz of the air-conditioning kicking on and off and the occasional clearing of someone's throat.

"OK, kids," announced Ron as the time drew close. "I need your clients' windows up and ready to go. Be ready to hit Enter on each window as fast as you can. Don't screw up and hit things twice or delete the message accidentally."

The drones sat at attention, knowing any screw-up would result in serious repercussions.

"On my command…here it comes…five…four…three…two…one…hit Enter!" shouted Ron.

In rapid fire, each drone clicked the various message windows for their respective clients, then hit Send, OK or Enter on the highlighted window, depending on the program and command required.

Pamela started to cry as the fear of messing up overwhelmed her, but she managed to complete her assigned tasks.

"OK, now back away from your workstations and don't touch a thing. If anyone needs to go to the restroom to relieve themselves or throw up, whatever the case may be for you, now's the time to do it…Joe, I'm still watching you."

The Blather, Facebook, Twitter, and social networking messages were sent out to the entire global community. In a matter of seconds, the messages were lost in the morass of ongoing communication that spread like wild fire across the Dallas-Fort Worth area. It took only a few milliseconds for the devices, with the 3D chip-stack assembled in China, to decipher the trigger code and short out.

"ҔI love ɾ Host˜ess → ˡTwinkies!ɛ"—Ashton Kutcher fans saw on his Blather account. They were used to crazy statements coming out of Ashton sometimes, so this wasn't really anything new. What they couldn't see were the binary-encoded characters that sent a veiled message to each of their systems; the only telltale signs were some strange characters displayed within the triggering message. It seemed like there was a lot more gibberish coming from Ashton's Blather account lately, but for those tracking him, they just figured maybe he was having fun with his fans.

Chapter
(Thirty-3)

"**Ricky Bobby to Stingray,** target ETA, ten minutes," came the lead F/A-18 Hornet from the USS *Truman*.

The squadron launched from the carrier five minutes ago, and were closing quickly on tanks starting to cross into Iraqi territory at the Khosravi entry.

The lead pilot thought they might catch some radar action from the SA-300 surface-to-air missile systems they suspected the Iranians had. As such, the pilots were coming in very low and very fast. At a few hundred meters above the ground, the SA-300's radar wouldn't likely pick them up until they were close enough to launch some HARM missiles to take them out preemptively. However, if the Iranians had the new SA-400s from the Russians, they could be in trouble. So far, no radar activity was detected, which may have been due to their low-level approach, or the lack of surface-to-air missile systems being engaged. The latter didn't really make sense if they were staging a full invasion.

"Ricky Bobby, this is Stingray. ETA, ten minutes confirmed. We're tracking your position. You are clear to engage. I repeat, clear to engage."

In the East China Sea, the Raptors were also quickly closing in on their targets, though they had orders to show force—and not engage unless engaged with.

In the President's Situation Room, the staff monitored events in Dallas, the Gulf and China, simultaneously. All events were happening at once, and potentially grave consequences threatened each location. The President became more frustrated at the cell phone traffic that was growing by the second. Clearly, people weren't going to wait an hour to begin checking status on developments. Even the President had grown impatient with things.

Still stuck on I-635 near DFW, Shannon had finally made it through to her mom.

"Mom...Mom! Quick! Do you know what's going on? No, Mom, we're OK, I don't have much time...I'm on 635—OK, you got my message. I didn't listen to yours. I just wanted to make a quick call.... Yes.... We're OK.... Un-huh..."

Shannon slunk down in her seat, but others in cars nearby saw her talking on the phone. Their reaction was mixed—some drivers glared at Shannon, trying to guilt her into putting her phone away. Others decided to maybe take a chance themselves, to at least get on the Internet to check what the local news station had to say. After all, how could it hurt anyone, really?

The older driver of the Lexus next to her caught her eye. He just shook his head at her with a look only a well-practiced father knows how to give to a kid—to make them mind in public.

Of course, Shannon caught the look and felt her guilt creep up on her.

Just like my dad, she thought.

Just a few seconds more, she thought. I'll be off soon enough.

The President was dealing with his own patience issues.

"I'm concerned this Iran threat is a hoax—that Iran is trying to take advantage of whatever happened in Atlanta this morning..."

Carl quickly interjected, "That's a possibility, but the consequences of being wrong, of there being just a delay, are tremendous. I don't believe we can accelerate the schedule on the lifting of air and vehicle travel around DFW...there's just too much risk right now."

"Agreed. There's too much at stake."

"Mr. President, we have fighters on their way to attack forces on the Iran/Iraq border right now. Our concern now is that if we provoke them, they may choose to go ahead with an attack since we originally said we'd stand down."

"Carl, they don't have a remote control that can reach DFW all the way from Iraq. If anything, someone controlling an EMP device has either been thwarted from using it, or is concerned they wouldn't be able to escape the area afterwards. Didn't you tell me we can locate the source of a pulse with pinpoint accuracy?"

"Yes, we can. The reality is that until we determine the exact cause of Atlanta, any country can make threats that we'll have to take seriously. Iran may just be the first. We've got to get this solved and develop any countermeasures needed to stave off further attacks…"

"Mr. President, look at the screen," said Ned.

Suddenly, cell phone traffic around DFW died out. Not all traffic, but a significant drop—all at once; and not just in the five-mile danger zone, but in areas as far out as Carrolton and Lewisville.

Something just happened.

The President's stomach sank. "Carl, what are the chances your message to shut down power finally got through?"

"Not a chance. I never left one. Shutting down all grids is a pretty serious matter. I needed to talk directly to TXU's President…"

"Well, then…"

The pundits on CNT were suddenly interrupted by the lead anchor: "We have to interrupt our experts here immediately. We have reports of fires breaking out in the Dallas-Fort Worth area. Whether this is related to the President's warning, we're not sure…"

The President looked around the Situation Room at each of his staff members in what looked to be a mix of anger and somberness.

"Well, fuck me. We don't have to wait for CNT to validate; we can see from the cell and internet traffic that we've been hit to some level of severity. Damn it to—Henry, shut down those sorties. Do it now!" The President ordered.

Henry picked up the conference phone already on speaker with his war room.

"Dale, this is Hank. Stand down and pull back…pull those birds back now. Do not delay! Do you copy?"

"Yes Sir, sending the order now."

The President had called Iran's bluff and lost, so it seemed. He was still in disbelief that Iran had the capability not only to detect their oncoming strike, but remotely call their own strike in retaliation. He felt a sense of panic rising in his chest, something he hadn't experienced since college, when he was going to fail an exam miserably—but this was public. Was it possible that he was going to fail on this? He had the smartest team with his current staff—unlike his first administration, where he picked staff based on political favors. Even so, everyone seemed powerless right now.

Chapter
(Thirty-4)

*T*he **US President didn't** know that he had been right about Iran. They didn't possess the ability to strike anywhere at any time in the US. They also couldn't have known the strike on their own forces was imminent. They were only following orders from an anonymous voice that called their embassy in China with updates.

This unknown source had originally contacted Iran years ago. For all they knew, it could have been the Chinese government itself, though this was unlikely. The contact had only asked them to trust him and give him a chance. If he delivered on the first, test case, then they would trust him on bigger ticket items.

Of course, the items all had a price, and a big kickback to go along with them. But for a nation used to running on bribes and smuggling, this wasn't unheard of.

At first, the items were arms and banned goods. Since the rest of the world had banned these sales to Iran due to their attempt to build nuclear capability, this was most beneficial. Next, much to Iran's delight, was the completely anonymous transfer of plans for strategic missile guidance systems. After each, favor, or sale, the government would transfer funds to a bank account in Switzerland. The unknown source always delivered. What he offered was exactly what the Iranian government seemed to need at the time. It was almost as if the source had his spy working within their system.

With the crack team the Zhonghua Nine Leader had assembled, it *was* like having a spy within the Iranian government. Zhonghua Six was from the intelligence community in China. They were able to hack into every major defense system in the world. Though Iran was a somewhat closed environment, Chinese Intelligence had the means to gather critical data on all allies and would-be enemies. Foreign nationals working in each country, still loyal to China, helped with the continuous flow of information. Plus, the vast number of listening devices and remote electronic eavesdropping capabilities at China's disposal—all aimed at getting information out of the Iranian Embassy—certainly didn't hurt. The Chinese Embassy in Tehran was like one large antenna, pulling in any and all information available through the airwaves, internet and nearby conversations. Regular updates from Zhonghua Six afforded the Leader a significant amount of information with which to make informed decisions.

Initially, the Leader viewed the funds gained from his efforts as necessary to continue the work of the Zhonghua Nine. It was like "priming the pump" for bigger and better things. In fact, the funds gained from early deliveries to countries such as Iran, North Korea and Russia helped fund bigger and more ambitious activities. The size of Zhonghua's operations had grown to where he was able to offer his inner circle of Eight significant compensation. This also allowed the Leader to do a more efficient job of recruiting and bribing. He found that when a new conscript was offered the option of generous payment for their loyalty or death, the choice was much easier for them. Government officials were also much more likely to look the other way when given a large sum for their silence—this was no surprise.

However, with this last plan, the revenue projected from the Iran endeavor was going to be much greater than any thus far. Iran's anger towards Iraq and their protracted war with that country was still in many religious leaders' minds. Still, this was almost trivial compared to Iran's hatred towards Israel. Iran leadership's abhorrence of Israel was deep-seated in their history. They wanted Israel destroyed.

The Leader asked for only $500 million for a first strike on the US and $500 million for the next. He assured Iran that these strikes would ensure the US would stay out of their business. Iran would have to pay for the potential to wipe Israel from the map, gaining land and resources from Iraq along the way. As a bonus, the Leader implied he might be in a position to inflict long-term punishment on the US for supporting Iraq during their war, and for their ongoing support of Israel. Payment was made only after each attack was successful.

Though the fee demanded was hotly debated by the leaders in Iran, their final analysis showed that the sum was a mere drop in the bucket compared to the cost of developing a military that could force the US to stand down during an invasion of Iraq. If a weapon really existed that could be used to attack a city at any time and place, how could they not take advantage of it?

Chapter
(Thirty-5)

Partly due to the scowl from the man in the neighboring car, Shannon was quickly getting off the phone with her mom.

"OK, Mom, I'm going to have to get off the phone. You know I'm not supposed to be on, but I thought a few secs wouldn't hurt. I'll call you la—"

At that moment, the Blather message from Ashton Kutcher's account finally made it through the system to Shannon's phone. Deep inside the device, the main-processor chip stack shorted out. The direct short to a fully-charged Lithium-Ion battery immediately caused it to flame and explode.

Shannon felt the heat on her hand before she heard a loud *pop,* and the glass of the phone shattered against her face. All her mom heard was the phone go dead.

Chapter
(Thirty-6)

*"**They struck us** and we didn't even see it coming. That radius of impact has got to be ten miles!"*

"That's impossible, Mr. President. With that level of damage, we'd be seeing a mushroom cloud by now. The only way to get the energy required for an EMP that strong is to use a nuke—flat out. We'd be getting hits on DSP right now if that were the case," Robert stated surely.

DSP was the acronym for the Defense Support Program—the Defense Department's satellite system for monitoring flashes from the earth's surface that could be either a launch of a strategic missile or a test of a nuclear weapon. It was developed for monitoring the former USSR during the Cold War, but was still an important part of the overall defense strategy with continued nuclear proliferation. DSP had been recently upgraded with the latest technology in the Sensor Based Infrared Systems satellites, and the Secretary of Defense had full confidence they would pick up the thermal from a nuke, even a very small one.

"Then what the hell caused that pulse, Robert?"

Carl interjected: "Mr. President, we have to hear back from our agents monitoring our ground stations to see if there was a field detected. We should be hearing soon."

The President hid his panic. "If they can attack at will…" his voice trailed off. He didn't want to think about that option. "There's just no way that's possible, right? Until we figure out what's going on here, we're sitting ducks. OK, everyone make your calls. We must make tactical decisions to deal with the DFW situation and its impact on the US—our systems and even our economy.

"As far as China and Iran…we'll need to stand down, and think about a strategic defense strike on Iran. With China, I'm inclined to just let them have these little islands. I'm not willing to give up a US city with another attack just to support our allies' claim of a few square miles of uninhabited rock…"

Greg and Dennis had been watching the developments from their spot in the corner at Starbucks. Though a few customers may have been following the news on the web, the vast majority had no idea that another attack had occurred.

CNT was just now getting reports of fires erupting all across the region, even as far out as Lewisville and Richardson.

"Greg, you know I once worked for Bell Helicopter—I know that area pretty well. That's a huge radius—gotta be ten miles! If there was any thought in anyone's mind that this was an EMP, this has gotta dissuade them. A pulse's energy dissipates exponentially with the distance. This attack fits our theory on a signal sent out to smart devices, we just don't know what signal, or where it's comin' from."

Greg's mind was drifting, mostly to Michelle and her safety. He needed to call and tell her to turn off her mobile and use only the home phone for the time being.

Just then a thought occurred to him.

"Dennis…where's our office exactly?"

"It's in Arlington, just south of DFW and Six Flags."

"So, they would have gotten the message to power down electronics, right?"

"Sure, they're in that area."

Greg paused, thinking. Dennis looked at him quizzically.

"I think I know what you're thinking…I don't want to influence you…but could you hurry it up a little?"

"Well, if someone has a smartphone…if they could turn it on right now and observe…observe what comes up in what order, then of course, see if their phone gets hit…"

"My thoughts exactly, Greg. I'll call in. Phone lines should still be up, even if cell phones aren't."

Dennis quickly pulled out his phone.

The phone just rang. Voicemail picked up.

"They're probably all on-site at DFW," Dennis said, thinking aloud.

Leaving a message would be better than nothing right now, he figured.

"Kelly, this is Dennis Wright, sorry I haven't checked in before now, but Greg and I got diverted to Huntsville this morning to check out a downed plane. I know things are crazy there and I hope you're all OK. Try to call me back in the next five minutes. There's an urgent test we need you to do to help verify the source of the attack. Please call me back."

Dennis' frustration was visible; there was a red flush moving up his neck onto his face. He was certainly agitated, that much Greg could tell. There was a great opportunity here to test their hypothesis, and it was slipping away.

"You worked there for years, surely there's someone else you know there to call," Greg prodded.

"Yeah, there's a buddy I had there that's a techno geek as well. He's always bought the family similar or identical phones if he can…just maybe…"

Dennis' voice trailed off as he thought.

"Sure, it's worth a shot. I've got his number stored."

Dennis pulled up the number. Dialing, his jaw was clenched and lips pursed in anticipation. He desperately hoped a clue might be waiting on the other end of this call. Time was running out.

"Hey Dennis."

"Jerrod. It's been a long time, buddy."

"Sure has, hey, I'd love to talk but things are kinda crazy down here right now, can I call you back sometime?"

"Actually, I need your expertise right now. It's related to the attack. Did you all get hit?"

"All our mobile phones and electronics are turned off, so, no."

"I figured, which is why I called your land line."

Jumping right to it, Dennis stated, "I need you to do us a big favor."

Jerrod hesitated. "Well, that depends."

"I need you to turn on all of your cell phones. Well, take them out of the house first."

"OK…we were waiting for the 'all clear,' but I suppose I could do that. We have four, mine, Leslie's and the kids'. All the same model…you know me."

"I was counting on that. Please hurry."

Moments later, Jerrod was back on the line, but standing outside the house. "They're booting up. What do I look for?"

"I think if something happens, you're gonna know."

After a few moments Dennis could hear a loud *pop* in the background followed by an expletive from Jerrod.

"Just back away!" Dennis exclaimed.

Dennis made direct eye contact with Greg and nodded. This was evidence they needed. Definitively, they now knew there was no EMP. The attack was caused by something else, and it had intelligence, whatever it was—a program, a timer, a message. But not a transient pulse.

"Hey, whose phones got hit, and what was the difference between them? Did you run different apps?"

"Just one phone—my son, Kenny's. He's got so much crap on there. He managed to get a virus or something, didn't he?"

Dennis was elated there was yet another data point with which to work, though he tried to mask that in his voice.

"Could be, but we don't know the details yet. I'll get you a new phone for him, but I've gotta run. This was really just what I needed to know. Thanks, Jerrod."

It was 4:25 on the East Coast.

Chapter

(Thirty-7)

*T*he President's staff was incredulous.

They had ruled out any type of electromagnetic pulse weapon. The sensors in the area hadn't detected any electromagnetic field aberrations, yet the hit was an even greater swathe than Atlanta.

Though the attack came fifteen minutes later than promised, it was somehow delivered about the time as the US's strike against Iran was called. Was it possible that Iran was able to detect the launch of aircraft? Was there an insider in the US government? Unlikely, but that was now something they had to investigate. Not much of this was making sense.

The President certainly wasn't in control of the situation, though he tried to speak as if he were.

"We don't understand how we were attacked, but we will get to the bottom of this soon," he said. "There is no super weapon that exists, and this is not magic. There's got to be an explanation for what happened, and therefore, a way to stop it. This was on our own soil for Chrissakes! For now, send a message to the envoy from Iran. I want to meet with them and hear their demands. At the same time, Robert, I want to have things prepared for a mass strike on Iran. Come up with a plan for both conventional and nuclear. I won't negotiate with a terrorist country. I'll shut down power to the whole United States for a day if that's what it takes to ensure we are safe while we take those motherfuckers out."

The President was nearly yelling. He was mad and he was serious, and uncharacteristically crude. But at the present time, he was powerless. He knew that whoever pulled off this most recent attack had the capability to do so again—anywhere in the US. It was only a matter of when and where.

In the Polaris Room, the Leader closed his eyes and rested his mind. The chaos unveiled on CNT ensured the US stayed would stay out of his way. But the excitement of the past hour had taken something out of him. He would check the balance of his personal Swiss bank account later. Even with the latest twists, everything was going according to plan.

He had no real personal interest in what happened to Iran. They were just the front, the funding source and the tool he was using to get his way.

"Zhonghua, I told you that you might be here a while, and you will be here a while longer. You can see how this effort has taken significant planning and flawless execution to succeed. You can also see the results. We've temporarily crippled the US in order to both capture what was taken from us—the Diaoyutai Islands—and deal Japan a significant blow. We dare not permanently damage either country, as our future wealth and prosperity depend on future customers— but we will soon secure our position of dominance in the world."

The members of Zhonghua Nine nodded their heads in agreement. The Leader proved to be a shrewd and cunning man—much more so than any of them had suspected. If they were somewhat reticent to ask difficult questions before, they were definitely fearful about asking now. Each had his part to play, and it was clear that playing each role faultlessly was paramount to their collective success.

Chapter
(Thirty-8)

"Before I call Teardown, I really need to check in with Michelle. She's probably getting anxious with everything that's going on. And I want her to stay off her cell phone for at least the next twenty-four hours. It's clear that whatever this is, it's only hitting the latest smart devices."

Greg was getting more concerned about Michelle as time went by. If there were another attack, he was sure Washington, DC would be a prime target.

"Sure, Greg, do what you need to do. But you've gotta hurry…we're onto something and we need to get word back up the chain through Donovan or Ben. We must try to get a few more data points to establish some certainty. We already know enough to get everyone prepared for another attack—as long as we can get the word out."

Greg dialed Michelle, but he wasn't quite prepared for what he got on the other line.

"Michelle, what's going on? Why are you crying, Honey?"

Michelle had seen the President's broadcast.

"Greg, I can't reach anyone on the phone, Facebook, Blather or email. Blather was going nuts right after the President's speech. I couldn't keep up with all the crap coming through. Everyone had to comment on the speech and how crazy this all was, even the stupid entertainers. Like anyone cares about what Bono has to say about what's going on there—he doesn't live there and he hates our country anyway. What's happening?"

Michelle cried harder.

"Honey…I'm sorry I can't be there, I just—well, the attack comes through the phone or other smart systems, like an iPad or iPhone. Somehow."

"How do you know that? Why can't they stop it, if someone knows that?"

"Michelle, that's what I'm doing, I'm investigating the attacks. That's why I called you. I need you to turn off your cell phone and not use it until I tell you it's safe to turn back on."

"Are you kidding? The phone is my *lifeline*! I can't be stuck at my computer to track stuff. What if someone has to get ahold of me?"

"Hold on a second...so you have Blather and Facebook on your phone?"

Michelle took a deep breath regaining her composure. "Well, yeah, of course. Everyone does. I thought you did, too."

"Well, Facebook, yeah, but I don't keep it running. I don't like to be bothered with it during the day. I just check it at night, and usually from my computer.

"Why, Greg? What does that matter?"

"Can you see if any Blather messages were sent around 4:15?"

"Greg, I just told you, there were hundreds of messages a minute! Of course there were."

"But were any of them strange? Random? Unreadable?"

"I don't see what this has to do with anything. All of them were crazy; the whole country has gone crazy. It's like everyone was fighting for attention!" Michelle exclaimed.

"Honey, I'm telling you that if you leave your cell phone on, you are putting yourself in danger. I want you to turn it off and just use the landline phone and our desktop computer. Promise me you will."

"Yes, of course. But get this thing solved, will you? I know you're smart enough; you were the smartest guy I knew in school. Don't worry about me. I know I'm a spaz, but I'm gonna be OK."

"Well, call from the house phone to check your voice mail on your cell—you know you can do that. You won't miss a thing."

"Yeah. Good idea. I miss you. I love you."

"Michelle, I miss you too. I love you. I'll call you later tonight, OK?"

"OK...but one more thing.... Naked!"

That made Greg laugh. "Whoa. Nice. Thanks Gorgeous. I totally needed that."

"Just want you to know I'm with you."

"Ok, later tonight. I will call the house phone. Bye, Princess."

After Greg hung up, he looked over at Dennis to see if he'd been listening. Dennis nodded his head and smiled.

"So you're thinking someone sent out a message through a social networking site?" asked Dennis.

"Yup, that's what I'm thinking."

"To specific people or to the phone itself?"

"To the phones and to smart devices."

"To a program? It would have to be, right?" Dennis surmised.

"Well, hopefully we can find out on my next phone call. I've got to get through to Teardown and call the prof working on those chips. And then we've got to visit Michael."

"Hospital, Michael? That Michael?"

"Yes. It seems like there were too many messages this afternoon to single out a trigger. That wasn't the case at 7:30 a.m. Eastern time. We have to figure out if Michael's phone was locked into real-time updates from one of the social networking sites—and if so, whom was he following? I bet one of those messages looks really strange."

Chapter
(Thirty-9)

The **President retired** to the Oval Office to think.

The US thwarted close calls from would-be terrorists on a weekly basis. Early in his first term, they narrowly averted the detonation of a dirty bomb. The resulting EMP would have taken out all of the electronics in a five-mile radius around San Francisco, spilling out reams of radioactivity in the process.

But that potential strike paled in comparison to today's attacks. And worst of all, the US seemed powerless to stop it. Resorting to the ultimate, big-gun solution wasn't something William was sure he was prepared to do. He had to weigh possible repercussions from other United Nations Security Council members, not the least of which were Iran's would-be allies, Russia and China, who had their own nuclear capabilities. A direct assault on Iran might not even stop further attacks on the United States. For all he knew, there was a splinter group within the United States itself. As a final wild card, it would likely be impossible stop the Iranians from laying mines in the Strait of Hormuz, a move that would cut off a significant flow of oil from the Gulf.

"Mr. President," Ned said, bursting through the door to the Oval Office. "We just got a message from the Chief of the Interests Section from Iran, and it's not good. I think we need to go downstairs."

Once back in the Situation Room, the President gave Ned a stern, expectant look.

Ned looked around the room at each Council member. "What I have to say must be classified at Top Secret, SCI Level. I know that's your call, Benevidez," he said, speaking to Daniel Benevidez, the National Security Advisor. "But divulging this information could cause grave, irreparable damage to the US."

"Go on," the President urged.

"The message we've received is that if the US does not completely stand down as previously requested, the next strike will be in a major city at a time of their choosing, and with no warning. They want the *Truman* pulled out of the Gulf region immediately as a sign of our compliance. They're giving us twenty-four hours."

Amanda Stevens, the Secretary of State, spoke up. "They've got to be working with another nation on this—there's no possible way Iran has this capability. In fact, how does *anyone* have this capability?"

"Well that, my brilliant Council members, goes to the very crux of this problem, doesn't it?" stated the President. "All fingers point to some other partner with good intelligence. Iran hasn't been able to do much of anything without help from their allies'—whether that's build reactors, rockets or guns. So even if we bomb them to kingdom come, there's a very good chance we would still get attacked. That means we've got to find out how they pulled this off, with whom, and preemptively stop them. So, which of your agencies is anywhere near getting to the heart of this? How are they doing this?"

Carl was first to speak.

"Mr. President, we certainly know what it wasn't. Since it was *not* an EMP, it had to be some type of low-level signal, in-system timer, or a virus."

"So a low-level signal that somehow resonates with all electronics and blows them up? Like Jamie Vendera singing a screeching high note and exploding a wine glass?" asked the President incredulously.

"Well, uhh…that seems very unlikely. But perhaps it's a signal over the phone system or the Internet to an embedded virus or Trojan on the systems."

The President looked at Carl in disbelief.

"I know," he continued, "a virus or Trojan on everyone's system is a little hard to imagine—most systems are well-equipped to catch those. But there are reverse IP address locators that can find out which computer is located where," Carl suggested, taking a stab at a theory.

Silence. Everyone knew they were grasping at straws. Aside from the background noise of CNT being continuously played on a large monitor, the room was quiet.

"So that's all we have to go on?" the President asked.

"Well, we've had most of our agents in preventative and clean-up mode the past few hours. We don't have a whole lot. But we're testing different theories," explained the Secretary.

The President looked at his team, lips pursed.

The President finally spoke. "If we can't solve this in, say, the next eighteen hours, we will have to explain to our allies why we've backed out on them. The Japanese Premier is already asking why we haven't done anything about China's aggressive behavior. Their ships are already at the Senkaku Islands, ready to claim them as their own. Not that they don't have some precedent on ownership, but so does Japan, and the international courts are working on it. As far as Israel...I don't know what we tell Israel, but we need to bring them up to speed. If Israel does a preemptive strike on Iran, then we're going to get pulled in, and if we don't have a solution to the attacks on our own soil, we're going to get hit again.

"Benevidez, you start working on a message to our allies. Robert, make plans to pull our carrier out of the Gulf—though I can't believe I'm saying that. Also, make sure your new CYBERCOM group is on this, now that we're thinking cyber attacks. Carl, redirect more of your staff to figuring out the cause of this mess—pull in the national labs. Those billions we pump into technology should count for something. I don't think anyone in your agencies should sleep tonight. There's just no time."

For the Zhonghua Nine, it was time to rest. Most of them hadn't slept but a few hours the previous night, and some not at all. The message back to Zhonghua Three was that the Chinese Navy was preparing to surround the islands. The value to China was so immense, both politically and from a natural resource perspective that they planned to station a small flotilla near the islands until ownership was clearly established by possession.

For all intents and purposes, the overt mission the Leader's cult members knew about had been accomplished. However, for the Leader, there were further gains to be made, not only financially, but politically and strategically. In fact, while things had gone according to plan up until now—perhaps even better than he had imagined—the next twenty-four hours would be the most critical in order to complete his overall mission.

The next important step was for the Chinese President to talk with the People of the United States.

Chapter
(for-tee)

Greg and Dennis quickly made their way back to Huntsville Hospital to see if Michael was lucid.

On the way, Greg called Trey, Teardown's lead engineer. Fortunately, he had already de-capped the phone's main integrated circuit package—which involved taking hot nitric acid and etching away the encapsulant surrounding the stack of chips inside.

Their habit of publishing high-level analyses of the guts of an electronic device provided some notoriety for Teardown. This was their main marketing tool. However, their main business was selling detailed reports to the device maker's competitors. Not only did this provide inside information, but it allowed competitors to determine if any of their patents had been infringed upon.

So it wasn't a coincidence that Teardown had already taken the Dazzle apart when it first came out. Still, what they found was surprising. In *this* phone, the die stack was different. The previous package they had dissected was already the most sophisticated on the market with six stacked die: a main processor, graphics processor, random access memory, flash memory, a GPS processor and a combination Wi-Fi/Bluetooth processor. The package inside the Dazzle they took apart today contained seven die. It was pretty unusual for a manufacturer to change die stacks mid-stream. So unusual that no one had ever thought to check for any changes.

"So there's an extra die in there? What does it do?" Greg asked.

"Well, the problem is that to dig into the function of this extra die is a lot more work," Trey grumbled. "These die are effectively welded together; it's not so easy to pull them apart. That's just the way these Through-Silicon Vias work. If it were the old bond-wire technology, we could pop these apart real fast. Or if the added die was right on top, we'd see the difference immediately."

"How long will it take?"

"A few days. I know that's not what you want to hear, but that's the reality. I took some liberties and gave one of my sources a call, though. I can't tell you her name right now, but I can tell you she's reputable. She says there's been no design change. That's just too expensive to do this late in the game with a device out in the market. You'll have to call Motorola directly to get any better information."

"I don't have contacts or that kind of time. I can try to make calls in the morning, but frankly, I'm worried that will be too late," said Greg. "If someone added another die in there, what would it have access to? Memory?"

"Everything. There's been some new standards that this stack makes use of. There's a common data, power and ground bus. Think of this new standard doing for integrated circuits what the IBM PC, ISA bus did for PC cards. You can mix and match all sorts of chips by just stacking them together. Anything that comes across the data bus, this chip can see."

"You mean like, Wi-Fi data?"

"Yup."

"GPS data?"

"Yup—I'm not sure which part of 'everything' you didn't understand. I mean, obviously data that's internal to each chip is going to stay inside its own local data bus, but if there's data transmitted over to the processor, that extra chip is gonna see it."

"OK, my head is spinning. This opens up a lot of possibilities."

"It sure does, but none of those possibilities work without software. I know you've got your hands full with this, and I wish I could help more. I'll be working on taking apart these die, but that's not going to solve all your problems."

"No, it's not, but it's more than I knew before," sighed Greg.

"Oh, yeah—one more thing."

"Yeah?"

"I know this chip is assembled in the Hon Yao factory in China, and that this same or a very similar die stack is used in almost all of the leading-edge phones and smart devices out there right now."

"That's *not* what I needed to hear…. Hey, one more question."

"Sure."

"You said the power lines, or bus, are all common as well."

"Yup. Ground, 1.2 through 3.0 volt—all of them."

"So, what happens if that extra chip is designed to short-circuit the power supplies to the ground?"

"Well, that would fry the die stack real fast; maybe even blow up the whole package. That power supply can deliver a couple of amps. If it's shorted long enough, it could smoke the circuit board with that amount of current on the power supply traces. As far as the battery, well, there's thermal overload protection at the power supply to keep things under control, but if it's sustained and you manage to heat the batteries, they could blow as well. That's the extreme. You'd probably get a variety in-between, depending on a lot of things. But that's a very specific, deliberate design—one to short out the stack."

"I know. But that's what this looks like to me," Greg said.

"There are fifteen different devices that all use a similar stack in their main processor package. You'd have to recall millions of systems if that's the case. Impossible."

"I know. Can you give me a call if you find out anything else? By the way, what's it cost to keep you on this all night?"

"Absolutely nothing. I've already called to let my family know I won't be home. In fact, I've called all my core team's families as well. We're all gonna be here. I'll call you if we find anything else to report on—we have to grind each layer off as we go, so depending on which die is the Trojan, it could be pretty fast or really slow. While I'm at it, I'll check the resettable fuses for the batteries—if this is an inside job, there's a good chance those are counterfeit or bypassed— that would seal the deal for a battery bomb."

"Alright. Goodbye for now, and thanks again, Trey, for all of your help."

Dennis was mulling things over while listening to Greg's half of the conversation. A lot of things were starting to make sense, but there were still missing pieces.

"Let me call Professor Jones real quick," Greg said, wanting to wrap things up on the smartphone investigation.

"Dr. Jones, Greg Cannon from NTSB.... Let me guess, there's an extra die in the stack...."

Still listening, Greg nodded to Dennis, confirming they were on the right track.

The President received notice from his Press Secretary that the President of China was making a public speech that would be broadcast on CNT at 5:00 p.m. This was highly unusual, and as his team gathered back in the Situation Room to listen to the speech. Neither the National Security Council nor staffers joining them knew what to expect.

"Do any of you have any information on what this is about?" queried the President.

Henry quickly commented, "Only that the press conference was called on short notice. No one is really up to speed on the subject matter."

"Well I don't like surprises, particularly when we've been trying to get through to him since this morning..."

President Li was on camera, preparing to speak. His words would be translated into English as he spoke.

"Fellow citizens of the world," President Li began, "and particularly citizens of the United States, I come to you today deeply troubled by the attacks that have taken place against the United States this very day. I offer my condolences, and want to assure President Brunson and the people of the United States that the Chinese government was not responsible. We will do our part to help investigate these crimes and bring any person or country to justice for their involvement..."

The President was struck by the oddity of this behavior from the Chinese government. The country's isolationist tendencies didn't seem to jive with President Li's stance....

"...as citizens of the world, it is all of our responsibility to ensure the free flow of commerce continues unhindered. What we have seen today not only affects the United States, but ultimately affects our global economy. Accordingly, China has taken action to protect territory that was unlawfully taken from us in the past..."

"There it is, final—" exclaimed the Defense Secretary.

"Shut the hell up!" the President countered.

"…the United States and its allies must protect against attacks that have taken place on their territory. Protection of the homeland is the ultimate test, and a worthy cause for any nation and its citizens.

"So in protecting our homeland, we stand today in solidarity with the United States and will do our best to help them protect theirs as well. I pledge to President Brunson that China will cooperate in investigation and prosecution of any enemy found to be responsible for today's events."

"Is he done? Is that it? He's trying to equate the attack on Atlanta and DFW to 'taking back' the Senkaku Islands?" said Robert, incredulous.

"Trying? He did more than that. With that short speech, the average citizen here in the US is only going to hear that China understands, cares about what happened, and wants to help. Do you hear France, England, Germany or any of our allies on the news sympathizing with us? Offering to help? Not yet," the President said, looking around the room at the Council.

Some members were starting to wonder if the stress was getting to the President. Yes, he was making sense, but this scenario didn't. He wasn't actually trusting the Chinese on this, was he?

The President continued, "No one here in the US knows about the Senkaku Islands, nor will they care about a few square miles of uninhabited rocks once they do read up on it. After all, the land was China's before the war with Japan in eighteen hundred something, right? President Li just gave us an 'out' for not coming to Japan's aid—how could we protect them when we have to protect ourselves? But if you ask me, this all lines up too well. A global appearance to sympathize with the US on the same day they take the islands, on the same day we, unbeknownst to US citizens, have to stand down helping our ally Japan because we're under attack by a nation friendly with China? But what choice do we have? We can't attack Iran or China, and they already have the islands surrounded. There's likely no additional territory they want right now, so we've lost what we're going to lose with China…. The bigger concern is Iran and their movement into Iraq. If China can actually help us shut down the Iranian-claimed attacks, let's use them. Ned, start preparing a correspondence to President Li accepting their offer of help. We'll play his game. It's not like we have any other choice."

"But he didn't deny that they had a hand in the attacks, Mr. President. He only said they weren't responsible," said Amanda.

"Shrewd, I know. They are in the loop somehow, even if it was only foreknowledge."

"Maybe the speech will put pressure on the Iranians as well," said Carl, thinking through things aloud.

"Or maybe Iran is blackmailing China with the same threat of attack. In any case, it's your agency's responsibility to get this solved, so enough conjecturing, Carl—get your agents moving faster."

Chapter
(Forty-1)

Greg and Dennis gently knocked on the door to Michael James' room and cracked it open. They were expecting to see Michael's parents, but surprisingly, they saw Sam. From the smile on her face, it was clear she had spoken with his parents, and possibly Michael.

"Greg! Dennis! What are you guys doing here?" cried Sam, looking much happier than when they had last seen her.

"Still working hard on getting all this solved," Greg replied, caught up in Samantha's exuberance.

Mr. and Mrs. James appeared pleased to see Greg and Dennis as well.

"We figured you'd be in some trouble from what we saw on TV. But I'll bet they're sorry they didn't talk to you before the incident in Dallas." Mr. James said, greeting Dennis with a handshake.

Turning to Greg, he asked, "So what brings you back here? Seeing if Michael is up for more questions?"

"Well, actually, yes…but first, how is he?"

"Well, why don't you ask him yourself?"

It was clear that Michael was doing somewhat better, though he was still in rough shape. The swelling and redness had gone down some in his face, and his eyes were open and not quite so glassy.

Though his voice was still scratchy, Michael managed to get out a greeting: "I'm sorry, sir…but I don't remember who you are…"

"Yeah, you weren't quite lucid when we first met. I'm Greg Cannon, and this is my partner, Dennis Wright. We're with the National Transportation Safety Board and we're trying to solve the mystery of what exactly happened on your flight this morning."

Michael just nodded, still foggy.

"One of the things we're focusing on may sound strange, but it's gonna be really important and you might be able to help. Earlier today, you stated that you left your phone on at the beginning of the flight. Do you use any applications like Facebook, Blather or Twitter?"

Michael thought for a minute, still fighting to remember much about the morning.

"Well…I use all of those…"

"Do those apps alert you when something new comes in?"

"Nah, that would drive me crazy. Well, but…that's right…this morning I left Blather on…Lady Gaga is having a concert in San Francisco…" his voice trailed off at the realization of where he was supposed to be right now—with his grandparents, on his way to move in with Jill. How could he have forgotten?

"Michael?" Mrs. James asked gently.

"Oh yeah…well, ticket announcements were coming out today. I wanted to make sure I didn't miss any Blahs…"

Greg looked over at Dennis. He was eager to get to their hotel to check Blather updates from Lady Gaga as soon as possible. His best guess told him that she sent one at 7:30 Eastern that morning—he didn't know what it would say, but he knew it would be the next clue.

"This has been really valuable," Greg said, "and we really hate to rush off, but we've got to move on this investigation. You gave us some good info. I hope we can drop by tomorrow to check up on you guys."

Dennis interrupted: "You have our business cards, so in case you need anything—or remember what you think is important—please call right away. We're staying…where are we again, Greg?"

"Over at Embassy Suites—on Monroe, downtown. It's really close…we can get back here in a flash."

Chapter
(Forty-2)

*T*he **President called** a meeting. His Secretary of Defense and Director of
National Intelligence had the most pertinent information he needed, now.

Robert started first.

"Mr. President, shortly after the pullback of our fighters, Iranian tanks
crossed the border, meeting little opposition. We communicated to remaining US
forces that they must refrain from any offensive or defensive action, save
defending themselves."

Shaking his head, the President said "This is unprecedented."

"Yes, Sir. It appears that there is confusion within the Iraqi Army. As we
speak, Iranian forces are advancing towards Bagdad and Basra."

The President provided his own update.

"When we pulled back the 5th Fleet, Amanda sent an early warning to the
Israeli Ambassador. It turns out Israel had already been updated through their
intelligence in Mossad. The Israeli's have some 'plants' inside Iran who are
actually French citizens, working on the Uranium enrichment centrifuges at
Natanz. The French are not supposed to be there, so it was easy to blackmail
them into reporting findings back to Mossad officers. Troop movement has been
rumored for days. Israel's already poised to nuke Iran should they push through
the Iraqi border into Syria."

"We wouldn't expect any opposition to Iran from Syria. Just look at the
naval port they allowed Iran to build in their own waters," said Henry.

"This is what happens when the United Nations aren't united. Iran's buildup,
especially on the nuclear side of things, hasn't been slowed in the slightest.
French helping Iran? I guess that's no surprise," said Henry. "But Israel's got a

good deal more nukes than Iran will have for a long time. Can we get Israel to slow things down their response while we find a solution?"

"That's exactly what Amanda is working on," the President answered. "They'll back down, but only if they see what we're seeing. Israel deems Iran's actions as immediate and bona fide threats."

"I can see that," added Robert. "Their best defense is a pre-emptive strike. If they wait too long, Iran can easily launch missiles close-in."

Henry reminded the men of the Iran's military capabilities. "True. Iran has no real Air Force to be worried about—they have a few old F-14 and MiG fighters with maintenance problems—however, they have a formidable Army made up of hundreds of thousands of well-trained soldiers and a few thousand tanks and armored vehicles. If those forces get close to Israel, this is a completely different battle. Likely, Israel has seen the damage to Atlanta and Dallas today, and feels vulnerable to the same type of attack."

Though he didn't want to provide information that would take away from any of the US's options, Henry understood the gravity of the situation and Israel's position.

"Well, we can't provide them real-time imagery. How about a ten-minute delay to let us scrub anything we don't want them to see?"

The President took a deep breath. He felt relieved, expecting this support would avert any military action from Israel.

"Good. A delay is important. No one can know details on China and Senkaku yet, that's just one of many items we'll have to filter. With everything happening right now, I don't want that leaked, not even to our allies.

"Hank, please call Amanda and let her know the plan. Israel's ambassador is waiting for an answer from our Secretary of State."

Chapter
(Forty-3)

Dennis was surprised he still hadn't heard from Donovan, especially since he could be instrumental in relaying critical information. Even if other agencies had discovered that the attack wasn't caused by an EMP, he figured he and Greg were likely a full day ahead of them.

"Greg, I've got to get something to eat before we keep going. Let's check into the hotel and get settled. Then we can get a bite before summarizing everything we've learned. We need to get a report out as soon as possible, but if we don't have the right frame of mind, that's not gonna serve us well. There are significant details that make this all come together. We may even come to more conclusions as we walk through it."

"OK, that sounds like a good plan."

Greg barely heard what Dennis had actually said. His head was full of thoughts, ideas and confusion about the events of the day. How could there be so many events packed into less than twelve hours? And it wasn't even close to being over.

Greg swung their Cadillac into a parking place near the front of the hotel and shut off the engine.

"I bet we sleep well tonight," Dennis sighed.

"Really? I don't think so. I don't think there's any way I'm going to be able to sleep at all," Greg replied.

"Well, I'm Diamond Level now with Hilton, so let me see if I can get you a nice room up on the executive level where I'll be," Dennis said. "The rooms are a little nicer up there."

"Sounds great if you can do it. But, any room will work fine for me."

Greg and Dennis made a bee-line for the front desk. Their singular focus would have been great, if it wasn't for what they were missing.

Until now, the swanky, gorgeous woman sitting in the corner of the lobby had been almost a permanent fixture through the afternoon. But when she spotted Greg and Dennis, she instantly woke up—if that's what you would call it. The look that began as a spark of vague recognition quickly transformed into a wide-eyed glare, like the woman had been briefly hit with an electric shock. She sat up straight and looked at them intently, following their every move.

Greg and Dennis certainly didn't look like criminals, terrorists or otherwise credible targets to Shelly, but this was the job she was sent to do and she didn't question her orders. Once the targets were identified, Shelly was alert and ready to go. Anyone observing the woman in the corner would have seen a dark shadow spread across her face as her countenance changed from one of observation and recognition to cool purposefulness. She quickly stood and followed the men to the counter, ensuring they checked-in ahead of her.

Constance, the smiling check-in clerk, was ready for them.

"Good evening! Welcome to Embassy Suites, are y'all checking in?" she said with a sweet, smooth southern drawl.

"Yes, we are," Dennis replied. He could be personable when he had to be. That was one of his best qualities. In fact, Greg was starting to think that if Dennis was just around more nice people, maybe he wouldn't be so gruff and crusty so much of the time.

"Can I have your names and IDs, and the credit cards you'll be usin'?"

The men handed over the materials with polite grins.

"Yup, here they are," Dennis said. "And Constance—by the way, that is such a pretty name—I know it's asking a lot, but as a Diamond Level member, is it gonna be possible to get my colleague here upgraded to an executive floor room? We've had a day that you just wouldn't believe, and we could really use whatever perks you have up your sleeve. We'd appreciate it so much."

"Mr. Wright, this is your lucky day," Constance said with a wink. "I'm a pushover for sweet-talk. Ain't that right, Tommy?" she said a little louder, so the clerk hiding behind a side door could hear.

"That's right, Connie," came the surprised response from an out-of-sight voice around the corner. Tommy was crazy about Constance and used any opportunity to be near her, even if that meant hovering near the desk on his break.

"You gotta know, I don't sweet talk just anyone…" Dennis started.

"Just the girls you want something from?" Constance quipped with another bright smile.

Dennis' blush seemed to silence him.

"What's wrong, honey, cat got your tongue?" she continued. "Well, that's OK, I've got your rooms all set up now, so you can talk all normal-like from here on out. You're both on the 16th floor, one of our two executive floors. We've got a fancy breakfast in the lounge up there and a happy hour and appetizers from five 'til seven tonight. All complimentary, of course, just don't get drunk and we won't have any trouble. Mr. Wright, I got you in room 1630, and Mr. Cannon, you're in 1601. Opposite ends of the building—I'm sure ya'll don't want to be right next to each other, just in case one of you has some *real* luck tonight."

Everyone was all smiles as Greg and Dennis turned to head to the elevator.

As Greg leaned down to grab his luggage, he saw spiky-heeled shoes and long, sleek legs. His eyes traced their line to the black dress and ample cleavage above. Greg felt the adrenaline in his body rush over him in a wave. That is, until he looked up a little further and saw the expressionless, cold look on the woman's face. There wasn't a smile or a frown, joy or sadness. It was just blank, as if no one were really there. Chills ran through Greg's body, mingling with the adrenaline already coursing through his veins. He quickened his pace and lowered his eyes.

Dennis merely gave Shelly a cursory glance, barely noticing that anyone was there. She hadn't really even registered in his mind, as his thoughts were somewhere else. He was focused on getting food and continuing their work.

Constance spied Shelly, though, and didn't like what she saw. This lady was trouble, she was sure. As the front desk manager, Constance didn't have to take all of the check-ins on her own. She used this as an opportunity to pull her doe-eyed colleague into the picture as she turned toward the back office.

"Tommy-boy, break's over. This one's yours—I need to go check on something in the pool," she said as she passed her admirer. "Call me if you want me. Well, I know you *want* me, but I mean if you need me to help out."

"Uh…OK," was all Tommy could stammer.

By now, Mary had caught on to what had just happened—her nasty demeanor had not only scared one of her targets, but had frightened off the front desk clerk as well. Clearly, this wasn't going to work.

By the time Tommy looked up at the next guest, he was staring at a completely different person than the woman everyone else had just seen.

"Hi there, Tommy," she purred, reading the boy's badge and extending her hand in warm greeting. "I'm here to check in," she continued, shaking Tommy's hand strangely. "Can you confirm my reservation?"

She had brought both hands up to gently take Tommy's, and slowly, as she spoke, slid her hand up to Tommy's elbow with a light touch. This was part of the neuro-linguistic programming she had been taught as part of her agent instruction. NLP was the art and science of speaking to and touching a subject in a certain way to trigger a particular response or behavior. While psychologists had been debating NLP techniques and their effectiveness for years in the academic community, intelligence communities had advanced its use far beyond scholarly pursuits. The rhythmic cadence of Shelly's phrasing, combined with her touch, smile and intense gaze, melted Tommy right there. He nearly forgot where he was for a second.

Shelly released the gentle grasp of her handshake—her fingers softly gliding from the break at Tommy's wrist down to his fingertips.

"My name's Shelly Chambers," she said, never taking her eyes off his.

Tommy quickly looked down to try to figure out exactly what he was supposed to do next…he'd forgotten all his front-desk training in a matter of seconds.

Check for her name, he said to himself. He had already forgotten it, though she had mentioned it just a moment ago. He stared up at her with a look of bewilderment.

"Shelly Chambers," she repeated knowingly, with a bright, seductive smile.

Tommy was able to type in Shelly's name before forgetting it again in his inner turmoil. Before he could look up her room number, though, Shelly interrupted his thoughts again.

"Tommy, you seem nervous. Do I make you nervous? I'm really nice once you get to know me," she purred.

"I'm n-not n-nervous," he stammered.

Genius, he thought, realizing he just confirmed his nervousness through his anxious stammer and totally brilliant response.

Tommy took a quick look over to the elevators, where Constance was visiting with those two men who had just checked in. He didn't want her to see him in a perplexed state of mind, so he was somewhat thankful she had suddenly decided to leave the desk.

"Of course you're not," Shelly continued. "I think you're doing well. In fact, I'm starting to feel kind of a connection between us...do you feel it?"

Tommy wasn't quite sure what all he was feeling. Confusion, arousal, nervousness, fear and excitement were all running through his mind right now.

"Well, Tommy, I just remembered that I didn't bring my Diamond Level card with me on this trip, I was in such a hurry. I was promoted last week, which feels so good...but it may not be in your system yet. I sure would love to have a room on the executive floor to celebrate my new level, if you have the authority to do that for me."

Tommy finally started to come out of his confusion and feel a little more secure in his decision making. Tommy figured that moving this woman to the Executive Level would be a good way to show that he had some clout in the hotel. After all, he heard Constance just give an upgrade to someone without any credentials at all. Tommy smiled and nodded.

Shelly continued to butter him up.

"In fact...well, if it's not too much trouble...and I don't see anyone else waiting to check in...maybe you could just escort me up after I'm checked out? I mean checked *in*...to make sure I can find the executive lounge area all right. Could you do that with me, Tommy?" she cooed.

That pretty much sent Tommy over the top. There was one room left on the Executive Level, and this woman was getting it.

"Ms. Chambers, that's no problem at all. I'm just glad you decided to stay here tonight. I'll be happy to show you around. In fact, if there's anything you need, just call down and ask for me—and I'll make sure it gets done. Here's your room key—15th floor, Executive Level. The lounge is on the 16th…which I'll show you to right away, if you're ready."

"Tommy, you are such a gentleman. And that's *Miss* Chambers, by the way," Shelly said with another broad smile. "I like a man that knows how to get it done. I think this is going to be a really good stay."

Chapter

(Forty-4)

"*Tommy*, thanks so much for helping me up to my room. This is going to make things a lot easier for me tonight," purred Shelly as she walked into her hotel room, making sure her stride was slow and her hips swayed sensually. Tommy followed close behind with her bags, not taking his eyes off of her. He had promised to see her up to the Executive Lounge, and they were making a quick stop at her room to drop things off.

"So, before we head up to the lounge, do you mind if I ask you something?"

"Sh-sh-sure" Tommy stammered.

"You have something for that Constance girl, don't you?"

"Excuse me?"

"Yeah, I saw the interaction down there. She knows you have the hots for her, and she just rubs it in your face, doesn't she?"

"Well…"

"Well, I'm not that type, Tommy. I don't use people," Shelly said with a slight smirk. "So why did you move me to the Executive Floor, help me up here with my luggage and volunteer to show me the lounge and everything? Were you hoping you just might get something from me in return?"

"Uh…what do you—I mean, no, I was just being nice."

"So you're this nice to all your guests? I'm nothing special?"

"Well, no, I didn't say, that, I mean, well…"

"I'm just teasing you. I know you hoped for something…every guy does. And I'll tell you what: to show you how much I appreciate what you did for me tonight, I'm going to give you something *extra* special in return," Shelly moved closer to Tommy, licking her lips slowly.

Tommy felt like running. He wasn't sure what he was dealing with now and really didn't want to get into any trouble. Hotel policy said he wasn't even supposed to be in her room…

Shelly was directly in front of Tommy. With her height and heels, she could look right into his eyes. He was backed up against the wall, so he really had nowhere to go. Reaching up to touch the sides of his face, she slowly, forcefully pressed her full lips onto his.

When their lips touched, what Tommy felt was unlike anything he ever experienced when kissing someone. Perhaps it was the fear and the excitement of the moment. All he knew was that this is what he wanted. It was *more* than he wanted. His desire to run away melted. In fact, for a moment, he even forgot where he was. The tingles he felt shoot down his spine, through his legs and arms, and down to his toes and fingers were exhilarating. It was almost as if something had flowed from Shelly's lips into his entire body.

Pulling away from Tommy for a moment, Shelly looked him full in the eyes. "I know you felt that. I felt it, too. And that's just the start."

As she turned Tommy and pushed him onto the bed, Shelly knew that the next ten minutes would seal his fate. He was already becoming submissive. He wanted this, but didn't want to be responsible for what happened. This was going to be easy.

Chapter
(Forty-5)

*T*he drones in the Hayward warehouse were getting edgy. Three hours had passed since Rick's untimely death, though for some it seemed like an eternity. The drones weren't allowed to do much besides sit, eat and rest as best as they could while waiting for their next instruction.

Pamela was nearly comatose. The agents gave her a couple of Xanax from her prescription to control her anxiety. It was either that or shoot her, Ron reasoned, and since he suspected they'd have one more assignment before the night was through, killing her wasn't an option. Killing Rick didn't have a big impact on the messages that were sent out, and in reality, since he was still logged in to his accounts, Ron surmised he could get things ready to go for the next set of messages as well as anyone. For that matter, he could likely kill all of the drones and just use their logged-in accounts if they decided to cause trouble, but that would be a lot of work and increased risk. He was getting paid well to make sure this all came off without a hitch, and so far, so good. He wasn't going to screw things up.

Ron hadn't been given the "all-clear" from his Zhonghua Nine contact yet, which is one of the reasons why he assumed they weren't quite finished. He surmised the hacks on the social networking sites had something to do with the attack on Atlanta this morning, and though Ron was cut off from the outside world like everyone else in the warehouse, he suspected another attack on a US city had occurred when they sent out the last messages. He just didn't know how it all worked. In his mind, his conscience was weighing whether the price of the murder he committed, as well as the likely attacks on US soil he enabled, were something that the money was going to be able to cover when all was said and done. Zhonghau's early-on, easy money had become more difficult for Ron to earn, while their tentacles became impossible to escape. They seemed to know his every move. He hoped this next payoff would be large enough to enable a disappearing act for him and his family, for good.

The waiting was maddening for everyone, even Ron.

"Hey, I know you guys hate me, and believe me, I'm not happy with the way things have gone here either. But we're all stuck here for a while; at least until I get a phone call that says we can go. I have some cards and poker chips in my bag if you guys want to play to kill time…"

"As long as you don't play," said Joe. "I don't think any of us are interested in playing games with a killer."

Ron took it all in stride. They were on the home stretch, and it wasn't going to help to get argumentative now. Getting the drones to do something to de-stress would be good.

"Fair enough," he said, unzipping his duffel bag and pulling out a poker set.

From his angle, Joe could see that there were more weapons stashed away. For a fleeting moment he thought he might be able to get access to the bag and grab one if Ron was distracted. However, he quickly extinguished that thought. After all, he was getting paid well for this, and it was the last gig. Just finishing the job and getting out of there was the best plan.

Most of the drones rolled their chairs over to the center table and set up for poker.

Only Pamela held back, staring blankly into space.

Back in his hotel room, Greg was preparing to investigate the messaging traffic on Blather from the top-followed celebrities and politicians to see if anything strange had gone out around the time of the attacks.

A thought occurred to him as he was about to get on Blather: most of the small commuter and private planes didn't have any form of on-board wireless available yet. It was just too expensive. Had any smaller planes crashed? Large planes had received all the attention on the news. If his theory was correct, there shouldn't be many small planes impacted, if any at all. Unfortunately, the DC office was closed, so this was something he'd have to dig into himself after he investigated Blather. Add that to the list.

Quickly booting up and getting onto the web, Greg went directly to the Blather website. It was simple, with a list of the top Blather-bees, as the site called them, alongside their latest status or thoughts.

Clicking on the top Blather-bee, Greg saw that Lady Gaga was obviously not on tour, on set, or doing anything really important. It left her with the ability to post nearly a hundred updates that day. Greg marveled at the ridiculous effort it must take to release such drivel into the cyber-world; a person would have to be on her phone at least every ten minutes to post this many times in a day.

7:20 —   Just finished showering. I love my new Frizz Control Shampoo
7:28 —   My hair drier just shorted out. So much for made in China
7:30 —   I Æ lov˜e the cñolor bluꝏe°
7:35 —   On my way to the airport! Goodbye NYC, Hello LAX!
8:05 —   OMG. Just heard about Atlanta!
8:15 —   At Airport. By the way, WTF? I love red, not blue!
8:18 —   Now I'm scared to fly

Right at 7:30—there it is, thought Greg.

The message at 7:30 not only had garbled characters, but it was obvious Lady Gaga hadn't submitted that message herself. The Unicode symbols were a sign that something had been encoded in binary that the browser didn't know how to print correctly. Was the destruct command buried in there?

Greg proceeded to check other leading Blather-bees for similarly encoded messages sent about the same time.

In the Executive Lounge, Shelly had been biding her time. Tommy had escorted her up about half an hour ago. He left, looking happy but completely confused. He was likely thinking he was in love with her by now, but she knew she would be long gone before he figured out what he should do next.

The happy hour was going to close at 7:00, but until then, she used the house phone in the lounge to call Dennis' room every now and then to see if he would pick up. She was too smart to use her own cell phone and have the number show up on someone's records later.

Brrrriiiiinnnng….. Brrrriiiiinnnng…the phone pulled Dennis out of his deep thought.

"Hello?"

There was no answer.

"Hellloooo?"

Wrong number, Dennis thought.

Shelly had gone back to her room to get things ready for her first target. She figured Greg would be the easier of the two, and she'd dispense with him first. Dennis, on the other hand…well, he seemed more experienced. She would have to come up with some means to lower his guard. She had been planning all afternoon while waiting in the lobby.

Shelly rapped on the door of room 1601 quickly, but softly. She figured it would be easy to get Greg to open the door, and she would simply step inside and put two bullets in his chest.

The door swung open.

Before Shelly stood a portly businessman dressed in blue boxers, white undershirt, and tall black socks. He was chewing on the nub of a cigar. His bald head was a far cry from the hair she was expecting—and had seen—on Greg.

"Greg?"

The older businessman took a look at Shelly and almost started salivating. "Greg? Well, I can be Greg if you want me to be."

He was assuming that such a fine looking lady, knocking gently on his door had to be some high-class call girl. He should know—he had made use of many escort services in his frequent travels. He leaned against the doorpost and smiled.

"I thought Greg Cannon was in this room," Shelly said.

"Oh…uh…well, I hate to disappoint you, but I'm not him. I got the guy who was supposed to be in here bumped back down a floor or two where he belongs."

Shelly's frustration was obvious.

"Hey, tell you what," the man continued, "looks like you may be out a client for tonight, but I'll pay you double whatever this Greg was going to pay you. I'm in a good mood, and you're one of the sweetest things I've seen all year."

It took Shelly a few seconds to comprehend what exactly this rotund little man was implying, but she caught on quickly. Her mind had been running a million miles an hour figuring out what to do next. He made it easy for her.

"Well, honey, seeing as if I've lost a client and you've made me a much better offer, I think we can make an arrangement," Shelly said with a sly smile.

"Let's get you out of the hall then, and into the room, so we don't have a lot of gossip and jealously going on," the businessman said as he turned to walk back inside. Whether he meant jealousy of him or her wasn't really clear.

Shelly followed. She placed her hand into her purse and felt for her Glock as the door shut behind her.

Continuing, the man said, "Now, I sure hope you're not one of those fine-looking girly men. Are you? Because I don't think I'm really into that scene…though I might have a look, you know."

Girly-man? Shelly thought. Oh no, he didn't…

"You're saying I look like I could be a guy? A chick with a—"

"Hey," the man responded gruffly as he shuffled into the suite, "those girly men in Bangkok are prettier than most women. Don't get so offended."

No way was anyone going to insinuate that *she* was a he. With barely time to aim, and certainly not much time to think, she emptied two shots right in the back of his head.

The businessman was dead before he hit the floor—with a *thunk*. The silencer had done its job in keeping things quiet, but the smell of gunpowder lingered in the air. It was a smell that Mary was used to, even enjoyed. Seeing the pool of blood developing around the man's head on the carpet gave her the smug assurance that he paid dearly for his disrespectful remarks. She might have even let him live had he not tested her patience.

Damn it, Mary, thought Shelly. Mary had prematurely jumped into the scene when she knew there was a killing opportunity at hand. The reaction hadn't allowed time for her to get off a clean shot—there was a mist of blood that had back-splattered onto her hands and dress. The original plan was to have placed two shots directly into Greg's heart—his clothes would have captured any spray of blood and she could have exited cleanly. Now she had to take time to clean off her hands and wipe off her dress before going out in the hall. And she would need to change, again, once back in her room.

What was worse, was that in the stress of the moment, Mary, was proving difficult to control. Shelly and Mary were going to have to do a better job of coordinating their skills next time.

Chapter
(Forty-6)

Greg sat back and stared at his computer screen. He cut and pasted all of the major Blather-bees' messages around the time of the attacks. In each and every case, there were garbled messages sent out at 7:30 a.m. and 4:15 p.m., immediately before Atlanta and Dallas had been hit. This couldn't be a coincidence. In looking at the messages before the attacks, there were garbled ones in there as well—about two hours prior for Atlanta and about an hour before for Dallas. Almost all of the messages looked like they came directly from the celebrity, but Greg knew if they hadn't, they had to have come from someone who knew them well, or at least knew a lot about them.

With the evidence from Teardown and the professor, the sequence of events on the surviving plane, and now this data, the picture was becoming clear. Greg had just a few more things to check into and his theory would be complete. But his hypothesis was so far out, he didn't know if he could get anyone to believe it. Well, there was no one better to bounce things off of than his crusty boss. He figured he better give Dennis a call to let him know it would be just a little bit longer before he was ready to meet; he wanted to have all of his ducks in a row before presenting his theory.

Dennis knew he needed to be working on the investigation, but between getting up early for the flight and the intensity of the day, he was having a hard time keeping himself awake.

Brrriiiiinnnng….. Brrriiiiinnnng…the phone pulled at Dennis' mind, and this time he was a little irritated by the noise. It had better not be a wrong number again.

"Hello?" Dennis said gruffly, expecting silence on the other end.

"Dennis? Are you OK? Did I wake you?" came the clear voice of Greg on the line.

What a relief. Not only a correct number, but someone he wanted to talk to.

"Greg! I was looking forward to talking with you."

"I don't want to disappoint you, but I'm not quite ready to meet yet. I've made really good progress, but I have a few more things to check out before I have my whole theory in place."

"That's great. You finish up what you need to do and we'll talk when you're ready."

"OK. For now I'm checking flight records. If my hunch is right, no small planes got hit anywhere around Atlanta this morning, unless they were on the ground and someone on board was using a cell phone before takeoff. Small planes don't have in-flight wireless, so any smartphone is basically disconnected from take-off until landing. The DC office is closed, of course, so I'm just checking flights myself, online, brute-force."

"I see where you're going with this. If you check the first ten flights and all are clear, I think you've made your case, statistically…so then pull your conclusions together, we'll discuss, and then track down Donovan to get this passed up the chain with the data to back it up. Sounds like you're doing just fine on your own."

"I'm concerned about another strike. If I'm right, there's nothing we're doing to prevent it, and it could happen again at any time. I'm moving as fast as I can. I don't know how long it will take, but I bet I'm done in about half an hour. I'll come up there and you can pick my argument apart."

"Yeah, let's go down to the cafe and discuss it. I need some food and coffee," Dennis said.

"Sounds like a plan. Talk to you soon."

Chapter
(Forty-7)

*I*n the White House, things had gone from bad to worse. The President's Security Council was headed toward self-destruction; alternatively blaming the NSA, the Defense Department, and the Department of Homeland Security for their failures in solving the underlying origin of the attacks. Homeland Security ruled out an EMP, which helped the investigation along, but didn't solve the problem. All believed another attack was imminent.

Back in his hotel room, Dennis was piecing things together. His thoughts were interrupted yet again. This time it was the vibration of his cell phone on the night-stand. He recognized it as Huntsville area code.

"Hello, Wright here."

"Dennis. It's Donovan."

Dennis was relieved to have finally made the connection back to the agent.

"Agent Donovan, great to hear from you. I figured you might get caught up in the whole DFW mess."

"Something like that…you said something about solving the problem…what do you have?"

"I think we cracked the code on how it all happens—the attacks. Greg's got it all laid out…how it works and how to block it."

"Are you sure?"

"Yes. We tested the theory after the DFW attack. It will make more sense when we explain it to you."

"Can he just explain some of it to me now, on the phone?"

"No, he's not with me right now, he's in his room working on the report."

"OK, where are you? I'll come down there right away."

"We're at the Embassy Suites, downtown. Let's plan on meeting at 9:00 in the lobby cafe."

"OK, I'll see you then."

"You probably won't believe it, but Lady Gaga, and Ashton Kutcher are partly behind this."

"What?"

Dennis thought he'd throw that in for a reaction.

"Yeah, though I'm trying to be funny, I'm actually very serious. It's different than you might think. You get over here and get briefed. Pass this on and you'll be a hero. See you soon."

Just then, there was a loud knock on Dennis' door.

Chapter

(Forty-8)

"LaShaunda, I know youse in dere!" came an angry yell through the door. It was clearly a female voice, and she was upset about something

In a higher pitched shrill, the voice came again after further pounding on the door.

"LaShaunda! I knoooow youse in dere! Open dis door right now ba-for I call da poohh-leece!"

The voice was tinged by a larger-than-life southern drawl. Dennis hoped he could take care of this obvious room number mix-up before someone called security.

"Hang on! I'm coming!" he called.

"Who dat? La Shaunda, you got a *man* in dere!? You git yo sooorry ass outta dere right now!"

For just a brief instant, Dennis thought he should call security and leave the door shut.

"Open dis door right now, girl!" came the yell, almost as if the lady were reading his mind.

"OK! OK! I'm opening the door! Just quiet down."

Dennis swung the door open. What he saw was an angry, beautiful African American woman, ready to kick LaShaunda's butt—whoever *that* was. She was tall and impeccably dressed. She didn't look at all how Dennis had pictured with that shrill voice. It took him a second to register what was happening.

Shelly could not have been more pleased.

"I knoooow she in he'a!" she continued. "Wher'r you hidin' her!?"

"I don't know what you're taking about," Dennis replied, his hands up in a defensive position in an effort to quell her anger. "We'll get this sorted out, OK?" His assurances clearly only made her more upset.

"Like hell we will! Yeah, we sortin' dis out riiiight na'o. LaShaunda, you OK?" Shelly yelled into the room.

"Hey, she's not here. Come on in and look for yourself."

"Well, fine den, I will, and if you done anythang to-er…well, I'll…" Shelly's voice trailed off as she marched into the room. Coming in to look for herself seemed to settle her a little, and Dennis breathed a little sigh of relief. He let the door shut behind him as he followed this stranger into the room.

"Girl, you come on out now, ya hear?" she called again, much more calmly now. "I ain't gonna hur-cha."

"See, I told you there wasn't anyone here but me," Dennis said.

Once she saw that the door to the room had closed, Shelly turned her back to Dennis, reached into her purse and swiftly pulled out the Glock.

As she spun around, her demeanor and voice suddenly changed. The drawl was gone, replaced by an ice-cold tone.

"Get the fuck onto the bed," she said almost softly.

Dennis was stunned. It was almost like someone had erased the stranger's facial expression and personality.

"Hey, she's not here. I didn't do anything. Why do you have a gun?"

"Dennis," she said with an evil smile, "Thank you for being stupid enough to let me in."

The look on her face sent a chill up Dennis' spine. He wanted to panic, run, fall on the ground and beg. Instead he just stood still and tried to stutter out a response.

"H-hey, do I know you? Wh-what do you want? Money?"

Her cold glare didn't change at all as she calmly responded, "I want you to do exactly what I tell you to do. That's what I want. Now, get on the bed."

A shock ran up Dennis' back. Nothing was as it seemed. He knew instinctively that this woman intended to kill him. He wasn't trained for this. He froze up completely, unable to move or talk.

"I said to get on the fuckin' bed, or I'm gonna hurt you so bad you'll be begging for me to finish you off. Do it now."

Suddenly, Dennis felt as if a hand were gently pressing on his back. The sensation sent a wave of calm through his body and gently pushing him down to the floor.

"On the bed you asshole, not on the floor!" Shelly responded, raising her voice just slightly.

Sliding to his knees, Dennis knew what he had to do. It was simple, and the most important decision he had ever made, forced into being by the impending end of his life.

"Get up or I'll fucking shoot you where you are!"

Dennis' prayer was short and to the point: "Jesus, please forgive me for all of my sins," Dennis cried. "Please save me."

Suddenly, Shelly, decided she'd had enough of this insolence..

"You stupid asshole, I told you 'on the bed!'"

As a wave of peace swept over Dennis, he was scarcely aware of what was taking place in Shelly. Why had he waited so long to dig deeper into the truths he had heard as a child?

You're forgiven, my child, spoke a clear voice in Dennis' head. He was caught up in the rapture of the moment; Dennis had no awareness of the kick directed at his face that would silence his own voice and mind in an instant.

With a shrill, blood-curling scream, Shelly directed her foot directly at Dennis' jaw. This alone was enough to immediately render Dennis unconscious. Shelly's alter, Mary Death, would have just plugged two holes in him. But the rage in Shelly hardly subsided. She continued to kick, punch, claw and bite at him.

When Shelly was done, Dennis' body had been pretty well decimated. His face was shredded, beyond recognition. But somehow he was still breathing. His breaths were coming in short, halting raspy gasps. Some of the blows had damaged his trachea.

This wasn't part of the plan…it was a disaster, Shelly thought. It would be better to put him out of his misery before he regained consciousness, lest he make any loud noises. She'd have to figure out how to clean things up after finishing him off.

Out of habit, Mary took three steps backward to avoid back-splatter; there was already blood on her clothes, in her eyelashes, even bits of flesh under her fingernails. She placed two rounds in Dennis' chest. The premeditated exactitude of the act stood in stark contrast to the animalistic attack Shelly had executed just minutes before.

The original plan was to have Dennis on the bed when she shot him, positioned to look like he had fallen asleep and started a fire while smoking. Unfortunately, there wasn't a story that fit with the savagely brutalized and murdered victim now lying on the floor. She still wanted to get Dennis up on the bed, even with the blood splattered on the walls and pooling on the carpet. In her rush she wasn't thinking very clearly. In moving Dennis, she was bound to get even more blood all over her dress. So be it.

Putting her arms underneath Dennis' and joining her hands at his chest, Shelly was able to use her strong legs to lift Dennis' body up enough to drop his torso onto the bed, where it was temporarily stable. Ignoring the blood, she lifted Dennis' legs and flipped them onto the bed. Rolling his body up to the fresh, white pillows, she tried to position him as if he had been sleeping there all along.

Blood was smeared all over when she finally finished wrestling him up there. Looking at her condition, Shelly decided it was best to shower before doing anything else to the room. Immediately, she stripped off her clothes and threw them on the bed next to Dennis' body.

Suddenly, there was a knock at the door.

Shelly felt a surprising anxiety rise in her chest. It wasn't like her to panic about anything, but this last scene and lack of control were unnerving.

Taking a breath to gain her composure, Shelly remained completely quiet.

"Dennis, are you in there?" came the call from Greg.

If only she was in a position to take him out now as well, her whole mission would be successful. Meeting him at the door, bloody and naked would certainly be a way to get his attention, she reasoned. She stood still.

Dennis' phone began to vibrate. Clearly it was Greg, calling to check on him.

Greg wouldn't be able to hear the phone vibrate through the door, but just in case Mary picked up a pillow and placed it gently over the phone on the nightstand.

After a minute or so, she heard Greg make his way back down the hall.

Shelly stepped into the shower. It took only a few minutes to get Dennis' blood off her body and out of her hair. Tossing the towel on the bed next to Dennis, she went back into the bathroom for Kleenex and began to wet them down. Walking naked back into the main room, she pulled a chair below each of the two sprinkler heads. She carefully wrapped the wet Kleenex around them, making sure the fragile glass water-triggering tube inside wasn't touched, yet ensuring the mechanism was completely surrounded by the cold, wet tissue.

Next, Shelly pulled a tightly rolled up, thin, slinky dress from her purse. She was thankful for her foresight, though she couldn't have imagined things might have gone so wrong.

Though she was concerned about any residual hair strands, Shelly relied on the fact that identifying Dennis' body was going to be the real challenge and would hamper the certain, concentrated investigation. No hairs would survive what she had planned next.

Picking up her purse, Shelly searched for the bottle of fingernail polish remover and a pack of Winstons. Pulling out a single cigarette, she placed the pack on the bed next to the bloody mess of Dennis' body. Shelly drizzled the remover all around and over Dennis, covering the bed, his clothes, and his face with the accelerant. She emptied the bottle over her blood-caked dress, for good measure.

Making sure she had all of her belongings and shell casings, Shelly lit the cigarette and pulled a long, deep drag, making sure the end was red-hot. Tucking the cigarette between Dennis' clammy fingers, she then placed his hand over the trail of wet polish remover—it lit up. Quickly, the fire followed the haphazard trail until the bed was engulfed in flames.

Taking two washcloths—one to cover her nose and mouth, the other to open the door and sully her remaining prints—Shelly peeked out the door before exiting the room, just as the curtains gave into the fire's call. Shelly knew she would have about ten minutes before the tissue dried out and the glass tubes in the sprinkler heads would heat up and burst, releasing water and setting off the hotel fire alarm. That would be just enough time to grab her already-packed bags and get on her way. By then, Dennis and the room would be incinerated, along with any evidence.

Chapter

(Forty-9)

Agent Donovan made it to the hotel lobby a little early, anxious to meet Dennis and get the full scoop on their investigation. Calling Dennis' phone, he only got voicemail. There was no answer in Dennis' room, either, when he asked to be connected at the front desk, so Donovan sat down in the lobby to wait.

"Hey, Agent Donovan," came a greeting from behind.

Turning, Donovan saw Dennis' partner coming towards him from the direction of the elevators. He couldn't remember the man's name.

Donovan acknowledged him with a small wave and head-nod, and stood to shake his hand.

"How are you? What a coincidence, I was just trying to reach Dennis. I was supposed to meet him here at nine, but I'm early. You'll have to forgive me, but I've already forgotten your name."

"It's Greg. Greg Cannon. I just left Dennis' floor. I went to his room, knocked on his door. Called. I figure he's over in the cafe. You want to look over there?"

"Sure. It sounds like we have a lot to talk about," said Donovan. "Look, I really don't want you to take this personally, but I've been ordered to ensure Dennis leaves tomorrow morning. This is all crazy, and there's fingers pointing and backstabbing going on. Dennis' statement on TV got back to Washington."

"Yeah, we saw the news, and he told about me your message," Greg said.

"It turns out that he's likely right—that it was a terrorist act of some sort."

"I'm glad you're here, we think we're figured out how it all works—the attacks."

"Who knows about your work?"

"We tried to relay the information up our chain of command, but haven't heard back. But it's just now that I've finished confirming everything, and the solution is *not* pretty."

"Let's get over to the bar and find Dennis. I want to hear this right away."

BLEEP BLEEP BLEEP... BLEEP BLEEP BLEEP...

"Aargh! What is that?!" exclaimed Greg.

BLEEP BLEEP BLEEP... BLEEP BLEEP BLEEP...

"That's the fire alarm. What timing. Let's wait a second to see if it shuts off."

"I'm gonna head outside to wait—my ears can't take this," Greg said. He put his hands over his ears and made his way toward the entrance.

Agent Donovan followed suit a half a minute later. If it was a real alarm, everyone would end up outside anyway, and they could all walk over to a nearby restaurant and talk there.

Sure enough, the alarm didn't subside. In fact, it was just a matter of minutes until a ladder truck, pumper and ambulance showed up.

"Looks like this is a real one," Donovan said, finding Greg with the hotel guests as they emptied out into the parking lot from the stairwells and front doors.

Looking up, Greg could see smoke coming out of the windows from a room on one of the top floors, with flames licking the side of the building.

"Donovan, look up there. This is the real deal."

"Greg, where the hell is Dennis? If he was in the cafe, he should have been right behind us," Donovan said.

Greg had a sinking feeling in his stomach. There was no way that room could be Dennis'. He didn't smoke. He didn't have a smartphone that could have lit up, either. Still, he wasn't out in the parking lot.

Shelly waited a short while before walking out with a group of guests heading toward the emergency exit on her floor. This is going to be easy, she reasoned, almost breathing a sigh of relief.

She hadn't been completely successful on her mission, but she had taken out the main target. Exiting the fire door with the crowd would leave a simple walk to the car where she could wait until her secondary target emerged.

Shelly was making her way down the sidewalk from the end of the building when she saw him.

Greg, the other target.

He was staring at the top of the building, along with everyone else. Taking a quick look up herself, she saw that the fire was spreading to adjacent rooms. A wave of pleasure came over her that piqued her confidence; it might be possible to complete this mission after all.

Shelly decided that with the crowd and commotion, it was worth a try. Her Glock was still in her purse, with a few rounds left. She'd stop off at the car first to drop off her luggage. Using her laser sight would let her keep more distance between she and her target.

"Greg, I don't like this at all," Donovan said. "My gut tells me that something's happened to Dennis. I'm going to go figure out what room Dennis is in—and which room is on fire."

A flicker out of the corner of his eye stopped Agent Donovan in his tracks. Instinctively, he shoved Greg sideways; a red dot swept across the back of Greg's head and onto his shoulder while almost concurrently, a *pffffft* sound signaled a bullet whizzing toward his jacket.

Greg plowed headlong into the guests in front of him, then onto the ground. His hands came up at the last minute to prevent him breaking his fall with his face. The bullet only grazed his shoulder, but the sting caused him to yelp as he felt its hot burn.

"Stay down!" Donovan yelled at Greg as he pulled his .45 from his vest holster inside his jacket.

Turning in the direction from where the laser and shot would have come, Donovan spied a tall, striking woman standing by herself in the parking lot—with a gun still trained on the crowd—seemingly waiting to take the next shot.

Shelly saw Greg get pushed to the ground and surmised her bullet had hit its target, but waited to see if another round was required. It was then she noticed a man standing with Greg had pulled out a weapon of his own.

Donovan saw the red glint of the laser as it swept toward his face and flat-out dropped to the ground. Rolling over to the curb at the hotel entrance, he yelled for everyone to get down. Pulling out of his roll into a prostrate position behind the curb, he was able to minimize his profile and make himself more difficult to hit.

Shelly calmly tried to track Donovan as he rolled. The darkness didn't help matters, but she squeezed off a shot. Despite her compensation, the bullet landed low, shattering the curb and spraying concrete dust into Donovan's face.

By now, some of the crowd realized what was happening and started to rush away from the scene. However, one courageous kid who was already videoing the fire on the 16th floor with his smartphone decided that capturing the developing parking lot battle was worth the chance of getting caught up in the cross-fire. He cowered behind the hotel shuttle van while recording the unfolding drama.

Agent Donovan squinted just in time to keep the debris out of his eyes, aimed, and got off one shot of his own. The bullet struck Shelly squarely on her right shoulder, shattering the end of her clavicle and scapula. Her gun flew out of her hand as she grasped her shoulder with a scream.

There was no time to lose. Donovan knew that if this nut job was also responsible for the fire and whatever might have happened to Dennis, she was well trained and not likely to give up. He sprung from his position on the ground and began a hard sprint over to where Shelly leaned against her car. His adrenaline was pumping in high gear, and it would have taken a Mack truck to stop him.

Seeing Donovan barreling towards her, Shelly tried to fight back the pain and make use her left arm. She intended to go for her gun, now laying about five feet on the ground in front of her.

"FBI! Get down on the ground, now!" Donovan yelled at the woman.

Instinctively, Shelly knew she had to finish this off. She also knew that if she went for her gun, she was likely lose her life to the agent. Her hesitation while thinking it through was all that Donovan needed to close the gap and slam his body full-force against her, pinning her to the car.

Donovan's athletic, solid body, knocked the wind out of Shelly on impact. Between the searing pain in her shoulder and the blow to her chest, she could only slump down and try to catch her breath.

By now, the local police who arrived to help tend to the fire had seen the commotion and made their way over to Donovan and Shelly.

"Police! Drop your gun and put your hands in the air!"

Just great, Donovan thought, the cavalry arrives and doesn't know who the enemy is! Still, he slid his gun behind him and put his hands in the air, still keeping his body pressed against Shelly.

"I'm FBI, and this woman is not only a suspect in this arson, but she's fired multiple shots here at government agents," Donovan stated over his shoulder to the approaching police.

The police held their ground. The lead officer yelled, "Fine, we'll get this sorted out, but for now put your hands behind your head and turn around!"

Donovan complied. As he backed away from Shelly, he could see that she was in bad shape and wasn't likely to try anything…at least not for now. He turned, fell to his knees and waited for the Huntsville police to advance.

As they got closer, Donovan loudly told them, "You realize I need this woman for questioning for Federal crimes after you 'get this straightened out,' right? We can cooperate on this, but she's leaving with me." He continued as another officer came up behind him: "My badge is in my front left jacket pocket…go ahead and look. But move it! I'm not at all exaggerating when I say that we have National Security issues all over this."

Meanwhile, it wasn't the first time that day that Donovan was being caught on camera unawares. Over in the shadows, the college student filming the action was catching the entire scene.

Chapter
(fif-tee)

It **was the middle** of the night in Iraq, and Iranian troops continued to progress into the country. For the most part, the Iraqis had been supportive of Iran since the pullout of the United States. After all, the Shiite-heavy parliament was supportive of Iran and its endeavors, and knew that any type of invasion was just a pass through on their way to somewhere else—hopefully Israel.

Many Iraqi troops, therefore, were also sympathetic to the Iranians, especially to those stationed at border crossings. In the past, at some of the crossings, Iranians had even been providing services and utilities for the Iraqis. Many Iranians were allowed to enter Iraq, to visit holy cities like Karabala and Najaf. Iraqi soldiers assumed that if there were ever a serious attack by Iran, the Americans—whom they knew were waiting in the Gulf—would have some type of counter-attack.

The attack—or rather, invasion—was underway. The United States had yet to respond.

For some older Iraqis, the thought of Iranian troops on Iraqi soil harkened back to the ten-year war of the 1980s. A lot had changed since then.

Since last night's invasion, which started in earnest shortly after the aborted US attack, troops had been making steady progress toward Baghdad. Any type of substantive resistance from the reluctant and off-guard defenders was quickly squelched with the overwhelming firepower readily prepared for this invasion.

"Shelly? Shelly Chambers?"

"Hit her with the smelling salts," Donovan demanded.

Shelly had been stabilized and brought the short distance to Huntsville Hospital by ambulance. Fortunately, Agent Donovan and the Huntsville Police soon figured out how to cooperate on the investigation and decided to divide and conquer. Donovan was convinced that the fire in the hotel was somehow related to this woman. Time was of the essence in getting her information and Greg's theory deciphered. The Huntsville Police were glad to help investigate the fire, given the background on the situation.

Dennis was still missing.

Donovan and Greg followed the ambulance over to the hospital—both to get Greg's flesh wound treated and ensure this "Shelly Chambers" was guarded and interrogated.

For all Donovan knew, Shelly was ready to take a cyanide pill. He really didn't know what he was dealing with. For that reason, he ordered Shelly to be forcibly strapped down to her gurney on the short ambulance ride and requested a Huntsville officer ride along for protection.

While Greg was tended to, Donovan made his way to Shelly's room for questioning.

As the ammonia fumes hit Shelly's sinuses, the small explosion in her nose started to pull her out of her stupor. Donovan was determined to interview her immediately.

"She's not awake yet. Do it again," Donovan insisted.

"But—" objected the nurse.

"Just do it. It's either that or I slap her into consciousness. Which would you prefer?"

"OK," she replied. "Shelly. Come on, wake up now."

A little bit of the fog lifted from Shelly's mind. It took her a bit to realize where she was. She had been in hospitals before, but that was to take care of unfinished business—targets who had to be eliminated after an initial attack had failed. She had never been in one as a patient.

The pain in her shoulder jogged her memory. It was all still foggy, but she remembered that she had been shot, and clearly was in the custody of the police.

"Owwww," Shelly moaned.

"Looks like she's starting to wake up. No pain killers until I'm done talking with her," Donovan ordered the nurse.

Turning to Shelly, Donovan spoke firmly and forcefully.

"Shelly, I'm Agent Tony Donovan, FBI. Nod if you understand what I'm saying."

Between the smelling salts and shoulder pain, Shelly was cognizant of her surroundings, though she still felt groggy. She nodded slowly.

"I suspect that, in addition to taking shots at me and others in the crowd, you also had something to do with the fire at the hotel and the disappearance of NTSB agent Dennis Wri—"

Donovan stopped short, realizing that he hadn't started things off correctly.

"But first, before we start, you have the right to remain silent…"

News crews arrived at the hotel only minutes after Shelly's capture. Fortunately, Donovan, Greg and Shelly were already safely absconded to the hospital. Unfortunately, the student with the smartphone video camera shared his footage with the crew, provided he got some credit (and money) for risking his life. But perhaps even worse was the willingness of the Huntsville Police to share "off-the-record" information about the investigation, including the possibility that a Federal agent and an assassin, wounded in a gun battle, may have both been associated with the fire and possibly even with the tragic events in Atlanta and Dallas.

With the video, a few unsubstantiated facts and off-the-record statements, the local CNT affiliate moved on the "real" story to add to their news-breaking coup that evening. They hurriedly figured out how to upload the student's video and were prepared to go live.

"This is Gerald Manning, investigative reporter from WAYA-TV in Huntsville, on the scene at the Embassy Suites downtown, where it appears a fire preceded a shootout between the arsonist and an FBI agent. From what we have gathered, an Alabama resident, by the name of Shelly Chambers, was a guest at the hotel and is a likely suspect in the arson set here earlier tonight. We have live footage from a college student, Jackson Gilbert, who was on the scene, and risked his life to video the gun battle and capture of Ms. Chambers just a few minutes ago. As you'll see in the video, the FBI agent involved in the capture appears to be the same agent on the scene this morning at the emergency landing site of American Flight 1225 on Highway 72, just outside Huntsville.

"As we start the video of the gun battle, Jackson Gilbert will describe what was happening…"

The edited video was about five minutes in length, and Jackson made the most of his on-camera time by adding dramatic flair to his description of the chaotic scene. Naturally, he made himself out to be a hero of sorts.

They popped up a still image of Donovan and Greg together as they were getting ready to leave the hotel parking lot in Donovan's government vehicle.

"Note, as we freeze the video on this scene, we see an FBI agent leaving with an injured agent or co-worker. You may recognize both of these agents from the scene of the aircraft landing on Highway 72, in Huntsville, this morning. Now, I'm showing you an image from this morning's report. From our investigation, we have learned that the FBI agent is likely Tony Donovan, attached to the local office here in Huntsville. The other agent has not been identified, but appears to be the target of Ms. Chambers' first shot.

"Here in another image from Jackson's video, is a still of Ms. Chambers. We have off-the-record reports that Ms. Chambers is from Birmingham, but we have no confirmation or further details as of yet."

The announcer from the anchor desk at WAYA-TV cut in. "So, Gerald, how do we know that Ms. Chambers is also suspected in the arson at the hotel?"

"Well, Ed, we don't know that. In fact, we don't even know that it *was* arson; however, initial reports from some of the officers on the scene indicate that this is being investigated as arson, and as such, Ms. Chambers seems to be a leading suspect. Things are so early in the investigation that we don't have anyone from the police, fire department or FBI who will go on record with any update for us."

"Folks, there you have it, a report from the thick of a breaking news story. We'll be checking in with our Huntsville crew periodically. Until then, we return you to coverage of…"

Chapter
(Fifty-1)

CNT headquarters picked up the story from WAYA-TV in Huntsville, making Gerald Manning part of the national headlines yet again. While the fire and shootout didn't have the dramatic impact of the attacks on Atlanta and Dallas, the story seemed important enough to get out to the public. Since a charred body had now been reported, the backdrop to the hotel arson story was growing more sinister.

Anyone tuned into the coverage on the attacks in the United States got word of the Huntsville fire and homicide. This included the Zhonghua Nine.

The Leader was hoping to hear that their agent in the US had successfully eliminated the government investigators. Instead, his staff monitoring the news alerted him to a breaking report on the capture of a suspected arsonist and murderer in Huntsville. Mulling over the implications of the report, the Leader knew it was time to launch Phase Four of Dormant Curse. Every risk and possibility had been accounted for in the Leader's planning. Each Zhonghua member had a prescribed plan for each phase of the operation; the Leader called for a final meeting of the Zhonghua.

"Zhonghua Nine, we just received word that not only was one of the government investigators we targeted in Huntsville not eliminated, but the agent sent to eliminate them has been captured by the FBI. This has serious implications for our mission, though it's nothing we didn't anticipate. We must push ahead to Dormant Curse Phase Four and finish our job here. We can then go home."

The Leader looked at each Zhonghua member intently. Most had no direct orders for this phase. However, those who understood the implications knew that calls needed to be placed to the drones, the Chinese military and finally, Shelly's handler. The messages were simple and direct, and would trigger a set of unique actions for each recipient.

"Dormant Curse Phase Four has begun."

The White House had not received any communication from Iran since their invasion of Iraq. In addition, no further attempt had been made to stop the Iranian troops. However, contingency planning was ongoing. There was the hope that once the means of the attacks was discovered and blocked, the US would be in a better position to deal with Iran. All options were on the table; in fact, Trident submarines with nuclear capabilities were already on the move to within striking distance of Tehran. An envoy had been sent to the Interests Section of Iran in DC with the clear message to Tehran: Any further attacks on the US would be met with assured destruction from the United States.

A key concern was the remote possibility that Iran could unleash the same destructive force experienced in Dallas and Atlanta across the whole of the United States or their allies. Plus, there was no assurance that completely annihilating Iran would shut down their operation, particularly if the attacks were based out of some other country.

Unfortunately, the government's science and technology communities weren't any closer to uncovering the method of the attacks. The Department of Homeland Security seemed stymied in their attempts to unravel the mystery and CYBERCOM, late to be pulled in, was just getting started. This much they had discovered: there was no EMP weapon and the attack appeared to hit only cell phone and smart devices with an internet connection. They had various teams investigating the possibility of a sophisticated smartphone or computer virus.

The secondary impacts of the attacks—voice communication and internet disruption, ongoing fires and social unrest—were taking their toll on all federal and community resources. Investigators diligently trying to do their jobs were thwarted by their inability to get their hands on an affected system that hadn't been extensively damaged. They were days from trying to recreate or test any developing theories.

Ron welcomed the phone call. There had been hours of mind-numbing card games and poker while he tried to keep himself, the other agents, and the drones from going stir-crazy waiting for some finality to the mission.

"Yes, I understand. Phase Four," Ron said.

He breathed a sigh of relief. He was glad to finally be at the end of this mission. He still had to dispose of Rick's body, but that would be an issue he would deal with later.

If only that drone hadn't blatantly disobeyed and lied about it, he thought, all this would have gone off without a hitch.

His agents and the drones were watching him carefully. While shifting his focus to the immediate task, the drones and team saw a hint of relief flash across Ron's face, even if for a brief moment. His determined expression let them know it wasn't over yet—but the change in countenance wasn't lost on the team, and provided some measure of hope. The relief of tension in the room was palpable.

"OK, drones," Ron said, almost enthusiastically, "open the folder named 'Phase Four' on your desktop. There's just one file inside and it's the one we're sending next. There's a short fuse on this one. We have five minutes to get it ready and send it. The good news is that this is the end of the mission. The other good news is that if you don't screw this up, you'll walk out of here unharmed, except for whatever mental damage Rick may have caused you by forcing me to kill an insubordinate, lying son-of-a-bitch."

The countenance on some of the drone's faces fell as they realized they were still dealing with a nut-job.

To his credit, Ron had only thrown in that last tirade to ensure the drones didn't think they could let up on their focus or absolute compliance with his commands. He expected they would all now do their jobs without any hiccups.

Chapter
(Fifty-2)

"...If you cannot afford a lawyer, one will be provided for you at government expense."

Donovan gave a big sigh. He was happy to have gotten that out of the way.

"Shelly Chambers. Is that your actual name?" he asked.

Now that Shelly was awake and fully aware of her pain—and her capture—she knew what she was supposed to do next. Kill herself. But no one had trained her for how she was going to do that when she didn't have access to any of her belongings—her purse, her gun, her pills. On every mission, she carried cyanide pills in an Amoxicillin vial. If agent Donovan had taken the time to go through her purse, he might have even found them, which would have tipped him off to the bigger picture of what he was dealing with. But he didn't. Figuring she couldn't do much of anything right now, Shelly's plan was to stay quiet. Donovan's question was met with only a glare.

"So, you want to play the silent game?"

Donovan was incensed. Time was short, and interviewing Greg was just as urgent as getting information out of Shelly. At least with Greg, he knew what the information was going to be about. With Shelly, he didn't know who, what, where or how she fit into the picture. He only knew she was bad…and she was responsible for two attempted murders—his and Greg's—and was likely responsible for a missing NTSB agent and a fire.

In his attempt to speed up the interview process, Donovan had tried to go through Shelly's phone and laptop while waiting for the medical staff to get her stable and set up in her room. The laptop was secured, of course. There was no getting into it, at least not with the tools he had available. The phone was a completely different story, and not in a good way. Shelly's phone was unlike any he had ever seen. The phone itself had no clear markings to identify its manufacturer. Beyond that, it was tough to tell how "smart" this phone was. The simple LED display showed only the number dialed. There was no call history. The device was designed to be obscure and appeared to be relatively low-functioning, beyond basic call capabilities.

It was clear that if he was going to get anywhere, he was going to have to pull out some tough stuff, and fast. As angry as he was getting, he did have some information that he'd recently received that would likely shake loose her tongue, but had been reticent in sharing it unless she wasn't going to cooperate. She wasn't cooperating.

"Well, Shelly, it's clear your actions today weren't the work of a lone ranger. You're obviously working with someone. However, you may or may not know just how ruthless they are. But I can tell you, your loyalty to them is misguided. Only ten minutes ago, I received word from our team in Birmingham. Using your driver's license, we had them quickly make their way over to your parents' house—if Steven and Celine Chambers are, in fact, your parents."

At the mention of her adoptive parents, Shelly responded, but not with the fear Donovan had been expecting; rather, her glare intensified, her breathing turned heavy, and Donovan felt hatred and violence projecting at him from her every pore. At least he had gotten some reaction out of her now. "Leave my parents out of this!" Shelly growled.

"Shelly, your parents are already involved," Donovan retorted.

"What are you talking about?" she demanded.

Shelly knew that her parents were in this, of course. They raised her, abused her, and trained her to become the multi-faceted killer that she was.

"When the agents arrived, the house was already in flames. Your parents haven't been found yet."

Donovan paused for effect. He was trying to study her face closely, to read whatever reaction he could as she processed the information. He should have been able to discern shock, sadness, anger, guilt or deceptiveness. There was just a cold stare. After a moment, Shelly glared at Donovan, and in her anger snarled, "If you did anything to them…"

"We didn't do anything. It's whomever you're working for, though…I can't be sure what they'd do. The fact is that the hotel fire, our battle, and your face have been all over the news. Likely whomever you're working with picked up on it and is covering their tracks. That's why you're not only under arrest, but you're in protective custody. Just tell me who they are and why you were targeting these agents, and I'll go after them."

"I'd never help you."

Donovan, getting exasperated at this point, kept his stoic stance and continued to try to convince her to talk.

"It's really in your best interest if you do," Donovan said. "I can't protect you or your parents unless you help me out and provide some information."

"Why should I believe you?" she countered.

"Because right now I don't believe you have any other choice. If your parents are in that charred house and the group you work for is responsible for their deaths, it's likely they're already trying to figure out how to get to you next."

Though Shelly was getting concerned about something happening to her father, she knew she couldn't help Donovan. Likely her mom and dad had escaped unharmed.

"Fuck you!"

This was getting incredibly frustrating for Donovan—without a partner he was forced to play "good-cop/bad-cop" all by himself.

"Answer me this. Why were you targeting these guys today? They were National Transportation Safety Board staff. They aren't trained in any operations—they don't even have self-defense training."

This was met with further silence.

"Do you ever call your contact?"

Shelly just sneered. Her father was her only contact, and she was loyal to him. No answer was required.

Donovan had to pause and think. He might as well jump to the chase and try to get to some meaningful information before he gave up.

"Were you successful in eliminating Dennis Wright?"

"What was that you said earlier about talking to an attorney? I want one."

Suddenly the urgency of the whole situation started to weigh on Donovan. He wasn't going to gain much headway by continuing this course of questioning. Even if Shelly had killed Dennis, and even if she admitted it, it wasn't likely that the information would provide any help in solving the larger problem of stopping the attacks on US cities. What he needed was to uncover the network that was giving her orders. The first step in that direction was probably talking to Greg.

"Shelly. We'll talk later. Right now you need to recover, and we need to make sure you're safe. You're under arrest for attempted murder, for starters. You and I both know there will be more charges added soon. That's enough to keep you here, not that you'd be going anywhere in your condition anyway. Nurse, you can drug her up all you want now," he said, turning to go.

Just as Donovan reached the door, Shelly's unmarked cell phone sprung to life.

I knew it—no caller-id, he thought. Shelly's contact is checking in.

Daddy, Shelly thought. The hope that she could hear her father's voice had briefly gone through her mind.

Looking back at Shelly, Donovan thought he saw a flash of expectation, which just as hastily was squelched. "Shelly," he said, suddenly taken with an idea, "I want *you* to answer."

Shelly was shaking her head as Donovan strode over to her bed and handed the phone to her good hand. She was torn. While not wanting to take the call and admit failure, she wanted to know he was safe and that he loved her still.

Shelly answered in a sweet voice, "Hello."

Over ten thousand miles away in Shanghai, Zhonghua Five heard the voice of the American agent sent to carry out the "seek-and-destroy" mission. When she answered, he hit the code "626622#" on the conference room phone in the Grand Hyatt Polaris Room.

Shelly was confused by the tones she heard on the line. It was as if someone accidentally dialed or was sitting on the phone. Donovan saw the look on her face and thrust out his hand authoritatively to take the phone back from her, not wanting to miss any dialogue taking place.

The only warning Shelly would have had that something was about to happen to her phone would have been the whine of the high-pitched charging circuit triggered to life by the code coming across the line. Its increasing pitch might not even be audible to someone without really good hearing. Donovan didn't hear a thing.

It only took one second of charge from the high-powered lithium-ion batteries to bring the on-board detonation capacitor up to voltage.

Before Donovan could take the phone from Shelly, the circuit dumped the energy from the capacitor onto a foil initiator. Within microseconds, a coin-sized, explosively formed projectile was vaporizing, creating a stretched-out rod of high-velocity copper, aimed straight at Shelly's head.

Donovan only saw a flash of light, then found himself dazed, laying on his back on the floor. His face stung, and his hand felt like it was being seared with a hot knife. He couldn't hear anything but a loud buzz in his head. Somehow, he had grit or sand in his eyes and he became aware that the room was filled with smoke. As the sound of the ringing in his ears started to subside, he heard the nurse. She was screaming. Trying to blink and clear his vision, he raised his hand to look at why it hurt so badly. He was bleeding. It looked like he had taken part of a shotgun blast. The shrapnel that peppered his hand was made from bits and pieces of plastic, metal and chemicals from various parts of the phone that had just exploded.

As Donovan grabbed the rails of the bed to pull himself up off the floor, the smoke from the room still hung in the air. Looking over the bed, he was snapped into reality by the screams of the nurse. Blood was streaming down her neck. She had what appeared to be a long shard of copper sticking out just below her ear.

"Help me!" she screamed to anyone who would listen. Her scream was soon muffled by the sound of the fire alarm, which woke up angrily just as the smoke reached its detector.

The Huntsville police on guard outside the door heard the explosion and screams, and after drawing their weapons, kicked the door open in case there was someone on the other side that needed to be caught off-guard.

What they saw was practically a battlefield.

Agent Donovan was trying to right himself as the nurse across the bed from him was screaming in pain…both were bleeding. Donovan's left hand looked bad, while the blood streaming from the nurse's neck soaked into her white blouse. Where a patient should have been was a body—but no head. Or at least, where the head was supposed to be, there was a bloody pulp of mess. The men stared at the figure. Blood was still spurting from the stump of the patient's neck. Body matter—brains, skin and tissue—were blasted all around, including on the ceiling. It was gruesome.

The police expeditiously surveyed the damage. One stayed to render first aid to the nurse while the other ran back into the hall to yell and radio for help.

Though Donovan was hurt, once he saw what was left of Shelly, his thoughts immediately turned to Greg. With what had just happened here, Greg had to be in danger. He was lucky to have survived Shelly's attempt at the hotel. He might not be so lucky next time. Whoever this unknown adversary was, he had the resources to make things happen.

No matter what pain he was in, Donovan knew he had to get himself patched up promptly and get Greg into protection…he knew right where he was going to take him.

Chapter

(Fifty-3)

*T*he **Leader addressed** his inner circle with a somber but pleased disposition. Entering Phase Four greatly sped up the final portion of their mission; however, none of the Zhonghua Nine were regretting the end. This had lasted longer than any of them had imagined.

"It appears that the last stage of Dormant Curse is almost complete. The drones will soon be taken care of, our unmanageable agent in America has been disposed of, and our Navy is now in control of the Diaoyutai Islands. The next step is for all of us to get back to our normal lives in the most discreet fashion possible. I cannot be seen with any of you, and of course, you must stay separate from each other upon your leaving. I will be exiting the building first. One of the guards will come with me; he will give Zhonghua One a call on the conference room phone to let him know when I am in my car. At that point, you each need to leave approximately five minutes apart. Make sure you gather your belongings, including your phones, at the door. We don't need any evidence that you were here."

What no one but the leader and those in the military command knew was that a call from Zhonghua Three to the military about an hour earlier had started a completely different set of players and events in motion. Phase Four meant that the end of the Zhonghua mission had come, but in military circles, it also meant the final cover story and strategic positioning of China's forces would start to unfold.

Every good mission needs a good cover story. For Dormant Curse, there were a number of stories already in play. The Chinese President had already addressed the entire globe over CNT when he declared his intention to help find the perpetrators of the attacks on the US. This was but the beginning of one of the stories they were weaving in anticipation of the exposure of the means, though not the source, of the attacks. Another part of the story would involve the factory that assembled the affected chips, smartphones and systems. Yet another would incriminate Zhonghua Nine itself. The final piece of the puzzle would play out in Iran and Iraq. And all of these stories woven together were a cover for the true intentions of the Leader. His personal role in the mission was almost complete; he had only one final scene to play.

Slowly standing up and nodding to the guard on his left, he deliberately made his way toward the exit. The Leader's crippled body, tired from the long time spent in the close quarters with the Zhonghua Nine, moved slowly, which only created additional tension in the remaining eight as they anxiously sat quietly, waiting for him to make it to the door. Some of them were mentally pushing him along.

As the Leader gathered his belongings, the guard closed the inner door to the main conference room to ensure any bystanders or guests passing by wouldn't be able to see into the Polaris room itself. Guests to the piano bar on the 53rd floor of the Jin Mao Tower were the only concern. With the elevators in sight, the Leader seemed to catch a second wind and started to quicken his pace. Of course, he knew what would be coming down that elevator at any moment, and he also knew he didn't want to be there when it arrived.

The Leader hoped that his timing hadn't been thrown off with the succession of events in the past few minutes. As they waited for the elevator doors to open, the guard noticed that the Leader seemed to be anticipating someone or something.

In the Leader's mind, the only exposure he was concerned about was his own. The rest of the Zhonghua Nine would not be leaving anytime soon.

Chapter
(Fifty-4)

"Do you even really know the true purpose of these messages?" quizzed Joe in a harsh tone.

Joe was looking directly at Ron when he made this inquiry. He was ready to send out the final Facebook, Twitter, and Blather messages, and had decided he needed to ask this one question before the mission was finally over. He didn't figure he'd get a response, but he needed to try, just in case. After all, in the movies, people spilled their guts when the end of a mission—or life—was near.

"Joe, I figured one of you smart drones would finally ask the obvious question. We don't have time right now to get into it, but after we send the message, we'll have time to shut down, pack up, and we can chat about it. After all, it's not like we are ever going to ever see each other again," Ron responded.

His tone was so sincere, it caught Joe off-guard. In fact it caught everyone off-guard, including the other agents. Ron's subordinates thought maybe he was losing it, which raised their concerns about getting out of here without any incidents.

"You'll let me in on what you know?" Joe said, almost elated.

"Joe.... NO, not really! Do you think I'm an idiot? And if you answer that rhetorical question I'll put a hole in your fucking head and finish your putz job for you. Now, just get back to staring at your damn screen and get ready to press Enter on my command. After this is done, no one needs to know anything more except that you're not to discuss anything about this with anyone, ever. Just take your money and go. Walk out and don't look back. That's all the info you need."

The agents breathed a sigh of relief. He wasn't going nuts at all. Ron was still the nasty S.O.B. they knew.

As mean as he had been to Joe all along, Ron had taken a particular liking to him. He was one, if not the only one, in this group that had a mind of his own. It was a pity they wouldn't meet again—he would be a good guy to have on a future mission. If everything worked out, however, Ron wouldn't need any more missions to make ends meet. He was looking forward to getting back to his family and figuring out how to take the payoff money and disappear for good.

Snapping out of his thoughts and looking at the time, he realized they had but a minute to go.

Standing up briskly, Ron announced, "OK, show time. We have less than a minute. I'll start the count-off at ten seconds to go."

The drones and agents waited anxiously. Ron didn't believe in "accidents" and he wasn't going to be easily convinced the drones hadn't intentionally disobeyed if something went wrong at this point. You paid for mistakes with your life.

"Ten…nine…eight…seven…six…five…"

Donovan found Greg waiting in his own hospital room, talking with Michelle on his mobile. Greg heard the explosion in the hospital, though it had been a few floors away, and heard the fire alarm go off, though it was quickly squelched. He knew there was something going on, but had no idea that he would be somehow linked to it. For Michelle—with all of the events of the day she was witnessing through the news, Facebook and Blather, and then not hearing from Greg—she had begun to panic. Though she was afraid, when she finally heard from Greg she was livid that he hadn't called earlier. Once he explained what had transpired that night, she was in tears. She feared for Greg's life and felt powerless to help. Greg had been careful not to share everything. He suspected that the investigation was going to be locked down tight in just a matter of time.

"Greg. How are you?" Donovan said.

With one glance at Donovan's face and bandaged hand, he knew something was wrong.

"Michelle, just a minute, Honey…"

"Is that your wife?" Donovan asked.

"Well…yes, it is."

Inside, Greg panicked. He hadn't shared anything he shouldn't have, he thought. But maybe he had. Had he put more people in jeopardy by talking with Michelle about what happened today?

"Great!" Donovan exclaimed. "Tell her to get her bags packed and be ready to be picked up by FBI agents in the next fifteen minutes. She's coming to Huntsville."

"But she's—"

"No 'buts' on this. This isn't a vacation; this is protective custody. Just do it Greg, I'll explain later. And after you're done, turn off that phone completely. Don't ask why, just do it. I have an FBI-cleared phone you can use for the next few days."

Greg broke the news to Michelle.

Donovan could hear the sounds of elation from Michelle on the receiver from a few feet away. At least one part of the day would go off without a hitch.

Greg was feeling upbeat after his conversation. Looking at Donovan while saying his goodbyes to Michelle, however, told him that something was awry.

Donovan swallowed hard; he had received a call from the Huntsville police department just before reaching Greg's room.

"Now, here's the hardest part…" with no time to mince words, Donovan just let him have it, "Dennis is dead."

Greg felt like someone had knocked the breath out of him. Donovan didn't give Greg much time to process before continuing.

"The protective custody applies to you, too. We need to go. Now."

Chapter

(Fifty-5)

"Mr. President, I'm sorry to wake you, but we have new developments. This is rather urgent."

The President had gone to bed at ten. The stress of the day had been high, and he needed to rest. He had planned on getting up around three in the morning. Apparently that was wishful thinking.

"What time is it, Ned?" the President said. He was trying to be quiet so as not to disturb his wife, Marjorie, who was sleeping soundly next to him.

"It's ten-thirty. I know you haven't had any sleep and I apologize for disturbing you. However, I can't really discuss this anywhere but the Situation Room—I have some overhead images you must see. You're going to have to weigh in on this and fast."

Just a few members of the Security Council were in the Situation Room by the time the President arrived. The Secretary of State and the Secretary of Defense were already seated, poring over images from the overhead assets as they came in. They stood up when the President walked in, giving him the respect due the Commander in Chief. Their expressions were somber.

"I can tell from your faces this isn't good. I'm not going to wait for the others to arrive—start filling me in on what's happening. What do you see?" the President said.

"Mr. President," Robert started, "we have so many locations to monitor everyday...well, with all that's been happening in the East China Sea and Iraq, combined with—"

"What did we miss?"

"Gwadar."

"Gwadar? Look I can't stay on top of every hot spot, I'm not even sure I remember what that is—I know it's not a country."

The President was now fully awake.

"You're right. It's a city. A small one at that. But it is also a port in Pakistan."

"OK, so what does a small port in Pakistan have to do with our current national and global crises?"

"Well, if Henry were here, he could—"

"Robert, just get started and he can fill in the rest."

"Gwadar is not just any port. It's been in major development the past decade, mostly just the past few years. It's at the southwest end of Pakistan, about 250 miles from Afghanistan. The Soviets would have loved to use it during their war in the 80s since it's so close."

"Well, why haven't we used it, then?"

"It couldn't handle large ships, including Navy vessels. Well, back then it couldn't. Now it can. The Chinese developed it, pretty much at their own expense, making it into a sophisticated deep-water port. They've also improved the airport and its runways. Plus, they've extended some major roads up to Islamabad."

"OK, I get it. They've been very active. It's coming back to me..."

"The development benefits Pakistan and China and their trading partners. It's used mainly for commerce—getting gas and oil out of there from pipelines that come in from Turkey and the Arab Emirates. You know the Chinese have also been working on high speed rail lines and highways—kind of rebuilding the ancient Silk Road in the process."

"Yeah, so good history lesson, but what's up now?"

"What's up is that in the process of developing the port for large cargo ships, Gwadar now has Chinese military vessels anchored there."

"I'm assuming the Pakistanis allowed this? Why are they there?"

"These Chinese Navy ships were there protecting cargo ships from the Somali Pirates who've captured quite a few vessels in recent months. They were there in a protective role."

"Are they just refueling? Doing repairs?"

"Well, I'm afraid not. If you look at the images I'm pulling up here..."

"Are those tanks?"

"Yup. This was taken late yesterday in a regularly scheduled sweep over the area. Images from two days ago were apparently jammed."

"Jammed?"

"Optical jamming with lasers. They must know the ephemeris of the observing satellite well enough to point a laser at it when it was overhead. I'm not sure why we didn't pick that up before, but in any case, we hit the target again from a different angle. We were previously using this asset to maintain a spotlight on Iraq so with this redirection we didn't get a long dwell, nor did we do any additional analysis of these particular images until this evening. We're getting a live shot of the area again within the next half hour."

"What are tanks and military vehicles doing there?"

"We don't know. It looks like they're getting cooperation, or at least no resistance, in unloading. The Iranian border is only twenty miles away. My gut tells me that either Pakistan is getting help fighting the local ethnic factions there, or they're getting ready to invade Iran. That area of the border doesn't have any major defenses. In fact, most of it is a wildlife reserve."

"What ethnic factions?"

"There are two groups there that want an independent nation of their own. I can't remember their names, but they constantly cause Pakistan grief. And they've caused the Chinese misery, too, launching rockets every now and then into the Chinese engineers' dormitories and stuff like that, just to shake things up. They're somewhat...out of control."

Carl and Henry walked in on the tail end of the conversation took their seats.

Henry knowledgably chimed in, "Yeah, the two groups are the Baluch and the Sindhi. They've been thorns in Pakistan's side for quite a while. I can see where China might help out, considering all their investments in the region over the years. Particularly if Pakistan requested support."

"Hank, don't you get it?" the President demanded.

"Get what?"

"Today of all days. This is not a coincidence. We're standing down in the East China Sea and in the Persian Gulf. Iran has their troops engaged in Iraq. And now the Chinese land right on their border? I almost guarantee you that the next images we see have the Chinese crossing the border into Iran—which is pretty much defenseless now."

"That would be a pretty gutsy and coordinated move, especially considering Iran could unleash the same attack on China they did on us."

"But what have I said ten times today? *Iran didn't attack us.* China has to be behind it. This proves it."

"Mr. President, respectfully, it doesn't prove anything yet. If they're in Iran in the next satellite images, I'll budge on my opinion. Besides, why would Pakistan help with an invasion of Iran?"

"Why did they hide Bin-Laden from us for so many years? They sell out to the highest bidder, just like many other countries. They don't know China's true intent..."

Amanda finally spoke up. "Or maybe they stand to benefit as well. You know how utterly poor Pakistan is—they have no oil or gas reserves like Iran; they're in subsistence mode. What if the Chinese, who apparently need every drop of oil and every whiff of gas they can get, promised some of the reserves in return? I'm sure Pakistan is tired of being the neglected Islamic nation. And everyone is sick of Iran's nuclear threats and radicalism."

"OK, Amanda, let's go with that. Say they're cooperating with China. I hope I'm wrong on all this, but if they are, what other inroads are there into Iran that China could use?"

Robert responded to this one, having already done a lot of analysis on the battles in Afghanistan. "None directly, of course. But the high-speed rail lines they've built go right through Afghanistan into Iran—those could be used. But there's a gauge difference."

"Please explain."

"Iran uses a different size width for their tracks. They have to change over at the junction. It can take hours."

"Who designed the rail lines?"

"China and Germany," Henry offered.

"But whose workers were used?" the President asked.

"Mainly Chinese. They have the most experience. They've built out all of China and the surrounding countries—Myanmar, Vietnam, Bangladesh..."

"Could any of the Chinese engineers also be military?"

"Certainly. We do that all the time, too. That's always a good way of infiltrating," Henry said assuredly.

"Then they likely know all they need to stage an inside attack, don't they? Hank, we need to get imagery of the rails—full sweep. Look for anything suspicious."

"Mr. President, that's a long rail line, and it runs East-West. It will take a lot of passes of our assets to capture all of that."

"Well, hurry and get on it then. And let's ask the hard question: What do we do if we see an invasion in the works? We've already pulled our forces back from the Gulf, and if China is really behind the US attacks, there's little we can do to stop progress."

"We still have options, Mr. President."

The President could tell from the serious look on Robert's face that the option he was going to present was one that the President thought he would never have to face.

Robert continued regardless: "We have subs within striking distance of Shanghai and Tehran."

"Secretary Goodwin, you are nuts. That is *not* an option," stated the President.

Robert judged the nuclear option viable, considering how things were escalating out of control. Before he could respond, however, the screen behind them went from a static image to a real-time video of the port.

The President was incredulous. "Where are the tanks? Where are the damn tanks?"

"They're on the move, Mr. President, or stored in hiding somewhere. We're programmed to scan the road, highway N-10 out of Gwadar, next. If we don't see them, we have a change detection pass scheduled with other assets."

The President shot a confused look over to Henry.

"I'm sorry…with our radar-based assets, like JSTARS and Predator, we can compare two scans of the area back-to-back. By doing some sophisticated analysis, we can see anything that's changed. In a desert environment it works really well—there's no change from blowing leaves, grass or animals. We can literally see tire tracks and footprints of who's gone where. If they've hidden the tanks, we'll see right where they went."

The images of the highway out of Gwadar started to appear. Everyone held their breath waiting to see what was next.

The President was wondering how they could have all of this information, but not much analysis or real intelligence to go with it. I hope to God, he thought to himself, that we don't find them in Iran.

Chapter

(Fifty-6)

*"F*our...three...two...one...now!" Ron exclaimed. He let a pregnant pause elapse before he continued. "Now we wait for a few minutes and then shut this all down. In fact, my agents here and I will shut things down for you. I have a mess to clean up anyway. You all take the next five years off..."

Outside in the front lobby, they heard a muffled scream through the insulated door.

What in the world? Ron thought. There was now pounding on the door. No sooner had Ron opened it than the woman monitoring the front desk ran inside.

"What the hell is going on!?" she exclaimed, her face flushed. She seemed out-of-breath. "Half the phones stored out there just exploded. Some are on fire!"

It took Ron a few seconds to process what she was saying and correlate it to the message that had just been sent out.

Could the messages have triggered the phones somehow?

Neither the agents nor the drones had been privy to the intent and impact of the messages they were sending, however, they had all seen the reports of the attack on Atlanta earlier in the day. Plus, when Ron was monitoring the accounts to keep the drones honest, he had seen some Blather updates on an attack in Dallas, not long after the first round of messages went out.

Could we be under attack? he thought. He wasn't going to take any chances.

"Everyone out! Now!" Ron shouted.

Unfortunately, Zhonghua had thought of almost everything, including how to shut down Dormant Curse without any trace. Taking care of the drones was one of the last steps in that plan. In fact, Phase Four was just that.

Above the overhead duct work, outside the workroom, and unbeknownst to Ron, agents higher up the chain had planted phones similar to the one that had taken off Shelly's head. The major difference was that these phones were strapped to a large block of Semtex and directly wired into the building's power. Each block was enough to take out a house.

The phones' charging circuits activated on the same Phase Four command, but needed time to build up enough charge to light off the foil initiator, priming the explosive.

Ron held open the spring-loaded door for the agents and drones. Though he had proven himself ruthless when he had to be, his natural instinct to protect kicked in.

When it was obvious that Pamela wasn't processing Ron's orders clearly or swiftly, Joe grabbed her by the arm and pulled her along. As he brought her up to her feet, she looked at Joe with confusion and gratitude. The human touch alone, after a day of fear and apprehension, brought her comfort.

The corner of the room opposite Joe and Pamela was the first to light off. The boom and flash from the explosion were simultaneous. The impact knocked them both to the ground as the searing heat hit their faces. Pamela was knocked unconscious immediately.

The explosion had taken out everyone near that side of the room—directly adjacent to the exit. Ron didn't even know what hit him. Outside the building, the blast blew out the front windows and started car alarms over a block away. The fireball could be seen for a mile as it billowed out the front and top of the building. It was only Joe and Pamela's delay that had kept them alive.

Joe immediately crawled under the table where their workstations had been only seconds before. The monitors had been blasted off the table and were now lying on the floor behind it. He dragged Pamela's limp body next to him as he tried to comprehend what had just happened and formulate a plan to get out.

The sprinkler system kicked on and was trying its best to knock down the flames from the explosion.

The force of the next blast came from above the utility room closet. It was much more intense, and broke into pieces the table that Joe and Pamela were under. The piece of table pressing on Joe's face and chest was on fire. He could feel its warmth. The sprinkler system's main feed into the overhead units had been fractured, and the water had stopped spraying.

As Joe lay there, straining to remain conscious, Ron's voice came echoing back to him from earlier in the day: *You made a deal with the devil and you all knew it.*

The heat from the fire sprung by the second blast was starting to sear his exposed arm and leg. The pain was becoming unbearable.

"NOOO!!" Joe shouted as he felt his body beginning to burn.

The blasts from the third and fourth phone-triggered bombs took place almost simultaneously, mercifully slamming the remains of the table against Joe and Pamela's heads. The impact drove shards of fractured skull bone through their brains, ending their misery.

The fires caused by the remaining bombs devoured their prey unabated. There were no sprinklers to tame their destruction, nor witnesses to testify their intent. Simultaneously, fires were springing up all over Hayward—exactly as Zhonghua had programmed. The devastation of the drone's warehouse space would likely be attributed to the general attack—a chemical or gas explosion caused by a smartphone short. In any case, its destruction would go unnoticed amid the noise of the night.

Chapter
(Fifty-7)

*T*he **Zhonghua Nine cult** had been waiting for the call from their Leader for about fifteen minutes. While his running late wasn't completely out of the realm of possibility, the anticipation of the end of the mission made the minutes tick by painfully slow.

The Leader made it down to the ground floor without incident or unnecessary attention. In fact, since it was eleven in the morning, he and his assistant blended in quite well with the other businessmen, hotel guests and tourists in the crowd at the entrance. There was a long line of guests waiting for taxis…but when the Leader arrived, the valet already had a black Mercedes limo waiting for him. Off in the distance, they could see the caravan of local SWAT vehicles making their way through the traffic toward the hotel's circle-drive. The Leader's anxiety faded as he realized the final stage of Dormant Curse was almost complete.

Greg and Donovan were speeding from the hospital in a small caravan of government vehicles. Things had been happening so fast that it was difficult for Greg to keep up mentally.

The hospital proved a dangerous place—it was better to get Greg somewhere secure, and fast.

Donovan looked terrible, and it was clear that he felt awful as well. If it weren't for his adrenaline rush, he probably would have been in a world of hurt. Donovan was still wired, though, and constantly scanned each direction and in his mirror for anything out of the ordinary.

Had Greg witnessed the scene in Shelly's room just a short while earlier, he would have feared for his life. But Donovan had decided not to share those details with him for the time being; he needed Greg's mind focused on the attacks—and their solution. Dennis' death was going to be difficult enough to process.

His thoughts still swirling, Greg ventured to ask the obvious question.

"Where are we going?"

"Redstone. Redstone Arsenal. We'll be there in about twenty minutes—well, fifteen with the speed I'm gonna drive."

Donovan's voice sounded like he just downed a triple-espresso—his speech would have been unintelligible if Greg hadn't been listening closely to every word. Greg was searching his memory to try to recall what Redstone Arsenal was. He remembered seeing some signs for it on the way from the airport, but that was about it.

"You mean...uh...we're going to go get some ammunition?" Greg asked somewhat sheepishly, figuring that he was missing something.

Donovan chuckled, perhaps for the first time that day. "Redstone is actually an army base. They do research, development, training...all sorts of stuff. The important thing is that it's protected and they have a SCIF," Donovan explained.

"Great...what's a SCIF?"

"It's a secure facility for storing and using sensitive compartmentalized information—deep black stuff—way above your clearance, if you even have one. You gotta have a lie detector test just to step foot in the door, and then it's all 'need-to-know.' However, you are on your way to brief folks in DC—even without a clearance, your stuff is likely Top Secret, SCI, so we need a secure video link. They have it."

"I'm wha—?"

"Sorry to spring this on you—too much going on. My superiors are getting through to the big chiefs on all ends so you can share everything directly. We're just waiting on word from the chain of command."

"Big chiefs?"

Donovan's voice sped up again as he answered, voicing the seriousness and intensity of the circumstances. "We're talking about networking you directly into the NSA. Likely the order will come from the Director of Intelligence, through the DOD, and to the four-star here, General Wood." He paused for effect, but couldn't bear to take too long of a break since he was so excited about all of it.

Greg wasn't sure how to respond; he just breathed deeply as he started to think about what he was going to say in that environment.

Donovan continued, "Well, I know it's hard to believe, but from the information you've uncovered, Dennis' *likely* murder, attempt on your life, and some stuff that went down in the hospital, everyone is convinced that what's inside your head right now is the real deal."

Greg tried to suppress the sorrow he felt in hearing the reminder of Dennis' death. He knew he needed to somehow be strong and focus on what was to happen next.

"OK…slow down…lots of questions here…NSA? I can tell you're serious, but that's overwhelming," Greg said.

"Believe it. It's gonna happen. If not a direct feed, then we're gonna tape it somehow and pipe it in shortly thereafter. We'll probably go live so you can answer questions, though. You can't question a recording."

"Questions? Am I in trouble?"

"Trouble?" Donovan laughed again. "No, at least not with the US Government. If you can solve this mess, you're likely gonna be a hero, though a SCI-level, classified hero that no one gets to know about. That's how these things go, man. Welcome to my world."

"OK, but what was that about the attempts on my life? You said attempts. Plural. I only know about the one that nailed my shoulder."

Donovan merged onto Memorial Parkway, being careful to remain in the middle of the caravan. As he considered what he should actually share with Greg, his cadence slowed considerably. "Greg, let's just say that the guy who took your room at the hotel? The businessman who bumped you back down to the consumer floor?"

"Yeah, how did you know about that?"

Donovan paused for a moment as the order came in over headset from the lead car to get into zone formation. One Suburban stayed ahead of Donovan and one behind as he merged over to the far left lane. Another of the four pulled up next to Donovan in the center lane of the highway, leaving the right lane open for cars that needed to get out of the way. They were somewhat protected on the left side by the concrete barrier between them and the north-bound lanes.

Fortunately, this late in the evening, there were few cars out, and they pulled over nicely as the convoy accelerated past.

Only then did Donovan continue. "Well, one of the hotel guests couldn't find his colleague after the fire…kind of like when we couldn't find Dennis. He was freaking out, worried that his buddy was the guy caught in the blaze—"

The radio crackled, "Linear formation." The road squeezed back to just two lanes again at the Drake exit, so the flanking Suburban now pulled in front of Donovan as the lead car sped up to make room for him.

Donovan's voice trailed off as his eyes suddenly caught sight of a black Chevy Camaro that had sprung to life on the shoulder. Its tires kicked up gravel and burned rubber as its lights came on. The vehicle fishtailed as it blasted onto the highway. Within a few seconds it was in the left lane and gaining on the caravan of Suburbans.

Donovan's eyes were glancing from his rearview mirror to his side-view mirror to the road in front of him, determining whether he should be taking any evasive action. Once it was clear the Camaro wasn't about to slow down, Donovan communicated with his team on his headset: "Ted, the Camaro behind you…take it out! Ken, I'm pulling up to second position, pull over and fall back!"

Whether the tail car's driver wasn't paying attention or had just delayed taking action, it was a fatal mistake. Before he could swerve, slow down to block, or say his prayers, a flash from the Camaro launched a Rocket Powered Grenade from under the front of the car. An RPG-32—developed by the Russians, manufactured in Mexico and smuggled across the border—was designed to take out tanks and infantry. A Suburban was no match for its firepower. The explosion blasted the vehicle high into the air as it tumbled end over end in space. As it hit the pavement, its momentum continued spinning the vehicle horizontally in a flaming barrel-roll, launching glass and metal as it traversed across the access road.

Donovan could see the fireball and flaming trajectory of the vehicle before it came to rest. There was no time to render aid or call anything in. In his vehicle, he had the answer to solving the ongoing attacks against the US…and he had to protect Greg at all costs.

"Ken, you have to stop him!" Donovan yelled through his headset as he and the lead car accelerated.

The lead car swerved toward the exit to Airport Road.

"Shit!" Donovan yelled. Agent Dickerson wasn't someone that Donovan trusted already—neither his judgment, nor his loyalty.

He's bailing out on me, Donovan thought.

"What the hell are you doing, Dickerson?"

There was no answer on the other end. He could see that Dickerson had shut off his lights and was speeding down the access road far in front of him.

I've got to outrun this guy, Donovan thought desperately as he cut his own lights—emergency, headlights, and tail lights. He would have to maneuver around cars as best he could without warning them with visual indicators. Instead, he flipped on his siren and started using his horn to alert them.

The Camaro, which slowed down and had fallen back to avoid being hit by any shrapnel, accelerated again as it started up the next overpass.

Ken, the driver of the, now, tail Suburban, knew the seriousness of this mission, his role, and what was at stake. He acted quickly and decisively. Hitting his brakes hard and sliding his heavy Suburban sideways across the lanes of the highway, he shut off his lights and jumped out the driver's side door with his automatic already out of its holster. In the Suburban's position on the down-side of the overpass, he had nearly blocked off the available three lanes. There wasn't enough room for the Camaro to pass him on the left side of the highway with the concrete barrier in place, and the half-width shoulder would make it difficult to go around him at high speed on the right. There was still a five-foot drop down to the access road, making it impossible for a sports car to survive a jump to the street below, even if it did somehow clear the concrete guardrail.

The agent positioned himself behind the front end of the vehicle, with his gun aimed where he expected the Camaro to come over the hill. He didn't have to wait long. The glow of the Camaro lights intensified and the engine roar grew louder and angrier as it approached on the other side of the overpass.

The driver of the Camaro wasn't prepared for what he saw just over the crest. He was expecting the flashing lights of the convoy. Instead he barely saw the glint of red and yellow reflectors from the front and rear side-ends of the black

Suburban. When he finally registered what he was looking at, it kicked in that he might not be able to stop in time. With the distance closing fast, the driver launched another RPG in hopes of blasting the Suburban out of his path.

The flare from the rocket gave Ken just enough warning to dive and roll for cover. At two hundred feet out, it should have been impossible to miss the Suburban, but the drop in height to where the vehicle was parked was something the Camaro's driver hadn't counted on in his haste. Had he waited only another second or two, he would have nailed the beast squarely in the side. However, as the target was ten feet below his own car, the rockets skimmed right over the top, continuing on for some distance before hitting the highway and detonating.

Donovan saw the explosion in his mirror, which only furthered his determination to outrun the assassin.

The driver of the Camaro tried his best to aim his car toward the narrow gap between the concrete rail and the back end of the Suburban while punching the pedal to the floor. The bullets hitting his car made the challenge that much more difficult. Drifting almost at a forty-five degree angle, he shot the gap, clipping the Suburban in the process. The impact caused the Camaro to fishtail back to the right and smash against the guardrail—but the driver made it through. Again, testing the limits of the power of his machine, he blasted down the exit lane and back onto the highway, sitting low in his seat to avoid being struck by the continued shots from the FBI agent firing from behind. Bullets struck the Camaro, but no vital parts of the car or driver were hit. Within seconds he was back up to speed and continuing the pursuit of his target.

Once clear of the attempted roadblock, the driver caught the shadow of one of the Suburbans in the illumination of the street lights over the highway—he had thought for a moment they might have exited. He accelerated, pushing the car to red-line in every gear as he powered forward.

Now almost out of reach of Donovan's short-range headset radio, Ken attempted to contact Donovan to let him know he had been unsuccessful in stopping the attacker.

"hissss…Camaro…ssss…unsucc..ful…on…hisss" came the distorted message.

"SHIT!" Donovan yelled.

Donovan saw the Camaro gaining on them. He hoped to come up with some plan before it got close. Catching a view of Greg in the backseat, he saw that his eyes were closed.

Is he so afraid he can't even look? Donovan wondered.

With no tire spikes to throw out and no second agent in his vehicle to fire defensive shots, all Donovan could hope for was that the overpass and curve coming up would keep him out of a line-of-sight shot.

"Dickerson, where the hell are you?" Donovan shouted into his headset.

The Camaro continued to gain ground. The Suburban, even at its top speed, was no match for the sports car.

"Dickerson! Our package has the answers to shutting down the attacks on the US…his life is more valuable than yours and mine together! Where the hell are you?" Donovan said into his headset, still trying to reach the lead car.

As Donovan came down the hill over Airport Road there was one final small curve before a half-mile straight stretch. The curve might be the last barrier he had before the Camaro was able to line up on them and fire off another RPG. The exit for Golf Road was coming up…for a moment Donovan considered taking it, but figured his best chance was still to try to beat the Camaro to the guard gate at Redstone.

Hitting the last straightaway before his exit, Donovan pushed the Suburban to its maximum speed and flipped his headlights, siren and emergency lights back on. The Camaro had spotted him; it was really no use trying to hide anymore. At 100mph, he passed other cars like they were standing still. He figured it would be about 50 seconds before he got to the Martin Road exit.

Still the Camaro continued to gain ground. The driver was hitting nearly 140mph now as he, too, came down the overpass at Airport Road. There was less than a quarter mile between them now—the killer would be within the 600-foot range of the RPG in about 30 seconds.

Time and speed were working against Donovan, and he knew it.

"Greg…almost there," Donovan said, as much to Greg as himself. "Hang in there."

The Camaro accelerated to over 150mph.

On the two-lane highway, a third lane created by the merging onramp also served as the exit lane for Martin Road. As it opened up, Donovan pulled into it and out of a direct line-of-fire. It was only seconds to an eminent launch of an RPG. If he could just make it to the beginning of the overpass a few hundred feet ahead, he knew he'd have a vertical obstacle to keep an RPG from hitting its mark.

As the Camaro started to move into the same exit lane as Donovan, a large black shadow moved directly into its path—Dickerson's unlit Suburban.

The Camaro hit a glancing blow. At its current speed, it was teetering on the edge of aerodynamic stability. With a little help from the front end of the SUV, along with its enormous kinetic energy, the car launched sky high, where it rolled slightly to its left as it flew through the air. Dickerson's Suburban might as well have been hit by a bomb—spinning around, off the highway, and back onto the access road where it came to rest facing traffic.

All Donovan saw were the lights of the Camaro disappear, the sparks of the crash, and the Camaro flying. When the car landed on its nose, the remaining RPGs detonated along with it, leaving a fireball as a clear signal the race was over.

Donovan's headset crackled with the word from Dickerson that he was OK and to continue to Redstone with the package.

I completely misjudged him, Donovan thought. Thank God I was wrong.

The danger now was passed, but with fellow agents dead and injured, Donovan let out an angry yell of frustration.

"ARRRGH!" he shouted, hitting the steering wheel.

All was quiet for a moment.

"Donovan, I'm sorry," Greg said.

"What were you doing with your eyes closed back there anyway? Are you OK?"

"Oh, yeah…I was praying. For protection for us, wisdom for you and safety for Michelle," Greg said.

Donovan let out a long sigh and shook his head. That wasn't a response he was expecting. God seemed pretty far removed tonight.

"Well, something worked. We were lucky to survive that."

Donovan fell silent. Greg knew not to speak, as Donovan attempted to focus on their next steps.

"Once you're situated, I'll call for a helicopter to bring your wife directly to the base from the airport. These attacks on us have got to be coordinated. We can't have your wife's safety in doubt—too easy to blackmail you."

"Is bringing her here is the right thing to do?"

"Greg, she's already on her way. No second guessing. She'll be safe."

"OK. After what we just went through—I totally trust you. I'll rest easier knowing she's alright," Greg said.

"There's not gonna be any rest tonight."

Chapter
(Fifty-8)

"So, Robert, I'm sorry to be right on this one, but there are your tanks."

The President noted the image of the tanks traversing toward the border from southern Pakistan into Iran.

"You're right. I stand corrected," Robert said slowly in agreement. "I never would have thought the Chinese would launch an invasion into Iran. I can't believe we haven't heard any scuttlebutt prior to this from our sources over there. It looks like they have one brigade ready to cross into southern Iran along a relatively smooth highway, and another going cross-country. I hope the Iranian troops at the border crossing see the Chinese from a distance and signal it to the military. They'll need to pull their troops back from Iraq to protect their border. There's no way they can cover two fronts at once. I'm guessing that to make matters worse, China has a sub nearby, too, ready to launch missiles if things get dicey."

"Just great. Could they have planned this any better? China invades Iran on the same day that Iran has already invaded Iraq? This is no coincidence," declared the President. "The only question is, what do we do now? If Iran really attacked us today, they could nail us again. On the other hand, if it was really China behind it all...we would still get hit with a similar Atlanta attack if we interfere, right? In any case, we have to stay away from Iran until we block the attack method."

The President was making a statement as well as posing a question. Fortunately, the experts in the Situation Room were smart enough to think about their answers a while and not give an off-the-cuff remark. This was a complex situation, and the answer to it would be complex as well.

Carl spoke first. "Mr. President, I agree. We can't risk provoking another attack."

"Well, if you all had found the cause and solution to the attacks, maybe we'd have something to work with," the President said. "And, Robert, before you suggest nuclear yet again—"

"Mr. President, actually, I don't believe we have a nuclear option at this point," said the Defense Secretary.

The President raised his eyebrows. Robert Goodwin always seemed a little trigger happy, so this was out of character.

Robert continued. "With this evidence…your supposition has to be right. Iran isn't the perpetrator of the attacks—it's likely China. And if we were to attack China, just where would we attack? Gwadar? The invading troops? Bejing? Our best attack on the Chinese invading Iran would be to launch air assaults. But we can't risk that, can we? I'm siding with Carl on this one. I don't know there's much we can do except open a dialogue with China."

"Dialogue? I don't have any bargaining chips!" the President exclaimed.

"Well, of course you do! There's the United Nations, economic sanctions…" Amanda added.

"That can take days or weeks to enact, and half the countries wouldn't even sanction China anyway. The nations on the Security Council do too much business with them." said Benevidez.

"What can we do to stop this *now*?" said the President, pounding his fist on the table and continuing to raise his voice.

The room fell silent.

Henry finally spoke up. "Mr. President, we do have a potential cause and, once we understand it, I'm sure we'll have a solution as well. I didn't want to bring it up until we debriefed the engineer who discovered the means, but given the circumstances, I felt I should at least mention that we have something in the works."

Carl reacted. "Henry, you're supposed to confer with us. Why wasn't I told?"

"Hey, I wasn't trying to hide anything. We just got a call an hour or so ago, requesting permission to get the guy into a SCIF down at Redstone to talk to our experts up here."

"Redstone, that's my facility, Henry. Why wasn't I told?" Robert joined in.

"Robert, there wasn't time, and technically, the Intelligence Community owns that SCIF. We needed to get him to a secure site as there have been attempts on his life today. His partner's already been assassinated."

"What? Why haven't we been told, damn it?" said Robert.

"Well, I'm telling you now! The guy is NTSB, not intelligence or military. It's a fluke he's discovered what he did, so cut me a break on this. We have extraordinary circumstances going on, and very little time to react. We've been doing this in real-time, OK? I haven't been trying to hide anything!"

Benevidez weighed in: "Why not just pipe him into all the agencies and the Situation Room at one time? If time is as urgent as you say, and I agree that it is, we all want to hear, digest, plan, and respond as quickly as possible. I say broadcast him here. Does the SCIF have video?"

"It sure does. That's a top facility we have down there," Robert responded.

The President decided for everyone. "OK, it's my call, pull up every agency that can weigh in. Call your top guys and get them to the closest SCIF they can get access to."

"But, Mr. President, what if he's wrong and we waste everyone's time?" asked Amanda.

"Wrong? More than one assassination attempt? Dead partner? Why would anyone want NTSB agents dead? If this guy's not onto something, he's just got really bad luck. Before you make your calls, I need to know—did you catch the assassin?"

Henry was quiet for a second. "She's dead."

He wasn't about to mention that they had her in their possession when her head blew up during questioning. He would let the Attorney General answer that one…after all, the FBI was *his* department. The Attorney General was already busy trying to contain the insanity at home. He had elected not to attend the National Security Council meeting that evening, as was his prerogative.

"This just gets crazier all the time," the President said, shaking his head. "Let's all hope to God that this engineer is right. By the way, what's he doing in Alabama?"

"Well, if you want to make things even stranger…you remember that 'agent' you called out this morning when he was surreptitiously taped stating this was a terrorist attack?"

"It's *him*?"

"No, that guy is dead. It's his partner. A kid…a recent college grad."

"Oh Lord, did we—"

"Likely CNT did, Mr. President, by broadcasting the clip. That's not the first blood that CNT's had on its hands and it won't be the last. After all, 'the public has the right to know,'" he said sarcastically.

"Hank, we'll have to discuss why you didn't get us this information right away some other time. But for now, check on that kid and make sure he's safe. And get him piped in to the secure system as soon as possible."

Henry nodded and hurriedly walked out the room to make his calls.

Chapter
(Fifty-9)

*T*he **Chinese Military Police** broke down the door to the Polaris room. The Zhonghua Nine had been expecting a call from their Leader. They had no expectation that the military would be appearing, frisking them for weapons, and forcing them to sit while judgments were pronounced.

The lieutenant of the military squad had his orders. He was told this cult was a danger to China—they were a revolutionary group bent on disrupting the establishment. The cult was planning a revolution, inciting the working class to protest their poor working conditions and take matters into their own hands, not unlike workers in Egypt and Libya. The military knew the dangers of worker riots and rebellions. The current economic climate, disparity in living conditions and pay in rural and urban China made this a real possibility.

He had all the details needed. There would be eight cult members and one guard in the Polaris room, and they were dangerous. His superiors had already passed judgment on the cult and provided him with a statement to read prior to their punishment.

The lieutenant had his team force each cult member into his seat and tied their hands behind their backs with cable ties. He, too, had heard rumors of the great Zhonghua Nine cult, and was shocked to find out they truly existed. He was disheartened to hear they were conspirators, not heroes.

He then read the prepared statement.

"Zhonghua Nine, you have been convicted by the Communist Party of crimes against the state: inciting riots, conspiracy to overthrow the government and plots to assassinate the President."

One at a time, the lieutenant pushed each Zhonghua Nine member forward and fired one shot through the skull and into the conference room table.

"The Leader! He has betrayed us!" Zhonghua Four yelled.

The same thought ran through each of the cult member's minds.

As each member echoed the same protests, the same reasoning, the same loyalty to the state, the lieutenant knew there was something wrong. These men were not who he was told they were. He wanted to throw up, run out, and erase this memory of the injustice he was sure he was perpetrating. But he knew that if he faltered in his mission, his second in command was ready to step in, finish the job, and finish him off as well. The sweat poured off his brow as he continued the executions.

"SHUT UP!" he howled to the remaining members, but to no avail.

His men felt the same trepidation, the same concern, but were too fearful to say anything. They looked at the squad leader closely, hoping that he might just realize his error and stop the killing, but knowing that if he were to pause, even for a moment, they would have to finish the job for him. Once the killing started, it could not be stopped.

The lieutenant could not get around to each cult member fast enough to quell the protests that would forever echo in his mind. Grab, push, place weapon, fire…as quickly as he could.

It took only a few minutes to dispose of the Zhonghua Nine, but it felt like an eternity for the cult members and the squad leader alike. Once it was finally over, he took a big step back. He looked at his firearm, and the blood splattered all over his sleeve and weapon, and closed his eyes. This would have been a difficult mission for even the most hardened mercenary. But a mercenary could leave at this stage; they still had work to do—a mission to accomplish.

Opening his eyes and making a final push to finish his orders, he yelled at his squad. "Take their IDs, and take photos!" he barked.

These were their orders. It seemed to the lieutenant that if the government knew so much about the group, they would know who its members were. But he had followed orders so far, and there was no reason to question or deviate now. The pictures were required immediately, and he didn't want to have to explain any delays.

Chapter

(Six-tee)

Bahram was up early. He had been up most of the night, thinking about what might be at hand. Not wanting to alert his family to his concerns, he kept his thoughts to himself. Bahram hoped what he had seen and heard this week was misinterpretation, and tried fervently to put it out of his mind.

The main room in their small apartment converted from dining to bedroom by simply rolling up the dining cloth and spreading out their mattress—the family all slept in the same room. They had no furniture to speak of, but neither did anyone else in their social sphere. The smallness of the space made it hard to disguise his mood.

His wife, Farah, sensing his unusual quietness, woke up early with Bahram to help make his breakfast.

"Bahram, have I displeased you?" she asked.

"Oh, no, not at all."

"Then why so quiet?"

Bahram weighed his response carefully. "I didn't know it showed…there's much on my mind."

"Why did you come home so early last night? Is your car OK?"

"Yes, it's fine. I got paid very well for my ride and decided to take the rest of the night off."

"That's rather strange, but I won't complain. I loved having you home."

"Well, it may not happen again soon, the customer was extremely generous."

"If the Lord wills, may you meet as generous of customers today!"

Bahram just smiled at his lovely wife. As his cousin, their families were close. Though things could be better financially, he was happy with his life.

"Do you hear those sirens?" Farah asked.

"You know my hearing isn't nearly as good as yours. You hear sirens?"

"Yes, police, ambulance."

Bahram cupped his hand behind his ear. "Yes, I think so."

"Bahram, I hear many. I hear car horns as well. Something is happening…let's go outside and see."

Bahram felt that same sinking feeling in his stomach again. Maybe this was unrelated to his unusual rides this week. He hoped against hope that it was.

Opening the door…the cacophony of sirens, horns and yelling could be heard.

"You stay here with the children and lock the door; I am going to see what is going on!" Bahram said, as he shut the door firmly behind him.

"Ali. Ali! Wake up!"

"Wha—?"

"Look, in the distance, is that a dust storm? I think I hear tanks!"

Ali looked out across the desert—the morning sun highlighted the plume of dust rising from the ground.

"That's too much dust to be tanks. No one but tourists come through here anyway."

"No, I hear something…give me your binoculars…"

Ali grabbed his binoculars from his stand and thrust them at Hassan, rolling his eyes. Hassan peered through intently.

"Yes, it's tanks!!"

"Tanks? Give me those. They'll never believe us. Why would anyone try to cross in broad daylight?!"

A sense of panic rose in Ali's chest. Gabd-Kumb border crossing wasn't supposed to be a risky outpost. There were no ongoing disputes with Pakistan. Their main job was to prevent smuggling. They weren't prepared for this.

"You're right. There are a lot of them! Call command and tell them to hurry with reserves, we can't stop this many!"

Ali tried to identify the specific type of armored vehicles approaching. Only the ones in front were readily visible, as dust was obscuring those behind.

"Hassan, they are not Pakistani. It looks like their tanks, but they have red stars on the front. Is that Russia?"

There was desperation in Hassan's voice as hung up his phone, "There's no response...nothing. What do we do?"

"There are tens, maybe hundreds of vehicles...lots of tanks. We are no match for them, there's just a few of us here."

As incredible as it seemed, this was their reality. Hassan tried to push his fear down and think logically.

"I say we stay alive so we can finally get through and alert command. If we're dead, who will tell them? They will be on their way to Tehran and no one will know!"

"You're right. You are so brilliant. I'll alert the others of what's coming. We need to take our radios and phones and hide. Maybe they will just pass."

Hassan was pleased that his companion was in agreement.

"They are maybe ten minutes away, let's hurry!"

The Iranian soldier's calls to military command would go unanswered. There would be no reinforcements.

In the heart of Iran, the primary target for Chinese troops was the capitol city of Tehran. On high-speed trains passing through the border checkpoints from Afghanistan, it was standard practice for customs agent to look the other way on cargo inspection...for the right incentives. Well-placed bribes ensured hidden payloads of Chinese weapons, armored vehicles, and soldiers would get through to Tehran—this would be the first notice of an invasion. Tanks rolling in from the South would follow shortly, blockading Tehran's major points of entry.

The Zhonghua Nine Leader's command had been delivered precisely on schedule. Phase Four was progressing just as he planned.

Chapter
(Sixty-1)

Once they had arrived at the US Army Materiel Command Building, Agent Donovan and Greg were escorted, under guard, to the SCIF deep within.

Now feeling safe, Greg initially had breathed a sigh of relief—however, once at the entrance to the facility, his apprehension spiked. The SCIF had only one way in or out, and its scowling, colossal guard was formidable. Greg showed his driver's license and signed his name, but no company identification was allowed. They only wanted a record of who he was; anything else was too much information.

One-at-a time, they were buzzed through the "man-trap" system, which prevented "piggy-back" entry. The second door could not be opened until the first was latched shut.

Inside the SCIF, the atmosphere was entirely different. Soft music played in the background, and any brief conversations in the hallway were hushed. As they walked, Greg observed private rooms, each with a card reader and cipher lock—in the doors was a small slot of a view window that could be opened only from the inside. Greg thought the whole place was a bit…spooky.

Once they reached the video-conference room, their escort swiped his badge and pressed the appropriate code into the scrambled keypad to allow them entry. The room was well-appointed, not at all like the tomb Greg expected.

"Please," said their escort, "have a seat. We'll get started soon. Mr. Cannon, I understand you may have information you want to present on your laptop?"

"Yes, I do. Will it be possible for me to hook it up…Mister…?"

"My name is not important. Better that you don't know it. You can call me Smith if you need to get my attention," the escort responded.

It was now clear to Greg that the escort had hidden his badge inside his shirt after swiping it at the door to disguise his name. Likely not a standard move, but

one to keep Greg from knowing too much, given he didn't have a clearance or
need-to-know.

"I'll get one of our techs in here to get you set up. Donovan, you have
clearance to be in the facility, even if you don't have the right compartments, so
you're his escort now. He touches anything and it's your neck, got it?"

Donovan nodded in response and Smith exited the room.

"Greg. Buddy," Donovan began once they were alone. "I know this has been
a lot to deal with today. The most important thing right now is to focus. In this
meeting, don't get bogged down in the details; keep it simple. Remember, these
are smart guys—they'll get it, and what they don't get, they'll ask about. Most
importantly, if you think there's something that will absolutely stop the attacks,
even if it seems like overkill, ask for it. These guys can probably make it happen.
Don't softball it," Donovan said.

Greg nodded his understanding. Still, Donovan could tell he was distracted.
Greg looked at Donovan straight in the eyes and asked, "So what about the
attempts on my life? You didn't finish…"

"You're right," Donovan pensively responded. "The businessman who took
your room…he was shot twice in the head. Those shots were meant for you."

Greg was speechless, but his shock registered on his face.

"And the agent who tried to kill you? Her head was blown off in her room at
the hospital while I was standing right next to her. That's how I got injured and
that's why I ran to get you out of there and ordered an armed escort for your
wife. Greg, whatever you know, you have to believe it's the truth…"

Just then, the door to the conference room opened and Smith came through
with his technician in tow.

"Well, boys, things just got more interesting…"

Smith paused for effect. Agent Donovan and Greg just looked at him with a
confused look. Greg wasn't sure how things could get anymore "interesting"
today. He just wanted the nightmare to hurry up and be over with.

"I've been told our conference is going to involve NSA. And you're not
gonna believe this, but even at this time of night, we're patching in the White
House Situation Room," Smith said almost gleefully.

Greg could almost feel his body floating as his mind reeled. This was getting to be too much.

"Cannon, I know this is all new and overwhelming. It's gonna be OK, buddy. We have your back." Smith had decided to lighten up with the cloak-and-dagger shtick since it was clear he had somewhat of a celebrity there in the room. "My tech will get your computer set up and we'll have a separate screen for anything you want to put up there. Hey, do you need anything to drink? Need a snack?" Smith offered congenially.

Greg nodded, "Sure, I could use some water, thanks." He appreciated Smith's sudden change in demeanor. Maybe he could get through this after all.

Chapter
(Sixty-2)

"So, Carl, we've had three attacks so far, that we know of, right?" the President asked.

"Yes, Mr. President. The last attack was on Hayward, California, done without any notice or provocation. It was at approximately nine o'clock Eastern time. There was nothing we could do to prepare the area. It was small by comparison to Dallas. Early reports show that entire warehouses have been leveled. This doesn't really fit. Some of us have been thinking this was a miscommunicated command."

The President was completely frustrated by their lack of ability to stop the seeming "fire-at-will" attacks.

"When are we on with this so-called 'expert?'" the President responded angrily.

Henry responded, "Mr. President, we are on in just a few minutes—waiting for all of the agencies to get on the line, Sir. Redstone is ready to go. I have to say that we're lucky this guy has survived—there was a third attempt on his life while under FBI escort to the facility. We lost at least one agent in the process. We don't know who's behind this, but they're obviously well organized and seem to know our every move."

"Hank, I'm already paranoid enough. I'm beginning to think we have a mole in our own organization, but judging from the little we know, I'd say they are just smarter than we are right now."

Henry took offense. "We're trying our best," he said gruffly.

The technical security officer in charge of the Situation Room interjected. "Sir, we have all agencies online now. Ready when you are."

"Mr. Cannon, we're ready to go live," Smith said to Greg.

The large, flat screen monitor in front of them switched from the generic US government backdrop to an image of the Situation Room. Instantly, the entire Security Council was in view, looking right at them, waiting expectantly.

Henry spoke first.

"Welcome, everyone. I wish we had time for formal introductions, but the fact is, we don't. To bring everyone up to speed, we've had three attacks on the US today of unknown source and origin. We have various theories about what might be the cause and means, but we have no conclusive evidence, and therefore, have no solutions.

"With us today is Greg Cannon. You've been briefed on his role in today's events."

There was so much that he had experienced that day, it was hard for Greg to believe that it all could be crammed into a "brief."

"We don't know exactly what Greg has uncovered, so that's what we are all here to assess. Greg, no doubt you've been under a great deal of duress today. I want to thank you in advance for your contributions to the resolution of this crisis. What have you got for us?"

The line went silent as those assembled waited impatiently for Greg's response.

Greg snapped out of his panic and swallowed hard. Or at least, he tried to swallow. He was so nervous that his mouth had completely dried up.

Where was that water? he wondered.

Greg grabbed the cup and took a swig, hoping it would jump start his mind and mouth.

"Mister…ah…Director…Mr. President…"

Henry interrupted. "Greg, no need to lean into the mic, we can hear you just fine. Take your time getting going, but then cut to the chase for us, OK?"

Greg breathed deeply, just like his high school speech teacher had taught him to do to relieve tension in his voice and body.

"As the Director stated, my name is Greg Cannon and I work for NTSB…OK, you already know all that. So, right…getting to what Dennis—that was my partner—and I uncovered today…well, based on our investigation, we observed that within a significant number of smartphones and tablet computers being used in the US, the main processor package has a chip stack…a stack of individual silicon integrated circuits, or chips, that include specialized devices containing functions for processing, memory, GPS, Wi-Fi, and the like. The chips are stacked to reduce circuit board space and cost. Most everyone is using this stacked-chip technology, as it's the least expensive and most efficient one on the market.

"Each of these chips in the stack are really thin…as thin as a piece of paper. When they get put together, it's nearly impossible to see what's inside. We dismantled a phone that was affected by the attack on Atlanta and found seven of these thin chips in the processor package. There are supposed to be six. One is a Trojan. Most new smartphones and tablets on the market are using a similar package."

"Greg, excuse me, NSA participant here, I need to ask—how do you know there's an extra chip in the stack?"

"I had a specialist in reverse engineering of chip designs take the package apart and validate the extra chip. Likewise, a Professor at the University of Huntsville took apart one of the blown-out phones from the plane and verified the specific package responsible for the fire on that device. It appears to operate by shorting things out, sometimes even igniting the Lithium Ion battery."

"You did all that today?"

"Yes, sir."

"But what was the Trojan chip? A timer?" came an unknown voice, probably from NSA.

"I'll get to that in a moment, if you'll uh…if you'll bear with me."

"Proceed," replied the voice.

"The Trojan chip itself appears to sit on the data-bus and listen for commands coming across from the cellular or Wi-Fi chip to the processor. When a particular command is sent to the phone, the chip activates and decodes a target location and radius sent in the message. Later, a second command actually shorts out the part if it meets the location criteria. There's enough time between the activate and attack commands for the Trojan chip to intercept location from GPS. In the Atlanta attack, there were two hours between commands. For Dallas, there was about one hour."

"But how does the phone get the commands?" someone asked.

"Great question. The messages came from one of the many social networking sites the user might have signed up for. Blather, Facebook, Twitter…they were hacked with encrypted messages prior to the attacks. The top-followed celebrities and pundits on the sites have been hacked, somehow. The messages I examined from Blather and Facebook had binary messages buried inside."

"You mean to tell me that my kid's smartphone and her obsessive interest in Justin Bieber's every move on Twitter just might cause our house to burn down?" another unidentified voice queried.

"Uh…well, yes," Greg said, unsure of how to process the skepticism in the speaker's tone. He remembered Donovan's words, took a deep breath and continued. "I am absolutely confident that this is the mechanism being used. In fact, all of the large commercial planes now have Wi-Fi onboard, so any smartphones or tablets could have received a trigger message while in flight. With the FAA's latest approval, tablets are even up in the cockpit in some airlines. The plane we examined had no smart devices up there, which is probably what saved them."

"Greg, this is Carl Johnson, Department of Homeland Security. Is there any chance you know where these chips are made?"

"Well, sir, the individual chips are made all over, but they're all being assembled in a Hon Yao factory in China, which is where the extra chip is likely placed into the stack. China doesn't have to actually make the main chips to have slipped this one in during assembly."

The President looked at each of his Security Council members with a knowing glare. This all made sense to him, and he wasn't even a techno-geek.

Greg continued, "As far as a solution, the commands are coming through the Internet via social networking sites. There's no guarantee they can't come in through other sources, but these seem to be the most efficient means for disseminating…well, this 'virus,' I guess. I strongly recommend shutting down the Internet immediately."

The look Greg got from the Director of National Intelligence made it clear that such an extreme solution wasn't necessarily viable, regardless of what Donovan said.

"…And if that's not possible," Greg continued, "you absolutely have to shut down all social networking sites as soon as possible—Facebook, Blather, Twitter, LinkedIn, and all others. This can't even be up for discussion. They have to be shut down. And in parallel, you have to identify which phones have this particular part in them and force the phone companies to pull a recall. I don't know what can be done about the Chinese assembly plant…but you have a serious problem on your hands there."

Donovan kicked Greg under the table to get his attention and gave him the finger-across-the-neck motion to signal it was time to cut it off. Greg got the message and fell silent.

"Is that it?" asked Henry.

Greg only nodded.

"This sounds like the most plausible theory we have to go on so far."

"Sir," Greg interjected, "no disrespect intended, but this is not a theory. I have the data and reports to back up each and every aspect."

"Hank and Carl, you have five minutes to confer with your staff and reach a conclusion," the President said.

"Mr. President, given the information presented, I have no problem ordering the blocking of all social networking sites immediately. I'm directing my team at NSA to do it now. Got it, guys?"

"Got it, Henry," came a faceless response.

"In the meantime, Greg, we're going to need you to stay there at Redstone where my staff can get access to your information," said the President. "We have all sorts of other issues to deal with now, in light of what you've uncovered. We'll be getting back to you, and soon. Robert, he's yours to protect now…you get things rolling there and we'll convene in a few minutes."

With that, the image of the Situation Room disappeared from view.

Chapter

(Sixty-3)

*M*ichelle Cannon's military flight had been redirected to land on Redstone's airfield, preventing any possible interception. The FBI was taking no chances that Michelle could be used as a bargaining chip to quiet Greg. Still, it had been decided that, depending on the results of the meeting, Greg and Michelle wouldn't be leaving the base anytime soon—for their own good.

She was brought to Cottage 58. It was the best the base had to offer—a three-bedroom structure nestled next to the woods a short drive from the airport. All three bedrooms were needed, as an FBI agent and a Redstone MP were both assigned to watch over the Cannons.

Michelle had been waiting on Greg for hours. When he and Donovan finally arrived, she was tired, but thankful. She embraced Greg with a warm hug and enjoyed the feeling and smell of her husband and the comfort he brought her.

Holding Michelle, Greg felt himself finally start to relax. He was glad she was safe.

"This is Agent Donovan," he said, nodding toward the agent with a look of appreciation. He felt like he could almost cry as relief, exhaustion, and immense gratitude that he had survived the day, washed over him. "He's saved my life a few times today. I think he might be the best friend I have in the world right now."

Donovan was touched by Greg's sincerity, but knew he had to maintain his guard regardless of pleasantries or casual introductions.

"It's great to meet you, Michelle," he said. "Your husband is one of the most respected men in the US at the moment—you should be proud. I have to warn you, though, that Greg's activities today are classified. He can't share details with you."

Turning to Greg, he said, "We're planning on getting up and going around eight. Michelle will stay here. You'll be debriefed then, Greg. We need to document every aspect of this mess before anything gets forgotten.

"Well, this has been an intense day for us all. You two go ahead to bed. There's much to discuss in the morning, but right now, I think everyone needs some rest."

The three said their goodnights and headed to their rooms. For Greg, this marked the end of what had been the longest day of his life.

Chapter
(Sixty-4)

*J*ust moments after the video-conference system was turned off, the Situation Room erupted in a clamor of heated discussion.

"Well, you heard him. The assembly of the computer chips was done in China, and that's where the placement of this Trojan—or whatever we want to call it—happened. I knew Iran wasn't responsible, and China's invasion completely confirms it," the President said.

"And that package isn't just used in phones, it's used in tablets, navigation systems, numerous other intelligent systems…" said Robert.

The President looked at Robert incredulously, "If you know so much about it, why didn't you clue into this problem a while ago?"

"Mr. President, we suspected that the package wasn't secure, which is why we didn't use it for any military systems. We've tried to keep a secure manufacturing supply chain, which has been tough given the amount of manufacturing headed to Asia, particularly Taiwan. There's pressure to do otherwise, but, fortunately, we've been able to resist, even at the expense of higher cost and sometimes less capable systems. But I never suspected something like this could have been pulled off. We were always more concerned about counterfeit chips than Trojans inside legitimate ones."

"Let's assume this Greg Cannon guy is pretty close to correct. We're on track to stopping the attacks on the US, right?" inquired the President.

Henry responded, "Yes, Sir. The social networking sites should be blocked within the hour, at the very latest."

"So we can now go back to running our defense without fear of retaliation?"

"I'd say so, but we have some more work to do before I can say that with complete certainty," said Robert.

"All right, we have to deal with what's going on in Iran and Iraq," the President continued.

"Mr. President, we need a complete analysis and risk assessment before we take action. It's likely that the Chinese anticipated the possibility of the US being able to regain control of our domestic situation and are positioning their forces for a possible retaliatory attack. We'll need to get JSTARS and UAVs up to provide additional, real-time assessment of the troops' positions, otherwise we'd be flying blind. I'll be getting our reconnaissance up and going immediately. We'll need to call in favors from Israel and perhaps Saudi Arabia as well. Mr. President, I'm going to suggest that we reconvene in two hours. I can't imagine that we'll have sufficient knowledge and an assessment of options completed until then," Henry concluded.

Amanda agreed. "I need time to contact our allies in the region as well. In fact, this is going to take communication with as many of our friends in the area and around the globe as we can muster."

"No snap decisions," stated the President. "In fact, by attacking Iranian troops in Iraq, we'd weaken their forces and reduce their chances of mounting a good fight against the Chinese. Better to let Iranian troops and Chinese troops battle it out and weaken each other while we strategize. Let's plan on getting back down here at 0300…"

Amanda picked up where the President left off: "And in the meantime, while I'm trying to get support for whatever action we'll have to take, I'll ensure all of the neighboring countries are informed of the status of the troop movements in Iraq and Iran. We're likely going to need their help before this is all over."

Bahram had seen the damage in Tehran. Traffic, typically a mess this time of day, was now at a complete standstill, and it appeared that there were fires spreading throughout every part of the city, adding gritty texture to the morning smog. Fire trucks and ambulances would have a difficult time getting through.

Racing home to turn on the news, the television seemed to be working fine, but the local news was at a loss to explain what was happening across the city.

It was clear that the Spiritual Leaders were already spinning things as best they could.

"…this morning, that Great Satan, the United States, attacked Iran with a new electromagnetic weapon. It appears that cell phone communication has been completely disrupted across the country. However, we have nothing to fear. Our Leaders will have everything back to normal very soon…"

Bahram shook his head. Everyone in Iran depended on cell phones, even the military—old phone lines were expensive and unreliable. This was a complete disaster for everyone.

"Liars!"

Farah looked at Bahram with shock.

"Bahram, why would they lie?" asked Farah.

He knew that he would have to tell her.

"Remember how I couldn't sleep? Let me tell you why. I picked up some army men three nights ago, they had been drinking and let it slip how there was going to be an invasion of sorts.

"And last night, the man who generously tipped me was from the Ministry of Defense, their offices were all lit up—they were all working late into the night. Our Leaders must have provoked this!"

Farah was still incredulous.

"How? Why?"

"I don't know. An invasion? A nuclear experiment? Likely some crazy action our leaders wanted to do to prove their might! Don't they know that we don't want to be mighty? We just want peace!"

Farah would have to trust her husband.

"What now, Bahram?"

"We leave. Now. We get out to the country while my gas tank is full, and before the fighting starts."

This was asking a lot. Farah raised her eyebrows. "Leave?" she asked.

"Yes! Pack what will fit—get the kids ready. We leave as soon as possible."

"What about the streets? You said they are jammed."

Bahram let himself smile. "I own these streets. I will find a way."

With no advance notice of the invasion, Chinese forces had already taken Bandar-E-Abbas, a primary port in southern Iran, used for the distribution of oil and import of goods. It was also home to the Iranian Navy. A portion of the Chinese entering through Pakistan had made their way across southern Iran, attacked their ground troops, and blockaded the key port. A newly-developed Iranian port in Syria was much too far away to provide any support, had they even been made aware of the attack.

From the sea, the Chinese Navy had already been firmly established in the Gulf region to protect against Somali pirates hijacking precious cargo ships. A year prior, they sent their sole aircraft carrier into the area as a show of strength as well as to provide humanitarian aid to Pakistanis victimized by natural disasters. With just one carrier, the Chinese Navy couldn't project a bona fide presence in the world. However, the ship served well as a launch point into Iran to take out any limited resistance they faced.

Chapter
(Sixty-5)

*I*t had been a rather uneventful day at the Hon Yao factory, that is, until the military police showed up unannounced and in force. The guards at the entrance to the facility were used to the local police and dignitaries arriving, sometimes unannounced, but this was completely different.

The sergeant-in-charge presented a list of names and a map of the facility. They demanded that the personnel listed be delivered to them for questioning, and that their team be allowed into the No-Man's Land area of the facility. They clearly knew what they were after, and were in a hurry to get it. Along with the military police, a crew of photographers and videographers were present. Typically, visits from police and dignitaries were kept somewhat hushed, unless there was a new expansion to announce by a local politician.

When the guards at the gate didn't understand the nature of what the military needed, the lead sergeant took his SKS and fired it into the air. He then pointed it at the factory guard and demanded access to find the culprits on the list.

By the time the military was finished, five staff, including the president of the company, were being led away in shackles, heads hung down, looking fearful. A group of soldiers followed, carrying a package of silicon wafers—the same type that had been secretly delivered every morning for dicing and insertion into the company's products. Video and photos of the scene would be used as propaganda. As soon as the staff and wafers were loaded into the military transport, the government press sped away to deliver their media to the editors preparing statements.

At three in the morning on the East Coast of the United States, select offices around Washington, DC and the beltway were lit up and busy. For most politicians, government workers, and civilians, the events of the day had left them drained, even if they were only observers. Most hoped that when they woke up, the government would have solved the problems leading to the various crises and they could go back to their lives as normal; they were looking forward to everything being wrapped up in a nice clean package in time for the markets to open.

However, US businesses with shipping operations in the Middle East knew something more was awry. Their shipping systems' navigation was dependent on GPS, and its accuracy had been severely curtailed. As the US military officially owned the satellites, the Secretary of Defense had ordered the degradation of the civilian access signal in the hopes that it might slow down or deter Chinese progress also dependent on the use of GPS.

When Chinese receiver accuracy changed from a few feet to a few hundred feet, they knew the US was aware of their invasion. The Chinese military had anticipated this, however, and was making use of highly accurate terrain maps to provide reference points where needed. For the advance troops, the degraded GPS accuracy was sufficient for their needs during the beginning of the mission. For those forces that progressed to positions near the cities and needed higher accuracy navigation, trained soldiers set up ground stations at survey markers previously placed during construction of the jointly-funded high-speed railway. Subtracting the ground station's tainted GPS position from the accurate position provided by the survey marker made up for the discrepancy. This error was then broadcast in real-time to any and all Chinese receivers nearby, including aircraft. For the Chinese military, the inconvenience was nothing more than an annoyance.

Chapter (Sixty-6)

"*W*here is he?"

"He's on his way. There were a few phone calls he needed to make," Ned responded impatiently.

"I've got to say, we were caught flat-footed on all of this," stated Henry. "We have been so focused on Afghanistan and Iraq the past few years that it's been an up hill battle trying to keep apprised of what's been happening in other regions. Frankly, I've been concerned all along that we'd been too patient with Iran and their nuclear program. Other nations have been asking for us to do something about Iran's aggressive behavior for years. I'm surprised Israel hasn't just acted on their own by now.

"But now we have China invading Iran for completely different reasons…at least that's what we all suspect, right? This is clearly about oil and gas and other natural resources—I would have thought with the lucrative contracts China had in place with Pakistan and Iran that a military action was not even a possibility."

"Well, clearly they're in Iran," Robert said. "Our reconnaissance shows they're all over the country. And we don't even have a full picture quite yet. Without communication with China, we have to assume the worst, which means we have to prepare for a retaliatory strike.

"Hank, do we know if Mr. Cannon's theory was good? Have we been able to validate that shutting down the social networking sites was the key to stopping the attacks?"

Just then, the President entered the room.

"Gentlemen," he nodded. "Please continue."

"Mr. Cannon sent us his files and we were able to validate his theory. Hacked messages went out over numerous social networking accounts—all with significant numbers of followers. The encryption was simplistic."

"What did the messages say?"

"The first contained a short latitude, longitude and radius message, and the second appears to be some form of trigger message—a unique code common to both the Atlanta and Dallas events. The third event, a smaller one in Hayward, was originally thought to be a fluke, but now it appears the coding that triggered it was a conglomeration of the set-up and trigger codes. In other words, instant destruct with no delay.

"In the morning, we'll contact the social networking IT departments to get the login IPs of the specific users who placed the messages. If needed, we'll do a complete dump on NIS, our server that captures all internet traffic data."

"Hank, that's going to take far too much time. I expect to leave this meeting with some decisions. If a strike in the Mideast or China is a next action, I need to know we can't be attacked on our soil again the same way."

"Mr. President, I would put the probability that we have this thing solved at ninety-five percent. It all seems to line up very well, and the additional investigation we've done only confirms Mr. Cannon's hypothesis. All social networking sites have been completely cut off, which will force them to work with us tomorrow. For now, no encrypted messages are coming through; in fact, no messages are coming through at all."

"Very well. So, we'll be able conduct an air-strike with no possible retaliation, if needed—at least no retaliation of the nature we witnessed yesterday," concluded the President.

Henry continued his report, "I have an Iranian status update, Sir. There's a lot we do know, and there's a lot we don't. First, it appears that Iran has also been hit by the same type of attack that was perpetrated on the US. Of course, this supports your premise, Mr. President, that Iran had nothing to do with the attacks on our soil. Why they were duped into making the statements claiming responsibility is anyone's guess, though I think we can expect to find China behind the curtain.

"Our overhead assets monitoring transmissions in the area saw a tremendous and almost instantaneous decrease in cellular and broadband chatter mid-morning. The decrease was pervasive, apparently impacting the entire country.

Their communications are effectively shut down. I can't imagine the collateral damage."

Knowing that Iran had blocked almost all social networking sites, Robert questioned whether the same method of attack could have been launched as was launched on the US.

"Nationwide? That sounds like a different mechanism."

"Good observation. We did some quick checking on that. It turns out that there's a morning schedule of prayer times that goes out via SMS to everyone's phone in Iran, part of the Spiritual Leader's attempt to keep everyone in check. Communications shut down right after that message."

"But you'd still need that chip, the one from Hon Yao, to short out the phone, right?"

"Exactly. The Republican Guard 'mafia' and their cronies, who are pretty much in charge of everything in Iran, years ago convinced the government that only an Iranian company was qualified to make a smartphone for their people. So, the smartphone market is pretty much a monopoly, with one major product, called the 'tPhone.' It all works well for them since the Guard's buddies own the phone company."

"That seems to be a significant conflict of interest," said Robert.

"On top of this, the phone isn't really original. It's a knock-off of an HTC, and therefore…"

The President was already one step ahead of Henry and jumped into the conversation.

"…let me guess. Since HTC is a Taiwanese company, the phone uses the same chipset."

"Correct, Mr. President."

It was hard for the President not to admire the intelligence behind this well-crafted plan.

Nodding, he said, "Whoever put this plan together was a genius. A hacked call to prayer? How ironic, and how pervasive for them."

"If we had been hit nationwide, we'd be in shambles right now," commented Carl.

"Which only goes to show that China likely wanted us to stand down temporarily, but not cripple us entirely," added Robert.

Benevidez agreed, "We're their top trade partner, and they hold over a trillion dollars of our debt. We're somewhat joined at the hip, though we don't trust each other."

"So what in the world are they doing? How do they think they can get away with this?" the President asked.

"The fact is that it's all happened so quickly—they *are* getting away with it," Amanda said.

"Which is why we have to *do* something. And right away!" said Robert.

"What, and start World War III? With the eyes of the world on us tomorrow, we have to present a case—a solid case—for why we would mount an attack on China or on forces in Iran," exclaimed the President.

"What, and let this invasion progress?" said Robert.

"Well, you may not be able to do much at this point," said Benevidez.

"Wrong, Dan," Carl quipped, "we can hold a nuclear gun to their heads."

"Really? Can we make good on that threat?" asked the President. "I remember President Jiang stating over a decade ago, 'I think you value Los Angeles more than we do Shanghai.' For all we know, they have their Shang-class nuclear subs parked off the coast of California in anticipation of a retaliatory strike. We can't act rashly on this. Henry, keep going on your situation report."

"Thank you, Mr. President. As of our last update two hours ago, they have made significant progress in establishing control of Iran. Iran's primary forces are stuck in Iraq, and communication with the remaining forces has been spotty, with likely few real-time updates. Chinese workers likely had everything mapped out and plans in place for some time. I believe the Chinese forces will have control of Iran very soon."

"What does that mean to you?" asked Robert.

"Control of communications or what's left of them, roads, railroads and perhaps most of the military. I can't imagine the military units coming back from Iraq will be able to even refuel at their own border when they get the message to come home."

"What's the status of our forces?" asked the President.

"We have the *Truman* in the Gulf of Aden right now, and within striking distance of Iran, but we can't mount a sustained effort without also having ground forces built up and ready," Robert explained. "We had plans for a preemptive strike against Iran, but the Chinese forces are moving 'at will' and we don't know where they'll be next."

The President tried to suppress showing any negative reaction to this latest update, though the situation was stretching his patience to its limits—at the same time he knew his staff was equally frustrated.

"Amanda, give me an update on your discussions with the neighbors."

"Mr. President, in spite of it being near noon in the Mideast, we have had considerable trouble reaching anyone with any knowledge of the situation, let alone authority. This is highly unusual. We have requests in to various dignitaries to return calls."

"No one? We're always able to get the Saudis on the phone, aren't we?"

"Yes, Sir. But this is the middle of the day for them. There are lunches, prayer services and other issues…"

Just then, the phone to the situation room rang. Few people had the number, so whenever it rang, it was worth stopping the conversation and seeing what it was about, especially at this time in the morning.

The Chief of Staff answered. "Yes, we're all here. OK, I'll put it on. Are you sure? Yes, that was the right thing to do, we'll drop everything and watch."

The President looked at Ned quizzically.

"Folks, we've been given notice that the President of China is about to make another address on CNT."

"What?!"

The large screen monitor lit up with an image of the Chinese flag in the background as a small, impeccably-dressed Chinese dignitary prepared the podium and microphone for the press conference.

"Can it get any stranger than this? This is the second time in twenty-four hours Li is addressing us through the press. What in the world is he prepared to tell the world that he couldn't pick up the fucking phone and call Washington to discuss? Is he going to offer an explanation for the attacks they perpetrated?"

The President was both frustrated and offended at the same time. After all, the US was the leader of the free world—the last remaining superpower. What business did the President of China have speaking directly to the world, let alone his own constituents?

"Why is CNT covering this anyway? Can't you use your authority to cut them off?" the President said to no one in particular.

"There's that pesky free speech issue…" Amanda said.

"Well, that's for US Citizens. He's not covered by our Constitution, and he has no rights here."

"CNT does."

Just then, the announcer broke in: "We interrupt our regularly scheduled programming to bring you live coverage from Beijing, where President Li will be addressing the global community concerning events in the US and abroad that have occurred in the past twenty-four hours."

Chapter
(Sixty-7)

"**C**itizens of the world, when I addressed the global community not less than twelve hours ago, the United States had been attacked with a weapon of unknown origin. I vowed that China would do all within its power to investigate the source of the weapon and help bring the criminals to justice. I am very sad to say that some of these criminals were Chinese citizens…"

"What! He's admitting this on global television? Where is he going with this?" grumbled Robert.

"…Some were also Iranian citizens, and the remainder were citizens from the United States.

"Our investigators were able to determine that the attacks were perpetrated by a global cult that, through bribery and coercion, infiltrated the electronics industry in China, the government in Iran and social networks in the United States. A specially-designed chip was inserted into smartphones manufactured at the Hon Yao factory in the Shenzhen Province, and these devices were shipped all over the world. What we know so far is that this chip, upon receiving the right command, can cause the system using it to catch fire or even explode. We regret to say that Chinese factory workers were responsible for the final assembly.

"We were also able to uncover that leaders within the Iranian government were responsible for the recruitment and directing of US-based citizens who delivered the attack commands to phones in the United States. These traitors in the United States delivered the attack messages through the various social networks used by the public…"

"How the hell does he know all of this?" Robert asked.

Henry responded, "Because they're really the ones who did it, that's why!"

"…able to confirm that the Iranian government claimed responsibility for the attacks, and were the ones who gave warning to the United States to stand down their military or experience an attack on Dallas, just prior to an invasion of Iraq by military forces from Iran. The US did not stand down and Dallas was attacked."

Finally, the President spoke, "OK, how would he know that? Do we have moles all around us?"

"He's twisting the truth to make us look responsible for the Dallas attack," muttered Amanda.

President Li paused, as if he had heard the objections, then responded deliberately: "Citizens of the United States, you can confirm with your government that Iran is the only country that has claimed responsibility for these attacks, and that United States-based social networking hackers delivered the attack messages to your very own communities. The Chinese military was able to find the location of the cult members in our country—and, unfortunately, due to resistance, had to use force to stop their continued actions."

At this point, pictures of the cult, shot execution-style in the Polaris room of the Grand Hyatt, appeared on the screen.

"We also found the perpetrators at the Hon Yao factory, confiscated the chips, and executed the managers who allowed their insertion into the consumer devices."

Pictures of guards carrying stacks of silicon wafers from the factory appeared on the screen.

"After uncovering the plot, we appealed to the government of Iran to stop the continued attacks on the United States; however, they were unresponsive to our pleas. In fact, the leadership threatened to cut off the supplies of oil through the Strait of Hormuz to the entire global community in retaliation for any interference we might present.

"Based on this, along with the chance presence of Chinese forces in the gulf region, I authorized our military to use whatever force necessary to prevent Iran from continuing to hold the United States and, effectively, the world hostage. In staging our own attack on Iran, we consulted with neighboring countries to gain support. We discovered that Iraq was already under attack from Iran, and other countries feared additional conventional or even nuclear attacks from Iran.

Therefore, we have entered Iran and are well on our way to containing the rogue nation."

In the Situation Room, the President spun around and looked at his Secretary of State, "Support from *what* neighboring countries?"

The anchor from CNT broke in: "We take you now to Kari Kelly, currently on site in Saudi Arabia, where King Abdullah is prepared to make a statement on behalf of President Li."

"Citizens of the world, it is with great consternation that I am addressing you this day. We were made aware of the invasion of Iraq by Iran late last night. At first, we were very surprised at the lack of response by the Americans. We have repeatedly asked the United States to do something about the build up of Iranian power and, in particular, their nuclear capability. The Americans have done nothing. Therefore, we welcome the peace-keeping forces from China that have now established their presence in Iran. We have committed financial aid and military support to China, to ensure the flow of oil and gas from and through Iran continues unabated to the world, and that the Iranian citizens no longer suffer under the dictatorial regime they were once subjected to. Thank you."

"And now," the CNT anchor said, "we switch to a broadcast, live, from the United Arab Emirates, where the President has also offered to speak his view on the circumstances today."

"The United Arab Emirates shares the view held by the King of Saudi Arabia, and also pledges to do its part in ensuring the stability and safety of the region. We wish to thank President Li for his leadership and bravery in addressing this serious issue directly and promptly, and encourage him to work with the other superpowers, such as the United States and Russia, in reaching a suitable short and long-term solution to the crisis that presented itself today."

The scene now returned to the image of the Chinese President, looking somber, gauging his next words carefully.

"I will be working with the leaders of the United Nations, the Presidents of the United States, Russia, and regional countries in determining a viable long-term solution. Now that the Iranian government is no longer able to direct attacks against the United States, the United States will be able to join us in adding stability to the region without fear of reprisal."

With that, the Chinese President nodded to the camera and walked off-stage.

Robert spoke up first. "This is total bullshit. We have evidence to prove it, too."

"Don't you realize what just happened?" Henry said. "Li presented an open-and-shut case. He identified the problem, came up with a solution and delivered the answer. Anyone who thinks for a moment that the majority of the United Nations Security Council won't have bought into this by the end of the day is being totally naive."

Carl joined in: "I agree. It will take us weeks to get this sorted out. Probably ninety percent of what he said is true. It's the other ten percent that's important. How do we prove that the Chinese government did or didn't know about this? What if it was this cult? We can't lie and say that Iran didn't claim responsibility—there're too many people who know otherwise. And it's likely that it was US hackers that passed the messages on the social networking sites."

"And the American public likes neat packages. He just gave them one," the Vice President said.

"But we know it's not true," said the President.

Carl agreed. "Of course it isn't, but we need all our ducks in a row before we claim that publicly."

Benevidez weighed in: "I agree, but here's what we don't know. Was the Chinese government in on this? The Chinese military? Sometimes they act independently, or at least they've seemed to in the past. What if their President was being honest?"

"They're all asking us to help dismantle the biggest threat to the region..."

"This speech changes everything," Robert said grimly.

After a moment of silence, the President did what everyone else thought was needed, but didn't have the authority to do.

"Colleagues, we're going to have to reconvene first thing in the morning. The United States, it appears, is now out of any immediate danger. The rest of the world could look totally different come morning. Be prepared to meet back here at nine. Our focus now is to prove China's role in this. I've got to get some rest and do some thinking on my own. You know where to reach me."

Chapter
(Sixty-8)

It was nearly two in the afternoon, and the sirens in Tehran were still blaring while smoke billowed from fires across the city. Bahram threaded his taxi through familiar backstreets, around stalled and burned out vehicles. Though his wife, Farah, was getting nauseated, their children squealed with delight at their fathers' seemingly erratic driving. Even with his expertise, progress was slow going. It was only fifteen or so miles to the outskirts of the city, traversing the South Tehran Highway toward his brother-in-law's farm outside Varamin.

By getting away from the big city, Bahram felt that he might avoid any type of panic and uprisings. Farah's brother would have food and room for them, and as family, he was obligated to take them in, for as long as they needed. However, at his current rate of progress, Bahram would be lucky to be out of the city by dinnertime and to Varamin by midnight.

There was a gentle rapping at the door to Greg and Michelle's room.

"Hello? Who's there?" came Greg's groggy response. Four hours of sleep didn't seem nearly enough, but it was going to have to do.

"Greg, it's Donovan," was the muffled reply through the door. "I'm sorry to wake you, but we've got to get going. Agent Kelly brought some breakfast in, so if you can get showered and dressed in the next five minutes..."

Five minutes? Greg thought as he rolled out of bed.

Ten minutes later, his hair wet and his stomach a little queasy from inhaling his food, Greg was riding with Donovan over to the same facility they visited last night. As Donovan suspected, all aspects surrounding the event were now Top Secret, SCI, and any discussions were going to have to take place in the SCI facility, except where it was impossible to do so.

"Greg, we'll spend a couple of hours or so getting debriefed about yesterday. Your laptop is likely going to have to stay in the SCIF. They can have a tech pull off anything that might be personal and unclassified."

Greg nodded his understanding. It was a government-issued laptop after all. Briefly, the thought of what notes from yesterday might still be on his smartphone went through his mind, but he decided he'd not risk mentioning it as he wasn't ready to give it up.

"What about my clearance?"

Donovan chuckled a little. Some sleep along with believing the worst was over helped his disposition.

"Good question, but I know that's not going to be an issue. You are at the center of this whole investigation, now. When we arrive, you may find you've already been upgraded...your lie detector tests will have to come later on."

Chapter
(Sixty-9)

*T*he **President kicked** things off. Though the prospect of further attacks was now significantly diminished, there was still a tremendous amount of work to accomplish in little time.

"OK, let's get started. As we might have predicted, there's an emergency meeting of the UN Security Council scheduled for this afternoon, called by China. We have to be ready with a statement and our proposed next steps. I wish we had enough evidence to allow us to act as a sovereign nation defending ourselves and our interests. However, after what I've seen so far, we don't have a defensible position to justify any type of independent counter-attack. With that said, what have we uncovered about China's role in all of this?"

Henry pulled up a slide that showed a number of dots placed on a map of the US. There was a high concentration located within the Bay area of Northern California.

"We are trying to trace the attacks back to their source. We contacted the support staff at each of the most highly visited social networking sites and had them identify the IP addresses of the users logging into the various accounts that had the hacked messages.

"What's interesting here is that it looks like the Atlanta attack logins came from all over the Bay Area—locations like homes and coffee shops. But the afternoon attacks all came from a proxy site that allows folks to browse the web without giving away their actual IP addresses…but it works both ways—all of the logins also came from this site. So, we've shut it down and have agents on their way to visit them. They're located in the Netherlands."

"This is pretty well organized," said the Vice President.

"Given the nature and sophistication of the attack, I wouldn't have expected anything less. However, the hackers logging in from various sites for the Atlanta attack clearly shows that some of them got lazy. In fact, we've sent agents to a handful of addresses already—but found no one so far. The danger is that some of these hackers are still out there, unidentified. It appears that most are just run-of-the-mill IT workers in the Bay area. We hope to have linked each tampered message to an identified hacker by the end of the day. We've put out APBs on those identified so far."

"I think we need to get their names and faces out to the press, to let any others know we're onto them…" said Amanda.

Henry wasn't so sure that would be a good idea. "That's a thought," he said. "But how much credence would that give President Li's address? We don't want the public thinking he's the 'good guy,' do we?"

Thinking the protection of the US outweighed any political issues, Carl offered his point of view. "Regardless of that issue, balance it with the need to diminish the chance of another hacking attack."

The President agreed, "Good point, Carl. Let's get names and faces out there. Hank, anything further?"

"No, Sir."

"OK, this is all good progress, but nothing here gives us any proof of China's involvement," said the President. "Carl, any progress in your area?"

Ned quickly interrupted.

"Mr. President, before we go to the Department of Homeland Security, there's a key issue I have to address immediately, as there's likely going to be a CNT report soon—and we'll want to weigh in before it goes on the air."

"OK, Ned, what's the issue?"

"Our office has received word from China that President Li set up a fund to help cover damages and plans to announce it this morning.

"And I quote: 'The Chinese government has set up a fund of *fifteen billion* US dollars to cover the cost of damage to the communities of Atlanta and Dallas. Though the attack was perpetrated by independent actors within China, Iran and the United States, as a show of solidarity with the citizens of the United States, the people of China wish to apologize for the actions of this small, rogue group and help repair any ill feelings caused that were beyond the control of our respective governments. The fund is to compensate US-based cell phone providers for the cost to replace both damaged phones and undamaged phones which used the faulty chipset. It will also be available to replace damaged aircraft. Finally, though no amount of money can replace a family member, the fund is making five million dollars available for each family member killed in the attack as well as covering the cost for medical care and missed work for any family member seriously injured.'

"The message goes on to officially request the US government's support in administrating the fund."

The room was silent.

"Mr. President?"

"I'm thinking…Do we have an estimate of the cost of the damage in Atlanta?"

"Early estimates come in at about one and a half billion, which could go up once all repairs are completed."

"What about Dallas?"

"Dallas was a bigger area, but much of the city was shut down in preparation. Rough estimates are in the neighborhood of three billion."

"OK, let's guess on the number of phones that were damaged or need to be replaced…"

"It could be as high as ten million phones and tablets or so, as a rough guess."

"Quantity price for a cell phone manufacturer?"

"Retail…maybe five hundred?" said Robert.

"Three hundred in quantity?" added Amanda.

"Let's go with five hundred to be conservative…total cost?" the President ventured. "About five billion, right?" he said, answering his own question.

"Sure…"

"OK, planes?"

"Nine crashed. More were damaged. Maybe twenty or so total…at ten to fifty million each."

"Assume a billion."

"500 or so deaths at five million each—two and a half billion."

"What are we up to now?"

"That's got the damage at almost thirteen billion so far," surmised Henry.

"Fifteen gives enough to cover known damage, plus headroom for injuries, hurt business…" concluded the President.

"All way too convenient," Amanda sighed.

"But why would they want to hurt us only to compensate us for it?"

The President looked over to his National Security Advisor, with a knowing look. "Benevidez, you know the answer, don't you?"

Benevidez had been his typically quiet self up to this point. A thinker rather than a talker, he had been calculating things in his head, weighing all that was being said against the facts he knew. "Yes. I know…do the math on what they gain…"

"What do you mean?" asked Carl.

"We'll start with Japan…you know those islands that no one seemed to really know about when we first brought them up yesterday? The Senkaku Islands?"

"Yes, of course, we almost went to war over those damn islands yesterday…a few rocks out in the middle of the ocean."

"Robert, you weren't listening. It's not the rocks; it's what's *under* the rocks—natural gas and oil. There's nearly twenty trillion cubic feet of gas estimated under there if they can drill and get to it. Japan wasn't going to give that up without a fight, especially with their increased energy needs after the tsunami. If China gets exclusive rights, since it's now right under their undisputed islands, well…that's…twenty trillion cubic feet…times fifteen dollars per thousand cubic feet going rate…that's worth about three hundred billion. And that doesn't include the oil. Fifteen billion doesn't seem like a big deal by comparison, does it? They'd go higher if needed."

"That's what this was about…"

"Yes. That and Iran's natural resources, which we can try to calculate as well…there's a field in the Kurdistan region that may hold up to twelve trillion cubic feet of natural gas. If you want something else to worry about, there's a field in Israel that's even bigger. If China doesn't find solutions to their energy shortages, they will be facing serious social unrest…these natural resources would all seem worthy targets."

"That's crazy, they can't buy us off like that!" said Robert.

"Really? But our communities are going to want that money...we can't really block that, can we? We'd have a political nightmare on our hands," declared Amanda.

"Mr. President, each of our states has the right to accept funding from outside sources, and the phone companies have the right to accept compensation for damages as well. What about the families that have just lost loved ones? I can't imagine asking any of them to turn this down unless we set up our own fund to compensate," added Carl.

"You all know it would take some time to set up an equivalent fund. This is like knowingly accepting and distributing a bribe. How soon will President Li need an answer?"

"Mr. President, they're going live on CNT in one hour," Ned said.

"I hate that damn news group. They'll cater to anyone for the ratings," the President snarled.

"If they don't cover it, someone else will."

"What do we gain by administrating the fund, and what do we lose?" the President queried.

"China has clearly had time to prepare for all of this—everything is in place, not only for the attack, but the cover story, and now the damage control," Benevidez responded.

The President closed his eyes and shook his head, "Really...I'm trying to sit here and put myself in the public's shoes. It's all very compelling, isn't it? I mean, what President Li is selling. What does the average resident in Dallas, whose car or home just got torched due to an exploding cell phone, care about the Senkaku Islands or natural gas in Asia, especially when she's being offered the money to have new carpet or what-not for her damaged house, or a new car or payment for time off? As far as she knows, from China's proactive messaging, we were attacked by Iran through hackers in the US, and China took out the enemy before we could even draw our guns...they know nothing of us being forced to stand down for China's gain. And China has the whole Mideast on their side. Let's think about that for a while before we do anything that makes sense to us but doesn't make any sense to the public."

Chapter
(Seven-tee)

"So, how did you like your debrief?" asked Agent Donovan.

Greg thought about his response for a bit, "It was pretty rough. I wasn't expecting quite that amount of pain, nor having my brains sucked out of me like that."

"Niiiiiice. Sounds like a wild time you had there—she really did miss you. Now, what did you think of your grilling in the SCIF this morning?"

"What? Oh, you meant…. Oh man, there was none of that, we were too tired," Greg said, embarrassed at Donovan's harassment.

"Aw, just messing with you, man. I was really referring to the debrief at the SCIF, but you set yourself up."

Greg had been fully indoctrinated and debriefed at the SCI Facility. It was a grueling time, but he knew there was a lot at stake. What he didn't hear about was the full extent of the global activities that had occurred in the past twenty-four hours. There was no need for him to know.

Chapter
(Seventy-1)

*T*he **White House Press** Secretary called his contacts at the major networks. The White House had their own announcement to give.

In working through the agreement to administer the recovery fund financed by China, the President requested the right to give the funding announcement first—after all, it was his country and they were his citizens. What business did a foreign nation have giving the US citizens money for something their own government should be handling? At the same time, the Federal and State governments were still broke. All entities had gone through their own budget slashing to try to balance things, and all had fallen short. The fact was that there wasn't funding to cover the losses from the attacks.

So with China's announcement imminent, the President and his advisors decided it was better to administer the funding than appear totally insensitive and out-of-the loop with what was going on nationally and globally. It took some time to set up a webpage providing information on how to request financial support, but the team at the Commerce Department, which would administer the funds, worked quickly…just in time for the announcement from the White House.

To appear completely informed and in control of things, the President gave the speech himself. His advisors decided that providing statements both confirming and countering the Chinese President's position were in order. In addition, President Brunson would disclose information he knew would get the Chinese President concerned about being exposed—that is, if the Chinese were as responsible as the President suspected they were.

"My fellow Americans, I am addressing you this morning with a heavy heart but with a confident mind and spirit. My heart is heavy for the losses in life and property that were experienced on our own soil in the attacks that occurred yesterday. However, I am confident that we have found the method and sources of the attacks and put measures in place to ensure they cannot happen again.

"As President Li of China stated earlier today, there was a conspiracy of sorts in these attacks. Parts assembled in China made their way into our smartphones, tablets and other intelligent systems. These parts contained Trojan chips, in the sense that additional circuitry was placed inside that caused the devices to self-destruct on command. The Chinese government has put a stop to the assembly of the affected parts and brought the perpetrators to justice. Likewise, in the United States, operatives were recruited to deliver triggering messages to the affected devices through our social networking sites. We have captured some of these operatives."

The President looked at the camera with a steely gaze, as if to send the message to the Chinese President himself.

FBI had traced two IP addresses back to locations in the Bay area—Joe's apartment and Pamela's condo. These were the only names they had been able to uncover so far. Using the names and addresses, the FBI quickly found associated cell numbers and traced their last known location—the Hayward warehouse. It was unclear if Joe and Pamela were actual members of the Chinese cult and had blown themselves up, or if they were victims in the same attacks they helped to perpetrate. In any case, it was unlikely that either of them would be found. It implied that maybe all the US-based operatives may have met the same fate. Nevertheless, President Brunson hoped that the Chinese didn't know for certain that the US-based operatives had been eliminated. It was a shot in the dark, but it was all they really had.

Images of Joe and Pamela now popped up on the monitor, side-by-side.

"These are photos of two of the operatives who delivered the messages from the Chinese cult to the social networks."

The President purposefully left Iran out of his statement, choosing instead to name the cult in China already acknowledged to have taken responsibility.

"Their names are Joe Klein and Pamela Giles. We have them in custody— due to the quick investigation by the NTSB, NSA and FBI, they were identified, arrested and are cooperating fully. They did not realize the full extent of the damage that would be caused by their participation with the Chinese cult, and are trying their best to help bring the rest of the accomplices to justice."

Message sent, thought President Brunson. I hope Li believes it.

Continuing his speech, he hoped to help take some credit for China's compensation for the US losses, though inside it was painful for him to announce. It felt like conceding defeat to a craftier foe.

"I am also here to announce that the government of China, in an effort to help remedy the losses caused by the Chinese-based cult and Hon Yao Industry Group, has set up a fund for compensation to those impacted by yesterday's attacks. This fund, totaling fifteen billion dollars, will be administered by the Department of Commerce."

There would be no time for questions. The President couldn't afford that. There were too many items he didn't know the answer to. If the subject of Iran came up, he would have to answer truthfully, and he didn't know what the truth was.

Bahram was nearly to the Tehran Freeway, the loop that circled the edge of the city. As he approached the street that would lead to the on-ramp, he expected that traffic would have abated this far from downtown. He was shocked to see, in the distance, cars still lined up. It was then he saw…the tanks.

Bahram pulled over to the side of the road.

Farah had been asleep when she felt the car slow down.

Ah, finally a break, she thought.

Seeing they were pulled over on the road, she was confused. "What are you doing?" she asked.

"Farah. I see tanks. They are blocking the highway in both directions. We can't go that way."

"Are they our tanks?"

"No, I've never seen any like those."

"What is happening? What will we do?"

Suddenly, Bahram turned his Peykan around and began driving over the dirt in the direction of the closest back road he could get to.

"I'm getting us out of here. I know the way. Trust me."

Farah had little choice.

"Farah, I don't know what is happening. We may never be able to go back. I don't know. We must pray for our nation and our leaders. We will make it to your brother's, God willing."

"Yes, God willing."

Chapter
(Seventy-2)

"**We're being set up** and screwed. We're still the most powerful nation in the world, and we don't have to settle for what's being offered to us," exclaimed the President. "When this is all done, we will have lost credibility with Japan, lost key positioning in the Mideast, and will have taken a bribe from China to make up for our losses. This isn't over," he continued.

"Of course it isn't," agreed Amanda, "but now in a way we know what it's like to be a small country that we ourselves have bribed into silence for years through the strings attached to our financial support."

"Really, is that what you think?" asked Carl.

"Yes, I do. In the past, Cuba, Colombia, and Nicaragua, were all bought off, and recently Egypt, Afghanistan, and Pakistan. That's the short list. And you know what we did to Iran in the 1950s."

"I don't totally agree. But even if there's some truth there, a lot of good it's done. Just look at today's events. Pakistan sold us out," Carl said.

"Exactly—you can only buy someone off for so long. Then they rebel. This was a wake-up call for all of us. It could have been so much worse."

The UN Security Council meeting was ready to begin, with Ambassador Kennedy at the table and the US National Security Council watching via live video feed.

While providing cooperation on a surface level, President Brunson had been pushing for any and all information implicating China that could be gleaned before the meeting began.

Unfortunately, timely information was in short supply. The Zhonghua Nine had done an impeccable job of covering their tracks. There was little information to be gathered from the Hayward warehouse where the contingent of drones had been assembled and massacred. The well-placed plastic explosives and ensuing fire effectively incinerated the place—though post-mortem analysis did show residual traces of the Semtex. It was also unlikely that the FBI would find a bona fide leaseholder for the site. The FBI traced the lease payment on the facility through its owner—a large lump sum paid out of a foreign bank account. The chances were high that it was a bogus account set with a fake ID, funded originally with cash. In other words, it was untraceable. But they were still hoping that someone had been careless along the way.

The investigation in Alabama wasn't yielding much fruit either, other than the valuable information from the NTSB agent. The sleeper agent killed at the Huntsville Hospital would have been a great witness, but Shelly Chambers was a mystery they wouldn't solve today.

The President hoped to gain support for a United Nations Security Council-sponsored investigation of China's actions—namely, the invasion of Iran and the capturing of the Senkaku Islands. He was convinced the evidence of the timing of Iran's supposed attacks on the US, coinciding with China's military actions, would indicate that the Chinese and Iranian governments had acted in concert. The President ordered his ambassador to the UN to press this point home with the Council. While the US might not have a smoking gun, he expected to have a persuasive presentation of the exact timeline of the movements of Chinese and Iranian troops, Chinese ships, US-based attacks, and the request from Iran to the US to stand down. It might all be circumstantial, but the evidence was going to be very compelling.

The Chinese Ambassador had prepared a speech, not unlike the one President Li had shared earlier in the day on CNT; however, he added some touches in response to the US President's televised announcement and some preemptive statements in anticipation of the US's petition for an investigation. It was almost as if they had inside knowledge of what case would be presented by the US Ambassador.

"This morning, President Brunson of the United States made us all aware of the capture of two US operatives. We encourage any and all means necessary to question these operatives, and make the interrogation results known to all nations who can provide assistance in furthering the investigation. We will do the same with operatives we have captured. We applaud the US authorities for their quick response..."

"China didn't flinch at all at our bluff. Either they know the operatives are all dead, or they figure they don't know anything that would lead us anywhere," said Henry.

"...would be a natural question to ask if the Chinese government was actually working with the cult. It is true that there were cult members that were moles in our government infrastructure and may have had influence over the actions of those who reported to them. However, there was no knowledge that commands were being provided by a cult member..."

"Don't they have to prove that?" asked Amanda.

"...those who feel that action against the Chinese nation should be taken, sanctions or worse, in punishment for the tragedy caused by a very small, independent group within our country. To those who would promote this thinking, I would ask if, within days of the tragedy of the 9-11 attacks on the United States, had the Afghani nation captured Osama Bin Laden, eliminated the Taliban, and made a reasonable attempt at compensation for their actions, whether the United States would have held Afghanistan culpable for the crimes committed by those within its borders..."

"That can't compare to this!" Carl hissed.

"Likewise, we are asking the global community and the Security Council to recognize the quick response by the Chinese government to dismantle the organization responsible for the attacks, including those forces within Iran who were holding the United States hostage to their demands. And we also ask you to consider the attempts we have made to compensate financially for the actions of a few rogue elements within our nation. Finally, we ask you to consider our request for support from the UN and from the Security Council nations to help manage the aftermath of the invasion that was required to stop the devastation by Iran. With so little time to act, the Chinese military had to respond without approaching the UN first, though we enlisted the help and support of neighboring countries. Please consider all of this evidence before casting judgment."

Around the room were nods of agreement from many of the Security Council representatives—Russia, Brazil and South Africa seemed to be buying the arguments presented at face value. It would be a hard sell to dissuade them, particularly when they stood to benefit from the potential division of assets and control as Iran was brought into compliance. Likely the US and China would have to abstain from a vote, as both had conflicts of interest; Russia alone could block the vote, as a unanimous vote from the permanent seats would be required for any substantive action.

"Hank, they've thought of almost everything, haven't they?"

"Yes, Mr. President, it is very compelling. I only hope our argument for further investigation is given a fair shake. But I'm afraid the politics of the situation and the conflicts of interest on the Council will make this a difficult choice for them. China is lobbying for use of the Yuan as a global currency— with the amount of control of natural resources they have and with the gold, silver and copper reserves to back up their currency—today could be the beginning of a lot more pain for the US if China gets their way."

The President closed his eyes and sighed heavily. Was his Presidency going to be the one that marked the tipping point of decline for the United States as a global leader? The momentum was shifting, and he could feel things slipping. But he knew the US's position in the world, the strength of his military and of the citizens—still, the signs were there. Former allies were starting to side with China. From now on, diplomacy would take precedence over might.

As the rest of the UN Security Council made their statements, the President's staff listened intently. They wanted to jump to the vote on the next steps to see how the US would fare. At the same time, they wanted to see which nations would cave in and buy the nicely packaged story, and which would question the motives, intent and knowledge of the Chinese government.

Chapter
(Seventy-3)

Shortly after noon, Greg and Donovan made it back to the "safe-cabin." Michelle had been waiting, somewhat impatiently, but she was trying her best to be understanding.

Though Greg and Donovan caught only snippets of the latest news over the radio on their way back to Cottage 58, Greg was anxious to get back and watch CNT for a bit to try to piece it all together. Unfortunately, he was going to be forced to get his information through the media machine rather than through the newly exposed classified channel to which he was now privy. He didn't have the need-to-know, so on much of this, he was going to be in the dark, just like everyone else.

Greg and Donovan found Michelle watching CNT. Since her favorite social networking sites were down, she needed something to keep her up-to-date on what was going on.

"Greg! You're back. I'm so glad you're here."

"Sorry we took a while..."

"That's not a problem. Kathy—er, Agent Miller here has taken great care of me. In fact, can we just stay here for a few days? I don't want to fly right now, and with all of this craziness, I don't want to be anywhere near DC."

Donovan smiled.

"Michelle, that's music to my ears. The fact is, we have orders to keep you both safe, and right now this is the best place to do that. Greg can work right down the road, and Miller will stock up on supplies."

This was news to Greg, but it all made sense.

"Greg, did you know that some Chinese cult was responsible for the attacks? The China President guy was on TV admitting it and showing how they killed them all and stuff."

"Actually—"

Donovan shot Greg a look.

"Actually, I didn't really know that," he said, following Donovan's lead. "What else is going on?"

"Well, our President got on a little while ago and announced a fifteen billion dollar fund to help the victims of the attacks. How about that? But you know who's coughing up the money?"

"Uh, the Department of uh.."

"The Chinese government!"

Both Donovan and Greg were shocked at this revelation. Michelle caught their look of surprise and was pleased to know something they didn't.

"And get this—they caught a couple of the cult members *here*. They were sending attack messages over Blather and Twitter *and Facebook*—that's why I can't get on anymore. They had to shut them down!"

Greg, wanted so badly for Michelle to know his involvement, but he could only remain silent and shake his head

"And did you know that China invaded Iran!? Iran was sending out the messages somehow and had invaded Iraq, so China kicked their butts and made them stop. Isn't that crazy? *Everyone* hates Iran, but nobody would do anything to stop them until China stepped in."

Greg and Donovan both looked at each other. What else had they missed in the past day?

"Honey, could you repeat that whole thing about China invading Iran?"

"Sure, that was part of the Chinese President's speech. It should come on again any time now—you know how they repeat stuff every ten minutes. The only problem is that so much new stuff is coming out...

"Anyway, they invaded Iran. I guess they're in control of it now, but are asking the rest of the big countries to help out and make sure it's all OK from here on out."

Michelle had a unique way of paraphrasing things, but it was indicative of how the US populace likely understood the reports. The way things were being presented, there seemed little notion of a Chinese government conspiracy—only their support of the United States and stability in the Middle East.

"Look, another news break—these have been happening all morning. It looks like something big…let's watch."

"We interrupt our programming to bring you an update from the United Nations. We have learned that just a few minutes ago, the United Nations Security Council convened at the request of the Chinese government. This was an emergency meeting to discuss the issues from the past two days…"

The President was incensed. Their regular supporters on the Security Council had, in fact, abandoned them. Of course, allies like England, France and Germany had sided with the United States and their borderline accusation of the Chinese government's involvement in the attacks—to them, the evidence was compelling enough for a full investigation. However, to other countries aligned with China and smaller countries receiving considerable funding from China, it was not such a clear case. The vote was close, but in the end it didn't matter. Russia's negative vote ended the call for an investigation. Instead, priority was given to finding a solution to the immediate problem of what to do with Iran. While most decisions within the Security Council received little press, the nature of this decision and its bearing on the United States made it a top story.

"See, the Chinese aren't *all* bad," said Michelle. "I think most people haven't given them a fair shake, you know? They stopped the attacks, they set up a fund for the victims, and now they stopped a crazy bully or whatever."

"Michelle, the Chinese are in Iran—and in control…" Greg said, almost talking to himself.

"Yeah, who could have predicted that?" Donovan said.

"I could have…" Greg said.

"What? How's that?" Donovan said. "What are you, a psychic?"

"No. But the Chinese are in the Mideast now, and I bet they're never coming out. In fact, they'll likely build up their forces," said Greg.

"How do you know that, man? Is Mideast politics one of your hobbies? Not even our—well, I don't know who would know that," Donovan said, more than a little incredulous.

"Look, I'm just lining some things up."

"Like what?"

"Two hundred years ago, in the early 1800s, no one would have thought there would be a nation of Israel again, right? Most of the world didn't care one way or the other, actually, and most Jews were scattered all over."

"Yeah, I'm not a history buff, but I know what you're saying. What's that got to do with China?"

"It's got everything to do with stuff written in the Bible…without an Israeli nation, there is no book of Revelation, and without Russia, China and, well, a lot of the world's forces gathered together in the Mideast, there is no *Armageddon*," Greg explained.

"Armageddon? Greg, you *can't* be serious."

"I'm just saying that what gets predicted from the Bible comes true."

Donovan's eyes narrowed as he thought about Greg's argument. "Yeah, people say that about Nostradamus, too. I've read his prophecies. You can read about anything you want into them."

"Hey, I agree with you, but when the Bible says that the Kings of the East cross the Euphrates on their way to Armageddon…that's pretty explicit. It's just that no one imagined how they'd get there."

"That's what you think this is about? Why do these 'Kings of the East' have to be China?" Donovan asked.

"They may or may not be. It might be another country. But it makes sense to me. Armageddon could be in a few years, and it could be in ten or twenty years, but the Kings of the East cross the Euphrates in Iraq in time for Armageddon. If those 'Kings' are China, they're not leaving."

"You're a smart guy, Greg—you proved that the past two days. Otherwise, I wouldn't even listen to this crap. I sure hope you're wrong. Or else, well…I don't know what else. I just hope you're wrong."

"I kind of hope so, too…"

"…and now we turn to the top analyst on the Middle East from the Bradley Institute, Dr. Norman Stanley, for a follow-up commentary. Dr. Stanley, what significance does this decision today by the UN Security Council have on the United States' policy and influence in the Mideast?"

"This shows that China has finally arrived as a true global superpower. Let's look at the facts: first, China was able to deal with the Iranian 'problem'—namely being a radical, destabilizing bully to its neighbors—where no one else, including the United States, was willing or able to deal with that nation. Second, China found the perpetrators of the attacks on the US; inside China, within the US, and also Iran. They dealt with them quickly and completely, while providing transparency to the world on the situation and funds to compensate for damages, even though the Chinese government was not responsible. Finally, the UN Security Council gave China a vote of confidence that it trusts China to lead an effort to maintain stability in Iran, while the other Council members work with them to find a solution moving forward. I would say that China has finally risen to the challenge of being a global leader. They don't have the military might of the US, but with the actions of the past few days, it's clear they have the political and economic strength to be major players."

"How biased is *that* reporting?" exclaimed Greg.

"Sounds about right to me," said Michelle.

Since none of the information Greg had could be divulged, he bit his tongue.

"...now with an alternative view is Dr. Craig Hornsby from the Heritance Group. Dr. Hornsby, do you have any thoughts on the latest news from the Security Council meeting?"

"I sure do. This all just smells. China captures the Senkaku Islands and invades Iran at the same time the US is attacked? That sure doesn't seem like a coincidence."

"Feels, seems and smells...those are all good facts, Craig," quipped the other analyst.

"I can't believe you don't see the correlation yourself," came the acerbic reply.

Dr. Stanley interjected, "The Chinese government stated that the cult had infiltrated the military—it may not have been a coincidence, but it doesn't show nefarious intent. In the final analysis, a destabilizing bully has been taken care of in the Mideast, and the US, as tragic as the loss was, is being made whole—"

"And it has suffered irreparable damage to its credibility and influence, particularly in the Mideast," Hornsby said.

"That may be, Craig, but the stability that can be achieved by China, the US, Russia and Europe all being involved in the nation building process in the Mideast is a good thing. For too long we've done it all alone, and we've failed. I say the Mideast is too valuable a region to let slip into chaos. The US already has troops in Afghanistan and a few in Iraq—we *all* have vested interests, so a balance of power is a good thing."

"Well, you're right about the troops. Within a few months, all nations will be pulled into this mess in the Mideast, if for no other reason than to guarantee their fair share. We had hoped for independent states; now it's likely we're all in there to stay for a while," Dr. Hornsby added. There seemed little dispute on this point.

Donovan looked at Greg. "Looks like you might just be right, buddy. Kings of the East, you say? I may just have to read up on that. I'll likely have some questions for you…"

"Anytime. You know as well as I do that nothing's going to be quite the same after this."

Donovan got up to leave. "Yeah, I know. But that's really outside my control and above my pay grade. We're seeing history being made, you know. I hope it's not our turning point."

Greg nodded. He knew his chance to speak his mind would fade if he didn't take advantage of this moment. "Donovan, you saved my life a few times now, and…well, I can't thank you enough. I hope to see you soon, under better circumstances."

Michelle chimed in, "Thanks, Donovan. It was good to meet you. I, too, hope to see you again."

"You too," Donovan said.

Chapter
(Seventy-4)

In the Lagoi Bay resort community on the north end of the island of Bintan in Indonesia, a small, nondescript elderly gentleman was settling into in his newly purchased home on the coast. Situated between high-end resorts like Club Med, Banyan Tree, and Bintan Lagoon, it was a heaven on earth, though a warm one. He seemed to be a man without a care in the world—with a smile on his face and a quick "hello" on his lips. He appeared to be an investor of sorts, for he would read a copy of the *Asian Times* each day and smile as he went over the financial section. Rumors within the community were that he was a wealthy businessman who had done well on the rise of China's economy and had decided to cash-out and retire while the going was good.

To anyone who cared to notice, the old man wore a unique gold ring that evidently had been specially made. Three Chinese symbols were engraved on the ring; one of which could readily be recognized as the number nine, the others were the symbols for Zhonghua. They lay on top of a detailed, elaborate backdrop of a five-toed dragon. It appeared to bring back fond memories for the old man, as he would sometimes glance at the ring and chuckle to himself with a twinkle in his eye.

The Leader had gotten away with it after all.

His reward for helping China reclaim the Diaoyutai Islands and secure access to oil, gas and natural resources in the East China Sea and Middle East, was a life of ease at Bintan. He had made peace with himself and the betrayal of his cult compatriots. After all, he *was* the cult, its originator, master and finisher; he formed it and he ended it when the organization had met its purposes. His conscience was clear; China was back on her way to former glory with additional resources to protect her path, and her past enemies were being punished for their evil war crimes. His family's souls might now rest in peace. Vengeance was complete, and life was good…for now.

Epilogue

"Greg, this is Trey at Teardown…"

Trey's voice sounded ominous.

Ugh—I forgot to call them back, thought Greg. I wonder if he's concerned about payment.

"Trey, good to hear from you. Thanks for all of your help with taking that chip apart. About the pay—"

"Sorry to interrupt, this isn't a courtesy call and it's not about money. We've uncovered more problems. On a hunch we decided to take a few other phones and computers apart. You know, there's a lot of other chipsets assembled at Hon Yao…"

"Yeah, I remember. What's up?"

"Greg, it looks like we've got Trojan chips on more final products coming from other Hon Yao factories—laptops, desktops and other tablets and phones."

"So, we could be attacked again?"

"Not physically…these chips are more sophisticated. They may 'listen-and-forward,' intercepting information and sending it on…it's too soon to tell, but I thought I needed to let you know right away."

Greg's stomach sank as he realized the implications of such a buried chip. Data, files, and conversations might be at risk—for individuals, corporations, and governments alike. They could already be compromised.

"This is really…really bad," Greg said, not knowing how to respond.

"It sure is. You may have solved the attack problems, but this is far from over.…"